ASCENDANT REVOLUTION

FADED SKIES BOOK 3

MATTHEW S. COX

DIVISION ZERO PRESS

Ascendant Revolution
Faded Skies Book 3
© 2018 – Matthew S. Cox

Cover and interior art by Ricky Gunawan.

ISBN (eBook): 978-1-949174-82-3

ISBN (print): 978-1-949174-83-0

CONTENTS

A TRUCE UNEASY

Wary of what the future held, Maya sat on the floor of her bedroom staring into space, the glowing, digital image of Vanessa Oman's condescending smile lingering in her memory. The woman had shot an executive dead with little reaction. Even though Tian Shen had sent men to murder Maya, watching her death on a live video call haunted her.

Sharing a bed with Genna had become sharing a bed with Sarah after her family moved down the hall. Neither the mattress in Genna's old place nor the new one in Sarah's room were as big or soft as the one in the penthouse she'd spent the first nine years of her life in, but that didn't matter. The warmth of having a real mother, or her as-good-as sister close at night more than made up for it.

This room had once been Sarah's, the same one she had snuck out of in the middle of the night to find Genna, an unfinished game of *Magic* left on the floor. She'd first slept here as a guest when her *real* mother vanished, and again when The Dad watched her so Genna could go on a mission for The Brigade.

She had been in this room the night men tried to kidnap her, when The Dad held them off long enough for the girls to escape out the window to the fire escape. Small dimples in the wall marked spots bullets had come through. Plaster and new paint helped hide the bad memories, but she knew right where to look.

This room had been Sarah's sanctuary for all eleven years of her life, but The Dad had lost his fight with cancer. More accurately, Vanessa killed him... somehow. He'd inexplicably gone from remission to dead overnight. She couldn't quite figure out what horrified her more—that the woman would do that, or that she had somehow weaponized cancer in such a way as it could kill in hours.

For the past sixteen days, this had been Maya's room, too. Sarah hadn't shown the slightest bit of hesitation at losing the 'privacy' of a bedroom all to herself. Then again, the girl didn't seem capable of being embarrassed—except when her old pathetic scrap curtain dress fell off around blueberries.

Genna liked the idea of moving, since this place had a second bedroom, bigger master bedroom, and slightly newer kitchen appliances. She also couldn't leave Sarah to be an orphan, and bringing another child into their one-bedroom place would've been too crowded. Much like Maya, her mother blamed herself for what happened to The Dad. In the span of about two months, the girl had gone from total stranger—the first other child Maya had ever met face to face—to friend, to best friend, to sister. After what they'd survived together, it didn't matter they shared not a single scrap of DNA, or even looked anything alike. Sarah had skin as pale as porcelain with long red hair, while Maya had been given 'media perfect' brown skin, perfectly straight black hair, and a genetic hodgepodge of traits tailor made to be appealing, like slightly-Japanese eyes, skin not too light or too dark, and cheek structure from Sudan. If someone asked her ethnicity, she'd have to answer "yes."

A few days clinging to each other in the most desperate of circumstances, believing that they only had each other left in the world, forged a bond as strong as any blood tie.

Well, Sarah did resemble her in one way: skinny—Sarah due to malnutrition, Maya by design.

Maya had developed a fierce, protective love for her as though they'd grown up together, the first time in all her nine years to experience that particular emotion. She also loved Genna like a mother. And Pope? She kinda liked him sticking around, too. Having a family would've been awesome—if not for her worry that Vanessa would destroy it all at any moment.

Faint thunder like a great boulder rolling overhead broke the stillness. The storm brought a welcome break from the heat and humidity of the past few days that had been so brutal Sarah disregarded the awkwardness of sharing a bed and slept with nothing on, not even a sheet over her. That had been her method of coping with heat her whole life, not even knowing such a thing as air conditioning could exist.

Maya couldn't quite bring herself to do the same, though the nightgown she'd worn her first night away from the Sanc was thin. Putting it on reminded her of her initial taste of 'freedom' from Vanessa, when she'd been stranded out in the Habitation District with only that nightie to wear.

Their apartment building still had the dead remnants of an air conditioner on the roof, but whatever had opened up the ninth-floor wall had also smashed the machinery. Whether it went beyond Zoe's skills to repair or she simply lacked the necessary parts, Maya couldn't tell. Granted, fixing it probably wouldn't help.

Outside the Sanc, electrical power tended to be an 'if you can get it' commodity. A few small providers sprang up, individual entrepreneurs who managed to put together a load of solar panels and battery storage would hand-run wires to buildings close enough, and charge by the month. Other places, like this high-rise, had their own panels... but they couldn't support the drain of personal air conditioning units in each apartment, much less the monster on the roof.

At least the rain cooled things off enough that she'd be able to sleep later. She'd never understood the stuffed animals, teddy bear, or doll thing, until she had a sister to cling to at night. Waking up from a nightmare with another living person's arms around her had been a bizarre, but awesome feeling. She'd been morbidly terrified of bad dreams in her old life, since she lived alone in a penthouse with only the emotionless voice of the house AI to soothe her after she'd woken up screaming. Back then, her nightmares had come from stupid, childish things like monsters under the bed or some grotesque bit of medical imagery she'd read about on the AuthNet. Not until a cybered-up mercenary clamped a giant metal hand over her mouth did she know what a *real* nightmare felt like.

She swished her feet side to side, studying the lay of *Magic* cards on the rug. This game relied on strategy, both in execution during play as well as the composition of the deck. Luck played a role as well depending on the shuffle. Had she any desire to excel at it, she'd have researched it online, but this apartment had no functional computer or connection to the AuthNet. Also, she only ever played the game against Sarah to spend time together, and didn't care at all who won.

Unlike Vanessa.

That woman doesn't care about anything but winning.

The last Maya had seen of her former mother had been the video call in which she'd shot Tian Shen, the woman who'd plotted to wrest control of Ascendant Pharmaceuticals from her—as well as sent men to kill Maya. Of course, the entire purpose of the call had been to point Vanessa at the traitorous executive; however, she hadn't anticipated gunfire. Vanessa rarely dirtied her hands in person. She'd expected something along the lines of the woman being fired, perhaps arrested, but generally removed from Ascendant so she would no longer be a threat to Maya's life.

More than witnessing murder on a live video feed, Vanessa's offer to leave her alone caused bad dreams and nights of fitful sleep. The woman never 'gave up and walked away.' Perhaps she did consider Maya revealing the traitor as some kind of gesture of truce. But that didn't ease her worries. Especially considering Zeroice had successfully hacked into the Ascendant network to obtain technical data related to Xenodril, the drug to cure Fade. Once The Brigade distributed it to the handful of other pharma companies that remained after the Third World War, Xenodril would cease being Ascendant's cash cow. Vanessa could no longer deliberately infect people with Fade to force them to buy an overpriced cure.

As soon as that happened, the shit would hit the fan.

Well, it kind of had already. Unrest in the Hab and the Baltimore Sanctuary Zone had steadily increased over the past two weeks. All the adults in the building talked as if they expected another actual war to break out, only not on a global scale. Opinions differed as to who would be shooting at who: Citizens vs. Nons with the Authority watching; Citizens and Nons vs. the Authority; Citizens, Nons, and the Authority against Ascendant's private army... or maybe everyone would simply go crazy and shoot at whatever didn't look like them.

Genna expected it to be Authority vs. Ascendant, with some confusion as bought-and-paid-for Authority sellouts sided with Ascendant. Either way, for the past eight days, Maya had been constantly sick to her stomach, dreading that it wouldn't be too long before many people died over what *she* started. That her video message to the Eastern Seaboard had been the catalyst to set everything in motion caused a conflict inside her. It *needed* to happen, but it bothered her to think people would die over her words. Then again, her ads for Ascendant products had already done that. If she needed to carry more guilt to cure the cancer Ascendant had become, so be it.

It probably wouldn't take Vanessa long to connect Maya to the hack of the Xenodril formula, not that she had a role more active than crawling through a pipe with a cable. Perhaps it would be simple vindictiveness, but some retribution would follow despite Vanessa's declaration that they had reached a truce. In the span of a day, the woman had gone from threatening to kill everyone in this building if Maya didn't behave herself to 'allowing' her to live with Genna if that's what she wanted, even offering to let her 'come home' when she became bored with slumming it.

Maya scoffed. *I am home.*

She didn't trust any sense of safety. Once Xenodril became worthless, Vanessa would be on the warpath. The woman knew Genna had ties to the Brigade, and even if she never associated Maya with the hack, Ascendant's retribution against people involved would sweep her family into the shitstorm.

Barnes didn't seem worried about fallout. He, Genna, and Pope had gone to a meeting about the Xenodril data an hour or so ago, right after dinner. The Brigade liked and ran with Maya's idea to share it for free to any company with the necessary infrastructure to manufacture it. Other companies would (hopefully) make it available at a much more reasonable price, thus eliminating the incentive for Ascendant to release the deadly bio weapon as a profit scheme.

Maya scowled, somewhat resenting being left out of that meeting. It *was* her idea after all. The Brigade treating her like a child sucked as much as it made her feel weird and confused. Despite being irritated at Genna and Pope making her stay home, she understood her parents did it to protect her. A nine-year-old, even one as ridiculously smart as her, didn't belong attending a clandestine meeting of a group still considered terrorists by the law, even if it seemed the real Authority had softened its opinion of them. She didn't belong in a room full of guns, explosives, knives, and people more than willing to use them if need be no matter how precociously adult she acted.

True, she doubted any other kids her age in the world had her particular 'maturity.' She knew hundreds of medicines, understood business concepts, could negotiate with executives, hell—she'd managed to manipulate a team of mercenaries into killing each other when they kidnapped her.

But she had no idea how to play with dolls. She couldn't fathom why Emily Chang pretended the building had faeries living in it. She *hoped* the girl pretended and didn't have mental issues that made her seriously believe the faeries existed. Trying to understand the reason behind the boys playing with little plastic spaceships or people figures left her bewildered.

I look like a little kid, but I don't feel like one.

She flicked at the cards in her hand. Her parents telling her to stay home for being too small to attend a Brigade meeting made her feel like a child in an almost insulting way. Maybe she shouldn't consider it a bad thing after all. If not for worrying where and when Ascendant would destroy her new—startlingly normal—life, she might've allowed herself to relax.

For as long as she'd lived in the penthouse apartment, all those days spent pining for Vanessa to show any trace of maternal love, she'd never been dealt with as a kid. The house AI talked to her like a tiny adult. Ascendant handlers, media people, aesthetic technicians, and employees all reacted as if she were a smaller version of Vanessa. This mostly involved terror as they expected annoying her would cause them to be fired or stripped of Citizenship. Not that Vanessa would've listened to her if she demanded someone's dismissal. She'd tried that once when Jerry Michaels kept picking on her and calling her a klutz for spilling coffee on him.

Who makes a little kid march around on a boardroom table wearing high heels... really.

Maya wouldn't have asked Vanessa to fire anyone unless they had been truly mean to her, like him. She rather hated how everyone stopped talking around her, refused to even look at her, and tended to regard her as dangerous as highly-volatile radioactive isotopes.

They were afraid of Vanessa, not me.

Now that woman would sometimes fire people for trivial things— like cutting her off in the hallway or trying to speak to her when they had no business need to do so. She probably would've fired (or done worse) to people who 'bothered' Maya, but that would've required the woman care about her at all. What kind of relationship might she have had with Vanessa if she also possessed the woman's cruel streak? Would they have shared dinners laughing at the poor people dying of Fade and making jokes about idiots at the office?

She sighed and glanced at the door to the hallway. Sarah had gone to the bathroom a while ago. Too long to still be in there. Too long to have decided to grab a snack from the kitchen.

Worried, Maya set her cards on the rug and stood, smoothing her T-shirt dress down. Genna had bought them a few more pieces of clothing, though she preferred to laze about in the comfort of an adult-sized shirt when not expecting to leave home.

She padded out into the hall. A short spur to the right led to the master bedroom, formerly where The Dad slept, now Genna and Pope's room. She crept to the door and peeked in, but found only the stacks of boxes containing the various military gear The Dad had stockpiled in the closet. Pope intended to evaluate it piece by piece, but so far, he'd only gotten rid of four hand grenades and two antipersonnel mines. He'd turned them in to the Authority, claiming to have found them in an apartment he'd recently moved into.

The thought that explosives had been so close to Sarah's bed for years made her shiver. Even if they'd been in a protective case, it struck her as insane to store them in that closet. Despite it being on the opposite wall from the one that connected the rooms, any one of them going off in the middle of the night would still probably have killed her, and The Dad, too. As awful as the thought was, Maya couldn't help but think the man's death had been a kindness—both for him *and* Sarah.

Maya backed away from the door and wandered past her room, around the L in the corridor, and up to the bathroom on the left. The door hung open, the room empty. She kept going to the living room, and found Sarah curled up on the couch in the spot where The Dad always sat. Her body shook with sobs, but she made almost no sound. Her pink dress with a unicorn head on the chest, a rainbow streaming from the horn, didn't at all match her mood.

Unable to think of anything to say, Maya crossed the room and sat beside her.

Another soft rumble shook the sky. Rain pattered against the sliding glass patio door to the right of the sofa. She placed a hand on Sarah's bare foot, gazing down at the rug while breathing in the scent of new paint. She hated not being good at emotional stuff. It scared her that she might be more like Vanessa than she cared to admit, but more likely, it came from having little experience (until recently) dealing with people on a human level.

"I miss him, too," said Maya in a near-whisper.

Sarah wiped her eyes. "Sorry for making you wait on the game."

"It's okay. The cards aren't important. You're sad. I understand."

Flashing red and blue lights flickered in the raindrops running down the patio door. An Authority drone passed outside in a gentle patrolling glide, unfazed by the downpour. Maya tracked it with a stare, almost wishing a lightning strike would take it down. While she nursed a slight nugget of new respect for the Authority, she hated the drones. Most Citizens hated the drones. No one liked living under an army of electronic eyes armed with .50 cal machine guns. She had once believed them all to be AIs like the Ascendant ones, but human pilots safe in bunkers somewhere operated the Authority drones.

"I don't know who to be upset with." Sarah sniffled and wiped her nose. "Vanessa for what she did. Dad for waiting so long to get help. Myself for not insisting he go to the VA."

Maya patted her on the foot. "It's mostly Vanessa's fault. Yeah, he should've gone to the hospital a long time ago, but he would've been okay if she didn't 'visit' him. It's also kinda my fault. She only killed him so she could keep you to control me. If I had asked Genna to take me back to the Sanc after she saved me from Moth, your dad would be okay." Her throat tightened. "If we never met..." She choked up.

"It's not your fault." Sarah pushed herself upright to sit and threaded an arm around Maya's back. "I'm really happy you're my sister now. You looked so lonely when I first saw you. I knew you needed a friend."

"I hate that woman so much," whispered Maya.

"Are you sure? I don't think you really hate her. You're too nice to hate anyone."

"She killed your father," said Maya in a teary voice. "And *so* many people."

Sarah leaned against her. "You hate what she did, not her. You're nothing like that woman."

"It's okay to cry about your dad. I miss him, too. He was cool... even if he did have explosives in his closet."

"Yeah." Sarah wiped at her face, but tears kept falling. She frowned at her dress. "Guess I'm breaking the law being sad while wearing this thing huh?"

"No. There's no law about how to feel. The Authority hasn't become that invasive yet." Maya fussed at Sarah's hair. "It's kind of a little too pink."

Sarah shrugged. "I don't mind wearing girly stuff."

"You shoot people in the face with a Hornet and pick locks."

"Yeah. Doesn't mean I can't be girly." She tugged at the fabric. "And it makes me look harmless so I can surprise people."

"It's so pink you'll never be able to hide in it," whispered Maya.

"You're really not good at being a kid." Sarah chuckled. "We shouldn't be thinking like soldiers all the time. And besides." She held up her arm. "I'm so white I glow in the moonlight. The pink doesn't make a difference."

Maya chuckled and raked her toes over the carpet. "The Dad taught you a lot of stuff."

"He did, but it was like living with two different people. Whenever he started showing me how to do something, he turned back into the person he really was. But he'd always wind up getting weird again after." Sarah looked down. "I kept asking him to teach me stuff because it kinda brought him back."

"Your dad was still cool even when he watched TV. He said a lot of funny things."

Sarah managed a weak smile. "Yeah."

"We could put the TV on and yell bad words at it. Maybe throw the footrest at the wall in his memory."

"Hah." Sarah poked her in the side. "Thanks, but that's not really how I want to remember him."

"Sorry," muttered Maya.

"It's okay. You didn't really see him any other way, except that time he showed us the Hornet. He taught me a lot of stuff, and he acted like a normal person then."

"He kinda talked to us like we were in the Army."

Sarah nodded. "Yeah."

"Do you think Pope is like a father? I'm not really sure. I've never had one before."

"Well..." Sarah wagged her head side to side. "He doesn't talk to us like we're in the Army. But he also doesn't do the stuff my dad used to do when I was little. Like carry me around on his shoulders or read me stories."

"Yeah. But, we're not little... so."

"That's true. And he's not really our dad, so I guess he's doing okay at trying." Sarah picked at her nails. "It's so weird having him say 'dad stuff' like 'get away from that ledge' or 'go to bed, now' and stuff."

"The Dad told you what to do sometimes, too."

"Yeah. I mean, more like Pope isn't my father in a 'got my mother pregnant' way, but he just started acting like it without me asking him to take care of me."

"You don't know how to let someone take care of you." Maya hugged her. "You're always playing mom."

Sarah laughed for a moment until she became sad again. "Yeah... I feel so guilty that I like it."

"Like what?"

"Genna and Pope taking care of me. I don't have to worry about feeding him or cleaning everything or..." She bowed her head into her hands, sniffled, and straightened. "Sorry."

"It's okay to be sad."

"Thanks." Sarah leaned on her for a while, neither of them talking.

Maya stretched her legs out and yawned. "Yeah. I'm not sure how a dad is supposed to be. I don't even have a biological father. They put me together like a pizza."

"I guess a father's supposed to be like Doc Chang. You see how he is with Emily." Sarah pulled her feet up on the cushions and pivoted to face Maya. She spent a while talking about how her father used to be when she'd been six and younger, before his mental problems worsened.

Maya listened, daydreaming about what it might've been like to grow up with a father instead of a house AI.

Rapid banging startled a yelp out of Maya. Sarah gasped and whipped around to stare at the apartment door. Genna had told them to stay inside and not open the door. But that worked *so* well when those fake workers abducted them.

"Faerie! Maya!" shouted Pick. "Help!"

Maya slouched with relief. Not a kidnapper, merely her six-year-old friend.

"What's wrong?" Sarah hopped off the couch and headed for the door, Maya trailing after her.

"Please help!" yelled Pick. "It's Naida."

Sarah undid the deadbolt and pulled the door open.

Pick, as usual wearing only shorts, stood out in the hallway, his puffy orb of brown hair surrounding a face streaked with tears—and marked with a large bruise that would soon be a black eye.

"What happened?" Sarah gasped. "Naida didn't do that..."

"No." Pick shook his head so hard his hair fluffed up. "A man's trying to kill her!"

2

COMPROMISED

Pick hovered in the doorway, shaking from fear, desperation, and anger.

"What?!" Maya gasped.

"Naida is working," said Pick in a low voice. "The man started hitting her. I tried to help, but the *pendejo* hit me, too."

Sarah growled and ran down the hall to the bedroom. Maya twisted to stare after her in confusion until the girl re-emerged carrying the Hornet. Her sister had gone back to being 'little Mom,' fury burning out of her dark blue eyes.

"We should get an adult," said Maya.

"Who?" asked Sarah. "Barnes, Genna, and Pope are off at that meeting. Brian?"

Maya scowled. "No. He's in the Sanc at work anyway."

"Come on," yelled Pick. "He's hitting her *now*."

Sarah hurried into the corridor.

"Book?" Maya scurried after them.

"He's an old man," said Sarah. "He'd only get hurt."

Maya jogged to catch up, still not used to the new carpeting in the hallway. "We're kids."

"He won't hit us, and I have a Hornet."

Pick stared at Sarah, then pointed at his developing black eye.

"Okay, fine. He might hit us, but he'd *kill* Book... and I have a Hornet." Sarah stormed into the stairwell.

They ran after her down to the third floor where Pick lived with his older sister, Naida. The woman had to be in her early twenties and worked as a prostitute out of the apartment. Of all the kids in the building, only Emily Chang didn't understand what that meant. Pick became quite defensive whenever anyone talked about her, or prostitution in general. Though she'd never witnessed it, Maya assumed the other boys had made fun of her at some point before she arrived here.

Sarah hurled her body against the stairwell door, emitting a diminutive grunt while shoving it out of her way. Maya ran beside her but Pick sprinted into the lead, racing down the hall to the corner and around the corner out of sight.

"Ruben!" yelled Sarah, not speeding up from her purposeful stride. "Wait for me."

"What are you going to do?" whispered Maya.

"Depends on what's going on." Sarah marched around the corner.

The door to Pick's apartment hung open. He hesitated with one foot over the threshold, barely fighting his need to run inside, staring back over his shoulder at the approaching girls. Grunting voices—both male and female—along with banging furniture and clattering emanated from within. It didn't sound at all like what prostitutes do, more like two people trying to strangle each other.

Maya lunged forward and grabbed Sarah's arm. "We should get Zoe. She's home."

"He's hitting her *now*," wailed Pick.

"I can handle one idiot." Sarah held the Hornet up in two hands like a cop from a movie. "We've done *much* scarier stuff."

Pick stared at her chest—specifically the graphic on her dress—and snickered.

"Yeah but we didn't have a choice then." Maya folded her arms. "And you don't really look scary."

Sarah held her head up high. "I am a fully functional attack unicorn."

Naida screamed in pain.

Pick started to run in, but Sarah grabbed him. "You two wait out here. I don't want you getting hurt."

The boy stared at her.

"Getting hurt any *more*." Sarah pushed Pick into Maya. "Hold onto him, okay? I'll be right back."

A heavy *thud* from deep in the apartment shook the floor along with a woman's scream of anger.

"Be careful!" Maya clamped her arms around Pick.

Sarah dashed inside.

The boy waited all of two seconds before overpowering her grip and breaking away. She chased him into the middle of the living room, where he stopped, looking back and forth from the hallway leading toward the bedrooms and the kitchen. Maya grabbed him again, but he dragged her into the kitchen despite her effort to hold him back. As soon as he reached up for a big cooking knife, she gave up trying to grab him around the body and seized his right arm in both hands.

"Ruben, no!" shouted Maya. "No knives!"

He growled, struggling to pull the giant blade from its plastic block holder.

"Stop!" shouted Sarah from down the hall. "Get off her."

Thumps, bangs, and grunts of adults throwing each other around continued.

"He could take the knife away from you and hurt Naida with it." Maya strained to hold the knife in place.

"I'm serious," yelled Sarah. "Stop it *now!*"

Pick gave up and slumped against the counter, breathing hard and crying. Seeing him wanting so much to protect his sister but being too tiny to make much of a difference hit Maya like a punch in the stomach. She kept clinging to him, both to comfort him and hold him in place lest he came down with a sudden case of stupid. Winded from her struggle, she gasped for breath, coughing on air that smelled of faint floral perfume and hours-old burritos.

The all-too-familiar *pthoonk!* of a Hornet dart firing preceded a soft electric *zzzzt*. A male voice cried out with a clipped gurgling scream while Naida yelped as if she'd grabbed a hot pot from the stove. Another *thump* shook the floor. Seconds later, Naida erupted in an explosion of furious, shrieking Spanish.

Judging by Pick's reddening face, she used all the bad words... and probably made up a few new ones.

Maya grimaced at the screaming, but took comfort in the woman sounding furious rather than terrified. Pick pushed off the counter. Despite being three years younger than Maya, he lifted her into the air instead of trying to break her grip, and started to carry her into the apartment. She clung to the edge of the sink, trying to stop him.

"Let go," said Pick. "I gotta see her."

"Please put me down."

He sighed and set her back on her feet.

"What's she saying?" asked Maya.

"Umm." Pick shrugged. "A bunch of stuff about his mother and goats. I don't know some of those words."

Sarah appeared in the archway between the kitchen and the living room, on the left side nearer the hallway to the bedrooms. "He's out cold."

"Are you okay?" Maya ran to her.

"Fine I"—Sarah jumped as Pick zoomed past her and scrambled toward Naida, turning to watch him go—"darted him."

Naida and Pick yelled at each other in rapid Spanish. His voice broke with tears while she sounded frustrated.

"What happened?" whispered Maya.

"This guy was on top of her with both hands around her neck. I told him to get off her, but he ignored me... so I darted him in the head." Sarah blew across the hornet's barrel like an Old West gunslinger.

"She's okay?"

"Yeah, I guess. Kinda shocked her, too, since they were touching each other, but it didn't knock her out."

Maya edged past her and crept down the hall. This apartment had the same layout as the one she lived in now. She ignored the bedroom that mirrored the one she shared with Sarah and kept going to the master, where all the noise came from. The jasmine perfume smell saturated this room much more than the rest of the house, with an undertone of slightly burnt meat.

Naida sat on the edge of the bed facing the door, holding Pick. Blood trickled from her nose, lip, and one earlobe where an earring had been ripped away. In addition to finger-shaped bruises on her throat, she wore a short powder-blue dress. Judging from the ripped shoulder strap, they hadn't quite gotten to the prostitution part before the fight started.

A man lay unconscious on the floor at the foot of the bed, presumably where Naida shoved him. Thirtyish, brown buzz cut, dark blue shirt with grey pants, he looked like most ordinary Nons living in the Hab. His grey poncho with breathing mask lay draped over a chair by the desk. The one-inch-long silver Hornet dart remained stuck to the side of his head, about halfway between his ear and eye, a small spark still dancing around the point of contact.

Maya stood in the doorway, mouth open in shock. Sarah tucked up beside her and put her arm around her. Pink walls tinged with age set off lime green curtains drawn closed over the windows. A small goldfish in a giant bowl on the floor in the corner swam in circles, oblivious to the goings on. Lingerie, dresses, and various shoes spilled out of one of a pair of closets. Two tiny tables lay on their sides, a scattering of little figurines on the rug, a few broken.

Pick stared at Sarah with awe. "You did it. You stopped him."

"I warned him." Sarah glanced at the Hornet. "Gave him four whole seconds."

Naida rocked Pick side to side, muttering to him.

Eyes narrowed, Maya walked over to squat beside the man and searched his pockets. She dumped some NuCoin on the rug, tossed a blister pack of headache pills aside, pen knife, keyring, two key fobs for who-knows-what.

"What are you doing?" asked Sarah.

"Trying to figure out who this guy is." Maya kept rummaging.

"Does it matter?" asked Naida. "Just another piece of—umm. Another garbage person."

Maya decided not to point out she'd heard (and used) *those* words. Perhaps normal kids weren't supposed to. She could pretend to be somewhat normal if it made the adults around her happy. That, and Sarah didn't really like swear words. She blushed whenever Maya used them.

"You think he's dangerous?" Sarah knelt beside her.

"I don't know. That's what I'm trying to find out." Maya pulled a small electronic device out of his pocket and turned it over in her hands.

"His minicomputer is probably locked." Sarah shook her head. "I can't open those."

"It's not a minicomputer." Maya pushed a button, which made it flip open like a tiny book, revealing a display screen. "It's a recorder."

"Why would someone carry a cheap recorder when minicomputers do everything?" asked Naida.

"I don't know." Maya tapped the touchscreen, navigating to the photo album. "But it's definitely weird."

She flipped it over and turned it on. A six-by-nine inch holographic panel appeared above it. The device held thirty-six photographs in its memory, all of them of Maya and her friends playing out in the parking lot behind the building. Three-quarters of the images focused on her.

"Oh, crap," whispered Sarah.

Maya glanced at her. "Umm. Pretty sure this deserves an 'oh shit.'"

Sarah blushed.

3

CREEPING DREAD

Back home almost an hour later, Maya paced around the living room while Sarah sat on the couch, the Hornet beside her on the cushion. They'd run to get help dealing with the unconscious guy, and stumbled into Genna, Pope, Barnes, and Mr. Weber returning from the Brigade meeting.

After a quick explanation—and showing them the device—Genna sent the girls home.

Maya teetered on the verge of screaming in rage one moment, crying in fear the next. The speed with which her emotions shifted kept her from surrendering to any one mood more than the rest.

"Stop pacing. You're making *me* nervous," said Sarah. "We're safe."

"I'm scared," said Maya, still walking in circles. "I'm tired of everyone coming after me. Why can't people leave me alone?"

Sarah stood, intercepted her roaming, and dragged her over to sit on the couch, holding her. "We'll be okay. Genna and Pope won't let anyone hurt us."

"I know. But they can't watch us *all* the time. Maybe we should hide in the wildlands or something."

"You'd miss our friends too much."

Maya thought about going far away, somewhere she'd never see the twins, Emily, or Pick ever again. Despite only knowing them all for less than three full months, she didn't want to leave, even if it meant danger. "I feel worse about putting everyone at risk. If it was only me who'd get hurt, I'd deal."

"Does Genna have the handcuffs she tied you to the bed with?" asked Sarah.

"What? No. I think they're still attached to that bed—which went flying out the hole in the wall. Why?"

Sarah folded her arms. "Because. I'm gonna cuff myself to you so you don't run off at night again like a dummy. If you do something stupid, I am going with you."

"I won't." Maya grinned.

"Promise?"

Maya nodded. "I still feel bad about scaring you last time. Every time we play *Magic*, I think about it."

"Good." Sarah squeezed her. "I forgive you, but *please* don't do that to me again."

"Promise."

They sat in silence for a few minutes. Maya felt better being with her, even if they didn't do anything more interesting than stare at the walls. Eventually, Sarah sniffled.

"What's wrong?" asked Maya, without moving.

"It's so quiet."

"Quiet makes you sad?"

Sarah sniffled into a chuckle. "Yeah. This place was never quiet. Dad always had the TV on. Or snored. Or rambled about how much he hated Koreans. Or peed late at night."

Maya giggled. "That was *so* loud."

"Yeah." Sarah wiped her cheeks and managed a weak laugh.

"Did he really poop while you were in the bathtub?"

"Ugh. Yeah." Sarah covered her mouth. "Emergency. He woulda crapped his pants. It stank so much I had to leave the room. I stood in the living room to avoid the stink, covered in suds and dripping for like ten minutes until the air in there wouldn't make my hair fall out."

Maya laughed herself to tears. "That's so awful."

After a while, the apartment fell deathly silent again.

"Maybe we should put the TV on football for background noise?" asked Maya.

"Nah. That'll make me sadder. I actually don't like football."

"You don't?"

Sarah shook her head and sighed. "No. I used to think he liked that game more than me. I still kinda hated that he spent so much time watching it."

"Wow. How do those men play so long?"

Sarah chuckled. "Aren't you supposed to be the smart one?"

"Yeah, why?"

"They're not constantly playing. That channel shows reruns of old games when the live one isn't on."

Maya twisted around to squint at her. "Why would someone want to watch a game they've already seen?"

"I have no idea why they'd watch a game more than once." Sarah scuffed her feet back and forth on the rug. "I don't understand why people watch it at all. Dad got into it though. Sometimes he'd forget he'd seen the game already and scream at players for messing up, even though he should've remembered what was going to happen."

"Sorry for what Vanessa did." Maya leaned against her.

"Not your fault."

"You hungry?"

"I guess." Sarah shrugged.

They sat without speaking for a few more minutes. Maya got up first and walked into the kitchen. She knelt by the cabinet doors, opened them, and stared into a vast hollow where boxes upon boxes of Veterans Affairs cheese sandwiches packed a corner so deep someone would need to crawl in there to reach the last box.

"Holy crap," muttered Maya. "That's gotta be like 500 sandwiches."

"They're cheap." Sarah padded up behind her. "And they last forever. We found some like two years ago while scavving. No one else wanted them, so I brought four boxes home. And dad used to get fresh ones from the VA office once a month."

Maya grinned. "Are you sure they're safe to eat? If starving people leave them behind, that doesn't say much."

Sarah raspberried her.

She plucked four of the thin packets out of the nearest open box, each about the size, thickness, and hardness of bathroom wall tile. The nutritional value of these self-inflating sandwiches might not even meet the standards of Tuna Blast cat food (which Sarah had mistaken for single-serving casseroles) but Maya couldn't get over the stigma of 'made for animals' and refused to even try it. Fortunately, Genna agreed with her.

She shut the door and took a seat at the kitchen table. Sarah collected her two sandwiches and squeezed the chemical ampule at the corner. Soon, the overly strong scent of artificial 'baked bread' filled the kitchen. Fifteen seconds after each capsule burst, the once rock-hard slabs had blown up into reasonable approximations of white bread and quarter-inch-thick cheese tiles.

Five bites into her first sandwich, the door opened. Genna and Pope walked in to join them at the table, almost matching in black T-shirts and green camo pants. Maya practically choked trying to swallow fast so she could speak. Neither appeared too emotional, so that helped her relax.

"Everything okay?" asked Genna.

Sarah nodded, but Maya shook her head.

"What's wrong, Baby?" Genna reached across the table to put a hand on her arm.

"That guy..." Maya looked back and forth between her parents, still not quite sure how to process *having* parents. "Those pictures."

Pope scratched at his short beard. "Don't think that guy is a perv. Not getting that kinda read off him. Or those images."

The word 'images' made Maya shudder, thinking about the horrible cartoon version of herself she'd seen on Mr. Mason's computer. She couldn't imagine what kind of awful person could hate her so much that they'd draw something like that. Worse, she suspected the one she'd seen had been relatively tame compared to the other few thousand images with her name on them.

"Still. Someone's scopin' her out." Genna drummed her fingers on the table. "Probably itchin' to grab her."

Maya hurried another two bites. "Why take pictures of me over several days then? Or pictures of the other kids at all? He'd been watching us for a week. He could've grabbed me at any time."

"That's a good question." Pope drummed his fingers on the table. "Maybe the guy just likes taking pictures."

Genna quirked an eyebrow. "I'd buy that more if he had photos on that thing *aside* from Maya and the kids in this building."

"Could be, he transfers them off to a terminal wherever he lives, doesn't leave them on the device," said Pope.

"It's kinda creepy he's taking our picture." Sarah shivered. "What does he want?"

"And..." Maya held up her sandwich. "If he's checking us out for whatever reason, why would he go to Naida?"

Pope coughed and glanced away while Genna bit her lip.

"I know what Naida does." Maya sighed. "I mean, I understand why a man would be with her. What I'm saying is, why would this guy who's obviously surveilling us—or me—take a break to visit her? And I don't think they did the prostitute thing. He had all his clothes on and so did she. It's like he went straight to punching her."

Sarah gawked across the table at her, a wad of chewed bread/cheese about to fall from her mouth.

"What?" asked Maya.

She finished chewing, swallowed, and shook her head. "Wow. You really don't know how to 'child.'"

Genna snickered.

"What should I be doing?" asked Maya. "Freaking out and crying? Maybe hiding under the bed?"

"Closet's better." Sarah wagged the sandwich at her. "Under the bed is the first place monsters look."

"Hiding in the closet is also way obvious." Maya rolled her eyes. "And there's no such thing as monsters."

"Vanessa Oman," said Sarah in a tone like 'checkmate.'

Maya cringed. "Ouch. Okay. Fair point."

Genna and Pope exchanged glances. Both appeared to be trying not to laugh.

"Still. Someone's snapping pictures of the kids without them knowing about it. No matter how you approach that idea, there's something wrong with it." Pope eyed Sarah's food and headed to the cabinet. "Either it's a creep, someone with mental damage, or someone is trying to get enough documentation of her day-to-day to establish a routine." He returned to his seat, dropped two sandwich tiles on the table, and crushed the ampule to inflate the third one still in his hand. "I don't think anyone's hired a PI to catch Maya cheating, so I'm at a loss to come up with a reason someone's lurking with a camera."

"Screw it." Genna stood. "I'm gonna ask him. And... I thought you hated those things."

Pope shrugged and ate about a third of the sandwich in one bite, muttering, "They're here," past a mouthful.

"Wait..." Maya glanced up at Genna. "You're going to ask him? He's still in the building?"

"Yeah, Baby. You 'member that room Barnes put you in your first day here?"

Maya frowned. "Yeah."

"Well, that man's in there now. Weber and Barnes didn't think it wise to let him run off on account of the contents of his camera. They're trying to figure out what he's up to... and I'm gonna go help."

"Oh. Okay." Maya picked up her second sandwich and squeezed the capsule. Heat radiated outward, spreading over the rock-hard tile. In seconds, it swelled up and softened.

"Be back in a bit." Genna kissed Maya atop the head before rounding the table to do the same to Sarah. "You two stay inside."

"Yes, Mom," said Maya.

"Okay." Sarah looked up with wide, nervous eyes. "Umm, Mom?"

Genna hesitated at the archway and backed up to take Sarah's hand. "It's fine if you wanna call me that, baby, but don't feel like you gotta. If it ain't comfortable for you, I ain't gonna make no big deal out of it."

"I didn't know if it was okay. My mother disappeared when I was too little to really remember her. I don't know what happened to her, if she died or just got tired of Dad being a head case and left."

"Sorry, baby." Genna hugged her. "The man never said a word about it to me."

Sarah looked down. "I'd almost rather she died than didn't love me enough to stay."

"Book's been here forever." Genna squeezed Sarah's shoulder. "He might remember."

"You think?" She perked up.

"I'll ask him on my way back. Now, stay out of trouble." Genna patted her on the head, lingered by Pope long enough for a brief kiss, and headed out the door.

MAYA LAY SPRAWLED ON HER STOMACH IN THE BEDROOM, CHIN propped up on her hands. Sarah knelt on the opposite side of a field of *Magic* cards, sitting back on her heels while studying her hand. The game had been going on for over two hours—a record—considering they both played 'for real.' They'd endured seemingly endless games before, but usually only when one or both of them were in a bad mood and didn't care about taking it seriously.

At the moment, they truly stalemated.

Luck had not been with Maya. Though she felt fairly certain she had Sarah beat in terms of strategic thinking, the girl had ridiculous luck. While Maya kept pulling useless cards from her deck, Sarah always seemed to get the exact thing she needed at any given moment. Though frustrating, Maya didn't let it bother her. One of the Ascendant audio technicians once commented about her being an android because she played video games without becoming the least bit upset at dying. He believed no genuine child could do that.

Maya sighed, happy to be totally rid of that life. The high-end video game system, she did somewhat miss... but it was most definitely *not* worth all the other crap that came with it. She'd rather live out in the wildlands with her new family eating bugs, having nothing but leaves and vines for clothing, than go back to that penthouse. *Especially* after Vanessa threatened to hurt Sarah in order to command Maya's obedience.

"Attack." Sarah turned three creature cards sideways. "And..." She dropped an instant that caused Maya's creatures to effectively become 'stunned' and unable to block.

"Sanctum!" Maya tapped her artifact card. The single-use item made her player life pool immune to damage for one turn.

"Argh!" Sarah laughed, picking up the 'no defense' instant. "This is such a rare card! Wasted."

Maya playfully stuck her tongue out while moving the artifact to her 'dead' pile. "So is this artifact. And it's been sitting right there. You knew I had it in play."

"Girls?" Pope appeared at the door.

They both jumped, Maya nearly shrieking.

"Sorry," he said in a low voice. "Didn't mean to scare you. It's bedtime."

"Okay." Sarah set her hand down and shifted her weight back onto her feet. "We can leave it set up 'til later."

"That looks like an epic cluster—umm, yeah." Pope chuckled. "Wow, are you girls playing a game or trying to cover the entire carpet?"

Maya hated that her reaction to having someone coming out of nowhere at the door was 'oh shit, I'm being kidnapped again.' She let a long, slow breath out her nose. "Yeah. It's a good game. Much better than a steamrolling."

"Yeah." Sarah pulled her unicorn dress off, evidently no longer hesitant about Pope seeing her with nothing on. She crossed to their beat up dresser and rummaged out one of her nightgowns, basically a man's T-shirt too worn out to wear outside.

Pope patted the doorjamb twice and wandered off.

Maya walked up beside Sarah, who held the 'nightgown' up, studying its holes and stains. "What's wrong?"

"There's so many holes in this thing, it should probably be surrendered to cleaning rag duty." Sarah shrugged and pulled it on.

Maya removed her T-shirt dress and wriggled into the spaghetti-strap nightie. A lot of bad memories had soaked into the silk, but for reasons of practicality, she still used it.

"I thought you hated that thing." Sarah sat on the edge of the bed.

"I do. It reminds me of when the blueberries took Genna and being all alone out there. But... it would be wasteful not to wear it while it still fits. And it breathes."

Sarah giggled. "You're so skinny, you'll still be able to wear it when you're grown up."

"Hah." Maya decided not to ruin the joke by pointing out she'd grow *taller*. "Probably."

Sarah scooted back on the bed and patted the mattress between her knees. "Hey, 'cause I have a little sister now.... Sit."

After a momentary head tilt of confusion, Maya shrugged and sat on the edge of the bed in front of Sarah. "What are you gonna do?"

Sarah hummed to herself and began brushing Maya's hair. "Since we don't have a fancy thing in the wall to do this."

"But you do this to those dolls sometimes. I'm not a doll."

She kept running the brush down the length of Maya's hair in slow, even strokes. "With dolls, it's like pretending to do something nice for someone you care about. I'm not pretending right now."

Maya opened her mouth to say something, but couldn't think of what. Sure, aesthetic technicians had sometimes run a manual comb around her head, but there hadn't been a scrap of emotion involved in that process—merely hired professionals trying to make her look perfect for the video recording.

With each pass of the brush over her scalp, Maya's mood swirled faster and faster into a storm. She feared that if she grew too attached to this new family, Vanessa would take it away from her. Still, she found herself adoring how the brushing felt, more so, the unspoken emotional energy, even the body heat against her back from sitting so close. The moment filled her with love for her new sister, hatred for Vanessa, and total dread fear that everyone and everything she cared about would soon be taken away from her. A strange man photographing her didn't help. As if every shadow out in the world held someone trying to hurt her, she shivered.

Maybe I should run away again. Go back to Vanessa so I'm sure she won't hurt them.

The brush scratched over her scalp, sending tingles down her back.

Maya closed her eyes, squeezing out a pair of fat tears that tumbled down her cheeks.

No. I promised. This is where I belong, and I will fight that bitch.

"Are you crying?" whispered Sarah.

"Yeah."

"Why?"

"Because my brain is screwed up. I'm happy."

"Sometimes that happens." Sarah kept brushing. "People cry when they're really happy."

Maya stared down at her feet, swinging them idly side to side. "I'm also really angry and really scared."

"Me too."

"But not at you."

"I know." Sarah chuckled.

"Is this what it was like for soldiers during the war?" asked Maya.

"What do you mean? I don't think they brushed each other's hair."

She almost laughed, picturing a pair of big men sitting in the grass brushing each other's buzz cuts, then glanced at the window on the left. "Knowing that people are gonna start shooting at any second, but not exactly when."

"I dunno." Sarah hesitated, the brush slowing. "I don't want to be shot."

"We're on the seventh floor." Maya raked her toes at the rug. "It's unlikely we'd get a stray bullet."

"You really think it's going to be that bad?"

"I hope not. But it's so scary right now."

Sarah ran a few more strokes down her hair before handing over the brush. "My turn?"

"Sure." Maya grinned.

They swapped places, but since Sarah's hair hung down onto the mattress, plenty long enough to sit on, Maya knelt behind her instead of trying to sit on the edge of the bed. Sarah clutched the blanket, gasping and twisting whenever the brush hit snags.

"Are you sure?" asked Maya. "One of the aesthetic techs, I think her name was Dianne, said red hair shouldn't be brushed."

"Oh, that's for the super-curly frizz monsters. Mine isn't *that* bad unless it's humid out... then the floof goes crazy."

"Super-curly frizz monsters?" Maya blinked.

Sarah looked back. "Remember that movie on Emily's computer with the princess who had a bow and arrow?"

"Oh. Yeah." Maya nodded. "Her hair was like"—she made an explosion noise and thrust her hands into the air.

"Exactly."

Maya hummed to herself trying to brush as gently as possible. Sarah's squirming and gasping lessened. Maybe five minutes later, Genna appeared at the door. "C'mon girls. Lights out time."

They scrambled around to crawl under the sheet. Genna kissed them both good night and turned off the light on her way out. Maya snuggled close to Sarah, grateful that the day-long rain had dropped the temperature enough to sleep comfortably.

She stared at the ceiling, happy to have a sister, and a family—but terrified she'd lose them.

4

SHOES

D espite the physical and emotional comfort of her bed, Maya couldn't fall asleep.

As usual, Sarah passed out within ten minutes. Genna had returned about an hour after she'd gone to interrogate the man who attacked Naida. He claimed to be a journalist named Ronnie Parker who wanted to write about the 'child who inspired a nation.' The man couldn't explain why he took pictures from a distance or never tried to speak to her, only stating he wanted to capture photos of 'Hab kids playing' for the article that didn't appear staged.

More worrisome, the man claimed not to remember being violent with Naida or even having tried to hire her as a prostitute. As far as 'Ronnie Parker' supposedly knew, one moment he sat in a car getting some 'nice shots for the story,' and the next, he found himself in a holding cell.

Maya scratched at her stomach, glaring at the ceiling. So much about this guy didn't make sense, at least not unless she believed some stuff she'd found in the Ascendant network while boredom clicking on random theoretical research files. For whatever reason, the access level they'd given her before she 'went rogue' had allowed her to read a bunch of 'hey, could we actually do this' type white papers. None of it had been more than brainstorming, but one did stand out to her.

She'd read it because the file had been titled 'Direct Synaptic Manipulation for Behavioral Control.' The white paper detailed a theoretical design for a series of nanomachines that could enter a target's brain and deliver tiny electrical charges to certain neuron clusters to effectively modify a person's desires or even take literal remote control of their muscles.

It sounded like something out of a movie, or a project the old government might have tried to come up with before humanity blasted itself to cinders. Even if a company like Ascendant could perfect that technology, it wouldn't make any sense to bother. World War Three had reduced the population to roughly eighteen percent of what it had been before the war. No government or nation organized enough to be worth a clandestine program of that scope still existed.

The man is probably lying, but even Naida doesn't know why he tried to kill her. She said he went from friendly to hitting her in the blink of an eye. Didn't say a word. Didn't even look angry.

Maya shivered.

Genna said he didn't have any cybernetics. It can't be a cortical interface malfunction. Either that guy took some bad drugs or someone's after me again—someone from Ascendant.

She rolled on her left side and stared down at the cards on the rug. Once again, she'd gone to bed with an unfinished game left out. This time, however, she wouldn't sneak off and run away into the night. For one thing, she'd only done that to save Genna—who presently lay asleep barely ten feet away from her on the other side of the wall. For another, she promised Sarah she wouldn't.

Besides. Vanessa won't know I ran away, and she could still hurt them.

The more she tried to stop thinking about the sinister implications of Ronnie Parker's inexplicable behavior, the more it unnerved her. *Something* was up, but she had no proof. Both Pope and Genna thought the man mentally ill, probably with blackouts and possible multiple personalities. Unless something else happened, the Brigade planned to check out his background, and if they didn't find any ties to Ascendant or other parties likely to want to abduct her, they'd cut him loose. She had to admit mental illness did sound more plausible than brain-manipulation that turned people into remote-controlled androids.

Maybe I'm becoming paranoid?

From the other side of the wall, a faint *bwee... bwee... bweee* broke the silence.

Or not. Maya sighed.

Ten seconds later, her bedroom door edged open.

Maya shifted her gaze to a man slipping into the bedroom, dressed all in black with an opaque visor and a breathing mask covering his face.

She whispered, "Are you here to kidnap me?"

The man raised his left arm, pointing a handgun in Sarah's direction before nodding.

Fear paralyzed her for a second, but she tapped the same detachment that kept her in control when Genna and her team of mercs had initially kidnapped her. Outwardly, she appeared the perfect picture of calm as she sat up. The faintest *squeak* of bed springs came from the other side of the wall.

Despite the man having a weapon trained on Sarah, she huffed a sigh. "Seriously? This is my third kidnapping in three months. I am *not* going coach this time."

The man tilted his head.

Maya peeled back the sheets and swung her legs over the side of the mattress, wiggling her toes at him before whispering, "I am going to put my shoes on before you kidnap me, or you can just go ahead and shoot me right now."

He gestured at her with his free right hand in a 'be my guest' motion.

She stood and walked over to the dresser. *I need to throw this guy off guard.* "I'm so sick of being kidnapped and stuck out in the middle of nowhere with only a nightdress on." Maya picked up her black BDU pants and pulled them on up under her nightie. After securing the button, she flung the nightie off and faced him, bare-chested, her hands on her hips while she did a spot-on impression of Vanessa reacting to a project delay. "Do you know how annoying that is?"

The guy fidgeted, clearly caught off guard, and whispered, "Get on with it, kid. We don't have all night."

"I'm going to put on real clothes first." She flung her arms out to either side. "Every time I get kidnapped, I wind up stranded in the middle of nowhere in my damn nightgown, barefoot. I'm *so* done with that."

He lowered his weapon somewhat away from Sarah. "All right, but keep quiet if you don't want your friend shot."

Jaw clenched, she turned away from him and opened a drawer, careful to move in slow, telegraphed motions so he didn't think she reached for a weapon. Also, going at a snail's pace fit her hopeful plan. She picked up a white T-shirt.

Sarah sucked in a small, sharp breath. Maya glanced out of the corner of her eye at the bed. The girl's blue eyes couldn't possibly get any wider, but she hadn't moved at all.

"Oh," she whispered. "Since you're kidnapping me, you probably want me to wear dark colors so I'm harder to see." She didn't look back at him, but half expected the guy to grab her out of frustration at any moment. After trading the white tee for a black one, she sat on the rug and pulled her sneakers on. She stood and faced him again, about to ask if he planned to tie her up, but at the sight of Pope creeping up behind the guy, she smiled.

"Okay. I'm ready for my kidnapping now. But... there's one more problem."

The man sighed. "Now what?"

"I have a daddy."

Pope pounced, seizing the man's left wrist and swinging the gun upward with one hand while clamping the other over his mouth. The kidnapper yanked a knife from his belt. Sidestepping the backward thrust, Pope flipped the guy over by his gun arm and pounded him chest-first onto the floor. The gun popped from his grip. Maya darted in, grabbed it, and backed up until her shoulders hit the dresser. She clutched the weapon in both hands, but kept it pointed at the floor in front of her, having no intention of using it.

A rapid series of thuds and grunts came from the hall leading to the living room. Maya bit her lip, picturing Genna taking on two or three people.

The man wrenched himself in a twisting motion, dislodging Pope from his back, but failing to throw him clear. Pope pulled the guy along for the ride, clinging to his back like some kind of koala crab while applying pressure to his throat. Maya squeezed and relaxed her grip on the handgun, thinking Pope reminded her of a character in a fighting video game she used to play—one that really annoyed her because he used all holds and grapples. The kidnapper emitted a strangled gurgle, and after a moment, went limp.

No longer having any need to keep herself together, Maya sank into a squat, shivering, too choked up to breathe.

"How are you so calm?" gasped Sarah.

Maya breathed a few times before she tried speaking. "If you have enough experience at something, it's not scary anymore. Besides... I wasn't sleeping. I heard the alarm go off. That's why I stalled."

"Damn. This building has a roach problem." Pope stood and dusted his hands off. He approached and eased the gun out of her grip.

Maya leapt into a hug. "Daddy..."

He scooped her into the air and squeezed her for a little while before setting her standing on the bed. "Hang tight, kiddo. Need a few minutes."

Maya backed up a step, nodding. "Okay." She sat on the edge of the bed.

Sarah clung to her from behind, shivering.

"Son of a bitch," muttered Genna as she walked in. "Found two out in the hallway waiting."

"Lucky they were watching for outside threats." Pope smiled.

"Nah. That just saved me two bullets." She kicked the unconscious guy. "What the hell now?"

"Not a damn clue. This guy say anything?" Pope glanced at Maya.

She shook her head. "I don't think they were going to kill me or he wouldn't have just stood there and let me get dressed."

"Dad's alarm used to be loud enough to wake me up." Sarah sniffled.

"I turned it down," said Pope. "Better the idiots breaking in *don't* know they woke us up."

Sarah swallowed.

Pope grabbed the back of the guy's shirt at the neck and dragged him out.

"Well..." Maya removed her shoes and tossed them to the rug. "I guess we're not sleeping tonight."

Sarah rubbed a hand up and down her back.

After sitting there for a few minutes in silence listening to Genna and Pope drag three unconscious men around, Maya changed back into her nightie and crawled into bed again. Even if she couldn't sleep, she could at least spend what remained of the night comfortable.

"Are you okay?" asked Sarah.

The question broke the dam.

Maya burst into tears, clinging to Sarah and sobbing. "No. I'm not okay. I'm sick of being kidnapped!"

"You weren't kidnapped," said Sarah. "Just attacked."

Crying morphed into teary giggles. "Semantics."

"What?"

Maya sighed. "Never mind."

"Hey at least he was gonna let you put your shoes on."

"I can't believe that worked." Maya grabbed her stomach and sighed out a long gasp of relief. "I hoped if I could keep him off balance, it would give Mom or Dad an opening."

"Whatever you did, it worked."

Maya rolled her head to the right, staring into Sarah's eyes. "Yeah, but I wish people would just leave me alone."

"They will." Sarah squeezed her hand. "As soon as the Brigade burns Ascendant down. They're only after you because of your connection to Vanessa. Once that company is gone, you're free."

"Maybe I shouldn't have asked Mom to stop when she almost shot Vanessa."

Sarah shook her head. "No. You had to be yourself. Killing is bad no matter who dies. Even someone like her."

Overcome, Maya couldn't say a word. This girl who'd lost her father not two weeks ago to that woman's cruelty would rather the bitch live than Maya have to witness her murder. She rolled on her side toward Sarah and huddled close, doubting it possible that she would ever feel safe again.

5

AN UNKNOWN QUANTITY

Megawaffle cereal blasted Maya's mouth with sugar.

She almost choked on the first spoonful, having forgotten its extreme sweetness. Even the liquid syrup she dumped on the toaster waffles didn't even come close. That stuff at least had some flavor. Or maybe super sweet appealed to her more when paired with hot food. Sometimes the video crews would have pastries delivered, and the one she liked was warm. Something rectangular with white icing drizzled back and forth on the top and fruity stuff inside.

Sarah, however, inhaled the cereal without hesitation, emitting soft murmurs of approval.

Then again, the girl had liked cat food. Compared to that, Maya would prefer Megawaffle, too.

Genna and Pope sat at the narrower ends of the kitchen table, both having buttered toast and coffee for their breakfast. Maya would've preferred it to drinking a bowl of pure sugar that someone stirred with a maple branch. She could probably lick a maple tree—if any still existed —and it would taste more like maple syrup than this cereal.

Genna had let the girls sleep in a little. But, honestly, it *was* summer. Not that it much mattered. Only about fifteen percent of kids in the Hab went to school. Citizen kids in the Sanc attended at about a sixty-two percent rate, with the rest homeschooled online. She'd once read on the AuthNet that before the war, the law required children under eighteen to attend school in person. No one cared if Hab kids got an education at all, and even in the Sanc, it hadn't been made mandatory. No, there they had a far more effective tool: citizenship. For those who didn't attend actual school, they had to pass an evaluation to confirm a high school equivalent education—or they lost their parentally-inherited citizenship on their eighteenth birthday.

Out of sheer boredom, Maya had already taken and passed the test online. Had she not been Vanessa Oman's legal daughter at the time, it probably would've been discarded as a prank. Soon after her ninth birthday, she'd effectively completed high school. She wanted to take university level courses, but the woman thought her too immature for it yet. And... during her more recent 'incarceration' back in the penthouse, she'd been on network lockdown. Maybe she could convince the Brigade to link this building to the AuthNet. As much as she hated Ascendant and all its drugs, having exposure to that world made her think it wasteful not to use her knowledge. Still, she couldn't quite decide between wanting to be a doctor, a chemist, a biologist, or some combination thereof.

Perhaps if she became a doctor, Vanessa would manage to do some good for this world by having ordered a genius baby... and Maya liked helping people. Only two medical schools remained in the Eastern Commonwealth States. The one right here in the Baltimore Sanctuary Zone had the unfortunate problem of being infected with Ascendant. Her ex-mother's company so infiltrated the school like a cancer, people couldn't tell where one began and the other ended. Alas, the other one was in Miami, and she really didn't want to leave her friends.

She didn't much think they'd take a kid her age anyway.

"Something wrong, baby?" asked Genna. "You're not eating."

Sarah had finished and sat staring across the table at her with a 'c'mon hurry up' face.

Maya glanced down at her half-bowl of cereal. "I'm thinking."

"They had a scare last night," said Pope.

"Actually, that wasn't too bad. If we had AuthNet access, I'd give that attempted kidnapping a four-star review." Maya leaned her chin on one hand, elbow on the table. "Did you kill them?"

Genna fired a 'can you believe this kid' look at Pope before chuckling. "No, actually... we didn't. Those idiots were operating under the misconception Ascendant would pay a ransom."

A sudden laugh with a spoonful of cereal halfway into Maya's mouth sprayed milk.

"Not so organized." Pope stood to grab a towel from the counter. "Three freelancers hoping to score a payday. Your mother told them an interesting story about how well that woman takes ransom demands."

"That and I promised if I ever saw them in our home again they'd better hope they made peace with whatever spirits they believe in." Genna scowled at nothing in particular and rubbed the bridge of her nose. "Maybe we should get outta this building."

Maya and Sarah both gasped.

"But our friends..." Sarah almost pouted.

"We can make this work." Pope sopped up the milk spray. "Need to add a few more bells and whistles, but we can get this place to the point fleas would have trouble sneaking in."

Sarah scratched at herself. "I don't have fleas."

"I know, baby." Genna rubbed her back. "It's just a figure of speech."

"I *have* had fleas. They suck." Sarah squirmed.

Maya giggled.

"It's not funny." Sarah scrunched up her nose.

"No, they really do suck... blood."

"Ugh." Genna shook her head.

"Did you ask Book about, umm..." Sarah bit her lip. "My bio mom?"

"Yeah... he, umm." Genna rubbed the bridge of her nose.

Sarah set her spoon down. "If she didn't hate me, I can handle it. Please tell me."

"Well, he seemed to think she died around the time you were two or three, caught up in some gang violence over in Block 12. Just walking by when a gunfight broke out and a stray shot hit her."

"Oh." Sarah looked down, tears gathering in her eyes. "I must've been small. I don't remember her at all. Always kinda figured she died, but I thought Fade got her."

Genna clasped Sarah's hand. "Book said Billy, umm, your dad, took it real hard. He figured that kinda broke him. He loved her a lot. As much as he loved you. Way Book explained it, he thought your dad kinda stopped caring if he lived at that point."

Yeah... the man wanted to die all right. Maya bit her lip.

"Thanks," whispered Sarah. "And, you're right. I guess he did kinda want to die. He always told me he knew he'd get sick from chemicals and stuff he'd been exposed to during the war. I just didn't think it would happen so soon."

Pope patted her on the shoulder and squeezed. "When we were over there, you wouldn't believe the destruction. Straight back to medieval times. No one really expected any kind of medical technology would survive."

"Yeah." Sarah looked down at her bowl. "I'm glad I know for sure now. At least she didn't abandon me on purpose."

Genna squeezed her hand.

"Mom?" asked Maya. "I was thinking about that journalist again. It's bothering me that he said he didn't remember hitting Naida."

"Guy's probably trained to lie. Seen that sorta thing before, but it wasn't my job to get the truth outta them." Genna sighed, shaking her head. "Though, he did play it way cool."

"I couldn't sleep last night because I kept trying to come up with an explanation for how he went from his car to the holding room and might not remember." Maya tossed the last two pieces of Megawaffle in her mouth and forced them down.

"This, I gotta hear." Pope smiled.

"Well..." Maya looked back and forth between her parents and Sarah. "He might've been infected by nanobots targeting the pre-frontal cortex to suppress short term memory while others stimulated the amygdala to stimulate desired decision-making branch process. Someone else could've been using that system to innervate specific neural pathways, creating external changes in action and mood."

Her entire family simply stared at her.

"Was that even English?" asked Sarah a moment later.

Genna raised one eyebrow.

"Okay, in English... someone might've been remote-controlling him. Or they just uploaded a set of instructions that took him over and made him do something. But... I think the system probably malfunctioned."

"Where the hell did you get that from?" asked Pope.

"I read some whitepapers in the Ascendant network about a project one day while bored." She wagged the spoon at him. "Also, his change of attitude happened after Sarah shot him in the face with a Hornet. The high-intensity electrical discharge could've overloaded the nanobots and killed them, which ended their override effect on his cognitive processing and allowed the guy to return to normal."

"You're just making up words now." Sarah stuck out her tongue.

"That's freaky as hell," said Genna. "But I heard some shit like that before. Was all theoretical though. Rumor went around my unit that the Chinese had something like that, but we never saw anything for real."

Maya nodded. "What I read was only a whitepaper discussing it in terms of feasibility. It didn't sound like anything existed yet."

"How long ago was that?" asked Pope.

"Umm." Maya squinted, trying to remember. "Maybe four or five weeks before Mom rescued me from that penthouse."

Genna shook her head, chuckling.

"Okay." Pope sank back into his chair. "Let's consider this might've actually happened. Is our journalist an assassin or an experiment?"

Maya shrugged. "Not sure. I haven't been going to Ascendant meetings lately."

"Heh." Pope chuckled.

"You think this is Ascendant's doing, baby?" asked Genna.

"Umm." Maya gave her a blank stare. "Who else has that kind of tech?"

"Doesn't have to be from Baltimore." Pope shifted his jaw side to side in thought. "Anyone could've brought a small lab setup in a van and grabbed this poor slob off the side of the road. Could be the California Washington Commonwealth randomly testing. Maybe they got a hold of the Chinese version? Or, hell, they had a lot of universities out there. Ascendant *is* pushing them to the brink of war."

"We kinda helped that out a bit." Genna cringed. "Blasting out the truth of Fade's origins has pissed off most of the world."

"What's left of it," muttered Sarah.

"Oops." Maya winced.

"It had to happen." Pope leaned over and patted her shoulder. "Fortunately, most of the rest of the world ain't in a position to do anything about it. At least not on any scale that presents a serious threat."

"Why would they attack us all?" asked Sarah. "It's Ascendant, not the people."

"Maybe they're waiting to see if we deal with it in-house." Genna drummed her fingers on the table.

"But why Maya?" Sarah gathered the empty bowls and stood. "Why are they taking pictures of her?"

"Well, this could be California, Europe, some other Pharma company, mercs." Pope rubbed his forehead in frustration. "I hate to say it, but everyone knows who she is. Not many people are aware that Vanessa disowned her."

"This is all so far-fetched." Genna leaned back and sighed out her nose.

"Can you ask Doc Chang to look at him?" asked Maya. "If he had nanobots in his system and the Hornet disabled them, they would most likely wind up in the bloodstream and filtered out by the kidneys. But it's been a while. He might've peed them out already."

"We can check." Pope stood. "I'll go have a chat with him."

"Is it still bad out there?" Sarah, already washing dishes, peered back over her shoulder. "Are we stuck inside today?"

"Word from Harlowe is things are tense but not as bad as everyone's thinking," said Genna. "Out here in the Hab, it should be reasonably safe. If anything starts, that powder keg's gonna spark inside the Sanc first. We should have time to react. Though, if you two do go outside, don't stray *too* far from the building, okay?"

Sarah nodded.

Maya swung her feet back and forth. Last night, three men walked into their home and tried to abduct her. Today, Sarah wanted to go out and be normal. Maybe the girl had a point. Hiding in here would only make her freak out more and dwell on being scared.

I flew on a drone into the Sanc to find Genna. I'm not scared of the Hab.

Grinning, Maya hopped out of her chair and ran over to help dry dishes.

6

LOOT DENIED

Children gathered in the basement with all the gravitas of a spaceship crew preparing to embark on a dangerous excursion down to the surface of an unexplored planet. Anton and Marcus had been restless as of late due to the group not having gone on a scavenging run since they scored the massive haul from the crashed drone. The big payoff left them overly excited and expecting another big windfall.

Marcus unrolled a large sheet of paper in the middle of the carpeted area Zoe set up for them. Six or seven layers deep and ringed by rolled rugs thicker than utility poles, it felt like sitting in a giant sandbox without the sand, a combination giant sofa and fort.

The paper contained a map of the Hab and a few blocks in either direction, something Book had helped with. While hand-drawn, the shapes of streets, sidewalks, and buildings had a degree of precision that baffled Maya. She wondered if, much like his head implant that contained all the novels he read to the kids, he also had something that let him copy images. Perhaps electronics took over his muscles and helped him draw this?

Pick flopped on his stomach, chin on one hand while pointing at spots on the map where they hadn't explored. As usual, he wore no shirt, but his khaki shorts with huge pockets on the thighs appeared somewhat new. The boy either shared Emily's aversion to shoes or simply didn't have any.

The twins knelt on either side of the giant paper, both in blue-and-white striped shirts and matching shorts. Sarah sat cross-legged beside Maya, wearing her not-so-white sneakers, the black BDU pants Genna got her, plus a dark grey tank top that bared her shoulders. She carried the Hornet in a hip holster, but covered it with a big scrap of tattered brown cloth she'd tied around her waist like a short skirt.

Knowing they intended to go out, Maya put on her 'little revolutionary' outfit, the black BDU pants with a black T-shirt and her black sneakers.

Unconcerned with the map or any planning, Emily Chang balance-beam walked around the rolled-up carpet logs bordering the padded enclosure. She still wore the overly fancy 'antique doll' dress that hung in tiered layers, but she'd added something new: a set of blue plastic faerie wings attached by sparkly silver elastic around her shoulders. The girl only trailed Maya by a year, but acted much younger. Or at least, Maya thought so. An eight-year-old shouldn't pretend to see faeries—or be one.

"We gotta hit this spot." Anton poked his finger at the paper.

"Naw," said his brother, Marcus. "That's kinda close to the Hab. If there's anything in there, it's long gone already."

"That's the thing." Anton smiled. "This one's locked up tight."

"Someone owns it?" Pick twisted a finger around inside his nose. "We's gonna steal a building?"

"No." Anton laughed. "It's like one of those limbo things."

"Limbo things?" asked Sarah.

"That's what Book said." Marcus scratched his head, making his in-need-of-a-trim afro wobble. "Said like no one owned it before the war, but a bank had four clothes. So, it stayed locked."

"Banks don't have clothes." Pick pulled his finger out long enough to shake his head.

Maya bit her lip. It probably didn't matter if her friends understood that or not, so she kept quiet, not wanting to be annoying.

"Sparkles!" shouted Emily, before jumping off the carpet roll.

For a second and a half, she seemed to hang in the air like a faerie, then landed with a belly flop in a pile of pillows.

"Okay, so if this place is locked..." Maya crawled forward to study the map. "How are we going to get inside that other people haven't already tried?"

"Maybe Sarah can get the door?" asked Marcus.

"Adult criminals can pick locks too." Maya sat back on her heels and folded her arms.

"Small windows or something Pick can fit through?" Anton tapped a finger to his chin.

Pick nodded.

"We haven't been much around that area 'cause it's so close to the Hab. If we can't get in there, we'll look around. Most of us still all got the NuCoin from the big haul, so this one's really for fun." Anton looked around. "Sound good?"

"Mission ready," said Marcus.

Maya suppressed an eye roll.

"Arr!" yelled Pick.

"Dude. This isn't pirates. This is Scav Team," whispered Anton.

Pick blinked, then jumped to his feet like a soldier. "Roger that."

At pirates, the twins let the six-year-old be the captain, but for scavenging, he had to sit back and listen to the older boys... or Sarah. As the oldest, she exercised a degree of authority over them all despite not actively playing their 'Scav Team' game.

Their mission decided upon, the twins rolled up the map, stashed it in the steel cabinet where it lived (which bore numerous hand-drawn 'badges' for Scav Team) and headed down the trash-strewn corridor to the basement stairs.

Maya followed close behind Sarah, and couldn't help but giggle.

"What?" asked Sarah.

"You're not walking funny anymore."

Sarah narrowed her eyes. "What?"

"You weren't used to shoes. Ever see a dog when they put doggie shoes on them and they step weird?"

"No." Sarah raspberried her, then sighed. "Still kinda feels strange."

"It's better to have shoes outside."

"I know, but that doesn't mean I'm used to having them. If it wasn't so dirty out there, I might leave them home. And I'm not a dog." Sarah play-punched her in the shoulder. "Come on, we're falling behind. Pick is gonna get hurt if we don't watch him."

"Am not," shouted Pick from the top of the stairs.

Anton led the way out the back door. The rusting husk of a large old car—the boys' pirate galleon—stood sentinel over a large, square swath of worn blacktop spider-webbed with trails of green grass growing up from cracks. Only one resident of the building had owned a functional car, Mr. Mason... and he would *not* be back. Merely thinking of him twisted Maya's stomach up in knots.

The kids exited the lot via the breach in the chain link fence. Anton and Marcus headed off to the left at a fast walk. All around her, the Hab carried on in relative normality. Here and there, the kids caught glimpses of gang members, none of whom paid them any notice. That woman with the realistic fake baby went by on the other side of the street, still trying to beg from people. She, slowed, eyeing the kids as if considering asking them for money, but changed her mind and kept going.

Paradoxically, Maya didn't feel comfortable despite being in a fairly large group. Both she and Sarah could pass for low-end Citizen kids due to their intact clothing and sneakers. The twins' clothes also looked new, but they still went barefoot. Only Pick still *looked* like a street rat, with his dirt-smeared skin and disheveled hair, but even he'd gotten a newish pair of shorts that had no rips or tatters. Emily's dress, though fancy, also appeared shabby due to her having worn it constantly for months. If she could do the impossible, and sit completely still, she'd look like a doll left in an attic for fifty years.

A new fear unsettled Maya: other street kids might come after them to take their clothes. Though, in a pack of six, numbers would probably keep them safe. Any other kids who'd band together in a group bigger than hers would be too old to wear any of the clothes they might steal from Maya or her friends.

Only one Authority drone passed overhead during the seven-block walk to the part of old Baltimore the twins had decided on visiting. Clouds of steamy air wafted from noodle counters, alleys, or open windows, scented with cooking food, chemicals, or sewer.

Grey-clad Nons went by, paying little attention to the kids. A few Frags rummaging in the trash eyed them, but kept their distance. One elderly, naked man with 'the end is near' painted on his chest waved his arm and shouted at them in a tone like he tried to warn them about something—but he'd drank too much booze to be able to create actual words. Still, he seemed harmless, so Anton merely walked past him. Sarah covered Emily's eyes before she could look at him.

The area the boys targeted for their scavenging trip wound up being only two blocks from the unofficial end of the Baltimore Habitation District. Due to its proximity to the Dead Space, the alleys and streets contained hundreds of improvised dwellings made of tarps, plastiboard cartons, and repurposed metal dumpsters.

Frags, though primitive, tended to keep to themselves, so Maya didn't worry too much that some adult might attack them to obtain clothes for their feral children, like the ones she'd run into on her trek to find Genna. As scary as that woman had looked, she'd fed Maya without hesitation, so maybe Frags wouldn't simply mug them for clothes, even if a good portion of them didn't have any. She wondered what they did during the colder months, picturing large groups huddled inside abandoned buildings, burning scrap wood while the 'hunters' ventured out to forage.

Ugh. We've gone back to tribal primitivism.

The twins marched onward with mission in their stride. Emily whined about them going too fast and kept asking them to slow down. Maya continued gazing around, wanting to be ready in case someone popped out of the dark and grabbed her. Aside from a handful of curious vagrants creeping out of alleys to check them out, no one appeared threatening. A new wave of stink rolled by on the next breeze, a rotting puke-tinged-with-ammonia awfulness that brought tears to her eyes. The twins coughed while Pick merely scrunched up his nose. Emily almost puked.

"Ugh, smells like Farnham," said Sarah before gagging. "Gah! What is that?"

Maya wiped her tears on her arm. "Someone drank too much booze and threw up, and it's been sitting in the sun."

An unpleasant noise emanated from Sarah's stomach. "I... didn't need an answer."

"Sorry," muttered Maya.

"Eww." Pick scrunched up his face.

Emily gasped and looked around at the paving. "Where is it? I don't wanna step in it."

"Fly over it if you're a faerie." Marcus made a fluttering wings gesture.

"I'm not a faerie yet." Emily bounced on her toes. "Eww. Eww. Eww. Where is it?"

"Probably over by the wall." Maya pointed.

Emily drifted into the middle of the street.

"Get out of the road," hissed Sarah.

"I don't wanna step in pee-puke!"

"That's better than getting hit by a car." Sarah pointed at the sidewalk beside her in a motherly 'get your ass over here now' way.

Head down, Emily trudged closer.

A few minutes later, the boys approached a padlocked gate in a chain link fence surrounding a twelve-story high-rise. They pulled it as wide as possible, enough of a gap for the kids to slip in. Pick entered after the twins, Emily close behind. Sarah waited for Maya to go in, then followed, bringing up the rear.

Various signs on the fence indicated it as 'office space for lease,' while the building itself had no markings other than '2065' in white letters above the entrance, probably the street address. Metal plates covered the glass portions of the front doors as well as the huge windows on either side of them. All the windows on the first three stories had plywood over them, liberally coated with graffiti.

"Whoa," said Anton, a note of disappointment in his voice. "This place is a damn castle."

Before Maya could say 'I told you so,' Marcus raced off yelling, "Let's check around back."

Maya's opinion of the general intelligence level of the human race plummeted when they reached the opposite side of the building. The fencing they'd squeezed through only went three-quarters the way around the property, leaving the street-facing side wide open—and the chain on the gate entirely useless.

The far side of the street held a bunch of abandoned buildings: a sandwich counter, a coffee shop, a store with mannequins in the window, and a pizza place. Only curious street kids and vagrants had been inside any of them for at least a decade. A few old brass casings from handgun bullets gathered in the gutter, collected by the wind in a pile.

"Hey, maybe we can get in over there." Anton pointed at a small paved area between the high rise and the street toward a ramp beyond the corner. Not giving anyone a chance to reply, he sprinted for it.

The group rushed after him.

A dock with two rolling doors sat at the bottom of a short road, the sort of thing semi-trailers would back up to. Based on the angle of the hill, Maya figured those doors led to the basement. Vast numbers of plastiboard cartons arranged like Frag dwellings lined both sides of the angled passage, but nothing moved. Whatever vagrants had lived here appeared to have either moved on or gone out for the day.

Anton ran down the hill, the clap of his bare feet echoing in the concrete canyon. Marcus chased him close with Pick right behind them. The girls followed but didn't bother running. Both twins scrambled up over bumpers made from scraps of old tire onto the dock. Pick, being shorter, had a harder time of it, but also pulled himself up.

Sarah stopped at the bottom of the ramp where the ground leveled off, about twenty feet from the dock. Maya hovered close to her, watching the boys while they poked around the rolling doors. Emily ignored everything, walking in a figure eight around Maya and Sarah, her arms held out like airplane wings.

"Yo, these shits are locked." Anton kicked the door. "Can you check it out, Faerie?"

Marcus squatted to examine dents. "Someone hit on them good. Gotta be stuff in here worth grabbing. And it's still in here 'cause the doors is still locked."

"Are," said Maya.

"Arrrr!" Pick struck a pirate's pose.

Maya sighed.

"Okay." Sarah approached the dock, which came up to her chin, and grabbed on to one of the tire-slice bumpers.

A scuff came from behind Maya.

She whirled around and squeaked at the sight of six men, all dressed in 'clothing' made from wires, appliance parts, plastic tarps, and even sections of plastiboard. They must have emerged from their shipping carton 'houses,' gathering in a group that blocked off the only way out.

None of the men had shoes, an unfortunate fact that had allowed them to creep frighteningly close before one of them had made a sound.

"Sarah," yelled Maya.

The redhead paused to look over her shoulder, one knee up on the dock bumper. She "eeped" and dropped back down.

Maya glanced from one guy to the next, noting two kept blinking and gazing around as if seeing things that didn't exist. Dried blood trailed down from another man's nostrils to his chin, like rust stains on a wall beneath a pipe opening. *That guy's on Fume.* Maya gulped. *Shit. Dosers.*

"Hey there..." A guy in a bright blue tarp-skirt patted a large machete strapped to his leg in a sheath made from Megawaffle cereal boxes. "Easy, kiddies. Not here ta hurt anyone."

Maya backed up until she stood next to Sarah. At least none of these guys looked at her *that* way. Much to her surprise, however, Sarah trembled. Already, her eyes had reddened. Maya glanced down at her sister's black BDU pants, the same style that the dosers once stole from her. Her beloved ones had been green camo, and she'd adored them since they'd been her first real garment. She'd basically *just* gotten pants again... and now dosers would leave them all bare-ass naked on the street.

At least Genna won't make us wait days before getting us new clothes.

"Get on down from there." A man with long, black hair slid a cheap katana off his back and wagged it at the twins. "You too." He pointed it at Pick.

Emily looked around for a place to run. Seeing no way out, she clamped onto Maya and shivered.

"We be nice to yous if you be nice to us-es," said a pudgy guy wearing a tabard made of plastiboard.

"Ouch..." Maya blinked at him. "You just perpetrated such a brutal attack on language, the Authority might actually arrest you."

"Huh?" asked the big guy.

A skinny man with bright pink hair kicked a yellow carton toward them. "Put all your stuff in there and you can go home wifout a scratch." He chuckled. "We ain't gonna hurt no one. Just need money."

Emily burst into tears. "Please don't take my dress!"

Crap. Maya gulped. *Sarah wasn't paranoid. Maybe we should wear rags when we go outside.*

The twins and Pick jumped down from the dock and moved up behind the girls.

Sarah slid her hand under the sash hiding the Hornet while muttering, "Sword guy's going down. Ant, you and Marcus, go right. Maya, all the way left. Run like hell. Scatter. They can't catch us all."

The men moved closer, a wall of humanity trapping the kids in a dead end alcove.

"Now!" yelled Sarah as she drew the Hornet, aimed, and fired a dart straight into katana-man's forehead.

The metal projectile hit him with a hollow *clonk* like a rock bouncing off a coconut. Sparks wrapped over the top of his skull and slithered down his back as foam flew from his mouth. He emitted a gargling attempt at a scream before lapsing into a twitching, flailing mess.

The twins bolted to the right. Maya dashed to the left.

Machete-man screamed a war cry and charged at Sarah. The fat one in the plastiboard tabard caught the twins in a double clothesline maneuver. Both boys folded in half, nearly kicking themselves in the face as their stringy bodies wrapped around his arms. Before they fell, he clamped on, holding them, laughing at the boys' attempts to punch him in the head.

Sarah pivoted and fired another dart, but missed Machete-man by inches. He crashed into her, knocking her against the dock wall hard enough to make her bark like a goose. The Hornet slipped out of her grip, clattering to the ground. Maya pivoted and ran back, flinging herself at him from behind while shrieking.

Machete-man palmed Maya's face and shoved her over on her ass, then flipped Sarah around to grab her from behind, holding her with his blade across her neck. She strained up on tiptoe, pulling at his arm and gasping.

Everyone froze statue still, Anton and Marcus with their fists poised to hit the fat doser.

"Now," said Machete-man. "I don't blame ya for tryin' ta run, so we can still do this all nice and shit. Put everything in that box."

Sarah struggled at the arm across her chest with both hands, unable to pull it down. She tried to get her throat away from the sharp edge, but couldn't lean her head back with it already against his chest.

"Okay!" shouted Maya. "Please don't hurt her."

Sarah let out a scream worthy of a horror movie actress seeing the monster for the first time. Her voice echoed off the high-rises surrounding them, startling some pigeons into the air.

The dosers found that hilarious.

Pick narrowed his eyes in defiance. Seconds later, the front of his shorts darkened.

"Don't matter. In the box." The pudgy doser tossed the twins to the ground one after the next, then took on a stance like a goalie in case they tried to run past him again.

Pick shot the guy a nasty look but shoved his pants down, his body two shades paler where the fabric had covered. Still glaring, he stepped out of them and kicked the soiled garment toward the box. Both twins began removing their shirts. Maya, her hands shaking, grabbed the bottom of her tee. Motion at the top of a ramp made her pause with it halfway off. An armored blueberry leaned past the corner of the next building, trying to stay hidden while watching the goings on.

Emily continued to beg the men not to steal her favorite dress.

Maya stared pleadingly at the distant blueberry, and mouthed 'please help us,' but the man made no effort to do anything. She scowled. *He probably thinks this is funny, watching Non kids being robbed.*

Machete lowered his blade from Sarah's throat and tossed her down to all fours. "Put all yer stuff in the box, kid."

"I haven't even had these for a week yet," whispered Sarah. "Please don't do this to us."

Marcus and Anton tossed their shirts in the box. Maya pulled hers off over her head.

"Damn, you is skinny," said the heavyset guy.

Maya glared at him.

"That blueberry's just gonna stand there, isn't he?" asked Anton.

"What the hell else would blueberries do?" Marcus shook his head. "We ain't no one to them."

Emily clamped her arms around herself, trembling. "Please don't take my dress."

A bald guy slapped the back of his hand into Machete-man's

shoulder. "Hey, why don' we skip that one." He pointed at Emily. "No one'd buy that little thing."

"People would buy your jock strap," said Machete-man. "It's NuCoin on the hoof."

Emily bawled, hands clasped at her chin, begging them to let her keep her faerie dress.

"Dude." The bald guy gestured at her again. "Come on. Look at her."

The five remaining dosers—Katana Man still lay unresponsive on the ground, twitching and drooling, a Hornet dart embedded in his forehead—exchanged glances and murmurings before nodding at each other.

"Fine. Whatever." Machete-man waved at Emily. "Get outta here. Keep that stupid thing."

Sobbing, Sarah removed her shirt. The twins' started undoing their shorts. Sarah couldn't bring herself to even open the button at the front of her pants. Maya started to push hers down, but before they made it a quarter of the way to her knees, she froze stock still staring past the dosers, unable to believe what her eyes told her.

Four blueberries ambled down the ramp toward them. One looked at Maya and made an 'up' gesture. She yanked her pants back in place.

"The hell, kid? *Off.*" Machete grabbed her shoulder. "That stuff is ours now."

"Holy shit." Anton gawked. "Seriously?"

"Whoa," muttered Marcus as he yanked his shorts back up.

Maya shoved at the guy holding her shoulder. "Get off me."

He grabbed the front of her pants, but before he could pull them down, he let off a squawk like a pigeon struck by a car. One of the blueberries seized him by the hair and hauled him backward. The other blueberries rushed the dosers, throwing them into the wall on the left and working them over with stun batons. The instant chaos erupted, Sarah scrambled back into her shirt.

Maya stooped to grab her T-shirt as the one who'd given her the 'up' sign hauled Machete-man away from her. The idiot took a swing at the officer, but the blade glanced off the man's armor with a plastic *click*.

"Oh, bad move, dude." Anton raised both eyebrows, still standing there shirtless. "Seriously bad move."

Maya cringed away from the vicious beating that followed. The twins recovered their shirts, making silent mocking faces at the dosers during the ass-kicking. Emily ran over and clung to Maya and Sarah, refusing to look at the armored officers thrashing the bewildered dosers.

"Holy crap," whispered Maya. "He wasn't standing there to watch ... he was waiting for backup!"

Within minutes, all six moaning dosers lay in a row, restrained in plastic cuffs. The officers ushered the kids together in a line by the dock. One picked up the Hornet and looked it over.

"You kids okay?" asked a blueberry.

Maya couldn't tell them apart without looking at nametags. "Yes, sir. Thank you *so* much."

He nodded. "What are you kids doing here?"

Pick retrieved his shorts from the ground next to the box, but didn't put them on.

"We're just exploring the old city," said Maya.

"What's with this?" The one holding the Hornet held it up.

"It's mine." Sarah bowed her head. "My father gave it to me for protection, but he died a couple weeks ago. He was a recon scout, LRRP/D with the 7th Cavalry."

A short, but stocky blueberry crouching by the dosers lifted Katana Man's head, admiring the one-inch silver dart nearly at the perfect center of his forehead. "Damn nice shot, kid."

"Couple weeks ago?" asked the blueberry on the far left. "Hawthorne?"

"Yes." Sarah nodded.

That officer opened his helmet visor. As soon as she saw his face, Maya's eyes bugged out. This man had been at the funeral, the guy in the dress uniform with the globe-and-anchor things on his cuffs. His nametag read 'Cabrera.' Sarah appeared to remember him as well, and choked up a little. He patted her on the head, took the Hornet from the officer holding it, and handed it back to her.

Two other blueberries tilted their heads at him, expressions unreadable under silver visors.

"She's a little young, but it's nonlethal." Officer Cabrera nodded at Sarah. "And her dad served."

The others all nodded.

"So, exploring?" Cabrera glanced at the loading dock.

"Yeah, we go scavenging around for anything that could be useful," said Marcus, a note of hesitant awe in his voice. "These dudes just ambushed us, tried to take our stuff."

A tilted his helmet at Pick.

"I wasn't scared." The boy held up the shorts. "I did it on purpose because they wanted ta steal them. Anyone takes *my* stuff, there's gonna be pee on 'em."

The officers chuckled.

While Cabrera and two officers recorded the kids' statements about the attempted mugging, the other two jogged back up the ramp and returned with a large, dark blue Authority personnel carrier complete with a .50 cal on the roof, which they backed down the ramp. They hopped out and began loading the dosers into the back.

Next came routine questions about where the kids lived, status of parents, and so on.

"All right." Cabrera nodded at them. "You kids go on home, okay. Things are a little tense and you should probably stick close to your building until this mess blows over."

"You serious?" whispered Anton. "We can like just leave?"

"Did you do anything we might want to detain you for?" asked another blueberry, a faint electric crackle in his voice from helmet-mounted speakers.

"Just being Nons," muttered Anton at the ground.

A blueberry, Officer Montez according to his armor, crouched to eye-level with the twins and opened his helmet visor. He somewhat resembled a grown-up version of Pick. "Hey. Look, I won't try and pretend that stuff didn't happen. I want you to understand that we're trying to clean house. You kids have every right to be on guard around anyone in this armor. But, I hope you'll eventually be able to see us as here to help everyone, not only Citizens."

The twins managed hesitant nods, both clearly dumbstruck.

"Why do you talk funny?" asked Emily.

Officer Montez laughed. "I'm actually from the New York Sanc. Reassigned here for a couple of months to help straighten things out."

"It's stuck in the skull," said a blueberry over by the vehicle. "She shot him inside the minimum range. Hell, the hit probably knocked him out before he noticed the zap."

"Screw it. Let the medics take it out. This dude loaded his pants. I don't want to touch him that long."

They shoved Katana-man into the metal-walled holding cell at the back of the truck, still with a Hornet dart protruding from his forehead.

Sarah clamped a hand over her mouth to stop herself from laughing.

"Okay, kids. Go on home, okay?" Cabrera clasped Sarah's shoulder. "Sorry again about your old man."

"Thanks." Sarah's lip quivered.

"Want a ride back?" asked Cabrera.

Sarah looked up at him. "Thanks, but it's not far and we should be okay in the Hab. Everyone knows Maya there and they won't give us trouble."

He looked at Maya. "All right. Heh. Didn't realize who you were the last time I saw you."

Maya smiled. "Neither did I. You didn't look like a blueberry in that green uniform."

"Kid seems a lot nicer than rumor made her out to be," added another man with his visor still down.

"Oh, I probably *was* snippy to a few officers, but it wasn't *their* fault. I had a pretty severe case of abandonment disorder, no real outlet for my emotions, and a mess of other problems." Maya smiled and put an arm around Sarah. "I'm better now."

The officers exchanged glances. One whistled. A few chuckled.

After thanking them again, Maya led the way up the ramp to the street, refusing to let go of Sarah's hand. Emily followed close, with the twins behind Pick who unashamedly streaked with his shorts in his hand.

Two blocks closer to home, Sarah finally screamed, "Holy crap!"

Her sudden outburst startled a clipped shriek from Maya, made the boys freeze in place, and sent Emily spinning in circles searching for danger.

"Faerie?" asked Anton.

"I can't believe what just happened." Sarah blinked. "The freakin' blueberries *helped* us."

"Yeah, wow." Marcus whistled. "That's even more messed up than them lockin' down the building and *not* leavin' us all in cuffs."

"That little drone was pretty cool." Anton grinned.

Marcus threw an arm around Maya and grinned. "She's changin' the world and shit."

She decided to tolerate the hug, despite Sarah giving her an 'ooo! He likes you' glance.

Pick wandered past everyone, casual as could be. Emily giggled.

"Umm," said Maya. "Aren't you gonna get dressed? You're naked."

"So?" He shrugged, holding the shorts up. "These have pee on 'em."

"Little man said he was gonna do that next time someone tried ta steal his threads." Anton laughed.

Sarah urged everyone into motion again. "Let's go inside. Maybe those blueberries are right."

"I dunno." Marcus shook his head. "It's *so* weird seeing them be like *human* to us."

Maya looked down.

"What's wrong?" asked Emily.

"This is what they were like to me before. Well, sometimes." Maya kicked a small chunk of concrete, sending it bouncing.

"Sometimes?" Sarah squeezed her hand.

"Even blueberries were scared of me. Or, really, what Vanessa would do if something happened. But, the ones who I wasn't nasty to, they talked to me the same way that guy just did. That's how they *should* treat people."

"We ain't people to them," muttered Anton.

"Maybe we is." Marcus tapped a finger to his chin.

"Are," said Maya.

"We're not playing pirates," snapped Pick.

"Maybe we *are*. Not we is." Maya laughed. "Come on. Let's go home."

7

LEARNING TO CHILD

Upon returning to their building, the kids headed to the basement playroom. Pick leapt over the carpet log and sat cross-legged by his box of comic books. The twins hit the air hockey table. Emily 'flew' again into the pillow stash, and crawled up to the mass of dolls.

"Uhh," said Sarah. "Ruben, go upstairs and put something on. You're not a Frag."

"But you—"

"Didn't *have* anything else," said Sarah in a louder voice.

He shrugged and hurried off.

"Hey..." Sarah prodded Maya forward.

After they climbed the carpet roll barrier into the square, she tugged Maya over and sat near the horde of various dolls, then kicked her sneakers off. With a shrug, Maya removed her shoes as well, figuring it more comfortable since they'd stay inside for the rest of the day.

"Okay." Sarah cracked her knuckles. "I'm going to teach you how to child properly."

Maya furrowed her eyebrows. "Child isn't a verb."

"What?" Sarah paused, elbow deep in the doll pile, looking back at her.

"Nothing. Just teasing you."

"Ugh. So serious." Sarah pulled out two dolls. "Okay. This is a Barbie, and this is... umm a Bratz." Both appeared old, likely made before the war.

Maya examined the dolls. "Tiny plastic people."

Emily scooted over to them with two faerie dolls and began playing, making voices for each one like they spoke to each other. With Sarah coaching her, Maya attempted to 'play with dolls.' It felt stupid and juvenile for a little while, until she tried thinking of in terms of making up stories instead of pretending to have a psychological condition. It became even less awkward when she decided to enjoy it as time spent with friends.

The twins kept swatting the air hockey puck around as doll drama unfolded. Doing something so exceedingly girly made Maya initially feel as uncomfortable as if she sat in a bowl of tepid oatmeal, but for most of her life, she'd *been* the doll that all the adults dressed up and filmed. She hadn't minded the makeup and the dresses (pinchy ones aside) as much as she'd hated the complete lack of attention from her 'mother.'

Guess there isn't much more girly than playing dress up with $10,000 gowns and two aesthetic technicians. She let out a contented sigh and tried to learn how to 'child.'

Pick ran in about twenty minutes later wearing a clean pair of shorts. The lack of dirt on his chest suggested Naida forced him to take a bath, probably after learning he'd peed himself. He clambered over the carpet log and pulled out his secret stash of comic books. While all the kids knew where he kept it, they all pretended not to at his request. Highly protective of his books, he usually wore plastic baggies over his hands whenever he touched them. Sometimes, he'd let the twins read one, but only if they kept the bags on their hands. Maya figured the comics to be quite old since she couldn't remember ever seeing a paper book before.

For about two hours, she found herself neck deep in dolls—and not totally hating it.

Brrzat!

A brilliant spray of sparks burst from something on the wall at the back end of the basement—and all the lights died.

Emily screamed.

"I didn't do it!" shouted Pick.

Maya dropped a pair of cloth-bodied dolls and looked around at the dark. One small speck of ember glowed in the distance by where the sparks had erupted. "Crap! They're coming for me!"

"Relax," said Sarah. "No one cut the power. This happens all the time."

"It does?" Maya turned her head toward the particular spot of darkness where Sarah's voice had come from. "I've never seen this happen before."

The smell of burned plastic found her nose.

"Okay, maybe not *all the time*," said Sarah, "But it happens like three or four times a year. Zoe will fix it."

"Think the roof's on fire again?" asked Anton.

Marcus chuckled. "Prob'ly not. The boom was much louder that time."

"I'm scared of the dark," whispered Emily.

"Hey, let's go up to Em's place and watch movies," said Pick.

Maya scratched her head. "How can we watch movies if the power's out?"

"It's probably only the basement." A sigh came from Sarah's direction.

Anton yawned. "She have anything better than little kid movies?"

"Umm," said Marcus, "Emily and Pick *are* little kids. Zoe won't let them see anything good."

"You two are only ten." Maya gestured toward their voices. "We're all considered 'young children.' None of us are even twelve yet."

"Whatever," muttered Anton. "Nothin' in them movies scary as 'end of the world man'."

Marcus laughed.

Emily sniveled. "It's still dark."

Maya groped around the mound of dolls until she found Emily's leg, and patted her way up to take the girl's hand. "Come on."

Thud.

"Ow, shit!" yelled Marcus.

"You okay?" asked Maya.

"Yeah. Banged my knee on something."

"Everyone stay still," said Sarah. "I'm going to open the door.

There'll be light in the hallway and then everyone can see enough to get out."

The carpet moved under Maya's backside. Rustling went by, then the soft patter of Sarah's feet on the concrete floor. A few plastic bottles skittered in the dark. Several soft bumps followed, but Sarah didn't cry out or even emit a weak 'oof.' Perhaps a minute later, crinkling and crunching came from the trash in the entry hallway.

With a metallic *squeak*, the basement door opened, allowing a little bit of light into the endless void.

"Grab my shoes please," yelled Sarah.

Maya managed to find them after some fumbling around, then followed the others toward the door, carefully navigating a minefield of old appliances, stacked tables, and chairs. The closer they got to the exit, the more light, and the faster everyone went.

"Ack!" whispered Sarah, stopping short halfway to the third floor landing.

"What?" asked Anton, right behind her.

"Blueberry," whispered Sarah. "Went into the third floor hallway."

"What's he doin'?" Marcus crept up.

"How should I know? I can't see through walls."

The twins advanced to the door and peered out. Overwhelmed by curiosity, Maya got down on all fours and slipped under them to peek as well. Three small heads hovered around the corner. Five doors from the stairwell, a man wearing Authority armor stood by Pick's apartment, helmet under his arm. He looked to be in his mid-twenties with black hair and a light tan.

Naida opened the door and practically fainted.

"Hey," said the blueberry. "Please relax. I'm here with good news."

"*Good* news?" Naida put a hand over her heart, clinging to the door perhaps to avoid fainting.

Sarah pressed the twins down onto Maya and stretched up on tiptoe to stick her head out as well. A curtain of red hair draped over Anton, Marcus, and Maya's faces. The boys puffed at it. Maya grabbed the tail end and held it aside.

Pick stepped out into the hall, unconcerned if anyone saw him. Maya grabbed his ankle.

"Yeah." The blueberry smiled. "I'm Officer Prentice, but feel free to call me Alex if you prefer."

Naida looked him up and down. Her expression made Maya think she expected the man to want to hire her. "What brings you here?"

"Sorry if it's a traumatic subject, but I'm here about the mandatory vaccinations."

Pick snarled.

"Umm..." Naida's expression shifted from 'give me a break' to terror.

"Please, Miss Gutierrez, don't be alarmed. The reason I'm here is to tell you that policy has been discontinued."

"What?" gasped Naida.

"The bi-monthly detention for vaccinations policy is officially terminated. Authority officers will no longer be showing up every eight weeks to drag you off." Officer Prentice shook his head. "I don't know what jackass thought that up, but it's gone."

She babbled something in Spanish.

Officer Prentice nodded. "*Sí. Está bien. No más.*"

Pick's simmering anger receded to hopeful confusion.

"However, there is a new policy in place."

Naida shivered, eyes wide.

"Hey, please calm down. It's not bad." Officer Prentice smiled at her. "If you, umm, are still working, you'll need to register. The whole way they're going to handle it is completely different now."

Appearing to regain some courage, Naida folded her arms. "So what is going to happen?"

"Well, you register and get an ID. You'll need to self-report to a clinic once every two months. They still want to keep you healthy, but those Ascendant bastards are gone. Whatever you do for a living, you're still a person. You'll need to report earnings, and the government will collect a portion of tax from it."

Naida bit her lip.

"Yeah, I know, it's a pain in the ass... but that tax comes with some medical care. Like if you get sick or injured as a direct result of your, umm, job... they cover it. Guess they figured certain vices keep the people happy."

Maya raised an eyebrow, noting the guy couldn't keep eye contact with her when he said 'job.'

Officer Prentice almost touched a finger to her cheek. "What happened there?"

"Some psycho attacked me."

"You don't need to be afraid of us anymore. If anyone gives you a bad time, call us. You know how we take care of our own."

She scoffed. "I'm no blueberry."

"No, but you'd technically be a 'city employee' once you register."

Naida stared down. "You almost make it sound like a real job. I don't like having to do this, but I have no choice."

He took her hand. "We all have choices. Some are easier than others."

Naida blinked at the gentle contact, gradually lifting her gaze until she met his eyes. "Two years ago, I waited tables in the Sanc. The manager got mad at me when I wouldn't go out with him. Lied, said I stole. Called you people. They couldn't prove I took anything because I didn't steal, but it was enough that no one would ever hire me in the Sanc again. It's on my record. If I was a Citizen, it wouldn't have gone on record."

Pick backed up into the stairwell out of sight, but kept leaning forward enough to watch.

"Records can be updated." He smiled, tracing his thumb back and forth over her knuckles. "No strings. I promise."

"Officer Prentice, are you flirting with me?"

"Perhaps."

"And you know what I've had to do?"

He let off a long, heavy sigh. "Stuff I've had to do on this job to survive, I can't judge anyone. Our jobs don't define who we are. The things any of us have to do to make sure we see tomorrow don't make us. It's only what circumstance forced on you."

Naida stared at him for a long moment, worry, hope, and something... else in her eyes. "If I had a chance for a different job, I'd take it."

"Do you have a minicomp?" asked Officer Prentice.

"I do." She leaned close and whispered at his ear.

He pulled a small device from his belt and rapidly keyed something in.

"Oh wow," whispered Anton. "Your sister's totally hooking up with a blueberry."

Maya covered her mouth to stop from giggling. Something about the two of them hit her as absolutely adorable.

"She ain't gonna be a pross no more," said Marcus.

Pick swung his arm to the right, pounding his fist into Marcus' crotch.

"Oomf." The boy grabbed himself and collapsed over backward.

Everyone ducked into the stairwell, hiding. Emily, still a few steps back, tilted her head in confusion.

"That's so cute!" whisper-squeed Sarah. "He asked her out."

"Dude, what the hell?" wheezed Marcus, cradling himself.

"Don't call my sister that." Pick glared down at him.

"It ain't a bad word," wheezed Marcus. "She *is* a pross."

Pick went to pounce on him, but Sarah caught him and held him back. "Ruben, stop it. He's not trying to be mean."

Anton peeked out again, but ducked right back. "Wow... First they help us, now they gettin' sweet on Naida." He leaned back, staring at Maya while shaking his head. "Girl, you *totally* broke the blueberries."

8

INERTIA

True to Sarah's prediction, the power outage had only affected the basement. The kids watched movies at the Changs' place while, fifteen feet away, Doc worked at his makeshift living room clinic, pulling broken glass out of a young woman's back. After the second film ended, Maya led a migration back to her apartment. Feeding the building's kids rotated on a schedule, and tonight landed on Genna. No one had ever offered much of an explanation why that started as opposed to everyone simply taking care of their own kids, but everyone ran with it.

The kids crammed themselves three each along the kitchen table's long sides with Genna and Pope at the ends. Genna handed out plates of spaghetti with turkey meatballs.

"What is this?" Emily prodded her fork at the noodles.

"Awesome is what it is," said Sarah.

"Spaghetti." Genna smiled.

Emily sniffed, looking suspicious.

"You've never seen spaghetti?" asked Maya in shock.

Sarah poked her. "I hadn't either until Genna made it."

The twins and Pick attacked their food without hesitation. Once they started emitting noises of pleasure, Emily tried a small forkful. Then a bigger one, her eyes widening with each bite.

"This is my favoritest food," cheered Emily after five mouthfuls.

Genna wagged her eyebrows in pride.

As the boys whispered about how much this 'Sanc food' had to cost, Maya fought hard to keep quiet, knowing the box pasta was reasonably cheap. The meatballs had been the most expensive part, but they could be skipped in lean times.

When Pope asked if they had fun today, Maya told Genna and Pope about the dosers and blueberries, and about watching another officer flirt with Naida. Her parents cringed in unison.

"Maybe you ought'a stay around the building for a while," said Genna.

Pope smiled. "Guess you really did light a fire under some asses."

"Yeah." Maya laughed.

"I did that once." Pick jammed another forkful of pasta into his grin.

"What?" asked Genna.

"Lit fire to my ass. Found a lighter. Farted."

Emily scrunched her face in disgust while Sarah almost choked on her food from laughing.

"Mr. Pope, she *broke* the damn blueberries but good." Anton scraped at his plate. "Is there any left? Can I have a little more?"

"Yeah, I think there's some." Genna got up and portioned out another tong-load of noodles, chuckling as Marcus also held up his plate.

"I don't envy them that mess though." Pope wiped sauce from his beard. "Trying to figure out which blueberries work for Ascendant, which are still Authority."

Genna shot a dire glower at the wall. "Just consider 'em lucky I'm not doing those interviews."

From there, the conversation took a wild—and somewhat embarrassing—turn when Emily commented that Maya liked dolls. At least Genna didn't tease her about it. Later, if she got the chance to talk to her mother alone, she'd explain that she did it to make Sarah happy, and wasn't as into the dolls as much as wanted to do something fun with her sister and friend. Though, since it had been fun, maybe she *did* like dolls. Or at least, didn't *hate* them.

The other kids headed home once dinner ended, leaving Maya and Sarah the task of cleaning up. Her parents would've helped, but Maya insisted they rest since they did all the cooking. Pope muttered something about 'this kid is broken' as they headed out to the living room.

"What's that supposed to mean?" whispered Maya.

Sarah glanced over at her. "Huh?"

"Dad said I'm broken because I told them we'd clean the dishes."

"Oh. See, there you go not 'childing' right. Kids aren't supposed to like doing work."

Maya mulled that for a moment. "Why?"

"Because it's work. And boring. And we're supposed to wanna play all the time."

"Oh. But they're tired." Maya scratched her head. "It's wrong to want to help?"

Sarah, elbow deep in dishwater, leaned against her for an armless hug. "Okay, maybe you're 'childing' right, but you're just a *nice* kid."

"You did work for The Dad."

"Well. I wasn't a kid. I had to grow up early."

Sensing a spike of sadness taking Sarah over, Maya hugged her. "You did what circumstance forced you to do. Now you can 'child.'"

"You got that from the blueberry." Sarah grinned.

Maya raised her hands. "Guilty."

DISHES DONE, THE GIRLS HEADED TOWARD THE BEDROOM, INTENT on resuming their stalemated *Magic* game.

"Maya," said Genna. "Got a minute?"

She paused halfway across the living room, turned on her heel, and walked over to the couch. "What's up?"

Genna and Pope exchanged an uncomfortable look.

"You're getting married?" asked Maya. "Awesome!"

They both sputtered into laughter. Genna might've blushed.

"Well, umm, regardless of what the future may or may not hold in that regard." Pope coughed into his hand. "We've been asked to do something neither one of us is quite keen on."

"But, Harlowe managed to convince me to at least mention it to you." Genna folded her arms, clearly annoyed. "I know what you're gonna say, and I don't think it's a good idea."

Maya sat on the coffee table facing them. "The Brigade wants me to do a mission, don't they?"

Sarah ran up, shaking her head. "She's a kid! Why can't everyone leave her alone?"

"That's the ultimate goal," said Pope. "Harlowe was able to talk Genna into considering the idea because the sooner we jiggle the handle on Ascendant, the sooner you two can have a normal life, like ordinary kids without worrying about revolution or overthrowing a toxic corporatocracy."

"English please." Sarah tilted her head at him.

"He's talking about Ascendant running the government." Maya rested her hands on her knees, squeezing. "I guess because you're even talking to me about it, it's pretty safe sounding."

Genna nodded. "Damn right. They made it *sound* safer than you walkin' to Foz's place."

"Dealing with Foz isn't exactly safe," muttered Sarah.

Maya grinned. "Worst he'll do is cheat."

"Try *not* selling to him." Sarah shook her head. "I heard about one gang he sent people after because they walked when he tried to cheat them."

"Seriously?" Maya whistled. "Should report him to the Authority."

"A month ago, I'd have thought you were making a joke and laughed." Sarah fidgeted. "Now I'm not so sure."

"What's the mission?" asked Maya.

Genna leaned forward and took her hands. "They haven't shared all the details yet, but there'll be a briefing for us all if you decide to do it. He only said something about a small-ass pipe and high technology."

Maya shrugged one shoulder. "Oh. Like what we did two weeks ago. Easy."

"I'm going," said Sarah. "I don't care. She shouldn't be alone."

"Hope these guys know what they're doing sending children on operations." Pope scratched at his beard. "Doesn't make any damn sense to me."

Sarah puffed her chest out. "I've done missions for the Brigade, but only like running messages or carrying small packages."

"Is this mission safer than riding a drone into the Sanc?" asked Maya.

Genna coughed. "Damn better be."

"Cheap shot." Pope brushed a hand over her hair. "I had no idea something like that would even be remotely a possibility when you went storming off to the Spread."

"That's okay." Maya leaned in and hugged him. "Neither did I."

"Harlowe was really on fire about this one." Genna shot an annoyed look at the wall. "He wants to move on it fast. Said it's way important. Made it sound like this could be what finally takes Ascendant down... and it's totally safe."

"Must be if you are considering letting her do this." Pope stretched an arm around Genna's back.

She leaned into him. "*Says* it's safe. I don't know why I'm even rollin' these dice.

"Why do they need Maya?" asked Sarah. "This sounds stupid."

"Well..." Pope sighed. "She offers, and I quote, a 'unique combination of small size and technical aptitude.'"

"Guess I believed him that it's safe," muttered Genna. "At least enough to let him continue explaining."

"You didn't tell him to go eff himself." Pope winked.

Genna chuckled.

"Yeah." Maya clutched her toes at the carpet. "Genetically engineered pizza at your service. Aesthetically appealing, smart enough to inherit a massive corporation, but tragically flawed with an overdeveloped conscience and sense of empathy."

"Aww, come here." Genna held her arms out wide.

Grinning, Maya climbed into her lap. "I was being kinda sarcastic. Not sad."

"Pizza?" asked Sarah. "What's a genetic pizza?"

Maya re-explained ordering pizza when she lived in the Sanc, and how Vanessa put together a list of options—like toppings—when she 'purchased' Maya.

"Aww, baby." Genna rocked her side to side. "Forget that damn woman."

"It's not that bad anymore." Maya cuddled against her real mother. "I realized that I only have about thirty-seven percent common DNA with that bitch. That's not even enough for her to count as bio-Mom. She's more like my second cousin or something like that."

Genna laughed.

"I still don't like sending her in on any kind of mission. Especially since Harlowe wouldn't share any details until she agreed to do it." Pope glanced at Sarah. "And I'm less thrilled about *both* girls going. If something happens..."

"You think I like it? But, I ain't never seen that man so optimistic about anything before. Not once. Something's different this time, so I'm at least willing to hear him out. And, nothing is gonna happen." Genna kissed Maya atop the head. "'Cause I'ma pull the damn plug on this shit if I don't like what I hear in the briefing."

"I'll help with anything that takes Ascendant down." Maya bent forward and reached up over her shoulder, tugging at her shirt. "I *really* want to get this stupid target off my back."

"Maybe you shouldn't have made that video," said Sarah in a small voice.

"I'd do it again." Maya leaned back against Genna. "All those Citizens, and no one else but the Brigade tried to stand up to them. The whole world already knew my face. I'd been feeding them lies for my whole life, helping that woman poison people for money. I *had* to do something. Maybe I am too much of a little girl still, 'cause I thought I'd do that video and everyone would be like 'oh, crap, Ascendant's bad!' and they'd get rid of them right away."

Pope patted her on the leg. "Stay optimistic, kiddo. You're steering an aircraft carrier, not a fighter jet."

"Huh?" asked Maya and Sarah at the same time.

"Fighter jets turn fast with little effort. Takes a long damn time to swing a carrier around and go the other way." Pope tapped his head. "Keep pullin' that wheel and you'll eventually get them pointed in the right direction. You've got a lot of inertia to overcome, but it seems like it's working."

"I still can't believe those blueberries *helped* us." Sarah gripped two handfuls of her pants. "I don't wanna lose these."

"Oh." Maya nodded. "I guess it was naïve to think everything would change fast."

"English please," said Sarah.

"That *was* English." Maya smirked.

"Isn't 'naïve' a Fre nch word?" asked Genna.

"*Je ne sais pas.*" Pope held up one finger.

Maya stuck out her tongue.

SHORT BRIEFING

Given the recent near miss with the dosers, plus rumors of increasing unrest, Maya didn't savor being outside after dark. Having her whole family going along for the ride gave her confidence, especially since her parents both carried handguns. Sarah reassured her in a different way. Despite the girl offering little in the way of fighting ability, her presence helped nonetheless.

Pope left his sniper rifle behind since they intended to go into the Sanc. Maya didn't bother asking how they planned to get past the checkpoint with guns at all. Obviously, they had a way to deal with that problem or her parents wouldn't have brought them. Then again, after they'd saved her from the penthouse, the Authority had let them walk in with rifles. Maybe stuff really *had* changed.

They stood on the street near their building for a few minutes, making no effort to go anywhere. Right around the time Maya's worry and anxiety built up enough that she opened her mouth to ask, a drab sedan in an unappealing shade of coffee brown rolled to a stop in front of them.

A chunky guy in a grey poncho, filter mask hanging loose down to his chest on straps, climbed out. Short dreadlocks sprouted from his head like some manner of prehistoric fern. His face, darker than Maya but not as deep brown as Genna, brightened with an enormous grin.

"Gen." The guy thrust his arm out.

They grasped each other's arms near the elbow before trading a quick hug. "Carl. Damn boy, you livin' the good life now or what?"

"Yeah, somethin' like that. Office job. Still, happy ta make time for the cause." He patted the car on the roof. "You said this one's gonna come back, right?"

Pope glanced around. "Damn sure hope so."

"We ain't plannin' on doin' anything wild," said Genna. "I'll leave it in the usual spot tomorrow afternoon."

"Sounds good." Carl nodded at her before clapping Pope on the arm. "Should I say 'keep an eye on her' or 'try ta keep up?'"

Maya glanced at Genna.

Pope laughed. "Both. I'll keep an eye on her while I'm trying to keep up."

"Good answer." Genna winked.

"Yo, heard about Binks." Carl bowed his head, shaking it. "That's some rough shit right there. Hope he at least saw it comin'.'"

"Damn drone," muttered Genna. "Thanks. Yeah. He died a soldier."

Maya stared at her sneakers, remembering lying face down with a drone hanging over her. Binks had charged into the open, shooting at it, probably afraid the drone had been seconds from hurting her.

"Take care of yourself, Gen." Carl stuffed his hands in his pockets and ambled off down the street.

Sarah hopped in behind the wheel. "I'll drive so you guys can shoot."

"Sorry, sweetie." Pope scooped her up and transplanted her to the back seat. "We need to return this one intact."

She raspberried him, but giggled.

Maya climbed in to sit beside her. Genna and Pope lifted the front seat cushions and stashed their guns in hidden compartments. She assumed the lining had signal dampening properties. Either that or rumors about the sensitivity of the Authority's equipment were overstated.

By car, the trip into the Sanc took only about forty minutes with Genna driving. At that hour, only two cars waited for entry ahead of them at the checkpoint. When their turn came to roll up to the gate, a pair of blueberries approached and chatted for a moment. The 'what are you driving into the Sanc at this hour for' conversation slid into a reminiscence of military memories. In a minute the Authority men laughed with Genna and Pope like they'd known each other for years. One peered into the back seat and nodded at the girls. Sarah squeezed Maya's hand, still nervous around the Authority, though she at least managed to keep her expression calm.

Six minutes after passing the checkpoint, Genna pulled the car into the parking lot of the Hangar, the bar-slash-restaurant the Brigade used as its Baltimore headquarters. The place appeared packed, a little past nine at night. She found a spot all the way in the back corner, but had to let everyone else out of the car before pulling in due to the tight fit.

After stashing their weapons under their clothes, Pope and Genna led the girls across the lot. When they headed for the back instead of the front doors, Maya couldn't help but "umm" in confusion.

"Too busy at the moment. Walking in there with a pair of kids risks the wrong kind of attention." Genna waved them to follow.

She trotted around the corner of the building, past a tiny loading dock, to a row of enormous plastic trash cans, all with electronic keypads on the lids. A blend of roasting barbecue and sour garbage hung in the air. Maya grimaced, not knowing if she should feel hungry again or nauseated.

"Seriously?" Sarah poked at one. "They lock their trash?"

"If it smells this weird, I understand why." Maya covered her nose.

"Yeah." Genna pointed at a sign on the wall.

If you're hungry, ask inside. Trash is garbage.

"Wow, we should've come here instead of begging at that soup counter," said Sarah.

Maya singsonged, "We were trying to."

"Okay." Genna stopped by the third from the last can and typed in a code that made the keypad chirp. "Meet you inside."

"Huh what?" asked Sarah.

Maya cringed. "We're gonna go in the trashcan, aren't we?"

"Yep." Genna chuckled and opened the lid.

Pope lifted Maya over the rim and set her down standing inside the empty trash bin. Still confused, she peered up at the rim, easily a whole foot taller than her, then leaned back to avoid taking a sneaker to the face when Sarah's feet came over the side. Genna lowered her in and reached for the lid.

"How long are we gonna hide in here?" asked Maya.

Genna grinned. "Not long at all."

Despite expecting it, Maya still flinched when the lid closed.

"Wow, they totally put us in a giant trashcan," said Sarah.

Maya opened her mouth to reply, but gasped instead when the can bottom sank out from under her. Sarah grabbed on, and they clung to each other as the mechanized floor descended like an elevator into a small room with bare cinder block walls and a single door that didn't have a knob. One small bulb at the center of the ceiling illuminated the area in harsh white light. The stink of sour kitchen grease and garbage hung thick in the air.

"Ugh." Maya pulled her T-shirt up as a breathing mask.

"Eww." Sarah looked around, still not letting go of her.

After five seconds, the platform they stood on began to rise. Maya leapt off, dragging Sarah with her. She spun, retreating from a single hydraulic strut pushing a square plate into the ceiling. Inch by inch, the girls backed away until they bumped into the room's only door. Buttons on a single keypad mounted to the wall beside it glowed with cobalt blue light.

Murmured voices echoed on other side. Maya listened for a few seconds, then calmed, realizing they'd taken a hidden entrance directly to the Brigade's underground command center. It probably also served as an emergency exit. The tiny elevator lowered again, revealing Genna and Pope in rather close company.

Maya giggled.

"Don't usually go two-at-a-time on this thing 'less there's an emergency." Genna winked at Pope. "But I'll make an exception."

He touched foreheads with her. "Hope this mission's quick. Can't wait to get home."

Genna stared into his eyes. For a few seconds, Maya expected them to do a bit more than gaze at each other.

"Try not to stab Harlowe if this is insane," said Pope.

"I'll do my best." Genna grinned, then crossed the room in two steps to the door. "But I ain't makin' no promises."

She punched in a code. The panel chirped, but the door didn't open.

Sarah looked around with fear in her eyes. "Something's wrong."

"Nah. They're just makin' sure who's ringin' the doorbell." Genna waved at the ceiling. "It's us."

The door rattled with a sharp *clonk*.

Genna pulled it open, revealing the hallway that ran past the two basement bathrooms. From the inside, fake cinder block facing made the door appear to be a dead end in the hallway, a dead end Maya had seen a few times without suspecting it to be an exit. She followed her down the corridor and through a sheet of hanging plastic strips into the Brigade command room.

Harlowe, Sidiqi, Carroll, and Ravi sat around the big round table, still littered with beer cans, loose ammunition, gun parts, and one hand grenade. Maya had a feeling the grenade had been decommissioned into a conversation piece, since no one had ever made any move to keep her away from it.

Maybe it's live and they trust me not to be an idiot.

"Genna..." Harlowe stood. "Good to see you." He nodded in greeting. "Maya. Pope. Sarah?"

"You know me," said Sarah.

"No... I do. I'm questioning why they brought you along." Harlowe chuckled.

"I'm going." Sarah folded her arms. "Buddy system and stuff. I'm almost as small as Maya and it's stupid to send her in alone."

Carroll raised both her snow-white eyebrows. "Right on, kid. Damn, little tiger has some nerve."

"Yeah." Genna patted her on the head. "A little too much sometimes. This better be as safe as you tryin' ta sell me on, or it stops before it starts. So what's going on?"

"Please." Harlowe gestured at chairs. "Have a seat and I'll explain the op."

Sidiqi fidgeted at a pen, spinning it around his fingers.

Once everyone sat, Harlowe opened a folder and unfolded a paper map. Maya couldn't help but smile to herself at how much this reminded her of the twins planning to Scav. Sometimes, the Brigade felt like a bunch of overgrown boys playing a game... only with real guns.

"Doctor Chang examined samples taken from the individual you detained in Block 13. They tested positive for nanobots."

"Wait, seriously?" blurted Maya.

Everyone looked at her.

"I was told you were the one who first mentioned that." Harlowe scratched his head.

"Yeah, but it was just a whitepaper. Theoretical. It's not supposed to be *real*." She shivered. "You know what that means, right?" Maya bit her lip. "Vanessa has the ability to mind control people."

Murmuring swept around the room. Brennan leaned back from his computer desk at the far end of the room to eavesdrop.

"Well, we don't have any substantive intelligence regarding the capabilities of these nanobots yet. Based on the information Doctor Chang provided us, we believe it appears to be less 'mind control' and more of an 'on switch' for random violence." Harlowe tapped a finger on the map. "But, I do think you are correct in terms of what Ascendant's end goal is. We think that man was a trial run of sorts."

"They are working toward the ability to make puppets out of people," said Sidiqi.

"So..." Maya leaned on the table. "This is like a prototype that merely turns people from calm to trying to kill everyone they see like a light switch?"

"That's how Doctor Chang categorized it, yes." Harlowe nodded.

"If that's true, don't you think it's just a *little* strange that he shows up at the building *I* live in?"

Everyone stared at Maya for a few seconds.

"Could be like testing new bombs in a place people you don't like live," said Carroll.

Ravi cringed, then shook her head. "And we thought Fade was the most evil they could come up with."

"Fade is more evil." Sarah looked off to the side and down.

"Damn straight," said Genna, ice in her tone.

Maya stood and raised her hands. "Stop. Fade is evil because it's indiscriminate. This new thing is evil because it steals free will. We shouldn't waste time arguing pointless philosophy. They're both evil. Deciding which one is worse gets us nowhere."

"Anyone got a PMRI?" asked Carroll, chuckling.

"I'm real." Maya folded her arms.

Harlowe tapped his finger on the map again to regain everyone's attention. "Zeroice managed to find some information about those nanobots in the data he liberated from the Ascendant network. In fact, your help in giving us that doorway in is part of why you're here now."

"Ugh." Maya flopped in the chair. "I'm crawling through another pipe, aren't I?"

"You ain't doin' nothin' until I understand what the hell's going on." Genna leaned her elbows on the table, eyeing Harlowe. "I agreed to consider it, but you still haven't said anything."

Harlowe raised both hands in a placating gesture at her. "I'm getting to that. Based on Zeroice's information, we were able to locate the likely facility where Ascendant is manufacturing these nanobots. It's located here"—he pointed—"Two-point-six kilometers west of the Hab, concealed under one of the bubbles at the Catonsville Growth Plant. The level of crypto on that file makes me wonder if that whole building isn't involved in something more than producing food."

"I'm gonna assume you're not about to ask her to put on that fancy dress and walk in the front door asking for a tour?" Genna raised an eyebrow.

Harlowe chuckled. "No. Zeroice obtained some schematics of the area going back thirty years, before the war repaved the whole district. Used to be a commercial strip there. Now, as you know, it's rubble fields and giant greenhouse bubbles."

Maya pictured the enormous half-buildings with solid walls and inflatable roofs that resembled gargantuan maggots. She'd once toured them with Vanessa, observing the long tanks of dark green liquid in which everything from potatoes to carrots to slabs of meat grew. The whole place stank so bad, merely thinking of the white, flexible ceiling five stories overhead made her gag.

I'm going to need a bath when I'm done. Ugh, that dress never smelled right again.

"Yeah." Genna leaned forward to study the map, her long dreads, bedecked with wooden trinkets and beads, dragged over the table. "Oh... that line there?"

"Exactly." Harlowe nodded to her before looking at Maya. "We located an old HVAC conduit that used to connect to an external AC unit before the war. The compressor structure and the office building or whatever it connected to are long gone, but the underground link between them should still be there."

"How'd an old air vent wind up connecting to the basement of a secret research lab?" asked Pope.

Harlowe laughed. "Best guess I have? Builders were lazy. Used the existing basement instead of digging out another giant hole."

Pope and Genna both nodded in a 'yeah, that makes sense' way.

"Okay. You're going to send me crawling through this duct," said Maya. "Why?"

Harlowe traced his finger over the map. "We've plotted a route that will allow you to sneak directly into what we believe to be a work area where you can access a terminal. You will install a wireless module our people can use to get in, then you take your butt out of there the same way you went in."

"Why aren't you sending in Ravi or Carroll as a fake worker?" Genna gestured at the women.

"Not feasible." Ravi poked her finger at the map. "We evaluated that as a possibility as much as we could without giving away that anyone hostile to Ascendant knew the facility contained more than tanks of vegetables."

"Maya is our option of last resort." Harlowe hooked his thumbs in his pockets and looked at her. He didn't seem entirely thrilled with the idea of sending her in.

Carroll pulled her snowy hair off her face. Though the woman had been nothing but friendly, Maya still found her slightly creepy. People shouldn't be *that* white. "There is an exceptional amount of security on that facility. The official story is they are conducting research on new growth mediums and prototype crops. Establishing an operative with enough of a falsified background to survive scrutiny and get in the door would take longer than we have. And it is likely to fail."

"All of our network people have been convinced for months that there's something major in this island network. The defenses around this place caught our eye a long time ago, as they're overkill for a hydroponics bubble. We've been looking for a way inside before we even knew about the nanobots. But, the security is too damn high. We don't believe anyone involved at this facility is even aware of this passageway. This is an opportunity we can't afford to miss. With the new intelligence about those nanobots, it could explain what they're keeping hidden here."

Genna bowed her head, both fists on the table. "I don't like it."

"Gen." Harlowe exhaled hard. "You know I wouldn't ask Maya to do this if I thought it didn't have a hundred percent chance of success—or at least a hundred percent chance of her safety... and no other options."

"I..." Genna pored over the map, studying the area around the target building. "Are you sure there's no other way inside? How do you even know this duct is going to work?"

"We don't. But, the beauty of that is... if it *doesn't* work, no one in that facility will know we even tried. If Maya can't get through, she turns around and leaves. Then we fall back on plan B and hope the crap-pocalypse waits long enough for us to set up a backstory."

"Shitpocalypse sounds better," said Maya. "And I'll do it."

Sarah stifled a snicker.

"What about HALO-ing with a PR9 rig? Roof's flexible material. Should be able to go in high." Pope made a flying-diving gesture.

Harlowe raised both eyebrows at him. "You're wildly overestimating our budget and resources."

The men chuckled.

"Had ta ask." Pope shrugged.

"Maya." Harlowe locked stares with her. "I want you to understand that you are to abort the mission if anything looks even remotely dangerous, and I mean *remotely*. If you see a giant damn rat in that duct, you turn around and come back. My people are telling me this should be as easy as what you did for Zero. Go in, plug a module in, get out."

"At least there won't be rat traps in a vent." Sarah smiled. "And I am going in with her."

Sidiqi pushed a handgun across the table toward Sarah. "Might need this if you're her backup. Heard your old man basically trained you up already."

Genna put her hand down on the weapon before Sarah could move. "No way. Bad enough we're sending children in there. We're not giving them guns. That'll only guarantee they get shot."

"How 'bout one of these then?" Carroll held up a pistol that looked like the Hornet, only green-and-black instead of yellow-and-black.

"I don't want my kids inclined to engage when they should be hauling ass."

Sarah looked up at Genna. "I'd rather have at least a Hornet in case we get cornered. Trust me, running is my favorite choice."

Genna stared at Carroll for a long moment before relenting with a nod. The skinny ghostly-pale woman rose from her seat like a spirit and glided around the table to hand the stunner pistol to Sarah. This one had a few more scratches and scuff marks, but otherwise appeared the same as the one she left at home except for color.

"Any differences?" Sarah dropped the magazine out to count darts, reseated it, sighted over the weapon, and checked the charge indicator. "I'm guessing this one is mil-spec instead of civilian, but did anything but color change?"

Harlowe, Ravi, and Sidiqi chuckled.

"Man..." Brennan—still at the far end of the room—laughed. "What the heck is it with the kids around here? One's super brain and the other one's practically a soldier already."

"Charging interface is different from the civilian model." Carroll tapped a finger on the bottom of the pistol grip. "Designed to fit the MOD-3, like every other bit of military electronics. Also, it's got better moisture seals."

"You mean, designed to fit the hunk of shit that never works," muttered Pope.

Genna guffawed. "You know it. We had three of them damn things catch fire on us."

"What's a HALO PR9?" asked Maya. "I guess it's expensive if the Brigade doesn't have one."

Harlowe gasped. "Holy shit. Someone get a picture. Maya didn't know something."

She smirked at him.

"Cut her a break, eh?" Ravi threw a French fry at him. "How would this kid pick up military stuff?"

"Video games," said Brennan, Carroll, Sarah, and Sidiqi at the same time.

Pope grinned. "HALO means jumping out of an aircraft at high altitude, falling with your parachute closed until you're close to the ground, and then opening it. The PR9 is the type of fall-arrest system my team used to go in on silent drops. It's an ion-thrust-assisted airfoil that's much smaller than a parachute. Basically a small backpack with folding wings. No parachute to get tangled in or leave behind to be found."

"That's all Delta Force Ranger shit." Carroll playfully scowled at him. "You guys hogged all the good stuff."

"I just wore the shit, never decided who got what." Pope stretched. "So... when are we doing this?"

Harlowe glanced at the girls. "If you two need to hit the bathroom, you should do it now."

"That soon?" Genna raised an eyebrow.

"I told you they'd be home in time for bed." Harlowe rolled up the map.

Maya stood. "Let's do it."

"Be right back." Sarah hurried off toward the bathroom.

Damn. Now I have to go, too. "Argh. Be right back." She ran after her sister.

10

TARGET OF OPPORTUNITY

Seated in the rear of the e-car, Maya stared down at the small wireless relay adapter in her hands. According to Harlowe, the military-grade component would automatically install a software interface as soon as she connected it. Once it ran, she could use it to initiate a connection back to the Brigade. Outwardly, it appeared to be a secondary CPU module, something most civilian technicians would never suspect as a hostile component. These things supposedly cost over fifty grand at the time of the war. Now, the Brigade salvaged them from old military storage depots for free—one benefit of a nearly-collapsed infrastructure.

She turned it over and over, letting the moonlight play off the metal parts. Open the terminal, find a modular slot, insert the component, and get out. *Sounds easy. But everything always sounds easy.* Maya took and released a deep breath to calm herself. Everyone with the Brigade, as well as Genna and Pope, kept telling her over and over again to turn back at the slightest scary thing.

Unfortunately, this mission didn't—as Genna hoped it might—offer a quick death to Ascendant. For something like that, she'd take bigger risks. The nanobot-mind-control project scared the hell out of her, and she agreed it needed to be stopped. However, she didn't feel the same sense of urgency as she would have if this mission could shut Ascendant down completely.

Killing the nanobot program wouldn't remove the target from her back. Honestly, it would probably make it bigger.

Assuming, of course, Vanessa ever realized what happened.

It seemed unlikely that people in this place would hurt two young girls if they caught them snooping around. Worst case scenario would probably be winding up on a helicopter back to one of Vanessa's penthouse prisons again. Then again, considering how that ended for Vanessa last time, perhaps not. Maybe they'd be held captive somewhere more difficult to find and kept out of sight.

I'll give this a decent try, but if I have to run, I will.

Sarah, sitting to her left, fiddled with the holster the Brigade let her borrow. It hung from an olive-drab web belt she'd found on a shelf in the command room, as well as a nylon strap around her leg that probably should've been at the wearer's thigh, but wound up closer to her knee. The military Hornet did look a little larger than the yellow one she had at home, almost too big for the girl's hands.

Enormous white forms rose from the debris field up ahead. Six 'greenhouse tents' stood in a long row, puffy inflatable domes swollen and glowing white from lights inside. They looked like some bizarre combination of spaceship and insect larvae, reminding her of this cartoon she once watched where an alien species used giant living creatures to traverse the stars.

Genna shut off the headlights once the complex came into view. Pope kept his handgun at the ready, eyeing the surrounding terrain for skeevers, Frags, or anyone else who might be drawn to a functional e-car out in the middle of the Dead Space. Maya once questioned why the places that grew all the food for the Sanc sat so far away out here, but she stopped wondering after having a whiff of the place. Citizens would rather pay armed guards to transport their food than put up with the stink.

"Almost there," whispered Sarah.

"Why are you whispering?" asked Maya. "The people in the place can't hear us all the way out here in a car."

"I dunno." Sarah shrugged. "We're trying to be sneaky so it felt like I should whisper."

Genna chuckled under her breath.

Maya looked down at herself. BDU pants, sneakers, T-shirt—all black. Sarah's outfit almost matched hers, except she had dirty white sneakers and the phrase 'It Must Be User Error' in small white letters on her otherwise plain, black shirt. Five months ago, the most dangerous thing she ever imagined doing would've been calling one of Vanessa's underlings an idiot. She hadn't realized how much she wanted to escape that penthouse until she'd been kidnapped from it.

Keep a mouse in a cage and it's happy there because it doesn't know how nice the world outside is.

She glanced out the window at miles of destruction. The faint suggestion of a former road cut a relatively flat line through mounds of concrete rubble and destroyed cars. A tailfin from a military aircraft jutted up from the ground about a quarter mile away.

Nice is relative.

The car rolled to a stop.

Maya swallowed, and replaced the wireless module in its protective carrying case. Brennan had rigged two loops of wire on it so she could wear the box like a tiny backpack. Genna and Pope opened the doors and stepped out. She scooted after them, her sneakers crunching pulverized concrete.

A steady, but weak breeze blew in from the east, flavored with ocean and dusted with the smell of ruin. She squinted out at the grave of a place once known as Catonsville, now little more than a vast swath of grey rubble.

"Baby" Genna grasped Maya by the shoulders. "You absolutely sure you want to do this?"

Maya looked up at her. "I have to at least try. Promise I'll turn around if it looks too dangerous."

"You turn around if it looks mildly annoying." Genna grinned, and handed her something that resembled a wristwatch.

The device consisted of a blank, black plastic square with two olive-drab straps and a small clip. She examined it, then raised an eyebrow at Genna.

"Tracker. I ain't sending you out of my sight unless you're wearing that."

"What about Sarah's homing butt?"

Sarah grabbed the spot. "I still have an implant."

"Yeah, but you two could always be separated," said Genna. "I ain't takin' that risk."

Maya shrugged and put the tracker on her left wrist. When she lowered her arms, it fell right off, landing in the concrete dust with a soft *piff*. "It's a little big."

"Wear it on your neck?" asked Sarah.

"I'm not a cat. And it's not *that* big." Maya squatted and picked the tracker up.

"Here." Genna took it and crouched.

Maya pulled her pant leg up out of the way as Genna secured the 'watch' around her left ankle. "Great, I'm on house arrest."

"Huh?" asked Sarah.

Genna chuckled.

After snugging the 'backpack' up on her shoulders, Maya walked toward where Pope searched the rubble. They made their way over a mound of smashed high-rise to a flat spot that still had yellow painted lines suggesting it had been a parking lot. Roughly thirty feet ahead, another immense pile of broken building, no piece bigger than a small car, created a veritable hill three stories tall.

"There. That's gotta be it." Pope pointed at a squarish metal outline half buried at the near side of the debris pile.

"What was it?" whispered Sarah.

"A really big air conditioner," said Genna. "The size of a little house. Too big and heavy to go on the roof of the building, so it sat next to it on the ground."

Maya climbed up on a chunk of concrete, gripping two spars of rebar for balance, and stared into the distance at the nearest 'greenhouse' bubble, which had to be at least 200 yards away, about two-thirds of that distance on the other side of a tall fence with concertina wire along the top. "I wouldn't call this *next* to it."

"Better than going two miles in a pipe." Sarah pretended to wipe sweat from her forehead.

Pope grunted and lifted a slab of metal away from a tangled mass of thin steel. It had probably been ductwork at one point, but looked more like beer cans run over by a truck. "This is it. It's a little jammed, but I think I can clear it."

"Hang on." Genna climbed over a jagged metal wall, probably the lower two feet of the former HVAC unit's outer casing, and helped him pull and bend sheet metal.

Sarah leaned closer to Maya, watching the parents work. "It's weird that she's stronger than him."

"It's not weird." Maya grinned. *My mother's a badass.* "She's got augments."

"Are we really about to let them do this?" whispered Genna.

"Seems that way." Pope tossed a piece of metal aside. "This thing is probably caved in. They're going to crawl in fifteen feet, find a blockage, and come back. We'll be home and in bed within an hour."

"Here's hoping." Genna chuckled, waving Maya over. "Careful by this sharp metal."

Maya approached the outside of the mangled housing, essentially a short wall of jagged steel fangs. "Umm. I think you should lift me over this."

Genna plucked her off her feet and set her down inside, next to a square hole in the ground. Three small, round pipes jutted up from the ground beside it, two full of wires, one empty. Maya crouched beside the hole, peering down a vertical drop about as deep as her height. At the bottom, it continued off toward the distant greenhouse.

"We might get unlucky," said Pope, his voice echoing.

"*Un*lucky?" asked Maya.

He leaned up and away from the vent. "All the crap covering the hole could've prevented stuff going down there to plug it. Inside looks fairly clean. She might actually make it into the facility."

Genna glanced sideways at him. Almost a minute later, still staring at him, she took a flashlight off her belt and handed it to Maya.

Sarah grabbed it. "I'll take point this time."

"No comms?" asked Maya, tapping her throat.

"Won't have any signal in that underground vent. Besides, you won't be in there that long." Genna took a folded paper from her thigh pocket and opened it to show the map. "This duct oughta be a straight shot to the work area with terminals. Don't matter which terminal you hit. Could be any one in the whole place. If the room's empty, meanin' no people, you scramble out the vent, plug that little thing in, and get your ass back in the vent before anyone sees you."

Sarah slipped past her and dropped into the duct.

"Like mice stealing cheese." Maya exhaled hard.

Genna pulled her into a hug. "Don't get caught in no trap, baby."

"Wow," said Sarah, her voice echoing. "It looks pretty clear down here."

Maya squeezed Genna tight, then stepped to the edge. Pope grasped her hands and lowered her into the aluminum-walled hole. If she stood on tiptoe, her fingertips came within a half inch of the top. Plenty of reach for Pope to haul her out when they finished.

"Be back in a few minutes." Maya got down on all fours.

Genna crouched over the opening. "Don't make noise. You're in a metal tunnel. Everything you do will project straight into the place. You gotta stay quiet."

Maya nodded.

She crawled into the shaft. Dust hung in the air, flavoring every breath with metallic dirt. She coughed and spat, trying to keep as silent as possible. The cone of a flashlight's beam wobbled in the steel-walled darkness up ahead, swaying back and forth with Sarah's motion.

This is a lot nicer than that pipe. The rectangular passage gave her enough room to crawl without her back touching the top, and she even had enough freedom to turn around if need be. If they ran into a blockage, she wouldn't have to shimmy backward the whole way out. Best of all, this place had no rat grates.

Maya advanced, careful not to make any noise. With the duct being underground, it didn't creak or make booming noises as loud as she expected. Rather than dangerous rusty flakes like the pipe, a layer of fuzz lined the bottom. Though it felt like she crept over carpeting, she tried not to think about what sort of foulness might comprise ancient dust so thick it offered cushioning. Fortunately, with no water here and nothing resembling food, the passage contained no rats.

After several minutes of monotonous silent crawling, Sarah stopped and leaned to the left side, allowing Maya to see past her at a pale brown sheet of wood covering the end of the duct. A little light leaked in around the edges, and the soft thrum of high technology emanated from beyond. She scooted up on the right, packing herself alongside her sister so they wound up face to face.

Sarah put her ears to Maya's lips and spoke in a feeble whisper. "I think it will come off if we push, but it will make a lot of noise if we drop it."

"Okay," whispered Maya. "Let's listen first. It's late. Maybe the workers went home."

Sarah nodded.

Moving together, they scooted the last six feet to the end cap. Maya examined what appeared to be a simple wooden box lid hung over the end of the metal ductwork.

"Someone has to be wrong," whispered Sarah. "This can't be a super top secret place. There's like *no* security on this vent."

"An adult wouldn't fit in here." Maya gestured at the walls. "They probably never thought anyone would send little kids in here."

Sarah's frown said 'neither did I.'

Minutes passed with only the electronic hum coming from inside. No voices, no footsteps, not even any mechanical whirring or clanking.

Maya gave a thumbs up.

Sarah reached out to the corners and pressed her hands against the wood. Little by little, she shoved at it until it gave way. After about an inch, the top slipped off the duct and hung on her fingertips. She froze, holding it there and listening, a faint tremble in her arms from the effort it took to support the weight. No one reacted to potentially seeing the cap move.

"It has to be empty in there," whispered Maya. "They would have heard that scrape."

"Yeah." Sarah eased the cap downward, revealing a flat metal barrier a few inches away. "Crap. There's like a cabinet or something blocking us in."

Maya's heart pounded. If some huge metal cabinet made it impossible to get out of the vent, they'd have no choice but to turn around and abort. That simultaneously relieved and angered her. As much as it upset Genna for the Brigade to trust Maya with a mission, some part of her felt a little proud. For all the evil she had helped Vanessa bring to the world by lying for commercials, anything she could do personally to help people felt like an attempt to make amends. Genna told her over and over that she'd been a child manipulated by her want for a mother's love. That didn't matter, despite Maya understanding it true. She still had a chance to do some good.

Sarah lowered the plywood cap straight down, but it hit the floor while still covering about three-quarters of the opening. "Umm..." She eased it to the left until they had a clear view of beige metal.

Maya scooted forward, sticking her head out until it touched the cabinet, and peered down at wheels. She didn't know whether to cheer or be annoyed that she couldn't go home right away. *Maybe I won't be strong enough to move this.* No sign of human presence had made itself known in the room, so she didn't hesitate in reaching out and pushing. Little by little, she increased pressure until she started to slide backward.

"It's too heavy," whispered Sarah.

"I've got no leverage."

"What?"

Maya sighed. "I don't have time to explain right now."

Sarah, her face smeared with grey dirt, stuck her tongue out at her.

"Hmm."

Maya pivoted around to put her feet toward the opening, and inched up to the end. She grabbed the bottom edge of the duct, pressed her sneakers flat against the cabinet, and shoved with both legs. The huge thing crept forward, wheels squeaking. She kept pushing until she created enough of a gap to squeeze out and stand behind it, sandwiched between the cabinet and the wall.

Icy air conditioning added to her worries, making her shiver as much from fear as from cold. With her shoulders against cinder blocks, she had enough leverage to nudge the cabinet forward until she could stand without being squeezed.

Still, no one shouted or at all reacted to a moving storage locker. Maya leaned to her right and peered around the side. A room three or four times bigger than the Brigade command area held several rows of workstations, all on fancy glass-top tables. Transparent display screens as big as mattresses hung from the ceiling on thin wires, showing graphs and numbers in bright blue text. A wall of frosted glass panels ran down the left side of the room, offering no view of what went on outside—but it also kept anyone from seeing her. Some sixty feet away, a sliding door at the end of the opaque glass bore the words 'restricted area' backward in red lettering.

Wow. Okay. Maybe I did step in poop.

Sarah shimmied out of the vent and stood beside her. "Can you do it?"

Maya nodded.

"Then do it fast. I wanna go home."

She crept out from behind the cabinet and pulled the 'backpack' off, holding it by one strap while scooting over to the nearest workstation terminal. Maya slid to a stop on her knees beside the desk. Two plastic latches later, she pulled the side of the CPU housing open to expose the motherboard, components, and a mesmerizingly beautiful array of glowing fiberoptic connectors. She wasted no time ogling it, pushing the pretty wiring out of the way. Beneath the nest of luminous cabling, three empty expansion sockets sat defenseless. Maya opened the case and took the wireless relay unit out of its foam.

Sarah broke cover from behind the cabinet and ran to her side, also sliding to a stop on her knees. She grasped the Hornet, but didn't pull it from the holster. The girl appeared awestruck by the guts of the advanced terminal, staring at the flickering light.

Maya held the glowing cables aside and seated the wireless unit. It snapped in place with a soft *click*. Two seconds later, an array of multicolored lights along the end exploded into a flurry of activity. She arranged the cabling over the unit to hide it, then replaced the cover on the CPU case.

Sarah gave her a 'that's it?' look.

Maya shook her head then stood, slinging the empty protective case once more on like a backpack. Leaving it on the floor to be found would be idiotic. She crept around the desk and peered at the giant thin-panel display screen. Of course, the Special Operations hardware she'd added to the machine didn't display any obvious install notifications.

Duh. That would be really stupid. Please stand by while we install your espionage suite.

Nothing happened when she hit the keyboard shortcut to open a command window.

Sarah glanced at her. "Is it broken?"

"No. I need to access a command window, but most companies lock that down. Just need to wait for the hardware to finish installing. It adds an override to the permissions."

"I won't even pretend I know what you said."

Maya grinned. A few seconds later, she retried the keyboard shortcut, and a text-only window popped up. "Sweet. It worked."

The spy module she installed added a hidden storage folder that remained invisible to the graphical operating system and could only be accessed by entering a 'change directory' command via this text parser. She switched the active folder then invoked a program named knock-knock.exe. Another text panel opened, displaying a massive stream of output scrolling by way too fast to read.

"What's that?" whispered Sarah.

"This is opening the doors basically." Maya pulled a small piece of paper out of her pocket with a network address and ran another command that created a VPN tunnel out to the system Brennan had set up to receive it.

A pop up box displayed, *Warning. Enabling this module may expose this terminal to unprotected content. Do you wish to continue?*

"I'll take that risk," whispered Maya as she hit yes.

A few more text panels popped up and vanished. Once again, the terminal looked as it had when she arrived.

"Okay. We're done."

Sarah exhaled with relief.

Maya started to turn away, but froze at the heading of one of the graphs on the monitor in front of her.

NVFP-8 Temperature Status.

A tiny squealing squeak escaped her throat. Her eyes shot open wide. Pure terror crashed full speed into shock, tackling it on top of rage. The mix of emotion left her barely able to breathe.

Another graph showed fluid levels for NVFP-8 in holding tanks, with digital controls for setting up distribution patterns to various pipelines labeled 'drone cluster 1' through 'drone cluster 8'.

"Oh, shit," whispered Maya.

Sarah rose to her feet and peered at the screen. "Mom is going to ground you if you keep swearing."

"This is worth a swear... or ten." She pointed. "This place isn't making those nanobots. Mom's going to kill Harlowe when she finds out where he sent us."

Sarah turned her head to follow Maya's finger to the screen. "Bunch of little pictures. Wheels, and like pots full of water?"

"NVFP-8," whispered Maya. "That's the official name... Nanovirus Fade Project, version 8. This is where they've been making *Fade*. We're probably standing a hundred feet away from enough of this stuff to kill every human left alive... ten times."

Sarah squeaked. "We gotta get out of here!"

"Not yet. There has to be some way to get rid of it." Maya attacked the console, pawing open menu after menu in search of any sort of flush or purge command. Screens flickered by as fast as she could swipe at the display.

"What are you doing?" whispered Sarah, tugging on her arm. "We need to leave *right now.*"

"This is a storage and processing center. This terminal has access to load and launch drones with Fade, and even program their distribution routes." Maya shivered with anxiety. "I can't just leave it alone. This is why they've been trying to get in here so bad. I bet they know exactly what's going on in here."

"They who?"

Maya glanced at Sarah. "You know... the B word. I don't wanna say it out loud in here."

"Oh..." Sarah twisted side to side, peering nervously at the frosted wall. "Someone's going to catch us. We have orders to get right out as soon as the device is active."

"What do soldiers call it when they're sent in to blow something up, but on the way, they see something else that's important, so they blow that up, too?"

"Umm." Sarah tugged at her arm. "A target of opportunity. But we're not soldiers, and we haven't been sent to destroy anything."

"Dammit!" whisper-shouted Maya. "If there's a flush command, this terminal doesn't have access to it."

Sarah pulled her toward the vent. "That sucks, but we can't do anything."

"Yeah, we can." Maya dashed away, ran down the aisle between two long tables of workstations, and crept up to the only door out of the room.

"Eep!" Sarah sprinted after her, too fearful of making noise to shout the message clear in her expression. When she caught up, she wrapped both arms around Maya. "Stop! What are you doing?"

Maya listened at the sliding glass panel, hearing no sign of anyone moving around outside. "This room is only workstations. There has to be a control room with an emergency purge or flush, or something like that. We have to destroy the Fade agent."

"*We* don't have to do anything but follow orders and get out. We did what we came in for. Mom is gonna be mad at us if we do something stupid and get hurt."

"I think she'd be angrier if we wasted a chance to destroy Fade. Think about Sam."

Sarah's hard sigh blasted the back of Maya's head with warmth. "That's not fair."

"We have to at least look."

"You have no idea where the control room is. Or if there even is one."

Maya rolled her eyes. "There's *always* a control room."

"What about security? Cameras, sensors, stuff like that?"

"If they had cameras, we'd be caught already. I think this place has all the security on the outside."

"That's stupid. If this is what you're saying it is, that means a lot of people would have to know Ascendant is making and using Fade. How is it possible that none of them have said anything?"

"Because." Maya twisted around to look at her. "This place is still a hydroponic farm. They would only need one or two people to run the actual bad stuff. Vanessa couldn't do it alone. Other people *have* to be involved, but not many. She's good at controlling people."

"How are you going to open the control room?" Sarah pulled on her again, trying to drag her away from the door. "There's no way it's open."

"You have your lock picks?"

"I can't pick keycards."

Maya bounced on her toes, whining in frustration. "Ooh... Wait. This is a farm. Why would the control room be locked? If they kept it locked, people might suspect something weird."

"I think they'd suspect weird from all the security out front." Sarah smirked.

"Not with all the attacks on the farms from people trying to steal food." Maya's eyes welled up with desperate tears. "Please. We have to at least try. For Sam. For Anton and Marcus' parents. For everyone who died to Fade."

Sarah bowed her head. "If we die, I'm going to kill you."

"Swear we won't." Maya winked. "I might be disowned, but I don't think they'd risk killing me."

"That makes *me* feel so much better." Sarah squeezed her.

"Wait here and cover me then. If something bad happens, you run out and get Mom and Dad."

Sarah bit her lip. "Feels weird calling them that. But, good weird. Do you think my dad would mind?"

"If it makes you feel safe and or happy, I think he'd be okay with it." Maya pushed the button to open the door.

A blast of foul, warm air hit her in the face, laden with the stench of earth, fertilizer, and strong chemicals that made her eyes water. After pulling her shirt up as a mask in a futile attempt to mute the stink, she peered out into the hall. To the left, the hallway hit a corner about twenty feet away while to the right, it ran more than a hundred yards with doors and other passages leading off from both sides. Large windows straight in front looked in on a massive chamber full of pipes and pumps, likely attached to the hydroponics tanks above them on ground level.

"Wow... so many doors," whispered Sarah.

Maya crept across the hall to the windows, peering into the maze of pipes and machinery. Numerous catwalks crisscrossed the room, suspended over a sunken floor another whole story deeper than the basement, filled with drab green fluid. The vast rectangular room took up about a third of the facility's space. Ten narrow tanks stood like a row of giant beer cans along the wall at the opposite left corner, each connected to pipes no bigger around than Sarah's arms.

Maya squinted at them. Even to her, it seemed pretty obvious that those tanks weren't part of the rest of the systems in this place. Much thinner, much shinier, and the complicated network of even smaller pipes leading away from them all went into the wall nearby—not up to the ceiling like the rest of the hydroponics equipment.

At the midway point of the long wall, a silver door caught her eye next to an observation window as wide as a small house.

"There. That's gotta be it." She pointed. "Looks like where the people who run the pumps would work."

"So?" asked Sarah.

Maya hurried to the right. "Look at the back corner. Those tall, narrow tanks. That's the bad stuff."

"Is that what stinks? Are we breathing it already?"

She scampered up to a set of double plastic doors. "No. That's the hydroponic fluid. Don't fall in it."

"Is it dangerous?" whispered Sarah.

"Probably... but it's basically liquid poop with a whole bunch of chemicals in it."

Sarah cringed.

"Not actual poop. Chemically similar."

"Whatever that means." Sarah rolled her eyes. "It's either poop or not poop."

The stink worsened when she brushed one of the doors open and stepped in onto a metal grating. Fortunately, crossing the room didn't require running a maze. A direct walkway connected this door straight across the large chamber to what she believed to be the control room. Made sense... managers wouldn't want to have to roam all over the place.

She walked at the middle, as far away from either railing as possible. Still, peering down through a grating at an undulating ocean of dark green liquid felt too much like being inside one of her video games for comfort. *Falling into green liquid is always bad.* It didn't help that the catwalk squeaked under her sneakers, wet with the chemicals. Sarah crept along behind her, refusing to release her two-handed grip on Maya's left arm. The elevated walkway bounced a little, raising a chorus of clattering into the room as the vibration traveled down branching pathways. Maya cringed at the noise.

By some miracle, no one came after them.

She grabbed the handle on the silvery door and twisted. Sarah gasped in surprise when it opened.

"See," whispered Maya. "If someone needs to reach the controls in an emergency, it can't be locked."

The room contained a big console-desk nearest the window covered in buttons, levers, dials, switches, and small monitors. Four ordinary desks stood behind it, each with a computer terminal. An enormous video screen made from nine smaller display panels took up most of the back wall, showing pump status and tank capacity for the hydroponics system. Graphical representations of fluid levels made it look like a computer game playing itself. Alas, none of it had anything to do with Fade.

"Hmm." She approached the big console and looked over the switches and knobs. "It's probably not going to be here. Normal workers would be at this station."

Sarah eased the silver door closed and pressed herself against the wall. "I'm really scared. I wanna go home."

"I swear I'll give up if I can't find anything fast. At least let me look for two minutes." Maya jogged over to the only desk with three computer screens. "This has to be it."

She flopped in the seat and tapped a keyboard. A password prompt came up. Despite not expecting much since the machine wasn't the same model, Maya attempted the same trick that got her into Mason's computer. Unsurprisingly, it didn't work. She checked under the keyboard, but found no sticky note with the password, so she proceeded to search the desk.

"What are you doing now?" whispered Sarah.

"Ascendant's IT people are really strict about issuing new passwords, and they make them stupid long. They don't even let employees create their own passwords, so almost *everyone* keeps breaking policy by having them written down somewhere."

"Seriously? Why even have passwords at all if everyone writes them down and leaves them around?"

"They're not supposed to. But with all the security outside... People are lazy and don't want to get in trouble for forgetting or not doing their work when they get locked out—aha!"

She pulled a piece of paper off the bottom of the middle drawer that contained the text: A957BoZ%94oEEo$97E3.

"Wow. People really are stupid." Sarah blinked.

Maya waved her over. "Look at this and tell me you'd remember it."

Sarah whined, but overcame her worry and broke away from the wall by the door. She scooted around the desk and pressed herself against Maya. "Oh, holy crap that's long."

"Yeah."

Maya found an employee achievement award on the desk for a Philip Gamsby. "Hmm. Pyramid of Excellence." She wagged it at Sarah. "When I'm big and have a real job, if I bust my butt for a place, they better give me something better than a $50 block of clear plastic."

"Hurry the hell up." Sarah pushed at her shoulder.

The first username she tried, pgamsby, worked. All three monitors flickered to life. The two on the sides displayed numerous icons over the faces of tiny children, a boy about two and a girl a year older. A woman's smiling face served as the middle monitor's background image.

"Wow, that's so wrong," said Maya.

"What? That's probably this guy's family. What's wrong with that?"

"The guy's got pictures of his wife and kids on a computer used to poison people with Fade. That's a little screwed up to me."

Sarah whistled. "Oh, yeah..."

She skimmed over the icons and identified six that she didn't recognize. One of those had to be the system that controlled the Fade tanks. She opened the first, but it turned out to be a charting application.

"Shit!" whispered Sarah. She ducked down and pulled Maya out of the chair to the floor. "Someone's coming."

Before Maya could open her mouth, the *clank, clank, clank* of boots on the catwalk outside grew louder.

She crammed herself into the space under the desk, Sarah huddling beside her.

A scrape of metal came from the control room door.

Maya closed her eyes. *Please don't be the guy who works at this desk.*

The squelch of wet boots on smooth tile moved to the right. Maya held her breath, afraid even the minuscule sound of air moving in her throat would get them caught.

"Huh... that's odd," said a man. "Someone here? Phil? Rohit? Terry?"

The footsteps resumed, drawing nearer. Maya clamped a hand over her mouth when a boot cut a shadow into the light leaking in under the front of the desk. She almost squeaked when the man leaned against their hiding place.

"Maybe he went to the can... Phil knows better than to leave his workstation unlocked."

Soft clicks came from overhead.

Maya peered up at the underside of the desk. Sarah shot her a pointed, accusing stare.

"Sorry, man. Gonna have to write you up for this one." He clucked his tongue.

Please go away. Please go away. Maya clenched her fists, trying to project her want into reality by sheer force of will. When that didn't make the guy leave, she stared apologies at Sarah.

Squishing footsteps picked up again, going off to the left, along with a man's humming. At least he sounded bored.

"Ugh. I don't know how the hell they can work in here. Stinks so damn bad..." The man coughed. "Hell with this."

Maya slumped in relief when the guard crossed the room again and the door squeaked closed.

"We are..." Sarah grabbed a fistful of Maya's T-shirt at her chest. "Going home right now."

"Not yet," whispered Maya. "He's still right outside. We have to wait for him to go back to his office. I've probably got two or three minutes."

Sarah shivered. She opened her mouth and closed it again a few times, unable to find a counterargument.

Once the clatter of boots on catwalk ceased, Maya crawled out from under the desk and stood tall on her knees, enough to reach the keyboard but not enough for her head to be seen past the monitors. The guard had again locked the workstation, but she logged back in and kept checking icons while Sarah emerged from their hiding spot, crawling up to the big command desk. She crouched behind it, peering out into the pipe room.

"I don't see him," she whispered.

"Good" Maya clicked another icon.

The fourth one she tapped opened a control panel that displayed a graphical representation of the Fade tanks as well as an array of digital buttons. She studied them for a few seconds and poked one marked 'EMRG-PURG.'

Another box popped up requesting the command authorization password from the 'red book.'

"Crap," whispered Maya.

She rummaged the desk drawers, tossing folders, media cases, and small boxes onto the floor. Near the bottom of the right lower drawer, she discovered a small three-ring binder with 'confidential' on the spine. It contained numerous sheets of codes that appeared to have some relationship with the day of the year.

"Ready?" whispered Sarah.

"Not yet. Hang on. I'm almost there." She sat cross-legged behind the desk, out of sight from the pipe room, and studied the code book. "This is an equation based on the day of the year and night or day. There are dummy codes though. I just need to do the checksums manually real quick to make sure I've picked the right one."

"Oh, sounds easy." Sarah lightly slapped herself in the forehead.

"Actually, it's a little bit of a pain the ass. I haven't done much logarithmic calculation. That stuff's beyond the school grade I completed, but I fiddled around for fun." She snagged a pen from the desk and started jotting down equations in the margin of the red paper. "The heavy math doesn't start until university level and I've only done stuff at grade twelve."

"Was that even English?"

"You ask that a lot." Maya grinned.

Sarah gasped. "He's coming back!"

"Get under the desk," said Maya, too focused on her work to have time to be frightened. "I'm almost... got it. It's this one." She poked her finger at a twenty-digit string of letters and numbers.

Sarah scooted under the control console. "He's gonna see me here!"

Ignoring everything but her code book, Maya propped up on her knees again and started keying in the confirmation code.

"What the hell are you doing in here?" bellowed a man.

Maya flicked her gaze up from the screen at a thirtysomething guy in a black BDU with matching black beret. She glanced at the half-entered code, at the book again, and back at the man before standing up to her full height. "Sorry, I don't think you've got high enough clearance to know why I'm here. You *do* know who I am, don't you?"

He tromped around the end of the desk and grabbed her right arm. "Yeah, I know who you are. And we know you've been declared a security risk."

Sarah, still unnoticed under the command desk, covered her mouth with both hands as tears poured from her eyes.

"Okay. You're right. I'm not supposed to be here." Maya looked away from Sarah to meet the man's gaze. "This place is more than a farm. Ascendant is using it to distribute Fade."

"Not my job to care what they use the place for. I'm just security." He tried to pull her away from the computer, but she clamped onto the desk.

"No!" yelled Maya. "It's a despicable weapon. How can you be part of this? How can you help them kill people?"

"The pay is good." The guard shrugged. "*Really* good."

Maya growled as her grip on the desk began to fail. "Ow! You're hurting me."

The guy jumped back when Sarah emerged. He released Maya's arm, but put a hand on the sidearm at his belt. She collapsed against the desk, staring at the screen. Six more letters to type in...

"*Two* kids?" He looked back and forth between them and flicked the retaining strap of his holster open. "Just what the hell is going on here?"

Maya reached for the keyboard.

"Hey!" the man yelled.

She typed in two more letters before he grabbed her by the back of the neck and pulled her away.

"Sare! Show this guy your bee stings," yelled Maya. "Maybe he'll let us go."

Sarah's eyes went wide.

"Damn, kid. You've got some mental damage. I don't wanna see no little girl's bee stings."

"Ow. Get off me." She squirmed. "Yeah, you're right you don't want to see her bee stings. But I really want her to show you." Maya stared at her. "Like right now."

"Oh, duh," muttered Sarah. "You can see them." She reached to pull her shirt up.

The security guard flinched away, trying not to look at her. "Dammit, kid. Don't do that."

Sarah drew the Hornet and fired a dart into the side of his head. Crackling tingles spread from his fingers into Maya's neck and crept down her back like an army of angry needle-legged spiders. Her arms and legs locked up, jaw clenched too tight to scream. After an agonizing two seconds, the man fell over backward, out cold. Maya collapsed in place, able to move but in too much pain to try.

"Ow, that hurt so much," whimpered Maya.

Sarah ran over to her and slid to a stop on her knees. "Maya!"

"I'm okay. Just. Ow." Growling past clenched teeth, she forced herself to all fours, her muscles still tweaking out with random stabbing shocks.

Sarah pulled her up to kneel and lifted her hair aside. "Oh wow, that guy left red marks on your neck."

"Guess he squeezed down hard when you zapped him." Maya braced one arm on the desk and punched in the last few characters before poking the 'execute' button.

The pipe chamber erupted into a sea of yellow flashing lights. A male voice over a loudspeaker announced a warning to clear the incinerator area due to highly toxic agents. Four seconds after that, a blaring alarm siren went off.

"Oops." Maya cringed. "I wasn't expecting alarms like that. Umm... we can get out of here now."

Sarah stuffed the Hornet back in its holster, grabbed two fistfuls of Maya's shirt, and shook her. "You're gonna get us killed."

"I'm sorry. Be mad at me later. Can we run now?"

"Argh!" Sarah grabbed her hand. "Yeah."

Maya scrambled along as Sarah dashed out onto the catwalk. More men and women in black BDUs swarmed toward the door at the opposite side. Sarah dashed to the right, dragging Maya down another walkway that took them out of sight behind a hydroponic fluid pump as big as a cargo van. As the security forces rushed toward the control room, Sarah hurried farther down the side passage, around a corner, and into a maze of pipes and machine housing.

Her eyes watered at the stink of the growth medium only inches below the grating. Barely able to see, she coughed into the crook of her elbow while trying to keep up with Sarah and not wipe out and go for a swim. The security people shouted about intruders, but no one said anything about kids, which Maya took as a good sign. That meant no one had spotted them—yet.

Sarah paused at the next corner, peering around it at the only door out of the room. "Crap. There's no way out of here without being seen. If they see us, the whole mission is ruined."

"They already know someone was in here, and as soon as that guy wakes up, they'll know *who* was here. He isn't dead. I'm screwed. But, they'll think I went for the Fade and won't have any idea about the module."

"Maybe..." Sarah glanced up studying the pipes overhead. "Hey. You up for a little climbing?"

"Will it get us out of here without being shot or kidnapped?"

Sarah glanced at her. "I think the term you're looking for is 'arrested.'"

"These turds work for Ascendant, not the Authority. It's kidnapping."

"Whatever. And yeah, I hope so. There's a vent up a little ways."

Maya nodded.

Sarah climbed the side of another giant pump, grabbing or stepping on pipes, housings, and valves. Maya followed as best she could. When she reached the top, Sarah pulled her over the edge but held her down.

"Stay low. Don't move," whispered Sarah, before scooting toward the middle of the pump and flattening herself out.

Maya crawled up behind her and did the same. Soon after, the blaring alarms cut off to silence. For the next few minutes, the clanking footfalls of security people scrambling around the maze of catwalks echoed over shouts of 'clear,' 'nothing here,' and 'where the hell did he go?'

At the 'he' part, Sarah stifled a giggle. Maya couldn't help but grin, too. Clearly these people expected an adult man to have snuck in here. The shouting migrated toward the door.

Sarah risked leaning up a bit to peek, but ducked back down in barely seconds. "They're guarding the door. We should be able to make it now."

"Okay."

Sarah crawled to the end of the pump away from the door. When she reached the edge, she stepped onto a pipe, leaned left, and proceeded to climb the tangle of metal tubes like an elaborate set of monkey bars. Maya didn't quite trust her arms to be able to pull her up, though two things gave her hope—she didn't weigh much, and she had terror pushing her.

Pipe by pipe, Maya scaled the foul-smelling warren of greasy pipes in her best effort to follow Sarah. She made the mistake of peering down at a roughly fifteen-foot fall into green liquid, and lost her nerve. In that instant of doubt, her fingers slipped from their hold overhead and her sneaker shot out from under her. She fell a short distance straight down, landing astride a three-inch pipe and clamping on. The dull *thud* of her crotch striking steel elicited a sympathetic gasp from Sarah.

"Oof," gasped Maya, stunned.

"Are you okay?" whispered Sarah from above.

"No. Not really. But I'm kinda super glad I'm a girl right now." She breathed in and out a few times, hard. "I can't feel my legs."

"Don't move. I think they heard that. Two guys are walking over here. Eyes go to motion. Stay very still."

Maya tried her best to do just that. The pipe had caught her in the groin with enough force to stun her legs. *If I was a boy, I don't think I'd still be one. Ow. Damn.* She clung to the pipe, fighting the urge to cry from pain. That she wanted to caught her off guard. The last time she'd cried in response to pain had happened so long ago she couldn't remember it. Tears didn't elicit any sympathy from the house AI, and she had a better chance of getting an emotional response from a computer than from Vanessa. If Genna saw her crying, she'd definitely react. Pope, too... even Sarah. Alas, clinging to filthy pipes deep in the heart of a top secret Ascendant murder factory with a security officer ten feet below her didn't bode well for her chances of ever seeing her parents again.

I'm sorry. I should've listened to Sarah and gone right out. This is my fault. I'm a dumbass. If the Brigade did know about the Fade here, that's probably why they wanted the module installed. They could've flushed it from remote... if they had the codes.

"Incineration routine completed," said a recorded male voice. "All personnel are required to clear the western quadrant for the next thirty minutes due to off-venting."

The man below her walked right on by, grumbling.

As soon as he disappeared around the side of a machine housing, Maya pulled herself up to stand on the pipe she'd landed on. Her groin ached, probably bruised, but the need to get back to her parents gave her wings, and she scrambled up the tangle of metal tubes without looking down. Sarah dropped back enough to grab her hand and help her up onto a fat two-foot thick horizontal pipe.

She clung to a vertical spar for balance while Sarah attacked the vent cover, using a lock pick to take a few screws out. Another guard walked by. Maya couldn't help but stare down at the top of his head. She didn't mind the second-story height so much—after riding a drone like a motorcycle, a mere twenty feet didn't scare her—but the green soup worried her as much as smashing her head open against some random pipe on the way down.

Sarah waited for the man to walk again out of sight, then shoved the vent cover up like the hood of a car. "C'mon."

Without a word, Maya shimmied over and crawled into the duct, taking a blast of air-conditioning in the face. Sarah scrambled in behind her and eased the vent cover shut.

"Holy crap," whispered Maya. "You were right. I should've listened to you and gone right out."

"I promise I won't be mad at you if we get out of here okay." Sarah patted her on the rear end twice. "All we need to do is get back to that room and go out the same way we came in."

"We're upstairs now." Maya shivered at the freezing gale, but at least the air didn't stink. "We'll have to find a way back downstairs."

"Vents?" whispered Sarah.

Maya crawled forward, but not as fast as she'd gone earlier. This vent didn't have earth packed around it. Each time her weight shifted, the thin metal banged and boomed. The passage connected at a T-join to a horizontal passageway. Air came from the right, but both directions looked about the same. Since left headed generally toward the room she wanted to be in, she went that way.

She crawled from offshoot to offshoot, pausing whenever she found a slatted cover. Every room she peered into on the ground floor had at least one person in it, workers in white clean-suits tending to food products in one capacity or another. Sarah followed her close and silent, her wide blue eyes conveying all the terror she didn't need words to express.

Finally, after nine unusable rooms, Maya spotted a vertical shaft leading down one level. She paused by it and looked at Sarah. "Sorry."

"Stop apologizing. Let's get out of here."

"Should we go down or keep looking for an empty room up here?"

Sarah shook her head and pointed at the shaft. "Down. There's too much security to go out the front door."

"Yeah. Good point." Maya swung her legs over the side to sit on the edge of the hole. "Umm. It's gonna make a lot of noise to jump."

Sarah patted her shoulder. "Turn around, lie on your front and let your legs hang. Give me your hands."

Maya shifted around and lay flat, then scooted back until her legs went over the side. Sarah held her hands, using her body as a counterweight to lower her gently. Of course, this pulled Sarah headfirst into the vertical spar. She slid forward, gripped Maya's shoulders, and climbed her like a squirrel descending a building upside down.

"You've done this before," said Maya.

"Once. Floor fell out from under us on a scav."

Maya gasped. "Maybe we shouldn't do that anymore. It's too dangerous for kids to explore old buildings."

"It's too dangerous for kids to run missions for the br—you know."

"Yeah, true."

Maya crouched and crawled into the vent, squeezed past a dormant fan, and wriggled around a rightward bend up to a slatted cover with faint blue light on the far side. She peered out at two rows of refrigerator-sized computer towers. Activity lights and status LEDs gave off enough of a glow to see a doorway out the other side. Eager to escape the ducts, she shoved it away and shimmied out onto cold linoleum, heading for the strip of hallway light up ahead.

Hoping that she'd gotten lucky, and this server room connected to (or was at least near) the workstation area, Maya opened the door with somewhat less caution than her situation likely demanded, and stuck her head out. The bright hallway glare made her cringe, but she recognized the frosted glass wall on the left. She grabbed Sarah's hand and took off running, rounding the corner some thirty feet away without hesitation— or caring that a woman in a black security uniform stood a ways down, clearly able to see them.

"Hey!" shouted the woman.

Maya threw herself at the door to the computer room... and bounced off. She grabbed the knob, but it wouldn't turn. "Crap! It's locked."

"The alarm," whispered Sarah.

"Eep!" Maya glanced at the approaching woman and sprinted the other way.

"Stop!" yelled the woman.

Maya ran as hard as she could, pumping her arms, her sneakers clapping on the floor, Sarah's squeaking right behind her. She veered left at the first turn, dashed past a row of small conference rooms, and rounded a right corner at the end. Five doors, four wood and nice, one metal and battered, lined a dead end.

"Shit," whispered Maya.

"No..." Sarah grabbed her from behind.

The tromp of the security guard's boots grew louder and louder. "Need backup in Q2. Couple of kids got in here somehow."

Maya eyed the doors. For no particular reason, she bolted for the beat-up one at the end. Sarah followed her into a room packed with dusty shelves, rust, and all manner of buckets, stray pipes, and unrecognizable machine components. Everything looked ancient, as though this space remained left over from whatever this building had been before the war.

"There!" Sarah practically shoved Maya behind the shelves on the right, pushing her toward the back corner.

A pair of grey steel doors stood at the opposite end of the room, marred with rust patches and secured by a padlocked chain. Sarah ran over and took a knee, fumbling her lock picking tools out. Maya ducked behind the nearby shelf and peeked around the edge. Out in the hall, the security woman poked her head (and a flashlight) into the first conference room.

"Come on out, kids. Nowhere for you to go. I don't know what you're doing down here, but this is no place for little girls."

Sarah couldn't quite get the picks in the lock, due to her hands shaking.

"Relax," whispered Maya. "She's not going to hurt us."

"I don't wanna get caught."

"I don't either, but we're not going to die." Maya put a hand on Sarah's shoulder. "You can do it."

The guard moved across the hall to the second room. "Come on, girls. I'm going to find you eventually. Are you hungry?"

"Holy crap," whispered Sarah. "I don't think she recognized you."

Maya shrugged. "Well, I am filthy and my hair's all over the place, hiding my face. It's going to take ten manicures to get this grease out from under my nails."

Sarah gave her the side eye.

"I'm kidding." Maya poked her.

A tiny hint of smile appeared. Sarah turned back to the padlock and bit her lip.

"I know you're probably in the old basement at the end." The security woman shone her flashlight into the third conference room. "But you also might want me to think that, and you're hiding under this table waiting to run once I go past you."

Snap.

The lock popped.

Sarah unfurled the chain and hauled the door open. Maya slipped through into a room only a little larger than the cargo elevator it held. An old forklift that looked like it hadn't moved in at least two decades sat half on the platform. She doubted the elevator would even work, but it had a frame to climb. Sarah tucked in and pulled the door closed.

"Up." Maya scrambled up the elevator frame, cringing at the soreness from her landing on the pipe earlier.

A pair of metal flap doors blocked off the roof, however time and warfare had provided a convenient rusted-out hole big enough for children to squeeze past. Maya gingerly grabbed the edge so she didn't cut her hand, then pulled herself up and out into clear nighttime air.

Searchlights swept back and forth, shining down from Ascendant drones orbiting the area like angry wasps defending their nest. A sickly, pale green fog clung to the ground off to the left—likely the off-venting from the fade burn. Despite being vaccinated, Maya held her breath. Of course, that could help them as no one would want to be here.

Sarah's long red hair billowed off to the side as her head emerged from the rust hole. She shrieked and launched herself upward, a woman's hand clamped onto her ankle. Maya wrapped her arms around Sarah, chest to chest, and pulled with all she had.

The security woman growled, but after a few seconds, her fingers slipped off Sarah's sneaker, and the girls flew over backward onto the ground, clinging to each other.

"That was too close," whispered Sarah. "What now?"

"The security gate is out front. We're in back." Maya sat up and gazed around at a large open yard surrounded by a tall chain-link fence. Random hunks of concrete debris littered the area along with some crushed fifty-gallon drums and a tire that appeared to belong to an aircraft. "We can climb the fence and get out."

Sarah gazed at the sky, pointing. "There's too many drones."

"They fly in pre-programmed paths. Genna showed me how to do this." Maya grinned, grabbed Sarah's hand, and ran with her to the giant tire, crawling under it.

She listened, timing the drones by tapping her finger on her leg. Every sixteen seconds, one went overhead. Maya repeated the count three times before working up the nerve to run to the next piece of cover, a concrete slab. Men's voices came over loudspeakers, announcing a perimeter breach.

Maya only waited one count of sixteen before running for a nest of metal barrels, several laying on their sides. She crawled into a drum, Sarah vanishing into another. As soon as a drone went overhead, Maya hurried back to her feet and kept going. She hid by a wrecked car, counted sixteen again, then darted over to a huge hunk of concrete not far from the fence. Sarah slid to a stop beside her, breathing hard. From her hiding place, Maya eyed a battered box truck on the other side of the chain link. The rear doors hung open, drifting in the wind.

"New idea," whispered Maya. "It's so open out there, the drones will see us. It's too far to go with nowhere to hide."

"So we stay here?"

"No. We have to get out from inside the fence." Maya pointed. "We're gonna hide in that old wrecked truck."

Sarah nodded. "Cool. Good idea... until they decide to search it and find us."

"Do you have a better idea? We'd have to run a long way over open field. The drones will shoot us. And we can't stay here. We can't even lie about accidentally getting in there because that one guy you zapped knows me."

"Okay. Okay."

They both flinched as a three-fanned Ascendant drone swooped by, a little lower than before.

"Crap." Maya ducked. "I think they're checking hiding places back here."

"Go!" Sarah swatted her back.

Maya launched herself out from under the big slab, sprinted the last fifteen feet to the fence, and climbed it like a squirrel on fire. She waited at the top until Sarah held the lowest strand of razor wire up so she could slip under it, then held it while Sarah crawled past. They shimmied down the outside of the fence side by side, jumped the last few feet, then hauled ass to the big, brown-grey box truck covered in tattered olive-drab tarps.

The rear bumper came up to the level of her chin, but she pulled herself up with the help of a small ladder at the corner. Stacks of not-ruined boxes inside surprised her, but she decided they offered an even better hiding place. With seconds to spare on the drone count, Maya hurried in, twisting sideways to shimmy between two walls of shipping cartons. At the inner end of the cargo area, a gap on the right with no boxes offered a more comfortable place to hide. She curled up on the floor with her back against yellow plastiboard.

"Wow." Sarah flopped down beside her, out of breath. "I can't believe we got out."

Maya desperately wanted something to drink, and swallowed a few times on a dry throat. "We're not out yet. If any of those drones saw us... wait, no. They'd have shot us. Ascendant drones are AIs."

Sarah threw an arm around her and clung. "What do we do now?"

"Wait here until they give up searching or Mom and Dad find us." Maya tugged her left pant leg up enough to expose the tracker around her ankle. "When we don't come out the tunnel, they'll start looking."

"We're *already* late. And they're probably freaking out because of the alarm."

"Try to be quiet," whispered Maya.

Sarah nodded.

Minutes passed as they listened to the constant whirr of drone fans outside and people shouting. Considering the number of curses flying around, Maya's confidence that they'd gotten lucky grew.

"They should give up soon," whispered Maya. "As soon as the drones go back in their nests, Mom and Dad will find us."

"Why did we do this?" asked Sarah, before heaving a long sigh. "If we escape, can we go back to being normal kids?"

"That's what I want, too." Maya brushed dirt off her arm. "Harlowe made it sound like this would get rid of Ascendant. As long as Vanessa's there, I have a big target on my back. Either she'll come after me, or mercenaries, or someone trying to take over the company, or... someone." Tears came unbidden. "I just wanna be left alone."

Sarah pulled her into a hug, patting her back. "That guy saw you. I think we should go into hiding."

"Doubt it." Maya wiped her eyes. "Vanessa won't be too angry with me for burning that Fade. They can still make more. All I did was cost them time, and she said she wasn't going to set any loose for a while. I probably did them a favor. If the Authority goes looking for Fade now, they won't find any."

"We gotta tell Mom and Dad what happened."

"Duh." Maya made a silly face at her. "Of course."

Again, they sat in silence for a while. Eventually, the ruckus of drones and searching security personnel died down to the soft susurrus of crickets and other insects. Sarah squeezed Maya's hand.

"We made it," whispered Sarah.

Maya tried to swallow again. "I'm thirsty."

Sarah smacked her lips a few times. "Yeah."

"Now, we just have to wait for them to find us."

"Yeah," whispered Sarah. "How long do we wait before we try to walk home?"

"I dunno." Maya shrugged. "I'm only nine."

Sarah snickered.

As the adrenaline of her narrow escape wore off, Maya yawned. She stared at yellow plastiboard cartons, daydreaming about the bed waiting for her at home. After a while, footsteps crunched outside.

Sarah sat up straight, a look of hope on her face.

"Damn annoying sons of bitches," muttered an unfamiliar man.

Maya shifted her gaze to Sarah.

The truck doors closed with a hard *whump*. Metal clanked.

"Uh oh," whispered Sarah. "I think I figured out why there's shipping boxes in this truck."

Maya leapt to her feet and hurried down the row of cartons to the back doors. They'd been sealed, and didn't have any handles on the inside. She banged her hands against them, calling, "Hey, open the doors!"

The low groan of laboring e-motors accompanied the truck lurching forward. Maya flew against the doors, bounced off, and landed on her butt. All the boxes around her wobbled and shifted from the rough ground.

Sarah crawled out from between the boxes and knelt beside her. "Hey, maybe this is good."

"Good?" Maya blinked.

"Yeah. That guy is giving us a ride away from here. He's probably going to the Hab, or maybe the Sanc."

Maya sat up and leaned against the side wall between the door and a carton. "Yeah. You're right. I bet he made a delivery, or he's buying food here and got stuck when we set off the alarm."

"Umm." Sarah's confidence faltered. "If he was making a delivery, why would the truck be way out in the middle of nowhere by the fence?"

"I don't know." Maya bit her lip, and huddled close to Sarah. "Wait for the truck to stop and run as soon as he opens the door?"

"Yeah." Sarah nodded. "That'll work."

11

OUT OF THE WAY

Two hours later, the truck continued to drive, though the ride had smoothed out somewhat and picked up speed, suggesting a road. Maya cycled through terror, anger, despair, boredom, and back to being sick with worry. Strips of small, rectangular LED lights ran the length of the ceiling at both corners. Though weak, they at least prevented total darkness.

"We're not stopping in the Hab," said Sarah.

Maya climbed to her feet and attacked the door. No amount of prodding, kicking, or pounding budged them.

"We can't open them from inside."

"I know." Maya folded her arms. "I'm just pissed."

"Well, the truck was sorta a good idea. We got away from the building. Mom and Dad are probably driving up behind us any minute now."

"Assuming this metal box isn't attenuating the tracker signal so much they can't read it."

"Huh?"

"This truck isn't as old as it looked. I thought it was a wreck from the war. It's not. The box we're in is metal. It might block the signal."

Sarah stuck out her tongue. "So why didn't you say block instead of ten-you-waited?"

"I dunno. I just did. Sorry if I make you feel like you haven't been to school."

"I'm not stupid."

Maya sat back down beside her and smiled. "I know. That's why I said 'not been to school.'"

One hour dragged into the next. Maya found herself growing angry again, mostly at herself for panicking too much to notice the obviously functional truck wasn't a wreck. Of course, being carted off to somewhere unknown beat having drones machine gun them to death in an open rubble patch. It probably beat capture as well. As often as she'd been around Ascendant and its employees, she'd never once before seen people in all-black BDUs like that, which made them more frightening.

Vanessa didn't take me on tours of the Fade plant.

Had those people caught them, it would not have ended well at all. They could've wound up locked in cells in that building, or killed, or interrogated. And she didn't think the two of them would have lasted long at all before giving away Brigade secrets.

She tried to feel grateful that the truck worked out, but couldn't help but dread they'd wound up in an even worse situation. Despite her anxiety, hours of monotonous driving in a dark, enclosed space caused a short blip of sleep.

"Gah!" Maya sat up, snapping awake.

"I gotta pee," said Sarah.

As soon as she heard those words, the need hit her, too.

Maya scrunched her knees together. "Did you have to say that? Now I gotta go."

"Gonna look for a bucket or something." Sarah wobbled to her feet and shimmied into the gap between the stacked plastiboard cartons.

She bounced in place, trying to think of anything except having to go. Sarah returned in a few minutes with an urgent expression.

"All the boxes are sealed. There's nothing here to pee in."

Maya cringed. "Don't stay that word."

When the truck hit bumpy ground, Sarah wobbled on her feet. A sharp bounce flung her face first into the boxes, but she managed to catch herself before smooching the ground.

"Sit down before you break your neck," said Maya.

"I can't sit. I gotta pee too bad. If I sit, I'm gonna mess myself."

"If you break your neck, you're gonna pee anyway *and* you'll be dead."

Sarah grabbed herself between the legs and managed to make it into a seated position without an accident.

Watching her squirm made Maya squirm.

Another almost-hour felt like ten. The need to pee had transcended simple need to actual pain. Maya pinned her knees together, trying not to breathe too deeply. Sarah started making wheezy sounds like a woman doing breath exercises in preparation for natural childbirth.

Every bump or jostle in the road hurt.

"How long is this guy gonna drive?" rasped Sarah.

"I don't know."

"Argh." Sarah grabbed the plastiboard cartons and pulled herself upright. "I can't sit anymore or I'm gonna make a mess whether I want to or not."

"We're almost there. Hold it a little longer."

"You just said you don't know. How do you know we're almost there?"

Maya bit her lip, cringing from the pain in her bladder. "Just trying to be positive."

Ten more minutes passed. Maya decided to stand as well, and found it helped—a little.

"Okay." Sarah opened her button. "I can't do this anymore. I'm peeing on the floor."

"No!" gasped Maya. "He'll know someone was here."

Sarah wobbled over to the back doors and shoved her pants down. "He's going to know anyway when we run past him."

"Please no. We don't know who this guy is or where we're going. We have to hide. We can't let anyone know we exist until we understand the risk."

Sarah pressed her forehead to the truck door and whined. After a moment, she stood and pulled her pants back up. "Okay, but I'm five minutes from no longer caring."

"What did you do when the Authority left you zip-tied all day?"

"What do you think I did?" Sarah glowered at the floor. "They tied my hands to my feet behind my back. I couldn't move. When I couldn't hold it anymore, guess what happened."

Maya shivered. "Eww. That's horrible."

"I slithered into the kitchen at least so I didn't ruin the rugs."

"Umm." Maya looked down at her sneakers. "Maybe we should stop talking about wetting ourselves."

"I've never had to go this bad. Ever." Sarah picked at the button on her pants. "I'm about to start crying it hurts so much."

The truck slowed down. Deceleration made the girls sway into the stacked boxes. Seconds later, Sarah slid into Maya, both of them pressed against the side wall on a turn. Clattering of rocks and mud clumps peppered the underside and the ride once again became bumpy.

Maya gritted her teeth and whined, trying not to have an accident while jostling about and bouncing. Sarah wedged herself against the truck doors with one leg up, sneaker pressed into the plastiboard boxes.

A few minutes after the truck left the smooth road, it rolled to a stop.

"Hide," whispered Maya. She rushed into the narrow space down the middle between the two rows of stacked cartons, and scurried into the empty space near the front end where they had originally hidden.

Sarah followed, but didn't even attempt to crouch down.

With a belabored *squeak* of metal, the doors opened, allowing sunlight to leak in along the roof.

Holy crap! We drove all night long.

A man muttered something that sounded drunk, though more than likely, the slurring came from exhaustion. Maya peered around the tower of cartons at a guy wearing a grey poncho and filter mask. He unloaded a few before carrying them away and grumbling.

"Now!" whispered Maya.

She speed-shimmied down the narrow passage and hesitated for only a few seconds at the end before jumping down to grass. Between her earlier fall on the pipe and having to go *so* bad, pain exploded in her groin as her feet hit the ground. She crumbled to her knees, grabbing herself, barely aware of a scattering of ramshackle huts spread out in front of her.

Another hut made of scrap wood and corrugated metal panels stood close by on the left. The voice of a man inside called someone lazy and told them to go empty the truck. Sarah climbed down on stiff legs. Maya forced herself to stand and turned in place, searching for anywhere to hide.

Forest to the left of the nearby building offered an ideal spot. She stiff-legged it over a short strip of grass, across a not-so-short patch of planted ground containing neat rows of various vegetables, and dashed into the woods.

Barely twenty paces into the trees, she became aware of the faint burble of a distant stream or creek. That sound made the idea of holding it for even another second intolerable. She shoved her pants down and watered the nearest tree. Sarah squatted almost close enough to touch shoulders and did the same. Proximity didn't embarrass Maya anywhere near as much as she expected it would. She pondered if boys using wall toilets ever felt awkward peeing while standing right next to someone else. Still, she had to go *far* too badly to care about something as trivial as privacy.

Sarah braced her forearm across the tree trunk and rested her head against it. "Ow. I've never been so happy to pee before."

"Yeah."

For a minute or so, Maya wondered if it would go on forever. Eventually, she finished, but didn't bother getting up, so thrilled with the absence of pain she couldn't summon the strength to move at all. Sarah also took a minute to breathe and enjoy not having to go anymore.

"How long were we driving?" wheezed Maya, finally standing and securing her pants back in place.

"A long damn time." Sarah let out a deep breath. "All night and a few hours. Ugh. I need to see Doc, I think. It still hurts and I can't go anymore."

"Your bladder isn't used to having to accommodate such a quantity of liquid. The membrane has stretched. It's simple soreness that should go away on its own in a little while."

"Did I ever say you stink at pretending to be a child?" asked Sarah.

Maya giggled. "Sorry. I used to read medical stuff on the AuthNet when bored."

"Really? Wow... what about that awesome video game system?"

"Even the coolest games get boring if you play them for 200 hours."

"Oh." Sarah grunted with discomfort as she stood and hiked her pants up.

Maya crept back toward where they came from, hid behind a large tree trunk, and peered around it at some manner of village. She counted around twenty huts that appeared to be dwellings, with three larger buildings in the center. Most looked handmade from scrap wood or metal, with a small number incorporating recognizable sections of box trucks or trailers.

The village had a definite 'main road,' albeit dirt, and even a well at the center of town, though it looked so decrepit she couldn't tell if it still worked or had been there from before. People wearing garments of leather or fur walked around or busied themselves with various chores. About three out of four adults had shoes, boots, or moccasins also made of animal hide. Of the seven or eight children she spotted over the course of several minutes, all were barefoot.

Maya's eyes widened. *Oh, shit. We're in the wildlands...*

"Ugh," groaned Sarah, lowering herself to sit on the ground. "That sucked *so* much."

"Sorry."

"I mean holding it so long." Sarah tapped her sneakers together. "Well, we got kidnapped again but we have shoes."

Maya stopped peering around the tree and ducked down to hide. "We haven't been kidnapped, technically. We're lost."

"Some guy drove us like ten hours away from home and we didn't want to go. Isn't that kidnapped?"

"He didn't know we were in the truck." Maya patted the tracker on her left ankle. "We just need to stay safe until Mom and Dad find us."

"They have to be going crazy... and what if we're too far away for them to get a signal from it?"

Maya fidgeted at the tracker, spinning it around her ankle. "Umm. If they don't find us in a day, we could ask the guy with the truck for a ride back to the Hab."

"This is the wildlands," whispered Sarah. "What if those stories are true and they take us as slaves?"

"You didn't believe that was true before." Maya poked her in the arm. "Didn't you suggest we go live in the wildlands to stay safe from Vanessa?"

"Yeah, but that was before."

"Before what?" Maya tilted her head.

"Before we were actually out here alone." Sarah flashed a cheesy smile. "It's a lot scarier being here."

"The people look kinda normal. I think they're better off than Frags."

"Really?" Sarah blinked.

"Yeah. I only see two people here running around naked, and both are toddlers. Frags, it's about half of them... and not just kids."

Sarah snickered.

"Probably because there's no deer to hunt for hide in the Dead Space. These people are all dressed like Native Americans."

"Duh. Of course they're native Americans. They grew up here."

Maya sighed. "You've never heard of Native Americans."

"You learned that in school, didn't you?"

"E-learns."

"That's technically still school, right?" Sarah folded her arms.

"Yeah."

"Well... Book taught me how to read. Dad taught me some stuff, too, but mostly survival skills and military history."

After a rough explanation of the difference between Native Americans and native (not capitalized) Americans, Maya stood. "I'm thirsty. There's a stream nearby."

"Is it safe to drink?"

"Why wouldn't it be?" Maya scratched her head.

"Umm, war? There's all sorts of toxic crap out in the wildlands. Radioactive fallout, contaminated groundwater, poisonous chemicals from things like factories or industrial facilities destroyed during the war. We need to test any water before we drink it. Even if it's radiation free, it could have dangerous meebas in it."

Maya stifled a snicker. "Amoebas?"

"That's what I said."

"Okay. How do we test it?"

"Umm. With a water test kit," said Sarah.

"Did you bring one?"

Sarah fidgeted. "No. It's home. Didn't think we'd need it for a fifteen-minute crawl in a vent shaft."

Maya sighed, about to apologize again but blinked instead. "Wait, you *have* water test kits?"

She nodded. "Yeah. Two actually. In my, umm, *our* closet."

"Well..." Maya walked toward the sound of the stream. "I'm thirsty as hell, and if I drink anything bad, they can fix it when we get home."

"It could kill you," said Sarah.

"So can dehydration." Maya continued heading toward the watery noise.

"Ugh." Sarah grunted, stood, and trudged after her. "At least boil it first. There could be meebas, bacteria, parasites, worms, spores, heavy metals, radiation..."

Maya kept going. "Boiling won't help radiation, and we don't have anything to boil water with."

A short walk brought her to a modest, but fast-moving stream flowing downhill to the right. Far in the distance, it joined with a river that divided the forest. She stopped near the water's edge, gazing around at the woods. If civilization had encroached on this place before the war, she couldn't tell. Considering trees didn't grow that fast, she doubted woodlands could've covered nuke-flattened land already.

The clean air caught her off guard. She gazed up and around at the trees, leaves whispering in the wind, and didn't know what to make of it. Never in her life had she seen so much greenery without it being in a video game or on a screen. Deep breath after deep breath filled her senses with the scent of nature, and offered a moment of calm.

Sarah scooted past her and crouched by the stream, scooping a handful of water and sniffing at it before letting it fall back into the flow. "It's fast-moving here, but that's not a guarantee it's safe. Fast-moving is better than stagnant."

"You're not thirsty?" Maya blinked. "My mouth feels like it's made out of cotton."

"It's barely been a day. We're not in danger of dehydrating. Two more days with no better options, I'd say okay we can risk it. I don't really wanna die from a bug in the water." She twisted left. "If there's a dead animal upstream, even if the water's fast, we could get sick and die."

"Grr."

Sarah stood. "What about the village? Did they look like they'd take us for slaves?"

"Umm. I don't know. What do slave-takers look like?" Maya shrugged.

"Well, did you see people in cages? Anyone like tied up or something?"

Maya shook her head. "No. They looked normal. Just wearing furs and leather."

"Okay." Sarah put an arm around her and guided her away from the water. "Even if we do get captured, I'd rather be a prisoner for a little while until Mom and Dad find and save us than poop myself to death."

"Eww." Maya cringed. "But if we get captured, what if they take the tracker away?"

"It will still be in this village. People here would probably think it's jewelry or something and one of them would wind up wearing it."

Maya nodded. "Okay."

She reluctantly backed away from the stream, deciding to trust what The Dad had taught Sarah in terms of survival. The girl might not know how to calculate the area of a square or how ions traverse sodium channels, but she could keep herself alive in the forest.

A few minutes later, Maya tucked up behind a tree at the forest's edge and surveyed the village. The truck that had brought them here remained where it stopped, the doors both closed. She figured at least the guy who drove it understood civilization if he made routine trips to the Hab for trade. Given the length of the ride, it couldn't be a something he did often, which also explained the huge truck to carry so much stuff at once. The size of that building suggested a trading post of sorts, likely to sell whatever he'd brought back from civilization. Solar panels on the building's roof also explained how the truck continued working.

Okay. Maybe they're not too primitive.

"If anyone tries to grab us, Hornet and we haul ass?"

Sarah nodded.

At a gurgle from her stomach, Maya pressed a hand into it, unable to tell if it came from hunger or fear. Somehow, she hadn't been as nervous about sneaking into the Ascendant facility as she presently felt about walking into a wildlands village. This place didn't have fences, security guards, or drones patrolling. All the dread came from things she'd read on the AuthNet over the years. What her senses told her disagreed with everything the Authority claimed.

She lurked for a little while more, watching the village children run around chasing a red ball. Except for their surroundings, they appeared happy and normal. The eldest, a girl, had skin the same dark brown as Genna. Two boys appeared Asian, another boy and a girl as pale as Sarah. Those two both had super-platinum blonde hair and wore short skirts made of vines and leaves instead of animal hide clothes. Maya figured them to be siblings, but struggled to understand why they'd want to wrap plants around themselves for clothing. Merely looking at them made her itch.

"What are you waiting for?" asked Sarah. "Is something wrong?"

"No. That's what's wrong. It looks too normal. Nothing like what I read."

Sarah scratched her head. "Didn't you say that Ascendant always lies, and they own the AuthNet?"

"Yeah. All right." She pushed off the tree. "Let's go."

The kids kicking the ball around played on a field beyond the other end of the village, too far away to notice Maya and Sarah walking into town along the dirt road. A small brown bird zipped by, vanishing into the branches. Some adults glanced at them, but other than the occasional nod of greeting, no one tried to talk. Even better, no one came running at them.

Maya headed straight for the well. A structure of wood planks and metal plates covered a hole about four feet wide, complete with a small solar panel array hooked to an electric pump. Sarah picked up a blue plastic bucket that appeared clean, shrugged, and held it under the spout. Maya pushed the only button on the pump housing.

The electric motor whirred to life, and within a few seconds, water bubbled up into the bucket.

They took turns drinking until neither one of them could swallow another drop. Maya leaned against the well for a while looking around at the shacks and people. An open 'courtyard' of reddish brown dirt surrounded the well. One of the village's three large buildings stood at the edge of it, perhaps thirty feet away. Trays of vegetables sat out like an open air market, suggesting it a trading post of sorts. Two young women, not quite adults yet, stood by the bins in a manner suggesting sales clerks. Windows to the left looked in on a room with shelves like a convenience store. Inside, a man about Pope's age tinkered with a small appliance at the counter.

"Wow, this kinda looks like a village from one of my old games. Only instead of stone and thatch, the huts are modern scrap. And there's no elves. This is like a town square or something."

Sarah snickered.

Maya decided to roam around exploring since they didn't necessarily have to do anything but wait for her parents to show up, following the tracker. As soon as she saw Genna again, she planned to do two things: say 'thank you' about five hundred times for insisting on the tracker, and promise never to do another mission until she grew up. She trudged toward one of the huts, drawn by curiosity.

"I messed up," muttered Maya. "You're right. I should learn how to 'child' and stop trying to fix what Ascendant broke. I only did it because—"

"You want the target off your back." Sarah poked her between the shoulder blades. "It's okay. We got out in one piece and maybe it's a good thing we're all the way out here. If Ascendant is trying to come after you, they won't be able to find us in the wildlands."

"Yeah but..." Maya grimaced. "They don't know that. They might go to our building and hurt our friends."

"You said yourself that Ascendant could just replace the Fade you flushed. Maybe they'll keep it quiet so no one finds out that they had so much."

Maya looked up from the ground, her mood slightly improved. "Maybe."

They roamed around the village for the better part of an hour. For no particular reason, perhaps the same nervousness that made Maya uncomfortable around Sarah at first, she avoided going near the kids playing with the ball. Right as she started to debate internally how she could be at ease with the children in her building but still intimidated by others, footsteps crunched up behind them.

Maya whirled.

A woman in a black tank top, green camo BDU pants, and combat boots approached with a curious, concerned expression despite the faint orange glow inside her eyes. Straight black hair hung to within inches of her belt line, a few errant strands wavering in the breeze. Her youthful face and delicate nose suggested she hadn't quite hit thirty yet. Small electronic components attached to her head at the temples, thin strips of dark metal set with tiny green lights trailed back over both ears. Her entire left arm well into the shoulder consisted of metal, scratched and scuffed in places that suggested she'd seen combat. The limb appeared only slightly thicker than her still-biological right arm, but generally mimicked the contours of humanity.

The sight of the cybernetic limb brought Maya straight back to being chained by one ankle to a bedframe with Moth pointing a gun at her face. She gasped and clung to Sarah, trembling, unable to speak.

Sarah stepped protectively in front of her, puffing her chest out.

"Whoa, it's okay." The woman raised both hands. "Don't freak out, kid. I'm not going to hurt you."

"What do you want?" asked Sarah. "Who are you?"

Maya shook off the bad memory and wrestled her emotions back under control... mostly. Still, talking remained out of reach.

The woman smiled. "My name is Kita. I saw you two wandering around and didn't recognize you. Just wanted to make sure you were all right. Got parents? Place to stay?"

"Kita." Sarah looked the woman up and down.

"It's technically Ankita, but most grunts can't handle three syllable words." Kita winked.

"My dad had a metal arm, too," said Sarah, her confrontational tone fading. "But it was a cheap one. What happened to yours? Combat injury if you got an assault model, right?"

"That's right. You ever see a movie or video game where a soldier picks up a grenade and throws it back at the enemy?"

Sarah nodded.

"Well, that doesn't quite work." Kita held up her left hand and clicked the metal fingers. "Lucky for me, it was a repack with crap explosives... and I had thick armor." She pointed at her left ear. "Went deaf on one side, but they gave me electronics."

"Oh, wow." Sarah leaned to the side for a better look at the glowing lights on the woman's head.

"Yeah. I can hear a flea fart in the grass at a hundred yards." Kita chuckled.

Maya let go of the last of her fear. "Sorry... A man with metal arms kidnapped me and wanted to kill me. I guess I'm a little more traumatized by it than I thought."

"Aww, you poor thing." Kita stepped closer and patted Maya on the shoulder with her live hand. "So, what's your story? How did you two wind up all the way out here?"

Maya looked at Sarah, who shrugged.

"Well," said Maya. "We're from the Baltimore Habitation District. Some bad people were trying to hurt us. We saw this truck sitting there abandoned and I thought it was a wreck, so we hid inside it. But the truck started driving and we couldn't get out."

Kita whistled. "Wow, you rode all the way here in the back of Oswald's truck? You're a long way from home."

"Yeah." Maya hooked her thumbs in her hip pockets and sighed. "But our parents are going to find us. We just have to wait for them. This is my sister, Sarah, and I'm Maya."

"If you two are hungry, you're welcome to have some of my food. There's plenty." Kita gestured at a distant building made of salvaged pieces with her living arm. "You're a little young to be on your own. I've also got the room if you'd like to crash until your parents get here."

Maya peered up at the woman. Nothing about her body language or tone radiated danger, and the look she gave them implied she thought the 'parents are coming' to be something the girls made up to not sound so defenseless. That meant she offered to take them in, so the woman seemed kindly in nature. "Okay."

"That would be nice," said Sarah.

"Come on then." Kita smiled and walked off toward the building.

Sarah glanced at Maya. "Seems nice."

"Yeah. She thinks we're lying about having parents and expects she's adopting us for good. I kinda feel bad for her. Combat wounded and lonely... when Mom and Dad show up, she's going to be sad."

Kita, about twenty yards away paused and looked back, smiling.

"Umm," said Sarah. "Did you forget about her super-ears?"

Maya bit her lip, and started walking.

When they caught up to her, Kita chuckled. "I'm not as lonely as you think, though I admit I wasn't quite buying the parents angle."

"I'm wearing a tracker," said Maya.

"Why would a girl your age have a tracker?"

"Because I have a bad habit of winding up *really* lost." Maya offered a weak smile.

Kita paused at a small three-step stairway connected to a porch deck that wrapped around two walls of a large rectangular dwelling. A set of sandals way too small for Kita at the top explained her statement about not being lonely. They wouldn't even fit Maya.

"You look kinda familiar." Kita studied her, tapping one metal finger to her chin.

"I'm not talking about *that* woman." Maya put her left foot up on the steps and pulled her pant leg off the tracker. "I have a *real* mother now. And it's kind of a long story."

Kita stooped to grasp the black square with two fingers, tilting it a little upward. "Hmm. Haven't seen a HVPT unit in a while. Assuming it's still got power, your people ought to be able to find you. How'd you get a piece of military hardware like this?"

"My mom made me wear it."

Sarah rubbed her forehead. "Umm. High value personnel tracker? Or something like that? Captains and up wore them."

"How's a little thing like you know that?" asked Kita.

"My dad was with a recon scout unit. He kinda had some mental issues. Thought the war was still going on and taught me stuff so I'd be 'ready when the enemy found us.'"

Maya rubbed Sarah's back.

"Come on in and maybe you can tell me about it?" Kita walked up the stairs, crossed the wide porch, and disappeared through a bead curtain.

Sarah, one hand on the Hornet, followed her. Maya brought up the rear, nudging strands of beads out of the way and poking her head in.

The interior didn't have separate spaces as much as the suggestion of rooms, courtesy of shallow partitions jutting out from the exterior walls that sorta-defined different areas. One space contained a small bed and a number of old toys. A larger bed took up the far right corner. A huge opening as big as a double-width garage door on the left side looked out over an even wider section of porch, more a deck. Hanging canvas flaps bunched up at both sides like an enormous shower curtain that could close off the house in the event of bad weather.

The sight made Maya shiver. This dwelling wouldn't be very warm in the winter, at least not without burning a ton of wood, little more than a giant tent with three wooden walls. Maybe Kita hung furs or something over the big opening during the cold season.

She approached a fireplace made of metal that sat in an area where the wooden flooring gave way to a round patch of bare dirt. Bricks formed a wall around it between the earth and the underside of the floor, so at least that spot wouldn't let creatures inside at night. Maya crept closer, curious what the large pot dangling over the fire pit held. The not-unpleasant aroma reminded her of vegetable soup with some unidentified spices. Atop the stove sat an odd statue of a four-armed man with the head of an elephant perched on a cluster of pillows.

"Here you go." Kita handed Maya a bowl of brownish-yellow stew. Her smile died when she realized she'd used her metal left arm. "Oh... I'm sorry. Didn't mean to scare you."

Maya took the bowl. "It's all right. I'm not afraid of your arm anymore. Just startled me at first. Thank you for feeding us."

"Yes, thank you." Sarah smiled and accepted a bowl.

They followed her over to the table which stood near enough to the open wall, they had a view of the nearby meadow where the kids continued playing with the ball. Maya sat and picked over the contents of the bowl with her spoon. It appeared to be a bunch of vegetables in a yellowish-brown sauce. She faintly remembered having something that smelled similar when she lived in the penthouse, but it had involved chicken.

"This is good." Sarah scooped up another spoonful. "What is it?"

"Oh, just some vegetables with a little curry and other spices." Kita took a seat near them. "The seasonings are a little difficult to get out here, but Oswald visits Baltimore once every two months or so."

Maya nibbled on a hunk of something that looked like broccoli but had no color at all, except for what the sauce gave it. Not recognizing a plant bothered her, so she made a note to look it up the next time she could get online. The food hit her with a bit more spice than she expected, but that made her like it more. "Oh, wow. This is really good."

"Told you," muttered Sarah around a mouthful.

"When's the last time you two had anything to eat?" Kita chuckled. "Never thought my throw-together stuff was *that* good."

"Last night for dinner," said Maya.

While they ate, she told Kita about Genna's group initially

kidnapping her and Vanessa doing the whole 'kill her I'll make another one' thing. She left out any mention of the Brigade, though did tell her about her new mother meeting Pope and the two of them becoming involved. To explain their presence out here, Maya invented a story about a bunch of dosers trying to steal her and Sarah's clothes, so they ran to hide on the truck—and became stuck.

By the time she finished explaining, the kids kicking the ball around dispersed. The two pale blondes waved farewell to the others and wandered off into the woods while the rest of the children entered the village. A boy around six in a deer hide tunic ran up to the deck and walked in. Though he did resemble Kita, his skin appeared much lighter.

The boy eyed them warily. All the exuberance he'd had running home tucked itself away under a thick blanket of shyness, and he scooted behind his mother.

Kita smiled. "This is my son, Anshad. It takes him a little time to get used to new people." She twisted around and ran a hand over his head a few times. "Baby, meet Maya and Sarah."

Anshad continued staring at them with huge brown eyes.

Sarah grinned at him and waved. Maya smiled.

He managed a faint smile in return, but didn't say anything.

"Well," said Kita. "You two are welcome to stay with us for as long as you need. If your parents had access to a HVPT, they probably have a tracer for it."

"Mom wouldn't have given it to me if she didn't have a way to use it. They should be here soon."

"Thank you for giving us food. Can we do anything to help? Maybe wash the dishes at least?" asked Sarah.

Kita's eyebrows went up. "You two are rather polite. It would be most gracious of you to help if you care to." She gestured at a sink, which consisted mostly of a basin with a pipe to the wall. No faucet. "Though, since you're used to the Hab, it's a little more rustic out here. You'll need to go to the well for water and heat it on the e-plate."

"There's power?" Sarah blinked.

"Yes, but not a lot. I've got a small panel on the roof." She pointed at an electrical outlet on the wall in the 'kitchen' section. "One outlet in the house."

Sarah took Maya's bowl, set them both in the sink, and picked up the bucket. "Be right back."

When she passed by, Maya stood and walked with her back outside to the village center and the well. A boy in his middle teens and two adult women formed a line waiting their turn to get water. All wore garments made of animal hide, some parts with fur. Both women had fur-lined boots while the boy wore sandals.

Sarah wandered up to the end of the line. At her approach, the others glanced back, both women nodding while the boy said, "Hey."

"Hi," replied Sarah.

Evidently uninterested in more conversation, he faced forward again.

Maya leaned over and whispered, "Wow. This is totally not what the AuthNet said the wildlands would be like. This is basically a little nice town... from 200 years ago."

"Gasp," deadpanned Sarah. She opened her mouth all the way and gawked at Maya for a few seconds. "Are you saying the AuthNet lied?"

Maya poked her in the stomach.

They both cracked up giggling, and couldn't stop randomly bursting into laughter during the five or six minutes it took them to reach the well pump. Again, Sarah held the bucket while Maya pushed the button. Washing a few dishes for someone who had the kindness to feed them seemed a small favor in return. In fact, aside from being a long way from home, the sheer normality of this village reassured her. Sure, it lacked even the limited technology they had in the Hab, no TV, no running water, and so on... but it didn't scare her.

Maya looked down at her sneakers.

Guess we haven't been kidnapped. She let off the button once the pail reached capacity. Sarah grunted under the weight, so Maya grabbed the handle as well. Together, they carried it, bumping shoulders on the walk back to Kita's house.

As nice as the town appeared, Maya didn't want to spend *too* long here.

Come on, Mom. Hurry up.

12

FOXES AND HOUNDS

Day progressed to early evening while Maya and Sarah helped with little tasks around Kita's home, mostly sweeping, hunting down a spoiled potato in the bin, and watering her garden. Anshad warmed up to them enough to say hello once, but otherwise hid in his little space by the toys and tried not to be seen.

Kita talked only a little of her time in the military. She had been an electronics warfare tech on a Navy boat until her vessel sustained too much damage to remain seaworthy. The survivors wound up on foot in Korea early enough in the conflict for the US Military to have the resources to replace her arm when the grenade took it. Within two days of her being declared fit for duty after recovering, things fell apart. She kept her head down while military forces broke up into separate fiefdoms. Her unit remained loyal to the country and continued trying to 'liberate' Korea, but eventually, attrition caused them to disband. She made her way back to the US, but grew disgusted with the new 'armed drones everywhere' society, so she decided to come out here. The woman didn't even remember the name of Anshad's father, only that he'd been a white guy she'd hooked up with in the Sanc.

Random shouts of kids playing or adults calling to each other echoed over the relative stillness outside. Having run out of chores to do, Maya wandered out to the deck and sat on the edge, letting her feet dangle. It didn't take long for Sarah to join her. After a few minutes, a tiny *chirp* came from the tracker around her ankle.

"Ooh. That's good, right?" Maya held her leg up as if admiring an expensive anklet.

"They'll find us." Sarah put an arm around her back. "It probably took her a while to put a team together and find a car that could handle this ride."

"Yeah." Maya leaned back, bracing her hands on the wood while staring at the sky. "It's so quiet here."

"No drones." Sarah shielded her eyes with her hand. "No electric signs or e-cars. It's kinda nice."

"Kinda."

Sarah lowered her arm and shrugged. "Not that I want to leave home, but if we wound up having to live in a place like this, I don't think I would hate it."

The quiet did have a certain allure. She hadn't come close to experiencing true silence since leaving the penthouse. High up off the ground inside thick walls, she'd been shielded for most of her life from the bustle of the Sanc, or the Hab. In her new home, the routine whirr of passing drones plus the concentration of many people in tight quarters kept the noise level relatively high, at least compared to this place. Living in the Sanc as an ordinary Citizen would be worse. Not only did more drones roam there, but constant advertising, tons of e-cars, and even more people, all added to the volume.

Faint whirring crept into the edge of her awareness. Maya tried to stop thinking about drone fans, but the irritating noise didn't cease.

"Wow. I'm so used to hearing drones, I'm imagining them."

Sarah leaned forward. "Umm... you're not imagining that noise, but it's not a drone." She twisted left, pointing at the sky.

A white object fairly close to the trees flew toward them, still a decent ways off. It appeared much larger than a drone, and not at all like anything Genna or the Brigade would've had access to.

"Kita?" called Maya.

The woman appeared in the open wall a few seconds later. "Yes?"

"Do you have any weapons?"

"No, child. I've given up harming others. Only a direct threat to my son's life would make me respond with violence."

Sarah jabbed her finger at the approaching aircraft. "I think there's about to be a direct threat to his life."

Kita stepped to the edge of the deck and peered at the sky. A high-pitched electronic whirr came from her head. "VT-93. Airborne personnel carrier. I've never seen one of those painted white before."

"You have electronic eyes?" asked Maya.

Sarah glanced at her. "They were glowing orange before."

"Duh. I meant to ask 'you have zoom?'"

"Yes," said Kita. "I lost mine in the explosion. They look pretty real though, don't they?"

"They do." Maya stood. "Can you see who's flying it?"

Kita leaned forward, squinting. "They're too far away to make out much of a face, but it looks like a man in white armor."

"Crap." Sarah shivered. "That's not good."

"Ascendant," muttered Maya. "What are *they* doing here?"

Her tracker chirped again.

"That could be your parents coming." Kita's eyes emitted another faint whirr. "Those units beep to let the person know someone's looking for them."

"Shit." Maya sighed. "They got the signal somehow."

"Why would Ascendant be coming after a pair of little girls with a military VTOL?" Kita kept staring at the distant craft.

"Because I've gone almost a month without being kidnapped and I'm about due." Maya scowled.

"We did kinda kick them in the balls pretty hard." Sarah got up. "We should go hide in the woods or something."

"Off on your own?" Kita spun toward her.

"She's right." Maya hopped down off the deck. "They might not hurt us, but they'll shoot anyone who tries to stop them from taking us. I don't want to be responsible for anyone here getting hurt." She looked up at Kita. "Thank you for feeding us and offering to let us stay here. We really do have parents who are probably right beyond those Ascendant idiots."

Kita glanced back and forth between Maya and the incoming transport, conflict plain on her face.

"It's all right," said Maya. "I can't ask you to fight like twenty guys for us when we can just run."

"They'll find us with the tracker." Sarah pointed at it. "Maybe we should get rid of it."

Maya bit her lip. "But... if we ditch it, Mom and Dad won't be able to find us."

"Do you want them to find us dead or have a harder time finding us alive?" asked Sarah.

"Fine." Maya took a knee and grabbed the mesh strap, but couldn't figure out how to open it. "Umm. I think it's stuck."

"Incoming!" shouted Kita.

Before Maya could even look up, the woman dove off the deck and tackled her, pulling Sarah to the ground as well in a hit hard enough to send them all sliding. A ripple of tiny explosions traced a line across the earth a few feet behind them, sending bits of grass and earth flying. Seconds later, the distant rumble of a machine gun came from the air.

"Oof," grunted Sarah.

"Oh shit! They're trying to kill us!" shouted Maya.

"Mama!" wailed Anshad.

"Stay inside." Kita let off a snarl and powered up to her feet lifting both girls. She heaved them up draping them over her shoulders like a pair of duffel bags, her arms tight around their legs, and bolted.

Maya clamped on as best she could, dangling upside down. At a second line of dirt puffs ripping up the ground close behind them, she screamed. Kita swerved to the left, ran a few steps, and jinked to the right. Sarah kept mostly quiet except for a continuous whine of fear leaking out of her nose. The VTOL tilted forward, the roar of its engines gaining volume and pitch.

A building blurred by on the left. Villagers shouted and scrambled for cover. Maya glared at the aircraft. *Come on. Follow me. Leave those people alone.* Kita carried the girls into the woods bordering the village, slowing to a stop perhaps thirty paces from the first tree.

"Holy crap," rasped Sarah. "You saved our butts."

Maya didn't have to work hard to hug her. "Thank you. But, please go back to your son. If I run, they'll come after me and leave the village alone."

Kita set them down and stared at Maya with a mixture of guilt and hesitation. "I can't let you two run off alone. Especially when they're shooting."

"You have a son. He needs you more than we do." Maya lifted her left leg and tugged at the tracker, but it wouldn't come off. "Grr. Dammit."

The VTOL craft swooped in and landed near the edge of the woods in a storm of leaves, dirt, and twigs kicked up by downblast from the engines. Men in white armor poured from a sliding door on the side.

"Eep!" Sarah pulled at Maya's shoulder. "Run!"

Maya looked Kita in the eye. "Please hide. Don't get hurt for us. Anshad needs you." She waited a second, then hauled ass, not looking back to see what Kita did, too focused on trying to sprint in thick woods while dodging around tree trunks, underbrush, and low-hanging branches.

Sarah pulled slightly ahead, but Maya found quite a bit of motivation in not wanting to die, and sped up.

Men's shouts echoed in the woods behind them, mostly 'over there' or 'I see her' or 'this way!'

Sarah drifted left and grabbed Maya's hand. "I don't wanna be kidnapped. Run faster."

Crack.

An explosion of splinters erupted from a tree way too close in front of them, the report of a rifle following in under a second.

Maya stifled a scream and ran faster. "They're not gonna kidnap us."

When another shot rang out, Sarah swerved to the right, pulling Maya along. A wooden *crack* came from even closer. That time, Maya squealed. Weaving between trees, she ran as hard as she could, the faint weight of the tracker around her ankle as much a ball-and-chain as a lifeline.

A few more gunshots followed, scaring birds into the air.

Sarah shrieked in pain, but didn't slow down.

No longer aware of any sense of exhaustion, Maya's world degenerated into a blur of green and brown, filled only with the rush of her hard breaths. Sarah hurdled a fallen moss-covered log. Maya attempted the maneuver but didn't clear it. Her leg clipped the top and she spilled forward, wiping out on her chest on the other side. The fall didn't slow her much—she tumbled in a somersault and sprang back to her feet.

Thirty or forty seconds later, a dull ache developed in the knee that bumped the dead tree. Men's shouts echoed in the forest over the rapid thumping of boots at their heels. Figures in white closed in on the left as if trying to corral her to run in a specific direction.

Sarah swerved to the right without warning, dragging Maya after her. Fallen leaves and twigs crunched under their sneakers, two smallish girls making as much noise as a herd of horses in her mind. The same instant she noticed they'd started to go downhill, the ground ceased existing at a cliff. Fortunately, she fell only about eight feet and landed before she could think to shriek. The steeper hill after the cliff threw her into a logroll. Sky and dirt traded places in her vision over and over until she spun out and slid to a stop flat on her back.

"Come on!" yelled Sarah, her voice coming from somewhere above and behind, a frightening distance away.

Crunching boots rushed toward her from every angle. Terror kicked Maya's pain and exhaustion aside. She flipped over onto all fours and looked around. Upon spotting Sarah only a few steps away, she scrambled to her feet. Sarah waited, grabbed her hand again, and sprinted, following the hill downward.

"Lost visual," shouted a man in the distance behind them.

Sarah dove to the ground and crawled into a patch of thick ferns. Maya followed.

"She didn't just disappear," called another voice.

Gasping for breath, Maya covered her mouth with both hands to keep quiet. She peered up at Sarah and almost screamed in anger. Blood smeared down the right side of her sister's face and on that shoulder. Seconds from a total freak-out, Maya's brain finished processing what her eyes told her: a splinter stuck out of Sarah's cheek, a finger's width from having hit her in the earlobe.

"I thought you were shot!" rasped Maya.

"Felt like it," muttered Sarah.

"It's just splinters."

Sarah shivered. "A bullet hit the tree right by my head."

"I'm sorry," whisper-wailed Maya, clamping on and bursting into tears.

"Shh!" Sarah patted her back. "Quiet."

Maya sniffled back tears and clenched her jaw to keep from whimpering apologies. She felt like a horrible friend for poking the wasp nest and not listening to Sarah's repeated pleas to leave. They could both be safe at home right now if she hadn't insisted on destroying the Fade store.

"Signal lock," said a man. "Over there in those bushes."

Sarah and Maya looked at each other. The expression on her sister's face dropped an F bomb without her having to say it.

Maya sprang to her feet and ran, Sarah beside her, inches ahead of a flurry of bullets chewing up the greenery where they had been hiding. More slugs ricocheted from nearby trees. Sarah shrieked and yelped, trying to keep running in a half-ducked stoop.

The same guy who spoke a moment ago shouted, ordering others in this direction. Tears streamed out of Maya's eyes, flowing back across her cheeks in the wind as she ran. Calls of angry men yelling commands and directions blurred to her awareness, no more meaningful than a baying pack of dogs that wanted to eat her.

Sarah's stride began to show signs of faltering; she wouldn't last much longer. Maya's legs threatened to turn to jelly soon as well, but the nearby *crack* of a bullet hitting a tree set off a second wind inside her.

One of the Ascendant men lost his footing and fell, tumbling down the hill while spitting curses. Maya spotted another ridge on the left and went for it, pulling Sarah by the arm. Twenty or so yards later, she skidded to a stop, arms waving, at the edge of a fall about twice the length of the last cliff.

"Too far." Sarah dragged her to the right, following the ridge at a wobbly run until the distance to the ground below lessened enough that she felt safe jumping.

Still holding hands, they leapt. Expecting the drop this time, Maya stayed upright when she landed.

"Hey look," wheezed Sarah. "There's a house."

A large wooden building stood at the edge of a river, visible perhaps a hundred yards away on the other side of thinning trees and a clearing. It had a short pier with a small boat moored to the end. She couldn't tell if the place had been abandoned at such a quick look, but her body would *not* put up with much more running.

"Boat," wheezed Maya. "Those guys won't be able to swim after us."

"Yeah. If we can get there... that's like forty yards of open grass. They'll hit us."

Maya looked around for other options, spotting a strange boxy object about a quarter of the way to the building, still in the trees. Somewhat larger than a passenger van, interlocking metal plates and white paint made it appear technological, but ivy had already grown around it. Figuring the machine to be something left over from the war, probably useless, she disregarded it. "We gotta go now or they'll get us for sure."

"Ugh." Sarah groaned but threw herself into a loping run.

Maya growled with pain and determination, forcing herself to keep the pace.

When they came within thirty feet of the box, it emitted an electronic buzzing snarl—and moved.

Sarah ran into a tree on purpose, clinging to it both to stay upright and as a hiding place. Maya stopped short, gawking as the once-cube unfolded itself, rising into the form of a robotic walker. Ivy ripped away as the war machine oriented itself upright and trained its weapons on the girls. Red symbols in some strange language marked its camouflage body.

Its boxy main body somewhat resembled a military tank, only propped up on seven-foot-tall legs. Short arms stuck out the sides, each holding up pods with a pair of gun barrels, the top cannon about twice as big as the one below it. Out of sixteen tubes arranged in two groups of eight on either side of its 'head,' four still contained missiles.

The robot towered over them and spoke in a language Maya didn't know. Too terrified to scream, she cringed, her arms over her face, peering up at its electronic camera eye face ten feet in the air.

"*O-lin-yee!*" shouted Sarah. "*O-lin-yee! Ulineun bimujang-ida!*"

"What did it say?" whispered Maya.

"It's Korean. I think it called us noncombatants. Hold your hands up."

Maya raised her hands.

"*O-lin-yee!*" shouted Sarah. "*O-lin-yee! Ulineun bimujang-ida!*"

The robot spoke in digitized Korean, a full sentence.

"Umm. Sorry." Maya shrugged. "I have no idea what you said." She glanced at Sarah. "Do you?"

"No," muttered Sarah out the side of her mouth. "Dad only taught me how to say 'I'm a child. I'm not armed.' At least... I hope that's what I just said."

The robot appeared to be 'thinking' about what to do.

That thing is Korean! What's it doing here!? Maya raised her hands, staring up the barrels of guns bigger around than her arms. "Olin yee!"

The robot pivoted upward with such a sudden motion that Maya fell on her butt and shrieked.

Boom!

Both large guns fired simultaneously. The concussion of them going off shook her bones. A puff of dirt spouted from the ground three inches away from Maya's leg—but she didn't hear the gunshot over the cannons. She clamped her hands over her ears, twisting around to look back. A line of white-armored men scrambled over each other to stop in time to avoid falling off the ridge. Two smoke trails rose from the sites of small explosions; three bodies flew into the air.

The robot's smaller guns thundered in rapid fire, both spitting long gouts of orange muzzle flare.

Hands clamped over her ears, Maya screamed—not that anyone heard her. An empty shell casing bounced off her head, painful enough that she let go of her ears to cradle the spot. Sarah grabbed her and pulled her standing, then into a run. They ducked between the robot's legs and sprinted across the last few meters of forested ground to the grassy area near the river where the rectangular building stood at the water's edge beside a dock.

Sarah bee-lined down the short pier to the boat and jumped in. A few bullets chased them, tearing up the wooden planks, a few striking the building. Maya shrieked and leapt into the boat, curling up on the floor in a ball.

"Hey!" shouted a man, half out of a door on the side of the building. "Get outta my—"

Another hail of bullets peppered the wood in a flurry of *snaps* and *clonks*. Tiny splinters rained like snowflakes.

"Gah!" the man screamed and jumped back inside, slamming the door.

Heavy thunder continued from the robot's machine guns, interrupted every so often by a *boom* from the cannons.

Sarah attacked a little outboard motor at the back. Sudden acceleration lifted the nose of the boat out of the water and sent Maya sliding into Sarah. Despite the near-silence of the motor, it put out a significant amount of power.

A loud *whoosh-boom* went off in the woods.

"It used a missile," yelled Sarah.

Small arms fire continued as distant chattering. A couple *bloops* hit the river nearby as well as a *click* or two that jarred the boat like sharp taps from a hammer. Once her brain processed that bullets had made contact with their boat, Maya screamed.

"Are you hit?" shouted Sarah.

Maya froze, sparing a few seconds to allow any sense of pain into her consciousness, but nothing hurt. "I don't think so. Just scared."

"Hang on!" Sarah swerved into a hard turn that shoved Maya against the left side.

The boat settled into its speed, the nose end no longer as high out of the water. She started to sit up, but Sarah grabbed her.

"Stay down. They're still trying to shoot us."

"Okay." She rolled toward Sarah and huddled low to the bottom. A little water collected, but not so much that she panicked.

A heavy *boom-boom-boom-boom* shook the air. More cannon fire followed, then another *whoosh-boom*. Maya pushed herself up enough to peer over the side of the boat. The Ascendant VTOL careened toward the river, flames pouring out of its left side. Still firing at it, the Korean robot tromped out of the woods into the clearing, putting six or seven more double-volleys from its main cannons into the faltering aircraft, which exploded into a cloud of fire, smoke, and shrapnel before it could hit the water.

Sarah abandoned the outboard motor and tackled Maya to the bottom of the boat. Debris whistled by. Splashing came from everywhere for a few seconds, then stopped.

"Is that all you got, capitalists?" said a heavily-accented voice over a loudspeaker.

The rain of aircraft parts over, Sarah let Maya sit up. They both stared at the robot strutting back into the woods in a manner that made it look like an overconfident rooster. It had a slight limp, favoring its left leg, but no sign of any Ascendant soldiers remained.

Maya shivered. "Did that thing kill them all?"

"Umm. It probably did. Unless they ran."

"What is it?"

"I think that's a KT3. My dad hated them. They had sensors and stuff that could find him unless he used his active stealth unit."

"What like a cloaking device?" Maya blinked.

"Nah. It didn't make him invisible to human eyes, just to electronics. But it ate power fast. Batteries would only last about twenty-five minutes."

"I think Genna said something about KT3s once, too. Why is a Korean robot here?"

Sarah crawled back to the motor, which also served as a tiller. "Who knows? They probably sent them here during the war and that one somehow managed not to get blown up. Guess it doesn't realize the war is over. Lucky for us."

"It's a robot. It doesn't *realize* anything. It just does what it's programmed to do." Maya rolled flat on her back, groaning. "Everything hurts. We ran too much."

"Running hurts less than bullets."

"You're shot."

"No. I'm 'splintered.'" Sarah chuckled. "Ow."

Maya crawled closer to her and sat up. She plucked a few slivers of wood out of Sarah's shoulder, tossing them overboard. Only the big wound from a splinter as thick as a pencil near her ear continued bleeding. "Sorry. I know it doesn't mean much to say 'sorry,' but this is my fault. We should've run when you wanted to leave. I promise, I'll always do what you suggest from now on."

"You're the smart one. I'm just some street kid. I'll always pick what feels safest. Not what needs to be done. My dad would've done the same thing you did. Complete the mission and get a target of opportunity." She sniffled.

"We're kids. I know I don't act like it, but you were right. We should've run. Heck, we never should've been in there in the first place. Mom is going to go nuts on Harlowe when she finds out that place was a Fade distribution center." She plucked another splinter.

"Ow!" Sarah gasped. "I thought Vanessa said she would leave you alone?"

Maya looked her over, but didn't see any more 'tree shrapnel.' "I... No. Those guys didn't even try to talk. They came in shooting."

"You're surprised?" Sarah pressed a hand to her big splinter wound. "You totally pissed her off."

"I doubt Vanessa had anything to do with this." She glanced back at the smoke plumes from pieces of destroyed VTOL littered all over both banks. "I think another war just started."

13

NORMAL GIRLS

Quiet forest stood on either side of the river, the calm broken only by the occasional trill of a bird. Since no one shot at them, Sarah slowed to a nice cruising speed in hopes of making the battery last longer. She wanted to cover more distance in case any of the Ascendant men survived.

Maya sat up, one arm draped over the side with her fingers in the water. Mostly, she gazed into the woods, never before having experienced so much greenery. At least, not in person. Of course, she'd seen forests and such in movies and video games, but the real thing came with all sorts of new smells and textures.

Here and there, a scrap of technology broke the splendor of nature: an old car, fragments of a house, even a crashed fighter jet with Chinese markings on the tail. In this place, the world gave off such tranquility that she briefly entertained the hope humanity might not be a lost cause. She daydreamed about bringing Doc Chang to that wildlands village for a visit. Maybe she should try and convince those people to move back to civilization? Then again, the Hab needed doctors as well. Only a cobbled-together attempt at an electric grid and more technology differentiated it from the wildlands. The level of primitivism actually wound up being quite similar. But at least the wildlands had quiet—and no dosers who'd steal their clothes.

A white butterfly drifted by. Maya held out her hand, but the fluttering insect didn't come close enough to notice her.

"It's kinda nice here," said Maya.

"I guess. But I still wanna go home."

"Yeah. Me too." She glanced back. "How long are we going to ride the boat?"

Sarah looked toward the shore on the right side. "Not much longer. Start looking for a good place to pull in."

"What like another house?"

"No. I don't think we'll find one. Just some spot without too many weeds or snakes."

Maya stared at her. "Snakes? Seriously?" She shivered. "Why did you have to say that?"

"I—"

With a soft *whuff*, the outboard motor burst into flames.

Sarah yelped and jumped away from it.

"Eek!" shouted Maya. "It's on fire!"

"I'm not blind." Sarah puffed at the flames, to little effect. "Crap! There's a bullet hole in the motor."

Maya reached over the side of the boat and scooped up water in two hands. She tossed it on the fire, causing an eruption of sparks.

"Stop!" yelled Sarah. "You don't put water on an electrical fire."

"Umm. Sorry."

"Get away from it. It might explode."

"Okay." Maya crawled to the front end of the boat.

Sarah reached out one leg and nudged the tiller to the side with her foot, steering them toward the shore. As soon as she straightened it, she scooted to the front and clung to Maya.

"Umm," whispered Maya. "We're not that far away from it. If it does explode, we're going to get covered in burning battery fluid."

"That's bad, right?"

Maya shrugged. "Only if you like having skin."

The motor cut out with a fizzling *snap*, leaving the boat drifting.

"Umm." Sarah eyed the small fire. "Maybe it'll burn itself out and we can paddle?"

Electrical crackling came from the motor a second before a *fwoosh* of fire shot out the left side like a tiny rocket.

"Crap!" shouted Sarah. "We gotta jump *now!*"

Maya screamed and leapt over the side, plunging headfirst into water so frigid it felt like she'd fallen into a bag of needles. She flailed her arms and legs in an uncoordinated attempt to move away from the boat. Sarah splashed in behind her.

Brilliant orange-blue light filled the air above the surface in time with a loud *kaboom* and a shockwave that hit her like a low-speed car. For a few seconds, a dazzling eruption of bright blue sparks danced overhead, raking her face and hands with tingles.

She continued flailing around but couldn't figure out which way to go. A hand grabbed her by the back of her shirt collar and pulled her upward until her head popped above the water. Maya whipped around and clamped both arms—and both legs—around Sarah. A short distance away, the last few inches of the boat's nose disappeared into the water.

"Ack." Sarah's face went under for a second before bobbing up again. "Let go. We'll"—she went under again briefly—"both drown."

Maya kept clinging, too frightened to process rational thought. "I can't swim."

"I can't"—Sarah went under again for a few seconds—"Either. Never did it before."

A bit of white bobbling along on the surface by where the boat sank caught her eye. "What's that?"

"Take a deep breath. Float on your back." Sarah gently pushed Maya out to arms' length.

"I don't know how to float!" wailed Maya. Panic started to set in when her face went under, but Sarah pushed her up.

"You're kinda swimming. Keep kicking. Dad said people naturally float. Go still on your back, and stay calm."

Maya flapped her arms in an effort to orient herself onto her back. She took as deep a breath as she could manage, hoping more air inside her would help her stay floating. Gingerly paddling, she managed to keep her face out of water and concentrated on holding as still as possible and breathing. Sloshing grew distant, then came back soon after.

Something bumped into her.

"Grab on," said Sarah. "It's a lifesaver from the boat."

"Isn't that candy?"

"No, an actual lifesaver."

Maya rolled over and clamped onto a big white ring, which appeared rather insistent on not sinking. Sarah had a death grip on the other side. They huddled together, clinging to the flotation device, and drifted with the current.

"It's so cold," whispered Maya past chattering teeth. "It's summer. Why is the water this cold? It *hurts*."

"I don't know."

"Crap. The Hornet," said Maya.

"It's okay... I think. It hasn't shocked me. I guess it's sealed. It's a military model, right? Be kinda stupid if it couldn't handle water."

"What do we do now?" Maya looked around, whining out her nose upon realizing she couldn't feel her fingers anymore.

"Umm." Sarah shivered, teeth chattering. "We need to get out of the river as fast as we can."

"I know that. But *how*?"

Sarah leaned into the ring and started kicking her legs. "Do like this. But on the same side."

"Okay." Maya held onto the lifesaver and kicked in her best effort to copy what her sister did.

After all that running plus freezing water, Maya's legs barely moved. She only lasted about twenty seconds before going limp and floating along as Sarah guided them closer to the riverbank. She'd nearly run out of energy as well, her kicking halfhearted. Hypothermia crossed Maya's mind, and she growled, forcing her legs into motion again. The current tried to keep them away from shore, but she fought hard.

A few minutes later, they reached the bank and climbed up onto solid (mostly) ground. Maya collapsed with a squish in the wet, muddy grass. From the look of the sky overhead, they probably had less than an hour of daylight left.

"I am *so* tired," muttered Maya. "It hurts to breathe."

"Yeah. We need to find a place to shelter, fast. And get out of these wet clothes."

Maya groaned and sat up. The idea of more walking made the concept of a hypothermic death seem not too bad. Sarah grabbed her arm and helped her upright. With all the grace of zombies, they staggered away from the water into the trees. Fortunately, they only had to walk for about two minutes before Sarah spotted a large, rectangular shape that appeared promising.

It turned out to be an old US Army truck, a boxy cargo transport similar to the one that drove them out to the wildlands, but double the size. Sarah marched over to the back and shoved the giant slab of door aside. A creaking groan of metal made the hairs on Maya's neck stand. The cavernous trailer contained only a few piles of folded canvas.

Sarah pulled herself up inside.

"Are you sure it's a good idea to get in *another* truck?" Maya clung to the trailer's edge, shaking on her feet. "That didn't work well last time."

"The front end's blown off. This one isn't going to drive anywhere." Sarah sighed, then peeled her T-shirt off.

Maya climbed in and fidgeted. Undressing outside felt wrong and embarrassing, even if it might be medically necessary at the moment. *Oh, hell. We've taken baths together. It's only as weird as I think it is.* She unceremoniously removed her clothes, dropping everything in a sopping wet heap. She folded her arms across herself, shivering, with only the tracker on. Every time a droplet leaked from her hair and ran down the back of her leg, she shook harder.

"Wring stuff out," said Sarah. "Hold it out the back so the water goes outside."

She picked up her shirt, walked to the end of the trailer with her toes over the edge, and stood beside her sister, twisting the fabric until it stopped releasing whenever she squeezed. Once she'd gotten it as dry as possible, she hung the shirt on one of the a cargo-tie-down slats covering the trailer's walls. She and Sarah repeated the process for the rest of their clothing, teeth still chattering the whole time. Soon, all their things hung up to dry.

Sarah walked deeper into the truck and crouched over one of the lumps. She rummaged around for a while, then pulled out a large sheet of olive drab canvas. "C'mere."

"What's that for?" Still trembling from the cold, Maya crept over. "My legs are totally numb. I'm so tired I don't even feel tired anymore."

"Sit." Sarah pointed at another bundle of folded canvas that would probably work for a cot.

Maya lowered herself to sit, feeling ridiculous at being outside with nothing on. But, Sarah knew survival stuff and many Frags back in the Hab lived with nothing to wear. If anyone saw her, they'd probably assume her to be feral rather than pointing and making fun of her. Sarah sat beside her, pulling the canvas around them like a blanket.

Maya gasped at the coldness of her sister's skin touching her. "You're freezing!"

"So are you. We need to share body heat. That river was *way* too cold. Can you feel your toes?"

"Umm. I don't know."

Sarah grabbed her leg and tucked Maya's foot under her arm. The girl's skin almost burned her. "Eek. Your foot is total ice."

"Yeah." Maya squirmed at the feeling of water trickling down her back from her hair. "What are you doing?"

"Hopefully stopping you from getting frostbite."

Maya thought that over. "Umm. It's summer. We're out of the water and no longer covered in wet clothes. I think we should be safe from frostbite."

"Hmm. Okay. Yeah that makes sense." Sarah dropped her leg, but still huddled close under their improvised blanket. "We're kinda stuck here until our stuff dries. Unless you want to carry it."

"I don't want to move right now." Maya mushed her hand into her thigh, cringing at how sore her leg had become.

"Me neither."

"It'll be dark soon. We might as well sleep. This is kinda soft."

Sarah nodded. "Yeah. Beats dirt. It's bad to sleep right on dirt. The ground steals body heat."

"You know a lot of stuff." Maya ducked her head under the canvas 'blanket' and stared at the green strap around her ankle. It made her think of when Genna had handcuffed her by the leg to a bed. Though this device had no physical connection to anything trapping her, the ability for Ascendant to find her again scared her even more than a one-inch chain. "Can you get this thing off me?"

"I don't wanna open the blanket yet." Sarah shivered.

"Okay."

"Should we keep it or get rid of it?"

"Umm." Sarah rolled her head side to side while thinking. "Not sure."

Maya spun the tracker around and around her ankle. "You know, Mom's never going to let me do another mission."

Sarah giggled. "Is that bad?"

"No. I don't think I wanna do this again."

"We could just be normal kids."

"What do 'normal kids' do?" asked Maya.

"Well..." Sarah smiled. "They talk a lot. Like, we could talk about how Marcus likes you."

Maya stuck out her tongue. "Let's not. What else do normal girls do?"

"Not sure I know." Sarah shrugged. "I'm not exactly normal either."

"You grew up fast to take care of The Dad." Maya lay back down and cuddled close, sliding her arm around under Sarah's back. "That was really awesome of you to do that for him."

"Thanks." Sarah sighed at the ceiling. "I guess some normal girls play with dolls or tinker with electronics. Video games if they have one. Some girls imagine faeries flying around or like fancy clothes."

"Some pick locks." Maya grinned.

Sarah laughed. "That's not normal. Speaking of..." She sat up, crawled over Maya, and left the warmth of their improvised blanket before hurrying over to where her pants hung on the wall. After plucking a lock pick from her pocket, she scurried back over and sat once more on the canvas 'mattress,' then pulled Maya's foot into her lap.

"Is it locked?"

"Umm." Sarah poked at the strap with the pick for a few seconds before tugging. "Nope. Only stuck. And we were kinda in a hurry. If guys weren't shooting at us, you could've opened it."

Maya pulled the tracker off and held it up. "This thing is either going to kill us or save us."

"Yeah."

Sighing, she decided to put it back on. "Mom told me to keep it, and that robot killed all the soldiers. I don't think they'd send more right away."

"Okay." Sarah limped over to replace her lock pick in her pants, then returned to the 'bed.'

Maya tucked up beside her, much like they'd done when sharing the sleeping bag in Genna's room before everyone moved to Sarah's old apartment. Her sister still felt cold, like she clung to a pack of uncooked chicken right out of the fridge. She clutched the rough canvas tight like a blanket, wondering how long it would take her to stop feeling frozen.

A big spider wandered along the ceiling overhead, but she couldn't summon the strength to move or even shriek. Rolled-up canvas made for a surprisingly comfortable bed, though her over-tired body had much lower standards for comfort than usual. The material on top of her, though scratchy, did help warm her up. Sarah's icicle-like fingers grasping her arm made her gasp.

"There's also movies. Normal girls watch movies sometimes. And board games, the cards, spending time with friends, too."

"Yeah..." Maya yawned. "That sounds much better than being shot at, kidnapped, tied up, swimming in the sewer, and taking a ride on a boat that blows up."

"No kidding." Sarah groaned. "I think that was a storm drain, not a sewer."

Maya raspberried at the ceiling. "Technicalities."

Sarah laughed.

"Sorry," whispered Maya. She stared at the small, bloody splinter wound right in front of her nose, and choked up from guilt.

"Please stop apologizing. I said if we lived, I'd forgive you. And right now, I'm too tired to talk."

"Yeah, me too," said Maya.

She closed her eyes, hoping that the tracker would lead her parents to them before more Ascendant thugs came.

It didn't seem terribly likely they'd stumble across another functional KT3 robot to save them from the next batch.

14

KEEPSAKES

Uncomfortable warmth dragged Maya awake.

She lay on her side facing empty floor, Sarah wedged between her and the trailer wall, clinging from behind. Sweat trickles crawled over her body, the steady puffing of her sister's breath at the back of her head. For the briefest moment, jumping again into the cold river approached tempting. Her arms and legs ached from all the running yesterday, leaving her uninterested in moving, even to escape the oven the cargo trailer had become.

Enjoying stillness lasted only a few more minutes before her stomach and bladder urged her into motion. She groaned in annoyance and lifted Sarah's arm from around her chest, then rolled off the canvas bundle onto all fours.

Why am I naked?

She blinked.

Oh... the river. Freezing. Wet clothes. She yawned, sat back on her heels, and wiped her eyes.

"Morning," half whispered Sarah in a sleepy drawl before rolling flat on her stomach, stretching her arms up over her, and releasing a giant yawn. "Wow, it got warm."

"Well... it *is* summer. At least for another week or two. It was kinda cool last night, but it's hot today." She half crawled toward Sarah to inspect her ear. "The bleeding's stopped."

"Cool." After another yawn, Sarah flung the canvas blanket aside and got up. She stood there for a moment fanning herself, then padded toward the doors—right past the clothes on the wall.

"Umm. What are you doing?" asked Maya.

"Gotta pee."

Maya opened her mouth to protest, but... they *were* in the middle of nowhere, and it did seem somewhat inefficient to get dressed only to right away push her pants back down. She crept to the end of the truck and crouched, peering out at the woods to make sure no one would sneak up on them.

Sarah disappeared into the trees. Maya bit her lip, but didn't hesitate long before jumping down and finding a spot to go. Once finished, she scurried back inside the truck and grab-tested her clothes. Satisfied that her shirt and pants had dried completely, she pulled them on as fast as her weary muscles would permit. A dunk in river water left her hair somewhat stiff and sticky, but not as bad as after falling in the storm drain under the Sanc.

Sarah climbed up to sit on the edge of the trailer, legs dangling. She stared into space, her eyes still half closed.

"Aren't you going to get dressed?" asked Maya.

"Yeah... eventually." Sarah swayed as if about to pass out again. "I'm too tired to breathe and overheated. Just enjoying the breeze. It's too hot in that truck."

Maya's legs weakened. "I'm tired, too. Even after sleeping. But I'm also really hungry."

A growl emanated from Sarah's stomach. She frowned at it, sighed, and pulled her feet up. Maya chuckled watching her grab at the cargo rails for help standing, thinking she moved like an old person—or a drunk. The girl trudged over to where she'd hung her clothing, most of her face hidden behind a wall of red hair. Sarah pulled her shirt and pants back on, though not with much urgency.

Maya stuck a hand into her sneakers. Finding them still damp inside, she stuffed her socks in her pockets to keep them dry, then put her shoes on, squealing at the unpleasant clamminess. "Shoes are still wet."

Sarah snagged her socks off the railing and jammed them in her thigh pocket, then checked over the Hornet. "Looks like it's okay. We're not defenseless."

"So, what do we do now? There's no food or water here."

Sarah waved toward the woods, then sat on the floor to put her shoes on. "Easy. We go back to that village and find Kita. Oh, ick. These feel so nasty."

"I hope she's okay." Maya cringed at her sneakers. "Yeah. I think it'll take them a couple days to dry."

"Did you hear her scream or anyone yell at her?"

"No."

"Then she probably listened to you and went back to protect her son."

"Sorry."

Sarah bounced to her feet. "I'm not yelling at you for not listening to me. Come on. We don't have to go fast, but we have to move. The village should be that way." She pointed. "We couldn't have gone far, even with the boat, so I think we'll get there in like two hours."

"What about that, umm, robot?"

"I don't think it will bother us since we're kids."

"Umm. It kinda looked like it couldn't decide what to do with us before it shot that guy."

Sarah shivered. "That dude would've hit us if the robot didn't fire on him. Look at it this way, the robot saved us." She headed to the back end of the truck and jumped to the ground. "C'mon. I'm really hungry."

"Okay."

Maya hurried to the trailer doors, eager to escape the stifling interior. Despite the day being quite warm, the woods felt cool by comparison to the trailer. Dressed all in black with long pants didn't make for comfort. *Is this why those two blonde kids wore leaf skirts? Or are they like even more primitive than the villagers?*

The tracker wobbled around her ankle, reminding her that its presence could be life-saving—or the exact opposite. Exhaustion clear in her stride, Sarah trudged around trees, avoiding thicker underbrush in a meandering path that cast doubt on their ability to keep going in the same direction. Alas, without a machete or big knife, some patches of understory wound up being impassable, or dangerous. Hiking so soon after the mad sprint away from Ascendant soldiers didn't agree with her legs. After a mere five minutes, Maya wanted to sit down, but hunger kept her going.

Sarah's sluggish pace suggested she, too, didn't much like the idea of walking.

Over the next forty or so minutes, the burbles of a few different streams awakened Maya's thirst, but Sarah didn't change course. She likely distrusted the water and didn't feel lost enough to risk it yet. Daydreams of home, the nice bed they shared, the soft rug with *Magic* cards all over it came and went. Maya caught herself having fond thoughts of the super-modern bathtub at Vanessa's penthouse and frowned. While she wouldn't mind soaking in a luxurious bath to let hot water leech the soreness from her muscles, she'd gladly never come within a mile of such an ostentatious apartment ever again if it meant she could keep her loving family.

With each step, she felt more and more like a selfish idiot for agreeing to the mission. Did Genna ever feel that way when she did something for the Brigade? The last time, she didn't seem happy about leaving, but she did anyway. *Am I upset that I almost got Sarah killed because I'm a kid, or do adult soldiers feel like this, too?* She sighed. *I'm nine. I shouldn't be 'doing missions' or being shot at... but someone is going to always be coming after me because of who I am.*

"It's been like that forever." Frowning, Maya punted a pinecone. It bounced off a tree a short distance away and fell out of sight into the brush.

"Huh?" Sarah paused and looked over at her.

"I was just thinking about the mission and how it would be better to be normal kids and stay safe at home, but then I realized that because of who I am, I've *never* been safe. Bad people have always been trying to hurt or kidnap me to exploit my connection to Vanessa and Ascendant. I just never *saw* it because I lived in a fortress. There could've been thousands of attempts to kidnap or hurt me before Genna's team finally got inside."

Sarah stopped walking and grabbed a fistful of Maya's shirt at the base of her neck, pulling her nose-to-nose. "If the next thing you say is 'I should just go back and let Vanessa have me' I will punch you in the nose."

"I wasn't going to say that." Maya hugged her. "My point is... I'm in danger no matter what I do, so the mission wasn't as completely stupid as I was making it out to be."

Sarah released her fistful of fabric and returned the hug. "A couple of kids sneaking into a top-secret base *is* stupid no matter what the reason. I still can't believe Mom let us do it."

"Yeah. Harlowe really sold it. And, I guess it *would've* been safe if I wasn't stupid. Not listening to you when you said 'let's get out of here' was dumb. I'm sorry."

"Oh, stop already." Sarah shook her head and resumed walking. "I told you, my dad would've done the same thing if he saw something *that* important that command didn't know about while on a mission."

"Yeah, but your dad was a trained soldier, not to mention an adult."

Sarah kept walking.

"Thanks. If you didn't go with me, I'd have gotten myself caught."

"Well... that's why I went. You're like book smart, but you don't really know how the world works."

Maya gazed up at the scraps of blue between wavering leaves. "I'm scared."

"They'll find us."

"Which they? Ascendant or our parents?"

"Umm, I meant our parents. I really hope Ascendant isn't sending more guys." Sarah paused, then giggled. "I wonder if they think *we* took out that whole platoon? Imagine that?" She lowered her voice to mimic a man: "Sir, the men we sent after those little girls are all dead. It's too dangerous. Those kids are super deadly. We should just sit here and hope they're not mad at us."

Maya snickered. "Somehow, I doubt they'll say that."

A spot of white moved among the trees up ahead.

Sarah stopped short and pulled Maya down into a crouch in the middle of the trail. "Don't move."

Nearly losing her balance, she caught herself on all fours and whispered, "Shouldn't we hide in the woods?"

"It's better to sit still than move. People see motion."

The white spot glided along behind a dense row of trees. It didn't seem high enough off the ground to be an Ascendant security officer in armor, nor did it make much noise. They held still for a minute or two watching, until a skinny little Asian girl walked out from behind the last tree.

Her waist-length black hair hung straight and perfect despite her grimy appearance, though her tattered white dress bore numerous holes, tears, and stains. The girl appeared around Maya's age, and spotted them within seconds of stepping into view. She changed direction and strolled straight toward them with a big smile.

Sarah glanced at Maya. "It's a kid."

"Yeah," whispered Maya. "And she sees us. I thought not moving was supposed to make it hard to see us?"

"It doesn't matter. She's not armed."

"She's barely dressed," whispered Maya, standing. "I think your old curtain was in better shape."

The barefoot girl stopped three paces away and waved. "Hi! My name is Ji Yeon. Would you like to be friends? What are your names?"

Maya gazed into the other girl's eyes, which seemed a little too big. She didn't look like Emily, who had a Chinese father and white mother. This kid had to be all the way... whatever she was, but something about her face bugged Maya. She resembled a more realistic human version of those cartoons with the eyes oversized to make them cute, though not so much she entered genetic freak territory.

"I'm Sarah. This is Maya. Why are you out here alone?"

Ji Yeon clasped her hands in front of herself and stared down. "I'm lonely. I really want to have friends. Will you be friends with me?"

"Maybe." Maya tilted her head. "Why are you alone?"

"My father is not feeling well." Ji Yeon bit her lip. "Actually, he's dead."

Sarah gasped. She took a step closer and grasped the girl's hand. "I'm so sorry. Mine died, too."

Ji Yeon lifted her head and made eye contact. "I'm sorry you lost your father and are alone like me."

"Thanks," said Sarah. "But I'm not alone. Maya is my sister. We have parents."

"That is nice." Ji Yeon smiled, no trace of sadness left anywhere on her face. "My father was not my biological father, but he took care of me. Good people do that."

Maya glanced at the sad white dress. "What happened to your dress?"

"I used to live somewhere with many angry people who tried to hurt each other all the time. Things exploded and mud rained from the sky all the time. Sometimes buildings fell apart. I did not like it there. Sergeant James brought me here where there is no fighting and it is quiet."

"*Yeoboseyo. Naneun Salada,*" said Sarah.

"*Hangug-eoleul hal jul aseyo?*" asked Ji Yeon.

Sarah cringed. "Umm. I think you just asked me if I speak Korean. Not really. Just a few important phrases."

"Are you from the village?" Maya pointed off into the woods, having no real idea if she'd indicated the right direction. "We're going there."

"Do you want to see my home?" Ji Yeon bounced on her toes, still smiling. "It is not far from here. There is food if you are hungry, and water."

"Umm," said Sarah, seeming nervous.

Maya shrugged. "Sure. I'm really hungry."

"Awesome!" chirped Ji Yeon. "This way!"

The girl spun around and skipped off.

"Something's strange about her," whispered Sarah.

Maya glanced at her. "What?"

"Well, she's like nine or ten and speaks Korean. She said she's from a place where a lot of fighting happened, but she's too little to have been alive during the war."

Maya put a hand on Sarah's shoulder. "People didn't stop speaking Korean when the war ended. And if you believe the AuthNet, there's still places where the different groups fight... and not only over there. The whole world isn't as peaceful as the Eastern Seaboard. Spaces between Sanctuary Zones aren't really all that quiet."

"Hmm."

"Hey." Maya rubbed her back. "Are you scared of her because she's Korean?"

Sarah blushed. "Maybe a little. My dad always told me how they could be sneaky. But he had SoKo friends. I don't think he feared *all* of them, just the NoKos. I know I shouldn't instantly distrust someone for being Korean. Sorry. I'm just scared, and Dad talked about it *so* much."

Maya leaned close and whispered right in her ear. "There *is* something a little weird about her, but I don't think she's dangerous or trying to trick us."

"Okay."

"And a lot of people are racist against them. When I first got kidnapped, Moth kept calling the one guy Korean even though he was Chinese."

"Moth had issues," muttered Sarah.

Maya made a *pff* noise. "Yeah. Serious issues."

Ji Yeon stopped about thirty yards away and whirled to look at them. "Are you coming?"

"Yeah," called Maya. She hurried over to catch up, groaning at her sore legs. "Sorry. We've had a bad couple of weeks. We're a little shy around people we don't know."

"Bad couple of weeks?" Ji Yeon clasped her hands in front of her self.

Maya shrugged. "Oh, you know, kidnapped a couple times, almost killed, shot at, falling into a sewer, starting a peasant revolt, stuff like that."

Ji Yeon giggled.

She thinks I'm joking.

"Come, follow me," chirped Ji Yeon. Again, she skipped off like a wingless forest faerie.

Sarah furrowed her brows.

"Yeah," whispered Maya. "That girl's far too happy and cheerful for having a dead father and a dress that looks like she lost a fight with a lawnmower."

"What's a lawnmower?" asked Sarah.

Maya sighed. "Not worth the explanation."

Ji Yeon led them through the forest. After a few minutes, they reached a modest-sized creek with water burbling over rocks and even a few fish darting in and out of darker spots. They followed alongside it for a little while until arriving at a bridge consisting of a fallen tree sawed to length and braced with rocks. Ji Yeon climbed up to stand on the old log, held her arms out to the sides and balance-beam walked over it with graceful ease as if she'd done it a thousand times.

Maya stepped on the piled rocks bracing the near end, placed a foot atop the log, and nearly fell after three steps when slippery moss took her sneaker out from under her. She recovered her balance in a flailing fit. Gingerly, she stepped forward, her shoes slipping almost every step of the way. Not that a fall would be dangerous—the creek appeared less than four feet deep—but she didn't want to get wet again. Certainty that she would fall in and become soaked made her briefly consider stripping naked and wading across while holding her clothes over her head, but she decided to keep going.

Ji Yeon waited patiently on the other side. Maya nearly fell six times, but made it to the opposite end. The girl offered a hand to help her down from the tree. Sarah managed the crossing almost as smoothly as their new friend, but at half the speed.

The Korean girl emitted a satisfied little noise and resumed walking.

Maya glanced from her to the log-bridge and back to her. *Weird. Maybe it's easier barefoot? Sarah's got shoes and didn't fall.* She sighed at the reminder of being the pampered rich girl who never left the apartment. Sarah had been climbing things like that her whole life.

A few minutes after crossing the creek, they arrived at a ramshackle house with two camper trailers as its left and right ends. Someone had built them together with a reasonable attempt to recreate the general shape of a house with panels of wood and scrap metal. They'd even added a front door and small porch. A single green-painted metal chair sat to the left of the door.

"This is home." Ji Yeon walked up the two steps and went inside.

Sarah grabbed Maya's shoulder and tugged her back when she tried to go in after the strange girl. With one hand on the Hornet, she crept in front and approached the door. Maya followed close. The porch area smelled like old, wet cigarettes mixed with damp wood. Happy childish humming came from inside, along with the clatter of metal pans. Sarah leaned in the door, looked around for a few seconds, then relaxed.

The space between the trailers formed a single large room with an eight-person rectangular table and chairs at the middle between a pair of posts holding up the piecemeal roof. Wood planks raised off the earth on a grid of two-by-fours formed the floor. On the left and right, the trailers formed additional 'rooms.' Ji Yeon stood near the opposite wall, opening cans and dumping the contents into a pot.

A vast worktable spanned across the right side of the room except for an opening that allowed access to the trailer door. Various small pieces of military gear covered it. Another green-painted metal chair by that table held a corpse so far gone it had become mostly skeletal and no longer smelled much. Dark stains and silver mold saturated the floorboards around the remains.

Sarah jumped back and screamed.

Maya had seen plenty of depictions of skeletons and even some corpses in medical documentation related to Ascendant's drugs, but being in the presence of exposed bones for real shocked her mute.

"What's wrong?" Ji Yeon peered back over her shoulder.

"Umm," said Sarah, her voice wavering. "Your father's body is still here."

"Yes. He is dead and cannot move anymore." The girl turned away and resumed stirring the contents of the pot.

Whoa. Maya let a long breath out her nose. *This poor kid.* She crept toward the dead man, careful not to step in any discoloration on the floor. A few places where blackening from decay fluids had spared his clothing remained green camouflage, and a handful of US Army patches survived as well. *This man's been dead at least a year or longer.*

Sarah stood by the front door, making soft grunts and grabbing motions in the air at Maya that probably translated to something along the lines of 'what are you doing! Get away from that guy!'

"Sorry you died," whispered Maya, leaning closer.

No obvious causes of death (such as bullet holes in bone or gouges from a blade) stood out to her. *He probably died in this chair.* She cringed at the momentary thought that The Dad would likely have also died in his favorite spot in the sofa had he been left to his own devices and avoided seeking treatment.

She glanced away from the dead guy and surveyed the table. Rifles, pistols, empty magazines, bullets, a couple hand grenades, a large box she assumed to be some manner of radio, knives, round things that looked an awful lot like land mines from video games, and a whole mess of electronic parts lay in a disorganized spread.

The soft, repetitive *scratch, scratch, scratch* of a metal spoon against a metal pot seemed like the loudest noise in the world for a moment.

Maya eyed the junk. "Umm... Sarah?"

"What," hissed Sarah, still over by the door.

"Check this stuff out. What is all this?"

Sarah emitted a strangled gurgle, but approached, head turned to the side to keep the dead man out of her view. "All what?"

"On the table. Are those land mines?"

With a gasp, Sarah whirled around to stare, forgetting entirely about the corpse. "Oh, crap. Yeah. And grenades. Those rifles look like FN-Sabres, and that ammo's probably live. This entire table is full of things we shouldn't touch... or even be around without an adult."

"Well, it's good you're trained and I'm overly mature." Maya took a step back. "Since there aren't any adults anywhere close."

"I mean, we shouldn't be in the same room with some of this crap." Sarah pointed at the mines and grenades. "They could blow up."

"The explosives are not so old they have become brittle." Ji Yeon carried two bowls over to the table in the middle of the room. "I've warmed up some food for you."

Maya approached her, gazing up at a few tiny gaps between sections of ceiling where light leaked in. Sun beating down on a large swath of green fiberglass painted the back corner of the room the same shade. Ji Yeon waited for her to sit, then slid a bowl in front of her, which appeared to contain something approximating beef stew. Sarah took the nearest chair. Ji Yeon set Sarah's bowl down in front of her, then walked around the table to take a seat facing them.

"Thank you," said Maya. Her first mouthful burned her tongue. "Mmm!"

Sarah blew on her spoon a few times before risking a bite.

Maya blinked in astonishment at the girl, wondering how she'd carried a metal bowl with her bare hands when the contents were so hot. Then again, Mr. Nori from the noodle place often did similar things. Maybe a person could acclimate to handling hot bowls after enough practice. *All the nerves in his hands have to be dead. This poor kid.*

"I'm ten years old," said Ji Yeon. "How old are you?"

That seemed like an odd thing to ask, but she might not have been comfortable with English, despite having no discernable accent when speaking it. Asking someone how old they are sounded like a basic enough question to be early in the process of learning a language.

"Nine."

"Eleven." Sarah shoveled another spoonful of stew into her mouth.

Ji Yeon bowed her head. "I am sorry if Sergeant James' body disturbs you."

Sarah almost choked.

"Umm. I'd offer to help you bury him, but I don't think Sarah wants to touch him... and I kinda don't either." Maya managed a sheepish smile. "Burying the dead is something adults should do."

Ji Yeon nodded. "Yes. But I'm alone. There are no other adults here. I am happy that you and Sarah are my friends. There is enough food here to last many years, but most of it is military packet rations."

"Guess your father didn't like visitors." Maya ate another mouthful.

"We did not have any, so I do not know if he would have liked them."

Sarah glanced sideways at Maya.

"The location of your home presents certain logistical challenges that made interaction with others problematic. Do you think he selected this location by design?" asked Maya.

"Wow." Ji Yeon giggled. "You use big words for a little girl. I think you are right. He wanted to avoid people."

Maya nodded. *Okay... this kid's not new to English.*

"Why are you talking weird?" Sarah gave her the side eye.

"She is playing a game," said Ji Yeon. "Maya wanted to see if I am smart, like her."

"Yeah." Maya laughed, hopefully not sounding *too* fake. "Sorry. People tried to kill us yesterday. I'm still freaking out."

"I heard the gunshots." Ji Yeon looked frightened. "A war robot, right?"

"Not exactly." Sarah shook her head. "We ran into a KT3, but it kinda wound up helping us. It shot at the men who wanted to kill us."

"Why would men want to kill you? You are children." Ji Yeon scrunched up her nose.

"Have you ever heard of Ascendant Pharmaceuticals?" asked Maya.

"Oh. You are the girl in the box." Ji Yeon pointed at her.

"In the box?" Maya raised an eyebrow.

Ji Yeon nodded. "Before Sergeant James brought me here, I found a box that made pictures. It had people inside it that did things. Sometimes they made me laugh. Sometimes they scared me. You look like the girl in the box who wanted people to buy medicines."

"Oh. You found some kind of video player." Maya sighed. "Yeah. That was me. Well, those people want to hurt me because some other bad people did a lot of bad things and I told on them."

"Now you are talking to me like I am five, not ten." Ji Yeon grinned.

"Sorry." Maya ate two spoonfuls fast. "Just trying to paraphrase."

"Oh."

"Huh?" asked Sarah.

Maya nodded to her. "My sister didn't know what 'pity' meant. I don't think she understands 'paraphrase' either."

"Grr," said Sarah with a hint of a chuckle.

While they finished off the rest of their stew, Maya explained her running away from Ascendant, the resulting fallout her video message caused, and—while omitting any mention of the Brigade—told of their sneaking into an Ascendant facility and destroying a whole bunch of Fade virus.

Je Yeon's eyes widened. "That stuff is evil! I am glad you destroyed it. The person who made it deserves punishment. I do not understand why anyone would create such a thing."

Maya smirked. "I'm not entirely sure Vanessa qualifies as a person."

"Heh." Sarah snickered.

"You can stay here if you want. I very much would like not to be alone anymore." Ji Yeon stood and collected the empty bowls.

"Oh, you don't have to cook *and* clean up for us." Sarah got up. "I can wash these."

Ji Yeon smiled. "Please. It is fine. You are guests. If you decide to live here with me, then we can share the chores. I have not had anyone to cook for since Sergeant James died. I miss him."

The girl carried the bowls over to the sink.

Sarah glanced at Maya and twirled her finger around by her head.

Maya shrugged.

"Slave?" mouthed Sarah without giving it voice.

After shaking her head, Maya stood and went back over to the work table, heading for the electronics.

Sarah rushed up behind her. "Get away from this stuff, you could get hurt."

"I don't care about the explosives." Maya opened a laptop. "I'm wondering if any of the technology works. Is there a dish on the roof? We might be able to communicate with Mom and Dad."

"There is no dish." Ji Yeon turned a plastic handle on an improvise faucet to rinse the bowls. "I know there is a network in the big city, but we cannot reach it."

Maya spent a few minutes fiddling around with the radio equipment. Evidently overwhelmed by curiosity, Sarah picked up one of the FN-Sabre rifles. It reminded Maya of a gun from a video game, with the ammo magazine at the end of the butt stock and a built-in scope. Sarah pulled the charging handle back and peered into the chamber before flipping it over, squeezing another button, and breaking the rifle in half.

"Careful! You snapped it," said Maya.

"No, silly." Sarah giggled and flexed the gun back and forth. "It's supposed to open like this, for cleaning."

Ji Yeon looked over at them. "Please be careful with those. Children should not handle guns. But... you do appear familiar with it. Since Sergeant James is dead, you can take them if you want. I do not want the guns at all. Things that kill people are bad." A sudden expression of despondence came over her. She bowed her head and shied away from them, sniffling.

"Aww," whispered Maya. *Someone probably killed her parents.*

Sarah slapped the Sabre closed, picked up a magazine, and loaded it in.

"What are you doing?" Maya gawked.

"This thing has a lot longer range than a Hornet."

Maya shook her head. "But... but... that's a *gun*. A real gun. It'll *kill* people. We're too little. People will shoot us instead of ignoring us."

"Maya..." Sarah frowned and pointed at the small bloody mark in front of her ear. "Ascendant guys are *already* trying to kill us. I won't let them hurt you."

"Your sister is very protective," said Ji Yeon in a half-whisper. "That is so nice. You should be grateful to have someone who loves you like that."

Maya choked up. Unable to speak, she nodded.

"I mean, I'm not gonna go hunting morons. But if we get cornered." Sarah patted the rifle. "Anyway, there's a problem."

"What?" asked Maya.

"Dad said never go into a fight with an untested weapon. I haven't fired one of these before, nor have I tested *this* rifle to know it works at all. But I also don't want to shoot it because the bang could make bad stuff come looking."

"Won't a gun that big hurt you?" Maya scratched her head.

"Nah. The Sabres fire 6.55 millimeter rounds. Dad always called it a toy. Oh, heck with it." Sarah walked over to the front door and nudged it open. "Hold your ears."

Maya stuck her fingers in her ears. Ji Yeon continued washing the bowls and pot.

"Gonna shoot at the dirt so the bullet doesn't hurt anything." Sarah widened her stance, raised the rifle to her shoulder, and sighted over it. A few seconds later, a sharp *bang* accompanied a flash of orange from the front. She barely moved. "Crap that was loud as hell."

"Yeah." Maya pulled her fingers out of her ears. "It works."

Sarah glanced at the rifle long enough to flick a switch near the pistol grip, and walked back over. "I don't want you touching this, okay?"

"Okay."

"Are you gonna get in trouble for touching it?" asked Maya.

Sarah shrugged. "Maybe. But if Mom and Dad find us, they're welcome to take it away from me."

"You can stay here until they find you." Ji Yeon put the washed dishes in a wire rack repurposed as a strainer, then dried her hands. "Oh. You are thirsty. I will get water for you." She snagged a pair of coffee cans from a shelf and disappeared out the front door.

"Wow," whispered Sarah. "That poor kid. She's so lonely she's acting like a servant or something. Do you think the dead guy kidnapped her?"

"Not really. She seems to like helping. And we *are* guests. She could be overly polite."

Sarah furrowed her eyebrows. "There's something off about her."

"I know. She's been living in a place with a dead guy for at least a year."

"How can you tell?"

"Body's decomposed mostly to bones. I don't know absolutely a hundred percent, but indoors in a temperate climate, I think it takes about a year or so for a corpse to reach that state of decomposition."

Sarah's stomach gurgled. "I don't really want to stay somewhere with a dead guy."

"I don't either, but there's food and shelter here." Maya pointed at the trailer. "We can go in there?"

Ji Yeon glided back in, both coffee cans full of water. She marched up with a big smile and handed one to each of them. "We have a water tank out back. I take it from a stream and boil it before filtering it."

"You have a purifier?" asked Sarah.

"Yes. It's from the Army. There's a tank on the roof that Sergeant James ran a pipe to. Only one faucet."

Sarah took a sip, swished it around her mouth like one of the Ascendant board executives tasting wine, nodded, then chugged several gulps. Maya clutched her coffee can in both hands and drank as much as she could before her body demanded air.

"So, will you stay with me?" asked Ji Yeon.

"People are trying to hurt me." Maya ground her sneaker toe into the floor. "I don't want you to get hurt, too."

Ji Yeon shook her head. "I am not afraid. Sergeant James has listeners set up and warning alarms. We will know if danger approaches." She darted over to the inner left corner of the room, close to the trailer. "We also have a hiding place under the floor."

"That won't help so much." Maya raised her left leg to show off the tracker. "They will find me down there."

"Can you take that off?" asked Ji Yeon.

"Yeah."

The small Korean girl held out her hand. "I will hold it for you so you can hide. If the men who tried to hurt you come here, I will tell them that I found it on the ground."

As nice as this girl had been, something about her tweaked Maya's sense of wrongness. She couldn't quite put a finger on why, but hesitated at the momentary worry the girl might destroy the tracker. Maybe she wanted friends so badly she'd break it to prevent anyone taking her new playmates away from her.

For a long two minutes, the three girls stood in silence, Maya staring into Ji Yeon's eyes. Time spent observing Vanessa and high-level people at Ascendant trying to outmaneuver each other had instilled within Maya somewhat of an ability to read when people attempted to scam her. She sensed nothing at all in this child's demeanor that suggested she planned to do anything to betray them.

"You don't want to be alone anymore," said Maya.

"No." Ji Yeon shook her head. "Being lonely is bad. I am sad all the time."

Hmm. She might not destroy it if she doesn't think she has *to.* "Our parents will also use this tracker to find us. You should come with us when we go home. A house with a dead person in it is no place for a kid."

Ji Yeon's expression lit up. "Really? I would be *so* happy to go with you."

"What did Sergeant James set up around the house?" asked Sarah.

"There are eight PXD-13 units in three concentric detection fields around the house. We also have twenty remote-detonated antipersonnel mines, but he did not show me how to operate those. One of the control boards on the table has buttons that set them off." Ji Yeon pointed at a large lump of cloth. "Under that sheet are video monitors connected to cameras on the roof. He intended to watch dangerous people on those screens to know when to use the bombs. But I do not know if any of them work."

"Holy shit," muttered Maya.

Ji Yeon twisted to face her, making a face like she might cry at any second. "Children should not use bad words. Especially girl children. It is rude even for women to talk like that."

"Riiight," muttered Maya. "If you're going to stay with us, you'll need to get used to that. Mom uses a lot of bad words."

"Okay." Ji Yeon nodded. "It is different here than where I am from. I understand, but I still don't want to use bad words myself."

Maya stooped and took the tracker off. She again hesitated, but stood and dangled it toward the girl. "Right now, more than anything, I want to go home and be with my parents. This is the key to them finding us. But... bad people could also use it to find us. It's kind of a catch-22."

"Huh?" Sarah twisted away from the table to stare at her.

"A problem from which there is no escape outcome due to conflicting dependent conditions," said Ji Yeon.

"Umm..." Sarah glanced back and forth between them. "I don't understand either one of you."

"I gave you the definition of catch-22." Ji Yeon faced her.

"Did you memorize a dictionary?" Sarah giggled.

"Yes," said Ji Yeon.

"Whoa." Maya blinked. "Umm, basically it means it's a situation that's a conflict. Keeping the tracker is bad because it could get us killed, but tossing it is bad because then our parents can't find us. Both choices have a bad result."

"Oh." Sarah nodded. "I get it. What the hell does twenty-two have to do with that?"

Ji Yeon opened her mouth, closed it, smiled, then said, "It is the title of a really old book."

Maya handed her the tracker.

"I will tell the bad people that I found it and thought it pretty. I will not tell them you are here." Ji Yeon stooped and put the tracker on her right ankle.

"Thanks." Maya stuffed her hands in her pockets, already feeling like she'd made a major mistake. She glanced at Sarah who didn't show any outward objection.

Ji Yeon stood and smiled at them. "Shall we play a game?"

"You have games out here in the sticks?" Maya blinked. "How do you get a 'net signal?"

"Yes, but not the kind of games you are thinking." Ji Yeon pointed at the trailer on the left. "We could play a nice game of chess. Or, I have a whole pile of other board games."

Maya glanced at Sarah, exchanged shrugs, and looked back to Ji Yeon. "Sure."

15

THE FIRE WITHIN

For the rest of the daylight hours, the girls played a mix of board games while lounging on the floor of the old camper trailer on the left, which served as Ji Yeon's bedroom. In addition to stacks of plastiboard cartons, it contained enough toys, dolls, and games to supply a small village. Of course, not every game had all its pieces.

Once it became dark, Ji Yeon offered to let them have her bed for the night, but neither Maya nor Sarah wanted to make her sleep on the floor. Since she had a queen size and none of the girls took up much room, they wound up all sharing it. Ji Yeon slept in her dress, not that she appeared to own anything else in the way of clothing. Maya and Sarah removed their shoes, otherwise remaining fully dressed to sleep.

Much to Maya's discomfort, Sarah leaned the loaded FN-Sabre against the wall beside the bed, close enough to grab without getting up.

UPON WAKING THE NEXT MORNING, JI YEON SHOWED THEM TO A tiny outhouse behind the main structure, then went back inside, leaving them to use it. At Sarah's urging, Maya went first. She braced for a horror show, but the thing smelled more like damp wood than foulness. *Huh, that's weird. It doesn't even really stink.* Once done, she waited nearby for Sarah to finish so they could walk back to the 'house' together. By the time they entered, Ji Yeon had already set out two plates with suspiciously square eggs next to an unidentifiable reddish-brown lump.

"Aren't you going to eat?" Maya poked the lump. "And what is this?"

Ji Yeon giggled. "I finished mine already while yours warmed up. It is a breakfast ration. Eggs with corned beef hash."

Sarah raised an eyebrow. "Dad always said the corned beef from the rations was a crime against humanity. He called it 'corned beef *harsh*' instead of hash."

"It doesn't smell bad." Maya took a test nibble. "Tastes okay."

"He probably had the real stuff before the war." Sarah sat and dug in. "Yeah, you're right. It's pretty good."

While they ate, Ji Yeon beamed with pride as though she'd made the food from scratch instead of simply heated ration packs. After breakfast, the girls sat at the table while their host cleaned up again. Sarah fidgeted, no doubt feeling guilty about being waited on.

Maya stared at the tracker around Ji Yeon's delicate ankle, roughly the same size as hers, only paler. She spent a little while feeling annoyed at Vanessa for having her made so small and insubstantial. Marcus once even said she had a body like an elf. Ji Yeon, aside from standing a little bit taller, had about the same build.

Sudden homesickness brought tears too fast for Maya to catch them.

"What?" Sarah pounced, putting an arm around her. "Why are you crying?"

"I'm sorry for being so *extra* at the facility. I should've gone out the pipe. I wanna go home." Maya decided not to fight the spontaneous upwelling of childishness, and sobbed into Sarah's shoulder. "It's my fault we're stuck out here."

"Shh." Sarah patted her back. "It's okay. I understand why you did it. That stuff is evil, and you're totally right for wanting to destroy it."

Maya cried a little while more before scraping her composure up off the floor. "You're serious?" She sniffled. "You're not like totally pissed at me?"

"No." Sarah sighed. "I'm scared and I wanna go home, but if I'm pissed at anyone, it's Ascendant."

"You not being mad at me is almost making me feel worse."

Sarah grinned. "Sorry. Not doing that on purpose. They'll find us.

And... if they don't show up in a couple days, I say we pack up a bunch of those rations and walk home."

"Seriously?" Maya blinked. "We drove in that truck for a whole day."

"So?" Sarah shrugged. "That only means it will take longer. If we bring food and water... and that Sabre, we'll be okay. It's only distance, not like we're stuck on the other side of a magic portal."

Ji Yeon jumped away from the sink and spun to face the door. "Hide. Go in the trapdoor now."

"What?" asked Sarah.

"Someone is coming." Ji Yeon hurried around the table toward the front door.

"How do you know that?" asked Maya.

"I can hear them." The girl pointed at the corner. "Quick. Hide."

Maya leapt from the chair and ran across the room. Only a throw rug appeared obvious, so she pulled it aside to reveal a trapdoor set in a concrete square. Ji Yeon grabbed a canvas strap and pulled, lifting the wooden panel to expose a cinder block shaft with a ladder down into another chamber. Sarah jogged over with the Sabre in hand, slung it over her shoulder on a strap, and climbed in first. Maya eased herself down a few rungs. Ji Yeon hurriedly closed the hatch, squishing Maya down. As soon as it shut, everything went black. Soft footsteps overhead hinted that the girl dragged the rug back over the opening.

Blind, Maya climbed by feel until her sneaker touched the floor. The scent of metal and dirt hung in the air, along with something like moldy paper. Sarah's hand alighted on her head, then moved to her shoulder.

"Don't move," whispered Sarah. "We don't know what's down here. There could be something dangerous."

Maya nodded. A second later, she felt stupid for doing so in a completely dark space and whispered, "Okay."

In the room above, Ji Yeon's pleasant humming continued for several minutes. No explosions, blaring alarms, or anything else happened. Maya bounced on her toes, anxiety building. Soft metallic clattering right next to her head made her picture Sarah aiming the Sabre up at the trapdoor.

"Don't shoot her," whispered Maya.

"I won't. Safety's still on. And stay quiet."

Footsteps *thunked* on the small porch, decidedly heavier than a little Korean girl.

Maya gulped.

"Hi! My name is Ji Yeon. What's yours?"

"Oh shit!" shouted Pope.

"Whoa," yelled Genna. "What the fuck is one of these doing here?"

"Please do not hurt me," said Ji Yeon.

Maya scrambled up the ladder.

"That's what they always say," grumbled Pope.

Ji Yeon's voice took on a tinge of pleading. "No, I am serious. I am sentient."

"It's got the goddamned tracker." Genna growled. "Where's the girl who had that?"

"I found it in the forest."

Genna yelled, "Fuck!"

Maya shoved the trapdoor up, creating a throw rug tent. She swatted it out of the way and climbed into the room. "Mom! Dad!"

Pope stood in the doorway, his big sniper rifle leaned around the wall, trained on Ji Yeon. For some reason, he appeared frightened of her. Genna aimed her M-17R2 combat rifle at the girl through a window. Both jumped at Maya's shout.

"Oh!' Ji Yeon glanced at Maya, then at Genna. "You must be her mother. She said you used many bad words. I am sorry for lying to you. People were using this tracker to attempt to harm her. So I pretended to be a decoy while they hid."

"Mom!" Sarah ran over. "Dad!"

Maya and Sarah plowed into a four-way hug. Pope spotted the wound on the side of Sarah's head and went off in a flurry of questions about what happened. The strong protectiveness in his voice brought her to tears and got Maya sniffling as well.

Genna swept the kids off their feet, clinging to the pair of them, her body shaking with emotion. Maya burst into tears, stammering apologies. It took a few minutes for her to calm down, but once she quieted, her parents finally set her down on their feet.

Genna stared her in the eye. "What happened? Why are you apologizing?"

"And what the hell are you doing in the same house as a rad

orphan?" Pope gestured at Ji Yeon. "What the hell is one of them doing here?"

"Oh, crap," whispered Sarah, glancing at the girl. "No wonder she seemed a little odd."

"Please." Ji Yeon clasped her hands in front of her chest. "Do not hurt me. I... you are correct. I am an android, but I am not a robot."

Pope's expression resembled that of a confused caveman. "That doesn't make sense."

"I am sentient." Ji Yeon let her arms fall at her sides. "I have emotions and am self-aware. I do not want to hurt anyone. All I want are friends and not to be lonely."

Genna raised a delaying hand. "Hang on. Those 'bots never admit to being 'bots."

"Okay. You got a point there." Pope lowered his rifle. "Can't say I've ever heard of one admitting to it. Are you armed, kid?"

Ji Yeon looked down and shed tears. A moment later when she spoke, her voice barely had any strength. "Yes."

Maya blinked. *We slept next to a nuclear bomb...*

"Umm." Genna took a step back, lowering her weapon.

"I hate it." Ji Yeon stomped. "Sergeant James was going to have me disarmed. I *want* to be disarmed so I can just live and be happy. I *hate* being a weapon."

"Umm." Maya glanced up at her parents. "We've been here for a day and she's been really nice to us. A little odd, but that all makes sense now... why she didn't eat or use the outhouse."

Ji Yeon stooped and removed the tracker from her ankle. She walked closer, holding it out. Both Genna and Pope leaned back. Maya stood her ground and took it from her. Sarah shivered, but didn't seem sure if she should be frightened of the girl.

"So..." Pope rested his hands on the backs of Maya and Sarah's heads, pulling them close to his chest. "What the hell happened in there?"

Maya explained everything about the mission. At the mention of the Fade storage facility and drone base, Genna's eyes practically burst from her skull. She stormed around in circles, cursing and mashing her fist into her other hand.

"I see what you mean." Ji Yeon turned her head back and forth, following Genna. "It is a little embarrassing to hear a woman use those words, but I understand."

Pope chuckled. He said something in Korean to Genna that made her scowl and Ji Yeon laugh. Both adults stared at the android. The artificial girl bounced on her toes while speaking rapid Korean in the pleading tone of a kid begging her parents for a puppy. She pointed at her chest, stomped her foot and burst into tears.

"What's she saying?" asked Maya.

"Tellin' us how much she hates having a bomb." Genna folded her arms. "She sounds a lot more genuine in Korean."

Ji Yeon asked something in Korean again.

Pope said a few words back to her then switched to English. "Can't for cannot, for example. Or Don't for do not."

"Oh. I think I get it." Ji Yeon nodded. "Please don't be afraid of me. I swear I won't explode."

Genna sat in one of the chairs by the table and pulled Maya into her lap. "So, what happened after that?"

"We snuck out a different way and found this truck..." She explained the long ride, Kita, the Ascendant VTOL coming after them, the KT3, the boat exploding, and winding up here.

"Oh, that bitch is done." Genna bowed her head against Maya's. Her body shook with anger, but she contained it well. "So much for that bullshit offer of a truce."

"I'm not sure it was her." Maya tapped her fingers on the table. "She's a total bitch and all, but I don't think she'd have ordered that."

"The bitch *told* us to kill you over the vid." Genna squeezed her tight, muttering apologies into her hair.

Maya reached up and clutched the arms encircling her. "I almost believe her that she expected you wouldn't do it. She's good at bluffing. But I also think she wouldn't really have cared too much if you did it. But not caring is different from actively sending people to shoot me."

"Not by much," muttered Sarah.

Pope edged closer, eyeing Ji Yeon warily. "Well if Vanessa didn't do that, who did?"

Maya flung her arms up in exasperation. "Who knows? Take your pick. Another Tian Shen. Someone else trying to get me out of the way so they can take the company from Vanessa. Maybe it's whoever was in charge of that Fade storage doing it without getting permission. I don't know."

"How did they hack the tracker?" Sarah tightened her hug on Pope.

"Probably lifted the signal while you were in the facility. Nothing they noticed while you were there, but later, they could've pulled it from data logs. Since they *did* use it, that means they had some equipment in there that scanned for any transmissions." Pope scratched at his beard.

Maya laughed at him.

"What?" He raised an eyebrow.

"You moved from that tunnel into the Hab, and you're starting to look *more* like a wild man." She smiled. "It's touching your shirt now."

Pope glanced at Genna with a raised eyebrow.

"It's fine. Much longer than that and I might sneak you with a trimmer at night." She tried to smile but it didn't really work. A long sigh leaked out her nose, and she again squeezed Maya. "You ready to go home?"

"Hell yeah," said Maya. "Umm. Mom?"

"Yes, baby?"

Maya twisted around to flash a cheesy smile. "Can we bring Ji Yeon with us? She's lonely."

Genna's face lost a little color. "Umm. I... Baby, you realize that th— she's capable of destroying the entire Hab?"

Sarah let out an "Eep!"

Ji Yeon slumped into a chair, head bowed. "I understand. It won't offend me if you refer to me as 'that thing.' You are a veteran and you have bad memories. I'm too dangerous to be near lots of people. I guess I have to be lonely." She sniffled, covered her face with her hands, and broke into crying.

Pope looked away, fists clenched.

"Damn," said Genna in a half-whisper. "Feels almost wrong leavin' her here."

"That's what they do," said Pope, his tone neutral. "They're designed to beg for help, to be taken in, then once they're around a crowd..."

"I was on a base with Sergeant James for three weeks in Seoul. I didn't go off."

"Why not?" asked Genna, a catch in her voice.

Ji Yeon looked up from the floor, staring into her eyes. "I don't want to die."

"That's a first." Pope raised both eyebrows.

"Wait, aren't they hardcoded to detonate when they detect a certain number of military personnel within the blast range?" Genna shifted her gaze to him.

"Yes." Ji Yeon wiped tears from her cheeks. "I overrode the software. I'm not a robot. I'm an android."

"Whoa." Sarah held her hands up. "Hang on. You were actually in Korea during the war? Are you really ten?"

"It's complicated." Ji Yeon swished her feet back and forth. "I have existed for twenty-seven years. I have been *alive* for sixteen. However, I am a child as far as my ability to process and react to my environment and other people. Although I am fully sentient, I cannot mature and will always behave like a ten-year-old."

Pope crept around the table, cautiously walking over to her. "How did you, umm, become alive?"

"I was created by the People's Army as a weapon and set loose roaming the streets. I do not have memories of that time since it predates my awareness. I remember waking up on a table surrounded by people who looked like a gang. An older man told me they took me off the street and reprogrammed me. They didn't have the necessary equipment to remove the weapon, but they did give me the ability to ignore the trigger routine. I met Sergeant James fourteen days later, and admitted to him that I was an android, but had become sentient and would not explode. He took me to the base after asking me some strange questions about killing puppies. No one there trusted me, but since I hadn't exploded, they left me alone. When the Army fell apart, he brought me here."

"Damn." Pope paced around. "He took a hell of a risk bringing you to that base. Surprised his commander didn't court martial him."

"He wanted to. But I threatened to go off if they did that to him." Ji Yeon looked up with an innocent face. "But I wouldn't have. I don't want to die. I just lied to protect him. They were confused like you are that I admitted to being an android."

"Yeah. Okay, so let's say we buy that you're 'alive.'" Pope looked her over. "Can you guarantee you won't ever explode?"

"No." Ji Yeon shook her head. "I cannot control the actions of other people. If someone shoots me or there is a hardware malfunction, I am a risk." She looked down and sniffled. "But, Sergeant James was going to have me disarmed. Will you take me to the tinker?"

"Tinker?" asked Genna.

"I really want to go home." Maya squeezed her mother's hand. "But, I can wait... can we help her? Please?"

Ji Yeon stared at Maya. Her slightly large eyes made sense. She'd been designed to appear as cute as possible. "Will you please still be my friend now that you know I'm not made out of meat?"

"Yeah." Maya nodded.

"Umm. Okay." Sarah fidgeted. "As long as you promise not to blow up. Friends don't kill each other with nuclear fire."

Ji Yeon nodded. "I swear. But I would prefer being disarmed. I do not want to die. And I do not want to hurt anyone."

"What's involved with this?" asked Genna. "Where is this tinker?"

"Ooh!" Ji Yeon brightened. She bounced off the chair and scrambled over to the work table. "There is a map. He lives in a place north of here, but it will take a few days to walk there. That's why Sergeant James had been putting it off. His leg was bothering him... but he wound up dying."

"Umm, Mom?" Sarah crept closer.

"Yes, baby?" Genna looked at her.

She pointed at the FN-Sabre over her shoulder. "You should probably take this. There's also a bunch of grenades and mines on that table."

"Baby, why are you carryin' a rifle?" Genna plucked it away from her.

"Well..." Sarah ground her sneaker into the floorboards. "We *did* have soldiers trying to kill us... and it was there. And you guys weren't. Sorry."

"I'm actually kinda worried that there's a functional KT3 roaming around in the area." Pope crossed to the table and checked over the grenades and landmines. The first mine he picked up, he nearly threw into the air. "Oh... these are empty shells. All the explosives are gone."

Ji Yeon looked up at him, offering a folded map. "Sergeant James used them to make the traps around the house. This is how to get to the tinker. Thank you!"

Pope about fainted when she hugged him.

16

A LITTLE ERRAND

Wasting no time, Genna ushered the kids out the front door. They walked for a little over fifteen minutes to a clearing in the forest, where a black Humvee waited. Given the threat of potential attack combined with no further need to find Maya, Pope turned the tracker off and stashed it in his pocket.

Ji Yeon climbed into the back seat, looking around at the vehicle with the awe of a child who'd never seen something like it before. Pope boosted Maya up while Sarah hauled herself in the opposite side. He and Genna got in up front, then sat there examining the map for a few minutes.

"I'm trying not to think about there being a nuke in the back seat." Genna flicked the safety of her rifle on and off.

"How do you think I feel?" asked Ji Yeon. "Everywhere I go, I'm stuck being next to it. I'm *really* happy you guys are helping me get rid of it. I hate it so much."

Maya took the girl's wrist, examining her fingers, turned her hand over, squeezed her arm, and whistled. "Wow..."

Ji Yeon looked at her. "What?"

"I can't believe how totally real you look and feel. You're even warm."

"Umm. I think I should probably be offended by that, but I

understand your reaction." She smiled, then hugged her. "You feel real, too."

"Ugh." Maya rolled her eyes. "Everyone thinks I'm an android, too."

"Why?" asked Ji Yeon.

Maya explained about the decoy robots that Vanessa placed in multiple apartments. "I've never seen one up close, but they're supposed to be good enough to fool people. So realistic you need a PMRI to even tell. They can even eat and pee and stuff."

"Can you?" asked Sarah.

"I'm capable of eating, yes. But I don't eat as much food as a person because it would be wasteful. I use some materials from food to correct wear on my body. My blood is full of nanobots that constantly fix me and keep everything working. I don't think they like the nuke either."

Sarah laughed. "No one likes nukes."

"You're not radioactive, are you?" asked Maya.

"I don't think the device is well shielded. I'm probably giving off radiation. But it is not so much to cause harm to you given the amount of time you have spent around me. That is another reason I wish to be rid of it." She blinked once, then burst into tears.

Pope poked the button to turn on the e-motors. "Right. Let's get this hot potato dealt with."

"What's wrong?" asked Maya.

"I probably killed Sergeant James. The radiation. We were together for many years." She bawled.

Sarah rubbed her back, but shot Maya a look like 'am I really comforting a robot?'

"Do you *know* you're leaking rads or are you guessing? Do you have sensors?" asked Maya.

Ji Yeon calmed her tears. "Umm. I'm guessing. I don't have a radiation detector. But the device inside me wasn't intended to exist for very long before going off. It would've been wasteful for them to build it well."

"Everything the NoKos made was cheaper than shit," said Genna. "Except those rad orphans. They had to make them damn near perfect to fool anyone. She's probably friggin' glowing in the dark."

"I'm sorry for being radioactive." Ji Yeon bowed her head. "Are you going to ground me?"

Genna barked a laugh. "Now if that ain't one of the most effed up things I ever heard."

"Nah." Pope steered around a crashed helicopter covered in weeds. "Not your fault, kid. You didn't, err, ask for that thing. And I have feeling they might've shielded the devices a little better than most. Hard to bring a cute little orphan into a base past the sensor suite when they're all lit up with rads."

"Heh. Not around where I was stationed. Couple blocks from the base, this one street was so filthy, anyone who walked down it had to go through decontamination."

"Ouch." Pope cringed.

"Yeah." Genna glanced out the window watching trees go by. "Some NoKo tried to backpack us, but his device malfunctioned. Instead of a mushroom cloud, it took a giant nuclear-tainted shit all over that street. Damn good thing he picked that way to come in... ruins six stories tall, mostly metal, whole bunch of tiny dwellings. Contained the bulk of the rads."

"Doesn't sound too good for the people who lived there," said Maya.

"Oh, baby, they'd been long gone already. Our dumb asses were the only people left anywhere within ten miles of that base." Genna rubbed the bridge of her forehead.

"War and killing are evil." Ji Yeon plucked a bit of lint from her shredded dress, a gesture as futile as polishing a rusty car. "I didn't ask to be what I am, but I'm still ashamed of myself."

The Humvee hit a bump that threw everyone a few inches up off their seats. Sarah and Maya screamed. Ji Yeon remained silent and calm.

"Remind me to complain to someone about the state of the forest here. These potholes need attention." Pope jerked the wheel to avoid something on the ground too low for Maya to see.

"Why did you both scream?" asked Ji Yeon.

"Great." Sarah leaned her head back and stared at the roof. "Now I have to teach two of you how to 'child.'"

Maya giggled.

"How to 'child?'" asked Ji Yeon. "I don't understand."

"She's using child as a verb for humorous effect." Maya put an arm around the artificial girl, and proceeded to try and explain why that was funny and why they screamed when thrown into the air.

"Hon," said Genna. "Crawl into the back and grab one of the canteens, please?"

Sarah glanced at Maya. They both shrugged at the same time, then did rock, paper, scissors. Maya lost, so she climbed over the seatback into the cargo area. Her parents had brought a box of military rations and about a dozen canteens. After picking up and tossing some empties aside, she found a full pair and returned to her seat. Genna took one while Maya opened the other and handed it to Sarah, who gulped down a few mouthfuls and gave it back. Maya drank her fill and let out a gratified gasp. She offered the canteen to Ji Yeon, who shook her head.

"Sorry it took us so long, baby. We saw you kick the wasp nest, and stayed there a while watching the place, hoping to catch them transporting you two out. Or seeing you escape. The tracker didn't come online for hours, and way off out here to the west."

"The truck." Sarah waved her hands at the ceiling. "It's walls blocked the signal."

"I'm kinda surprised at Harlowe," said Pope.

She eyed him back. "That he didn't protest us taking the Hummer?"

"No." Pope chuckled. "That you didn't kill him."

"Mom?" asked Maya. "Dad?"

Pope used the rearview mirror to look at her while Genna twisted around.

"I don't think I should do any more missions."

"You got that right." Genna winked.

"I want to stay home and be a kid, but I'm scared everyone is coming after me as long as Ascendant is in power." Maya picked at her pant leg. "Was I stupid for going after the Fade stores, or did I do the right thing?"

Both of her parents let off hard sighs.

"You should've gotten the hell out of there with that intel," said Genna. "You had no idea what to expect in that room. There could've been armed guards or security doors you couldn't get past."

"There *were* armed guards." Sarah frowned. "But lazy ones."

"Place had so much front-loaded security, they never expected anyone would get in." Pope tapped his fingers on the wheel. "If you weren't a kid, I'd say you did the right thing. You had a rare opportunity being inside that place close enough to strike. However, since you're nine, you should've gotten out."

"Okay." Maya clasped her hands in her lap. "So both good and bad."

"Mostly bad." Genna reached back and squeezed her hand. "But I blame myself for not telling Harlowe to go to hell when he asked about sending you in there. Goddamn Fade storage?" She grumbled. "Son of a bitch probably knew that... or at least suspected."

Pope shook his head. "He only sent her in there to tap the computer. Not like anyone expected Fade to be loose in the place. Plus, she's vaccinated."

"That's not the point."

"I know. Fade means high security, more risk." Pope patted Genna on the shoulder. "I still can't believe she managed to pull off destroying it."

Maya grinned to herself.

"Don't encourage her." Genna slid back into her seat and faced forward.

"No way." Maya held up her hands. "I'm gonna stay home from now on... at least until the next time someone kidnaps me."

Sarah started to laugh but wound up staring at her, worried.

Everyone sat in silence for a long while, near an hour. Eventually, forest gave way to open field strewn with the rubble of a once-city in places, sparse grass in others. Here and there, a recognizable sign stuck up from the ground or jutted at an angle from the side of a mound of concrete chunks.

"I have to pee," said Sarah.

Genna and Pope both groaned.

"Why is it that whenever someone says that, everyone suddenly realizes they have to go, too?" asked Maya, squirming.

"No idea. You're the smart one." Sarah stuck out her tongue.

Ji Yeon shrugged. "I don't have to pee."

Everyone laughed, including Ji Yeon.

Pope brought the Humvee to a stop near a debris mound. "Okay, quick pee break. Don't go more than ten steps away."

Maya almost blushed, but it made sense to stay close to her parents out here. She followed Sarah out the passenger side door and jumped to the ground. Much to Maya's horrified astonishment, Sarah dropped her pants and squatted right next to the tire without looking for any cover.

Genna went around front while Pope took a few more steps and watered the debris with his back to everyone.

Whatever. They're my family. Maya hid behind the giant tire and assumed the position.

Ji Yeon also squatted and pulled her dress up. The pathetic garment had been so short she barely had to. Maya almost yelped in surprise when the android urinated as well. Catching herself staring at the perfect illusion of humanity, she whirled away, blushing.

"Umm," whispered Maya. "Why are you peeing?"

"Aren't we supposed to?" Ji Yeon turned her head to look at her.

"Umm..." Sarah managed a nervous laugh, also unable to resist looking. "I think she means *how* are you peeing?"

"When I eat or drink, whatever the nanobots don't use comes back out. My original stupid computer brain had programming in it to do this in front of soldiers so they would think I'm real."

Maya wanted to fall into a tiny hole at the thought of how embarrassing it would be to have total strangers catch her in the middle of going to the bathroom outside. She hurriedly finished and hiked her pants up.

"That makes sense." Sarah stood and fixed her pants in place. "She cried, too. So she has water."

Ji Yeon stood and let her dress flop back down. "I know you need to ask about some things to get used to me, but it makes me sad to be talked about like I'm a machine. I don't mind helping you understand about me, but I would much prefer if you treated me like a friend, a person, instead of a machine."

"I'm sorry." Maya hugged her. "I've never seen, umm, someone like you for real before so stuff surprises me. Sorry for asking stuff."

Ji Yeon grinned. "It's all right."

Maya put a hand on the girl's chest. "Do you really have a bomb in there?"

"Yes." Ji Yeon grasped Maya's wrist and moved her hand down over her stomach, like a mother letting someone feel the baby kick—only the girl didn't appear at all pregnant. "It's here. The device is about the size of a large potato. I hate it more than anything."

"That's really sad." Maya sighed. "Like handcuffing a real kid to a bomb."

"Thank you." Ji Yeon hugged her again.

Sarah raised an eyebrow, but didn't point out the obviousness that Ji Yeon wasn't a real kid, though she did act damn close to one.

"Hide!" whispered Ji Yeon. She sprinted to the other side of the Humvee where Pope and Genna stood by the front bumper, gazing around while comparing reality to the map. "Someone's coming!"

Maya leapt into the Humvee, Sarah right behind her.

People rose out of the debris field, mostly wearing long scraps of pale grey cloth tied around their bodies like mummy shrouds along with poncho fragments. Some had armored vests, some helmets, and all covered themselves in concrete dust to blend into the surroundings. About half of the thirty or so figures carried guns, a mix of rifles and pistols, the rest brandished crossbows, bows, or blades. They emerged from hiding places amid the rubble, effectively surrounding the Humvee on three sides, trapping them against the mountain of former building.

"Well, shit." Pope spat to the side. "That's a little inconvenient."

"Skeevers," whispered Genna. "No point talking to them."

Pope nodded once. "Best chance is to go close quarters and hope they won't risk shooting their own people."

Maya huddled down behind the driver's seat, peering out the windshield at the approaching armed people. "What do they want?"

"Skeevers," whispered Sarah, a terrified tremor in her voice. "They'll probably eat us or worse."

"Umm, worse?" Maya gulped. "What's worse than being eaten?"

"Mr. Mason," whispered Sarah. "What he wanted to do to us."

Maya eyed the door and slapped the lock.

Outside, the small army of rag-clad people closed in, inches at a time. No one had taken a shot yet, but one loud noise would cause an explosion of violence. Genna and Pope both clutched knives on their belts. Standing back to back, they appeared to be waiting for the skeevers to get close enough to use their blades. Ji Yeon walked around the front end of the Humvee and stood beside them, calmly eyeing the scene.

"If Mom and Dad don't win..." Sarah reached into the front seat and grabbed the FN-Sabre rifle. "I should probably kill you and then myself. It'll be better than what'll happen to us if the skeevers get us."

A heavy shudder shook Maya's body.

Ji Yeon turned to look at Sarah through the windshield, and shook her head 'no' before facing the approaching crowd and raising her arms out to either side and shouting, "Stop!"

The skeevers all twitched. One guy fired a crossbow bolt that struck the side of the Humvee with a *thunk*.

For a second or two, the skeevers appeared confused, then they all recoiled from Ji Yeon.

"Go away and leave us alone or I will kill all of you." The tiny girl stepped toward them without fear, looking back and forth over the motley group. "You cannot run fast enough to survive if I blow myself up. If you shoot me, that will only make me explode. I will kill everything within two and a half miles. Leave these people in peace and disappear. You have ten seconds."

Maya gasped when the android girl turned her head far enough left. Both her eyes glowed bright red.

Genna started to reach for Ji Yeon to pull her back from the skeevers, but hesitated. Pope managed a spot on impression of a statue.

"Nine... eight... seven," said Ji Yeon.

The skeevers broke ranks and ran back into the rubble like cockroaches fleeing light. Ji Yeon stood with her legs wide, arms raised high, watching them scurry away, not moving even after the last of them vanished from sight.

"Umm." Genna glanced down at her. "Please tell me you're bluffing."

"My friends said these people would do bad things to them. Worse than death. They were about to end their own lives rather than be taken." Ji Yeon lowered her arms and turned to face the adults, her eyes no longer glowing. "I bluffed in the sense that I hoped the bad people would run away, but not in the sense of my being able to kill everyone. I absolutely did not *want* to, but I could have." Her lip quivered. "I don't want to die. But I couldn't let them do something so evil that your children would kill themselves to escape."

Genna whipped her head around to stare at the Humvee.

Sarah leapt out and ran to her, Maya following close behind.

"What is this kid talking about?" whispered Genna, while squeezing both girls in a hug.

"Umm." Sarah repeated her fears that the skeevers would've either cannibalized or done 'sex-type-stuff' to them all.

"Where'd you get that from?" Genna blinked.

"That's what Dad said skeevers would do if they caught me."

"Aww, baby." Genna hugged her and patted her back a few times. "He's probably makin' it sound way worse than it is to scare you into staying as safe as possible."

"Do you know that for sure?" Sarah shuddered. "Would you take that chance?"

"It's okay, baby. Stop thinkin' 'bout such bad shit. You didn't do anything wrong."

Maya figured she'd probably have a nightmare or two about skeevers chasing her. She forced herself not to think about being so terrified that she would've *wanted* Sarah to kill her instead of being captured, and hid her face against Genna's shirt.

Pope eyed the field around them. "No telling what to expect from some of the ferals out here. Rather not think about it. Kid, are you a hundred percent sure you can avoid triggering if you're around too many people at once?"

"I think I've overridden it, yes. But I can't say it's totally perfect. That's why I've stayed out here all alone instead of walking to a city. I didn't want to risk being a danger to people." Ji Yeon stared down at her toes.

Genna released her hug on Sarah and Maya after a moment, then took a knee in front of the android, brushing some of the child's long, black hair away from her face. "I... I'm not sure how to handle seeing, umm, you do somethin' like that. So damn human."

Ji Yeon fidgeted.

Gingerly, Genna threaded her arms around the frail artificial girl and hugged her. A few seconds later, Ji Yeon returned the embrace and burst into tears.

"I hate having people afraid of me," sobbed Ji Yeon.

Genna stood, picking her up. Pope gave them the side eye, like he didn't quite fully trust the android yet.

Maya took a step back, letting her mother carry Ji Yeon to the Humvee. She thought back to her first time visiting the Devil's Hangover. As soon as she'd walked into that bar, one old man went crazy, thinking she was the same kind of false child with a nuke. If Ji Yeon really was alive in a mental sense, people reacting like that had to be painful. And she'd just made people afraid of her on purpose to protect them all from a fate best left unimagined.

She might've been jealous watching Genna cradle some other kid who couldn't stop crying. But it made her happier to have found someone like her for a mother. Knowing she held an android, the woman still tried to comfort Ji Yeon. Pope, though, clung to some suspicion. Maya couldn't fault him for it, given what he'd seen in Korea. She'd read stories of soldiers falling for those rad orphans, causing the deaths of hundreds. Rumor claimed that once word spread of the androids' existence, soldiers shot actual street kids at a distance, not trusting them —sometimes fatally, sometimes only a 'test bullet' in the leg to make sure they were real.

Sick to her stomach, Maya climbed back into the Humvee and held on to Sarah.

No one spoke as they drove on for the better part of two hours. Eventually, Ji Yeon calmed down, but remained in Genna's lap. The clinginess matched what Maya had read on the AuthNet about the rad orphans. Their programming made them act like that, though they didn't usually acknowledge being robots or admit to having a weapon.

Maya swallowed the overwhelming want to go home and leaned against Sarah.

"Sorry," whispered Sarah.

"For?"

"Thinking about shooting us."

Maya looked up at her. "If the skeevers were gonna do *that* to us over and over until we died anyway, I would rather you shot me."

Sarah sniffled. "I don't like it out here."

"Stop!" yelled Ji Yeon.

Pope jammed on the brakes. The Humvee twisted slightly to the side, flinging her into a clump with Sarah against the left side door. Pope prevented a spin-out and skidded the truck to a halt, clutching the wheel in both hands. No one moved for a few seconds. Pope twisted around and stared at the small girl. "What? Why are you yelling like that?"

"Were you yelling at us to stop talking about the skeevers?" asked Maya.

Ji Yeon pointed forward. "No, I meant stop driving. There are mines in the ground ahead. I can see them."

"Shit." Genna plucked the map from the center console and looked it over. "We ain't that far. Maybe a quarter mile now. Not bad to do on foot."

"Right. We still have another problem." Pope leaned back in his seat. "Do we bring children across a mine field or do we leave them unsupervised with the Humvee?"

Maya raised a hand. "I prefer to keep all of my limbs attached."

"Mines are evil." Ji Yeon shook her head. "They remain in the ground long after war, and hurt the innocent. Why do people even make things like that?"

Pope sighed. "Humans have a unique drive to keep creating better and nastier ways to kill each other."

Her hating land mines is kinda like hypocrisy. Maya bit her lip. *Maybe not. She does hate her own bomb, too.*

"Do not leave your children here alone. It is dangerous." Ji Yeon smiled. "I can see the mines and lead us through the field without harm."

Genna glanced at Pope. "Disarm a swath? Or do you think they're too unstable?"

"What's the spacing like?" Pope squinted at the ground up ahead. "Is there enough room to make it without disarming? Any idea what kind of fuses these things have?"

Ji Yeon shook her head. "No. I only see round metal plates under the ground. They are spaced about fifteen yards in an alternating grid pattern."

"I'd rather disarm these with a rifle from a safe distance," said Genna. "But I also don't want to make that much noise now. However, if they're proximity fuses, it's too dangerous to try walking around them."

"I will go dig one up. I'm only an android so it won't matter if I explode."

Genna clamped onto her as she tried to get out. "Hold on, kid. If you set off a land mine, you also might set off something a little spicier. Besides, you seem like a lot more than just an android."

Pope glanced at her with a 'you really believe that?' eyebrow. "Where is the nearest mine?"

Ji Yeon pointed. "Do you see that piece of stop sign?"

"Yep."

"The mine is two-point-four feet to the right and nine inches past it."

"Hmm." Pope stared at the spot.

"I don't see a post." Genna leaned close to the windshield. "I doubt they're prox mines. Kid, you got zoom eyes?"

"Yes."

"Is there anything protruding from the ground by the mine like a small plastic tube?"

Ji Yeon stared at the spot. "No."

"Everyone stay put." Pope pulled a knife off his belt and slipped out of his seat.

He advanced toward the area where the mine supposedly lay buried. When he reached about six feet from it, he flattened out on the ground and advanced by crawling, prodding the dirt with the knife as he moved. Maya barely breathed watching him. Sarah couldn't look, and hid her face against Maya's shoulder.

Eventually, Pope dug something out of the ground. He fiddled with it for a few seconds, then stood.

"MAP-10s." Pope held up a green disc about six inches wide and two thick. "That's good and bad."

"Ugh." Genna groaned.

"Mine, antipersonnel, mark ten," said Sarah. "Pressure switch activated. Kill radius fifty feet."

Maya playfully swatted at Sarah's shoulder. "Stop that. I'm the one that's supposed to fail at being a child."

Sarah laughed and grabbed her hands to stop the 'assault.'

"How is it good *and* bad?" Maya stuck her tongue out at her sister.

"Good because they're pressure triggers," said Genna. "Bad because those damn things are so cheap a grasshopper farting six feet away could set them off if they're too old."

"So trying to drive around them could set them off?" asked Maya.

"Yeah." Genna nodded.

Pope set the disarmed mine on the ground and climbed back into the Humvee. "We can do it, single file. If you think it's worth it."

"Maybe it's reckless, but it's damn hard to think of this girl as an android." Genna made faces at the field ahead of them.

"You realize she is one. They're designed to pull at our heartstrings. Are we really going to risk our kids' lives for her?"

Ji Yeon looked down. "I can't ask you to do that. Thank you for bringing me this far. I can make my way through the mines alone to the tinker's place."

Genna remained quiet for a moment. "Nah. I can't leave her alone. One of *them* things wouldn't want to be separated from a caretaker. They'd beg. No explanation for this, but I don't think she's one of 'them things' anymore."

"Fair point." Pope frowned at the minefield.

"Do you have optics?" asked Ji Yeon.

"Yeah, in back." Genna pointed over her shoulder with a thumb.

"I can link to them and show you where the mines are so you can see them, too. They are spaced enough to drive carefully, or we could walk."

"As much as I don't like leaving the truck behind, it could set these things off from vibration. Just as soon leave it out here and safe."

"All right. Let me grab the optics." Genna hopped out and set Ji Yeon down on her feet before going around and opening the rear door.

Maya climbed down out of the Humvee and stared off at the barren wasteland. The hilly ground littered with rubble offered thousands of hiding places where danger could lurk. Both staying here with the truck and going forward terrified her. No amount of thinking could protect her here. One couldn't simply outsmart an explosive mine. Well, not walking into a minefield probably counted as 'outsmarting' a mine. She closed her eyes and shivered in fear.

"I have the MAC addresses," said Ji Yeon. "Gimme a sec. Linking. What's the password?"

Genna spoke a series of letters and numbers.

"Got it." Pope tapped at a headband that held small clear plastic squares over his eyes. "Holy shit... there's hundreds of them."

"Fuck," whispered Genna, adjusting her augmented reality rig. "Okay, that's a mess, but damn this kid is handy." She raised her rifle, flicked a switch, and aimed around. "Heh. Been awhile since I used targeting optics."

Pope walked over and picked Maya up. "Here's what's going to happen." He attached Maya to Genna's back. "Hang on to her. If you fall off, you stay put wherever you land. Do not move."

"Okay." Maya gripped the straps of Genna's utility vest and wrapped her legs around her waist.

Sarah hopped up on Pope's back.

Ji Yeon walked out in front, her head constantly sweeping left to right and back again. Pope followed her about six paces behind, with Genna six paces back from him. Maya looked around at the devastation.

"Wow, wherever we are makes the Dead Space look like civilization. There's nothing left."

"It's scary here." Sarah sputtered when the wind blew her hair into her mouth. "Why does this guy live here?"

"Some people *really* don't want the Sons of Jeva knocking on their door," muttered Pope.

Genna chuckled.

Ji Yeon stopped. "There is a man aiming a primitive ranged weapon at Pope. Eighty meters ahead at eleven o'clock."

Pope dove to the ground a second before an arrow flew through the air where he'd been standing.

Sarah rolled off him to all fours, then pointed at a small pile of broken-apart building a few yards away. "Clear path?"

"Yeah," said Pope. "Stay down."

Sarah scrambled over to hide behind the rubble.

Genna set Maya down, and she ran to hide next to Sarah. Ji Yeon raced over to the girls, squatting on her toes while gripping the edge of a long piece of old highway divider so she could watch the fight.

Maya, curled on the ground with both arms around Sarah, blinked at her. "Get down!"

"I have to keep looking so your parents can see the mines," said Ji Yeon. "And I'm an unarmed little girl. They will kidnap me before they try to hurt me."

"More skeevers?" whined Sarah.

"I don't know." Ji Yeon shrugged, gasped, then ducked down in a ball.

A loud *bang* went off, followed by a rapid scattering noise as if someone had dropped a bag of small rocks from a passing airplane. Small puffs of dust rose into the air all over the place.

Maya stifled a scream.

Pope laughed. "Watch that first step, dumbass."

Ji Yeon popped back up to peek over the concrete barrier.

A gun went off, then another shot. The aluminum clatter of an arrow bouncing off concrete followed. Two rapid shots preceded a man wailing in pain. Maya curled up tighter, shaking. Sarah draped herself on top of her. Another few gunshots filled the air. An arrow bounced off concrete nearby with a clatter.

"Someone's coming around left," whispered Ji Yeon.

Maya uncurled and sat up at the same instant a man in scrap leather armor rounded the end of the debris mound they used for cover. He carried a bow and arrow, aiming as if to ambush Pope or Genna from the side. He stopped short, surprised at the sight of the kids, but didn't appear interested in shooting them. The expression on his face made him look like a starving dog who'd found steak.

Ji Yeon screamed like a child seeing a monster.

Sarah drew the Hornet, aimed, and clicked the trigger—but nothing happened.

"Shit!" rasped Maya. "It's broken from the river!"

The man leaned back, both eyebrows up at the sight of the gun.

"Nope," muttered Sarah, annoyed. The Hornet emitted a soft *click*. "I forgot the safety."

With a wild, gleeful cry, the man started to run at them.

Pthoonk!

The Hornet spat out a dart, which struck the man high on the chest near the base of the neck. Tiny sparks lapped at exposed skin, crawling up the front of his neck to the chin and making his teeth glow bright blue. He stopped in his tracks, convulsing in place. Two red holes appeared an instant later in his chest, bullets tearing his leather armor like tissue paper.

Maya squealed and looked away, cringing at the *thud* of the body hitting the ground.

"You made me waste a dart," said Sarah in a wavering voice.

Rapid footsteps in the distance ended with another explosion and peppering of small fragments everywhere.

"Gah! Shit," yelled Genna.

"You hit?" shouted Pope.

"Shrapnel. Right in the goddamned tit."

"Need me to suck out the poison?"

Genna laughed.

"They're running. Clear on my side."

"Copy that." Genna coughed. "Ow. How can a tiny bit of metal hurt so damn much?"

"Are you okay?" whispered Sarah.

Maya sat up and huddled against the debris pile. "Yeah. Scared shitless, but I'm not hurt." She gestured at the dead guy. "*This* is the wildlands I read about on the AuthNet."

"Yeah. But, look at the bright side," said Sarah, still sounding scared and freaked out.

"Bright side?" Maya blinked. "There's a *bright* side?"

Ji Yeon tilted her head.

"Yeah." Sarah pulled Maya into a hug. "These guys don't know who you are."

"How is that a bright side?"

Sarah let out a nervous giggle. "You don't have to feel guilty that the attack is your fault. They'd have attacked anyone."

A lump swelled in Maya's throat. "Do, umm, normal girls hide in minefields during gunfights?"

"Only the same way Pick is a pirate captain," whispered Sarah.

Maya leaned back, forcing a smile. "Guess we're both not 'childing' properly."

17

EMPATHY

Genna sat on a chunk of debris, shirt open. Pope wiped blood off her breast and stomach after plucking a tiny scrap of metal out of her. A couple shots of GIB spray from a first aid kit mended the hole, and a spritz of NuSkin covered it.

Maya examined the bottle Pope had called GIB, wondering how Bioactive Syn-Stem Gel mutated into that acronym. "How do you get GIB from BASS Gel?"

"It's faster to say in the field.' Genna chuckled. "Means Guts in a Bottle."

"Or giblets." Pope grinned. "Guys in my unit used to call it 'gibbing' a guy to hit him with a missile meant for a KT3, since the biggest piece left of 'em would be about the size of a turkey gizzard."

"That's a conspicuous waste of ordinance." Genna shook her head.

"Oh, they didn't do it on purpose." Pope packed up the first aid kit. "But, people tended to miss a lot of hasty shots when trying to stuff a missile up a KT3's nose before it fired on them. Did you know an unarmored human torso is too soft to set off the impact fuse on an AA-6? Leaves a five-inch hole... that's usually on fire."

Maya and Sarah blinked at him.

Genna sat there a moment more watching him wipe nonexistent

blood from her exposed breast. "You tryin' ta polish it to a boot shine? Think you got all the blood."

Other than a thumbnail-sized spot of skin still a bit redder than the rest of her dark brown complexion, she appeared intact again.

As soon as Maya realized Pope probably liked touching Genna's boob and continued to rub it for reasons other than cleaning, she blushed and looked away.

"Maybe it wasn't the greatest idea to skip the armor," said Pope.

"Yeah. But we rushed. Wasn't thinkin' right with her missing." Genna pulled her shirt back on. "Little sore, but I'll survive. Let's get the hell out of here before we attract even more friends."

Once Genna finished putting her harness and gear back on, Maya hopped on her back. Pope carried Sarah the same way, navigating the minefield behind Ji Yeon. The augmented reality optics allowed them to see a marker wherever the android spotted something metal under the ground.

Before long, they crested a hill, which turned out to be an enormous pile of rubble from fallen high-rises. The uneven ground ended at a ridge overlooking a shallow canyon where a former warehouse still stood mostly intact. Steel plates welded in places patched war damage, a clear sign someone lived (or had once lived) there after the war. A zig-zag maze of chain link fence topped with coils of concertina wire took a circuitous route to a person-sized door at the left end of a row of four garage doors.

Genna pointed out two cameras watching the approach.

"Is he going to shoot us?" asked Sarah.

"I'd say that depends on how we go about walking up to the place." Pope looked back and forth down the slope in front of them. "Looks like we're on the other side of the minefield here."

Ji Yeon pointed to the right, along the canyon. "There are no mines on that side. Maybe he doesn't want people coming this way?"

"Probably has a bunch of cameras pointing that way or something." Genna set Maya down, then slung her rifle on its strap. "What kind of idiot sets up a shop all the way the hell out here?"

"Someone with both a valuable skill and an intense dislike of other people." Pope chuckled. He, too, slung his rifle after Sarah dropped down to stand.

Genna led the way on the treacherous climb, past broken furniture, slabs of drywall, tables, pipes, half-shattered bathtubs, and large panels of smashed concrete. Once they reached the relatively-intact street at the bottom, Maya hurried up to walk beside her, and the two navigated the back and forth pathway between chain link fence. A yard on their left contained numerous broken-down vehicles as well as large machines she didn't recognize and a scattering of big appliances like washing machines.

"This zigzag is a kill zone," said Pope, in a low voice. "If the man's got a weapon, anyone he doesn't like the look of wouldn't make it to the door."

"Is that blood?" Sarah gasped, pointing at a stain on the ground. "Oh, crap, it is!"

Maya forced herself to smile. "Look cute. Skeevers don't have smiling kids with them."

"Heh." Genna chuckled. When they reached the end, she knocked relatively hard on a steel door covered in rust and patched bullet holes.

"What'chu want?" A man's voice crackled from a tiny speaker over the door.

"You the tinker?" asked Genna. "Heard you could help us out with something."

"Gimme a minute," replied the man. "And yeah. Name's Murphy."

Footsteps scuffed up on the other side of the door. A loud *clank* made Maya jump. The door swung outward, revealing a man with wild dark brown hair wearing an olive drab T-shirt and brown coveralls as well as a ton of grime. His right eye appeared slightly larger than his left, and the way his hair went everywhere gave him an electrocuted look.

Murphy stared at Maya and sighed. "Not sure what you heard, but I ain't payin' any more than 2,500 NuCoin for it."

Maya scoffed and folded her arms. "I'm not an android."

"No kiddin'?"

"No," snapped Maya. "I'm a real child. We're not here to sell me."

"Jeebus Cripes," whispered Murphy. He leaned closer, peering at her. "You is the real one? You mind if'n I scan ya?"

She bit back the nasty response that formed at the tip of her brain. *We need his help.* "Are you going to kidnap or kill me if you scan me and find out I'm real?"

His bushy eyebrows shot up. "Of course not."

"Okay, fine. Whatever. Scan away."

"Come in, come in!" All smiles, Murphy backed away from the door, gesturing like a lonely grandfather who hadn't seen another person in years, though he couldn't have been much older than forty. As soon as everyone stepped inside, he shut the door and secured four deadbolts.

Maya let a silent sigh out her nose and followed him into a cavernous room containing rows of shelves all packed with junk. Tracks and rails ran back and forth on the ceiling two stories overhead, chains still holding up gripper mechanisms that looked beefy enough to move cars around. More than a few old android limbs sticking out of the shelving lent the place a graveyard eeriness that unnerved her.

She decided to stop looking around and followed the man down one of the rows. Genna stayed close behind, keeping a hand on her shoulder. Ji Yeon followed, with Pope and Sarah bringing up the rear. The lack of sunlight added to the creepy unease, though the man himself hadn't given her any bad feelings. However, this place had all the trappings of a horrible nightmare.

This is exactly what I'm going to see in my dreams when the skeevers are chasing me.

Murphy walked past the far end of the row, stepped around some plastiboard boxes, and approached a workbench. Maya approached and suffered a moment's worth of having a PMRI gun pointed at her.

"Oh my!" shouted Murphy. "It really *is* you. Wow. It's such a privilege to meet you." He shook her hand, grinning ear to ear. "I should have figured you were real since you look a little older."

"A little older?" Maya raised an eyebrow.

"Usually, I get people coming here to sell duplicates. But they all look like they're a year or two younger." He peered at Genna. "Forgive me, Miss Oman."

"Only 'cause you didn't mean that, I'm not gonna hold it against you." Genna narrowed her eyes. "I ain't that bitch."

"This is my *real* mom." Maya clamped on in a hug. "Vanessa doesn't own me anymore."

"Oh, you poor thing." Murphy cradled her face in both hands. "Never imagined they'd have slaves in the fancy place."

"It's complicated." Maya leaned back from his touch. "Thanks though. I'm okay. Can you help us with something?"

"Oh sure." He managed a cheesy smile. "Would you mind an autograph?"

Maya's eyebrows became a flat line. "Seriously?"

He grinned. "Please?"

She forced herself not to roll her eyes. "Okay."

Murphy rummaged around the desk and unearthed an eight-by-ten picture of Maya posing for an Ascendant ad. Fortunately, he didn't have the mortifying one of her in a bikini pitching abdominal-fat-destroying pills. She took it, plus a marker, and scrawled her signature along the bottom.

"Thank you!" He placed it back in the drawer like a sacred relic. "What can I help you with?"

Sarah's 'are you effing kidding me' expression almost made Maya laugh.

"We found a new friend, but she's got something dangerous inside her. We heard you can remove it so she's safe." Maya waved at the android, who stepped forward.

"Hi! My name is Ji Yeon."

"Ack!" Murphy almost jumped backward over the desk. "*Nogsaeg wising myeonglyeong du sa ahob.*"

Ji Yeon scrunched up her nose in an angry expression, balling her hands in fists. "I don't wanna!"

"Whoa…" Murphy gasped. "That's not right."

"What's not right?" asked Pope.

He pointed at Ji Yeon, his hand shaking. "That phrase is a command override. It should make them turn off."

Pope scratched his head. "Green phase command two four nine? Seriously? All you have to do is say that to them and they go to sleep?"

"Yeah, man." Murphy nodded. "Found that buried in their program code. Course, would've been nicer if I'd have made that discovery *before* the war ended. It don't make any sense. They ain't supposed to be able to disregard it. It's the only failsafe way of tellin' em apart from a real kid without opening them up."

Genna chuckled. "Evidently not failsafe if she ignored it."

"I am what you think I am." Ji Yeon bowed her head. "But I am sentient. I'm not running the original instructions. Please, will you remove the bomb? I hate it. I only want to be a real person, not a weapon."

"And that's equally messed up." Murphy scratched his beard. "They don't usually admit to bein' androids. Ehh... you really *want* me to disarm the thing?"

"Yes please!" whined Ji Yeon.

Maya put on her most imploring stare. "It would mean a lot to me."

The tinker wiped a hand down his face, pulling his eyes droopy for a second. "Okay. C'mon."

He walked off to the left, leading everyone into a room that resembled a crude doctor's office complete with a procedure table in the middle, overhead lights, and a handful of pushcart-mounted electronics. Two shelves on the left held various cybernetic implants, many with dried blood on them.

Murphy patted the table.

Ji Yeon walked over to it, removed her dress, and climbed up to lay flat on her front, arms folded under her head.

Murphy swung an overhead boom down from a machine on the ceiling, positioning the camera-like box at the end above the girl's back. He spent a few minutes looking at a small monitor on a pushcart that appeared to be some manner of x-ray scan. "Well, damn. You got a live one all right." He glanced back at everyone else. "No point backing away. If I make an error, couple extra feet won't mean a damn thing."

Maya shivered.

"Please don't make an error then," said Ji Yeon.

Murphy brushed the girl's hair off her back and pressed a thumb into the base of her skull while simultaneously squeezing her left shoulder like he attempted to do some bogus kung-fu movie magical grip. A split appeared along Ji Yeon's spinal groove. Previously seamless skin opened sideways in two panels, revealing shiny chrome ribs, grey bundles of synthetic muscle, wires, and some blinking lights. The metal structure resembled a real skeleton so much that Maya couldn't keep looking at her. Not that seeing bones bothered her, but a person shouldn't be 'alive' at the time.

Sarah, too, turned away at the sight, shivering. "That's too creepy."

"Don't make no sense," muttered Genna, still not having entered the room.

"What's that?" Pope twisted back to look out the door.

"Why'd Vanessa bother having Maya for real instead of using an android? Can't say it's cost, 'cause they have dozens of decoy androids."

"The decoys ain't as common as people think." Murphy continued prodding around inside Ji Yeon. "They initially made a few to do exactly what you suggested, but the units of the time couldn't project convincing empathy."

Maya folded her arms. "Neither can Vanessa. They'd be perfect for each other."

Sarah giggled.

"Headcrash checked out several sites before we went in, and they all had Mayas in them." Genna shook her head lightly, making the wooden beads and rings in her dreads clatter.

Curiosity got the better of Maya and she peered again into the room. The thin child laying naked upon the procedure table appeared totally real in every way—except for her wide open back, metal bones, and 'guts' made of electronics and soft plastic 'organs.' The sight of a girl with her innards exposed reclining there awake, tapping her fingers in boredom while a man poked around with tools inside her, exceeded some threshold of weird that left Maya unable to feel curious *or* repelled.

"Probably holograms." Murphy adjusted a headset with a huge array of lenses. He leaned back and looked at Maya, his eyes comically massive courtesy of a brick-sized rectangular lens across his face. "Have you ever seen one of your doubles?"

"No." Maya shook her head. "I've heard about them, but never saw one."

"Could they be lies, too?" Sarah risked a peek at the table, but cringed.

"Wouldn't surprise me." Genna pulled both girls close at her sides.

Murphy returned his attention to his work. A high-pitched whirr from his electronic screwdriver broke the silence in short bursts. Ji Yeon rested her cheek on her folded arms, gazing into nowhere, looking completely bored. One by one, the man placed removed screws on the cart beside him.

"You know..." Pope gestured at the tinker. "We should probably be a little more concerned about a guy named Murphy playing around with a nuclear weapon."

"Ha ha. Don't worry. I routinely break my own law."

Maya scratched her head. "He made a law?"

"Murphy's Law," said Genna.

"Oh. Duh." Maya biffed herself in the forehead.

"I'm totally lost" Sarah sighed.

Maya smiled at her. "At least *something* is normal."

Sarah raspberried her.

"Okay, now for the challenging part." Murphy looked over at everyone. "Got a choice of three wires. Which one I disconnect first makes a big difference. One will safe the device. Another will set her off instantly, and the last one would start a tamper countdown that would probably give us five minutes to live."

"So... nothing major," deadpanned Pope.

Ji Yeon's expression of boredom gave way to worry. "If you don't know which wire to disconnect first, you should stop. I don't want to kill anyone. I'll go back to where Sergeant James is and stay alone."

Murphy stuck his hand into her back.

Click.

Maya squealed, her knees no longer willing to hold her up. Sarah screamed and jumped into Pope's arms. A vein in Genna's forehead swelled up. Pope raised one eyebrow.

"Aah!" yelled Ji Yeon. "What did you do? I heard a click!"

Murphy emitted a wheezy chuckle. "I'll be damned. This is a first. This ro—I mean girl *is* actually sentient."

"Huh?" Sarah clutched her chest, shaking. "You almost nuked us."

He grinned back at everyone. "Nah. The hardware's all the same. I knew exactly which wire to unhook first. Wanted to see how she would react. And, well, damn... she *is* sentient. She showed greater concern for others than herself."

"That just means she's not a politician." Pope grinned.

"Ain't a whole lot of humans who'd be that selfless either." Genna fanned herself. "You scared the shit out of me."

"I'd do the same thing," said Maya. "A thirty-three percent chance of a good outcome with a sixty-six percent chance of death? It wouldn't be worth it."

"You could say that someone would choose that out of self-interest." Ji Yeon swished her feet back and forth. "It is true that I don't want to die, but if my device went off, it would have harmed my friends, and that would be worse."

Genna glanced at Pope and whispered, "Still worried she's pretending?"

"Jury's still out, but I think they're close to a decision." He smiled. "Gah, that's unsettling seeing her wide open like that."

"Almost done." Murphy picked up another tool. "Now, everyone try not to breathe too loud."

18

SPARE PARTS

Maya almost fainted in relief when the adrenaline wore off. Murphy had teased them all with the whole 'which wire do I disconnect' thing. She came close to screaming at him but decided that pulling a Vanessa on a man performing surgery around a nuclear device probably wouldn't be wise.

"Ooh!" chirped Ji Yeon. "The detonator is missing from my diagnostic senses. You did it! You disarmed me!"

"Hon?" asked Murphy.

"Yes?" Ji Yeon shifted a little to look at him.

"For the next, oh, minute... I need you to not move at all, okay?"

"I understand." An unsettling stillness came over Ji Yeon. She even stopped breathing. Her frozen facial expression and absolute lack of any motion finally made her look like a machine rather than a person.

Everyone observed in tense silence as Murphy gingerly lifted a cylinder about the size of a beer can out of her lower back, a few short wires dangling off the bottom end.

"So, we're safe now?" Genna subconsciously tugged at the girls, like she really wanted to pull them out of the room.

"Completely." Murphy didn't take his eyes off the object in his hands. "As long as no static electricity zaps the middle contact. If that happens, we won't have much to worry about ever again."

Sarah and Maya shivered in unison.

"Wait, a simple static shock would set that thing off?" Genna gawked.

"North Korean hardware. Cheap. Not much of a failsafe. Any voltage to that contact would set off the precursor explosive which would initiate the chain reaction and... we wouldn't have time to even *think* 'oh shit.'" Murphy gingerly carried it to the side of the room and lowered it into a black tray. "Dielectric box. Safe in here. *Now* we can breathe."

"Is it shielded?" asked Pope.

"Yeah. These suckers wouldn't be too effective if they set off rad alarms. It's not setting off my gear, so it's not leaking." He walked back over to Ji Yeon and resumed looking over her insides.

Pope eyed the dielectric box. "Well, I suppose we could bring it to our mutual friends or turn it in to the Authority."

"Neither one of those options sounds like a good idea." Genna set her hands on her hips, glowering at nothing in particular. "People on both sides would be dumb enough to try and use it."

"We can't just leave it here." Pope gestured at it.

"I can take it apart downstairs." Murphy chuckled to himself, then leaned his face close to Ji Yeon's. "I get the feeling you're a good girl."

"I try to be." Ji Yeon smiled. "Thank you for getting that awful thing out of me."

"Tempted to disable L12." Murphy tapped a finger to his chin. "Want me to?"

"Umm. I would not hurt anyone, but it may be helpful for non-violent reasons." Ji Yeon shrugged. "Whatever you think is best."

"What the hell is L12?" asked Genna.

Murphy poked his finger into Li Yeon's thigh, which squished much the way an ordinary girl's thigh should squish. "She has synthetic muscle fibers that do an impressive job simulating human biology in every way but one... they can be quite a bit stronger. L12 is a hardware limiter switch that keeps her only as strong as the child she appears to be. Disabling it would allow her to utilize her full strength."

"Whoa." Maya went wide-eyed. "Could she throw cars?"

"Heh." Murphy laughed. "If they ever made an adult sized one of these, possibly. Her, not really. Though she might be able to shove one aside if it's small enough. Still, depends on leverage. She doesn't weigh much."

Pope whistled. "Back to that nuke. How do we know you'll actually disassemble it?"

"Easy." Murphy reached inside Ji Yeon and stuck his finger between two metal ribs by the spine, near where a person's heart would normally be. "Come downstairs with me and watch."

"I don't feel any different," said Ji Yeon. "But I am calibrating now."

"All set, kid." Murphy pushed something at the bottom of her back cavity.

Maya cringed away as she caught a glimpse of a plastic bladder that probably served as the girl's stomach—or intestine given how close it sat to her rear end. The two panels of her back motored closed, and within seconds, any trace of a seam or gap in her skin disappeared. She once again appeared indistinguishable from a human.

Murphy picked up the sorry excuse for a tattered dress and tossed it into a wastebasket.

Ji Yeon pushed herself up and sat on the edge of the table. "Am I to stay naked?"

"Nope." Murphy patted her on the head. "That sorry rag they made you wear isn't much different than you having nothing on. I got some better stuff for ya downstairs. Real clothes, not a costume designed to make you look pathetic. You prefer a dress, or a shirt and pants?"

"I would like a dress, please." Ji Yeon beamed and swished her feet back and forth.

Why would this guy have kids' clothes? Maya glanced at Genna, but didn't bother asking.

After picking up the nuke-in-a-box, Murphy nodded toward the door. "Come on."

Ji Yeon hopped off the table and followed him.

"That kid needs a bath," said Genna.

Maya hurried after. "Ji Yeon?"

She looked back over her shoulder.

"Can you take baths? Or would water get inside you?"

"I like baths." She smiled. "I'm not afraid of water."

"Oh," said Maya. "That's cool."

Murphy crossed the warehouse to another door, which led to a stairwell down. Genna, Pope, and Sarah followed in single file, none of them too thrilled with being close to a nuke that could go off with one tiny zap. Of course, upstairs or downstairs wouldn't make the least bit of difference if it detonated.

At the bottom of the stairs, Murphy went left down a grey hallway lined with multiple battered metal doors. Bare metal piping ran across the ceiling in uneven rows, all carrying wires he'd likely installed by hand after moving in. A damp and somewhat moldy smell clung to the air, but the place at least looked clean. Ji Yeon walked behind him dutifully to the third room on the left. Inside, a large machine took up most of the inner wall, consisting of a big chamber with a thick glass window. The tinker set the dielectric box on a table, plucked the nuke out of it, and placed it inside the machine.

"I don't think that's enough shielding to absorb a blast if it goes off." Pope chuckled.

"Nah." Murphy smiled. "It's just a radiation shield. When I open that sucker up, it's going to be throwing off gamma rays." He walked up to a console and stuck his hands in two black holes. A few seconds later, a pair of robotic arms descended inside the shielded chamber and whirled into place over the nuke.

"Nice." Ji Yeon padded closer, peering into the box. "You're really going to break it."

Maya walked up behind her and put a hand on her back. Warm skin felt so natural under her hand that she couldn't imagine how it had opened before. Unable to resist, she traced a finger down the girl's spinal groove, mystified at being unable to feel any trace of a seam.

Ji Yeon giggled and peered back at her. "That tickles."

"There's no, umm... opening at all."

"Yes." The girl stared down, a note of sadness in her voice. "My skin is largely silicone, but it is permeated with nanobots that repair it. When the switches are pressed to access my insides for medicine, the same nanobots create cuts so I open like panels. Upon closing, they seal it again into one solid piece. That's why I can go in water."

"Oh. That's cool. I'm sorry for making you think about being non-biological. It's *really* super hard to tell."

"Thank you." Ji Yeon hugged her.

"Umm," said Genna. "You mentioned something about clothes for her?"

Ji Yeon shrugged. "I can wait. Making that bomb not work anymore is more important."

"Oh, yeah, no problem." Murphy glanced back at them. "Out the door, two rooms down on the right side. In there."

Pope appeared keen on watching the bomb disposal operation, either out of curiosity or to make sure the tinker kept his word and destroyed it.

"I got it." Maya took Ji Yeon's hand and led her out of the room.

She went into the second door on the right—and came face to face with her somewhat younger self. Another Maya lay draped in a chair, inert as a mannequin and wearing only a scrap of plastic wrapped around her like a short skirt. Except for the android not being tied to the chair, the sight came too close to that horrible cartoon she'd seen on Mr. Mason's computer.

Maya screamed.

Scrambling footsteps rushed up behind her. Genna rushed in and grabbed her. "What happened?"

"Maya?" asked Sarah.

Shaking, she pointed at her clone.

"Oh." Genna slouched with relief. "Just a decoy android."

Ji Yeon padded over to the left side of the room where a shelf held several boxes, some of which held children's clothing.

"Why's it naked?" asked Sarah. "Or mostly naked. Just has a plastic bag on."

"It's a robot. He's probably going to use it for parts or something." Genna winced at the sight of the false girl, and squeezed the genuine one.

"Mom..." Maya sniffled. "That guy liked me way too much. Why's he keeping that here? Do you think he's umm"—she lowered her voice to a whisper—"like Mr. Mason?"

Genna rubbed her chin. "Nah. Ain't gettin' that kinda vibe. These are just machines to him. There aren't many people left who count as famous. He's probably just thrilled to meet someone the whole world knows. Before the war, a lot of people went crazy about 'celebrities.'"

Ji Yeon took a white dress with puffy shoulders out of the box and tried to pull it on, but it wasn't big enough. She tossed it in a different box and tried a peach colored dress with plain sleeves, which fit her much better. After rummaging the box for a little while more, she found a pair of black ballet flats and put them on.

"Might as well grab a shirt and pants too, or a second dress," said Genna. "This guy doesn't need any of that stuff."

"What's he doing with girl's clothes?" whispered Maya. "That's kinda weird."

Genna patted her on the head. "He probably takes them from androids people bring here to sell him... at least the ones he breaks down for parts. And there's an abandoned city not far to the west. Could be scavenge."

"Some of them are already parts," said Ji Yeon.

Maya glanced over at her. The girl held up a pink T-shirt with a bullet hole in it, but no blood. She tossed it aside and kept digging.

"Eep." Maya shivered. "I hope that wasn't one of my clones that someone just shot."

"Yeah, me too..." Genna ran a hand over her head.

Maya approached the android copy.

Sarah grimaced, but followed.

The other version of her appeared about seven or eight years old. Other than dusty, she looked as real as Ji Yeon. Of course, sitting there utterly still like a mannequin destroyed any sense of humanity. Seeing this thing up close explained how Moth, Icarus, and Headcrash had fallen for her attempt at pretending to be a robot. It bothered her on a primal level, like a dream where she saw herself dead. The longer she stared at it, the greater her sense of impending doom.

"It's way too realistic." Sarah shook her head, a note of disgust in her voice. "Why did they give it a... you know." Her face turned red.

"If a kidnapper could just look there and know it's a decoy, they wouldn't be useful," said Maya. "These robots can eat, cry, sweat, do everything... and they pretend to go unconscious if someone uses chemical knockout agents on them."

"That thing is *way* creepy." Sarah backed away. "Can we get out of this room now, please?"

Ji Yeon looked down.

"I don't think *you* are creepy. You're alive. That fake Maya is a robot.

It's just sitting there like a thing." Sarah pointed at it. "Dead bodies are creepy, too, right?"

"Yes." Ji Yeon brightened.

Maya leaned around to examine her double more closely. A one-inch square of skin at the back of the neck stuck out like a tiny door, exposing metal spine and an interface plug. On impulse, Maya grabbed the robot's arm, but recoiled from the complete lack of body heat.

"Eww. It's cold like a dead person." She backed up and clamped on to Genna. "I'm going to have so many nightmares now. Chased by skeevers, chased by copies of myself, probably running around a building full of junk like upstairs. Ugh."

"It's only a robot, baby." Genna scooped her up. "It can't hurt you."

Ji Yeon approached, carrying a bundle of extra clothes. "Is it okay to take this stuff?"

"We should probably ask, but I don't think he'll mind." Genna guided Ji Yeon along with a hand at the back of her head.

She carried Maya back to the other room. Murphy continued working on the nuke, manipulating a pair of joysticks that controlled the robotic arms, which whirred around inside the shielded box. Flashing lights on the chamber painted the cinder block walls an eerie shade of pulsing red.

"Can I ask a silly question?" Genna quirked an eyebrow. "Why do you have a Maya robot sitting around in the other room?"

"With no clothes on," added Sarah.

"Oh." Murphy chuckled. "I've got four or five of them. Kidnappers figure out they get tricked, bring them here to sell for parts. No need to keep a T-shirt on a toaster oven. Better the clothes go to real kids in need. There's a village not far from here I usually trade the stuff to for veggies. Unless someone wanted to buy one of those robots whole and active, no need to waste clothes on 'em a real kid could wear. But no one ever buys them, they only bring 'em to me for coins. One dude came here awhile back, but, umm... I wasn't going to sell him one."

"Why not?" asked Maya.

"Because. And that's all I'm gonna say with a kid in the room."

"Oh." Maya nodded. "Was the guy's name Mason?"

Murphy coughed. "Aww shit."

"Wow." Maya shuddered. "Eww. Thank you for not giving him one of my copies."

"He didn't know I *had* some. Only that word's out I buy androids. Dude gave me a serious bad vibe."

Sarah clamped on to Pope.

Ji Yeon looked up at Genna with massive hyper-cute eyes. "Please don't kill me for parts."

Sarah leaned over to Maya and whispered, "She said 'kill' not 'take apart.'"

"She's sentient," whispered Maya.

"I don't know that much Korean." Sarah's eyebrows scrunched together.

Maya giggled. "Sentient means she has self-awareness. Like a person. She is not a robot, she's just a person who happens to have metal bones."

Ji Yeon whirled to face them and beamed. "Thank you for being my friends!"

"And she's apparently got *really* good hearing." Sarah blushed.

"Oookay," whispered Murphy. "Almost done... separating the precursor explosives from the nuclear material now. If you give me about an hour, I think I have enough lead upstairs to make a box for the nasty stuff."

"Won't it explode?" asked Sarah.

"No." Maya shook her head. "A nuclear detonation requires a high degree of precision in the arrangement of the components. Typically, there are two or more discrete masses of sub critical fissile material which are combined to critical mass with a high-energy explosive. The pressure wave of the primary explosive needs to compress it *just* right to set off a chain reaction. Otherwise, it just blasts radioactive crud all over the place, a dirty bomb."

Murphy twisted around to stare at Maya. "That PMRI said you're a real kid..."

"I am." Maya smiled. "I'm just smart. And I used to be highly bored, so I read a lot."

Sarah pointed a thumb at her. "She's a genetic pizza... with all the toppings."

Maya stuck out her tongue.

Sarah and Ji Yeon giggled.

"What does that mean? 'All the toppings'?" whispered Sarah.

"I'll explain later." Maya folded her arms.

Pope exhaled in relief. "Well, if you put the stuff in a lead box, I'll surrender it to the Authority. Let *them* worry about disposing of it."

FOR A LITTLE OVER TWO HOURS, THE KIDS PLAYED AROUND AISLES of scrap metal in the upstairs warehouse. Murphy had collected tons of things the twins and Pick would've loved to find scavenging. Old appliances, toys, tools, computers, furniture, and chunks of car engines. Though Maya initially thought of this place as scary, playing in and around the junk took some of the fear out of it.

Eventually, the parents came looking for them. Pope carried a box wrapped in fabric and tied with several cords. Murphy walked behind them, tired but appearing satisfied.

"All right." Pope smiled. "Ready to go home?"

Maya sprang to her feet and ran over. "Yes!"

Sarah cheered and followed.

Ji Yeon trudged over, a forlorn stare aimed at the ground.

"Why do you look so sad?" Maya grabbed her hand. "I told you we'd bring you home."

Genna nodded.

"Really?" Happy tears gathered in her eyes.

"Barnes is going to shit his pants." Pope snickered.

"We'll brief him." Genna waved Ji Yeon over. "No sense being deceptive since she's harmless. But we still shouldn't advertise she's anything more than a normal kid unless we have to."

"Umm." Ji Yeon ground the toe of her ballet flat into the floor. "I'm not going to grow up. Eventually, Maya and Sarah will be more like my mothers than my friends. It will be pretty obvious I'm an artificial person. But I don't mind as long as people aren't mean about it."

"Mean people suck," said Maya.

"Nice people swallow?" asked Sarah.

Genna and Pope sputtered and coughed. Murphy whistled.

"Huh?" asked Maya.

Ji Yeon shook her head. "I don't know why that made them uncomfortable."

Sarah shrugged. "I saw that on a T-shirt at Foz's place. Mean people suck, nice people swallow."

Genna lost it and burst into laughter.

"Oh..." Sarah's face went scarlet. "That's something sexual isn't it?"

"Right!" said Pope in a loud voice. "Let's go home."

19

AN OBVIOUS TRAP

Pope walked with Ji Yeon back across the minefield to retrieve the Humvee, while everyone else waited at the base of the canyon in the relative safety of whatever defenses Murphy had, plus Genna's rifle.

The Humvee rolled up along the old road about a half hour later. Pope grumbled about the easy ride in compared to the minefield.

"We still have too much Army in our heads," said Genna. "A pain in the ass straight line is our first instinct rather than a simple, but long way around."

He laughed.

Maya jumped into the back seat, eager to go home, but also gripped by the sudden fear that Ascendant might be waiting for her. She grabbed Sarah's hand as soon as she got in. Ji Yeon sat in the middle with her arms around them, admiring her new shoes.

For hours, Genna drove over barren landscape and the occasional swath of forest. Maya asked if they could stop by that village to let Kita know they were okay. Wanting to check out the possibility of a KT3 robot, Pope readily agreed.

They reached the village late in the day. The parents decided to spend the night since the ride back to the Hab would take a while. Kita appeared both surprised and overjoyed to find them okay, and agreed to watch the kids while Pope and Genna went off to recon the woods. As a precaution, neither brought a firearm so the robot wouldn't tag them as hostile combatants.

Kita told the kids that the villagers considered those woods cursed and no one dared go into them. Maya explained about the robot and guessed that someone not educated enough to understand robots saw it and invented the curse story to keep people safe.

Her parents returned soon, both clearly rattled. However, they had gathered up twelve combat rifles and a bunch of ammo, plus handguns. According to them, the KT3 would remain a dormant cube unless something came within a certain distance. Exploiting that proximity, they went back to the woods several times to scavenge some of the Ascendant armor.

Neither Kita nor Anshad suspected anything unusual about Ji Yeon, and the girl even ate dinner with everyone else. Maya figured she'd probably forget the whole android thing eventually—at least until it became overly apparent the girl wouldn't grow any older.

The girls all shared a sleeping bag on the floor near Anshad's bed. With three of them packed into it, 'cozy' took on new meaning, but it definitely beat laying on top of a piece of rolled up canvas not knowing if she'd ever go home again. Genna, Pope, and Kita stayed up late, reminiscing about Army stuff. Even though Kita had been a technician from a ship rather than a front line soldier, she had a good number of funny stories.

In the morning, they bid her farewell and piled into the Humvee yet again for the expected long ride.

"What if Ascendant tries to kill me again?" asked Maya.

"If they were inclined to do it, they'd have already been at our building." Pope grumbled something inaudible to himself. "I'll check things out when we get close. Best you two stay inside for a couple days until we feel the situation out."

Genna cracked her knuckles. "Oh, I'm gonna be feelin' Harlowe out real good."

"Heh." Pope chuckled.

"Really?" Maya blinked.

"Ain't gonna start off with the fist. Depends on what he says." Genna winked at her.

As it turned out, the Hab appeared normal. Too normal. No sign of any Ascendant presence, or even societal unrest greeted them upon their return. Even the protestors who had been a near permanent fixture since the video aired had vanished.

They headed straight to Doc Chang's apartment to get Sarah's cheek, ear, and shoulder looked at. She sat on the medical table, squirming and grimacing as he worked. Maya held her hand while he reopened and disinfected the largest splinter wound, plus a few others before using the spray stuff to repair the skin.

Ji Yeon and Emily ran around in circles laughing and playing.

"Thanks, Doc." Sarah sat up and brushed a finger at the tiny pink dot of repaired skin.

"Your new friend need a checkup?" asked Doc Chang.

"Umm." Maya fidgeted. "Probably not."

They gave him a brief explanation, which drew Zoe from the back room out of curiosity. At the end of a maybe twenty minute conversation, the adults decided that Ji Yeon would primarily live with the Changs. Zoe had the most technical training out of anyone in the building—not that they expected the girl to need much maintenance—and Emily had taken to her so well so fast. Maya couldn't help but feel a little disappointed, but also happy that she and Sarah still had the bedroom to themselves. It didn't hurt that most people couldn't tell a Chinese person from a Korean, and would likely mistake Ji Yeon for a biracial child due to her strange eyes. Having her 'officially' part of the Chang family helped her cover as a real person.

Due to the late hour and driving all day, the parents dragged Maya and Sarah home, upstairs one floor to the seventh. Both eager to be rid of the grime of travel, plus river muck in their hair, the girls shared a bath. In the midst of washing, the reality of 'home again safe' hit Maya hard. She started crying at the thought she'd almost gotten her sister killed.

"What?" asked Sarah, her voice echoey.

"I'm beating myself up for being dumb. We almost died."

Sarah twisted around and hugged her from behind. "We're home. We're safe, and we're *never* doing anything like that again." She paused. "Until we're grown up."

"Hah." Maya's crying switched to giggling. "I dunno if I want to get shot at even as a grown up. I'd rather help people."

Sarah proceeded to wash Maya's hair. "You'd make a good doctor. You're super smart, and caring. And you already know all the drugs."

"I guess. All I gotta do is live long enough to grow up."

"Stop thinking like that."

"Hey, while you're behind me, could you scrub the target off my back?"

A washcloth slid side to side over her shoulders.

"There. I don't see a target."

Maya sat cross-legged, elbows on her knees, chin in her hands. "Oh, it's there. And I'm tired of it." Helplessness and anger crashed together, bringing more tears. "I'm so damn sick of being threatened, kidnapped, shot at, and hated because of that woman."

"No one hates you." Sarah dropped the washcloth and poured more water over Maya's head.

"Sure they do. People see my face everywhere and they blame me for everything Ascendant does. I'm like the symbol of that company, so they hate me for what that represents."

Sarah hugged her again. "Those people are assholes."

"Sare!" Maya gasped. "You just used a swear word."

"Yeah. Sometimes they're necessary."

A knock struck the door three times. "Hurry up you two," said Genna. "I got dibs on that tub."

"Okay!" Sarah whirled around. "Do my hair real quick?"

Working fast, Maya reciprocated the hair wash while Sarah scrubbed herself. Soon, they rinsed off, dressed, and went to bed. Like a child half her age, Maya hid under the covers, hoping mere fabric might protect her from Ascendant's wrath.

MAYA SAT ON THE CONCRETE STEPS AT THE BACK DOOR TO THEIR building, Sarah beside her. Four days had passed since they'd returned, and things had thus far been calm. Genna and Pope still didn't want either of them going too far from home, so scavving trips had been put on hold. Maya wondered if she failed to 'child' properly again by not minding sorta being grounded. The parents wanted her to stay in or near the building out of protectiveness, not punishment. Also, she had little interest in going any significant distance (like more than one city block) away from home yet.

As expected, nightmares happened. Mostly Ascendant soldiers chasing her around some horrifying factory type place full of sharp things and rusty machinery. The worst one involved an army of Maya androids coming after her with knives, trying to steal her clothing. Though, having to share a bed with Sarah helped a *lot*. As soon as she woke up screaming, she had mini-mom right there to make her feel better.

Sarah's faded pink T-shirt bore the ghost of a cat-head decal, merely a silhouette of darker pink fabric that hadn't faded as much. She'd worn her white skirt as well, which convinced Maya to try doing the girly thing for once and also wearing a dress, a fairly plain sky blue one. Both girls had gone barefoot since they didn't plan on wandering much more than thirty feet away from the building at most, and neither expected a kidnapping attempt or attack in broad daylight. Plus, the insides of their sneakers were *still* damp. She didn't worry too much as Sarah had the Hornet (her original yellow one) close by.

Maya picked at the hem of her dress, a little longer than mid-thigh, and frowned, wondering if it would slow her down if she tried to run in it. It draped loose enough that she didn't think so, but wearing it instead of a shirt, pants, and sneakers somehow left her feeling vulnerable, almost as if she'd forgotten to put on armor.

I'm trying to be a normal kid. Normal kids wear stuff like this. Emily is super girly. Ji Yeon's not far behind. Sarah's just in a pink mood today. She doesn't care what she wears as long as she has clothes at all. She loves those Army pants. Maybe she's afraid to wear them now so no one steals them? She shooed a fly off her shin. *Do I hate being in a dress because they stink for fighting or am I mentally scarred from Vanessa forcing me to wear them for commercials?* She pictured an aesthetic technician's horrified reaction to her present garment, something that brand new *might* have cost about $20, not the $10,000 her old gowns did. Any of those people would've gasped as if she'd gone for a roll in animal waste.

Sarah randomly started snickering again, as if reacting to her thoughts.

She glanced over, mildly freaked out. "What are you laughing at?"

"Barnes..." Sarah snickered. "That face."

Maya forgot her worries and giggled along with her sister.

Barnes had screamed like a teenage girl in a horror movie at the sight of Ji Yeon. The face he made would've been awesome to put on a T-shirt. He nervously listened to their explanation, but didn't seem to calm down much until the girl admitted to being an android and explained about how she had been disarmed and was fully sentient.

"Yeah. I think he's going to have nightmares about her" Sarah stretched out a leg and tried to pick a dandelion with her toes. "At least you slept okay last night."

"My dreams are getting stranger. Last one had a bunch of android Mayas with giant metal arms like Moth."

"Whoa." Sarah gave up on the weed and folded her arms across her knees. "Mom's gonna kill you if she finds out you started taking drugs."

Maya laughed, leaned back against the wall, and looked over the parking lot.

Pirate Captain Pick stood on the hood of the huge, old car. In addition to his pair of ripped up shorts, he wore an improvised eye patch made out of a single plastic sunglass lens tied around his head with string. His sister wouldn't let him wear an actual eyepatch, since she worried it might mess with his sight.

Marcus stood in the back seat, chest deep in a moon roof, pretending to 'gaze out at the high seas' with cardboard tube binoculars. Anton occupied the driver's seat, 'steering' the ship by sliding his hands around a wheel that hadn't been able to turn in years.

Emily and Ji Yeon played on the swings Zoe'd built from old pipes. Looking at them made Maya's groin hurt with the memory of falling while climbing out of the giant room full of hydroponic liquid at the Ascendant facility.

"Did they tell Emily?" asked Sarah.

"No idea." Maya shrugged. "I don't think she'd care either way."

"The boys don't know."

"If Ji Yeon wants to tell them, she'll tell them." Maya leaned back and gazed up at the clouds. "She's basically alive. It's her choice."

Sarah swiped her foot back and forth over a thin scrap of grass growing out of a crack in the paving. Maya grinned to herself. *Getting her to wear shoes is like trying to put clothes on a cat.* Ji Yeon, on the other hand, adored her flats, the first shoes she'd ever worn.

"Do you think she feels as old as she is or does she not hold on to memories?"

"What kind of question is that?" Sarah shrugged. "I dunno. She's nice, and it's really easy to forget she's a robot."

"She's more convincingly human than Vanessa."

Sarah laughed.

The boys shouted about a 'ship o' plunder' approaching and engaged in a mock battle with imaginary evil pirates or some such thing. Maya watched them for a while, but didn't feel much of an urge to get up off the steps.

"Are we failing to child properly?"

Sarah looked over at her. "Huh?"

"We're just sitting here like parents watching the kids play."

"Heh. I'm *still* kinda tired and worn out from that trip. Just happy to be home."

"Yeah."

"Hey, you know." Sarah leaned close with a conspiratorial whisper. "Marcus keeps looking at you. The dress makes you pretty."

Maya rolled her eyes. "Are you trying to make sure I never wear it again?"

"Oh come on. Boys aren't *that* bad."

"Why don't *you* kiss him then?"

She stuck out her tongue. "Because he likes you."

Maya gestured at the car. "He doesn't *like* me. He's ten. I'm nine. We're way too small for that. And kissing? Eww. I don't even understand why people do that. It's a great way to spread germs. We might as well spit in each other's mouths."

"You are such a romantic."

"Huh?" Maya peered at her, confused.

Sarah snickered.

A woman wandered by on the sidewalk that ran along the edge of the parking lot, slightly stooped. One of the ubiquitous grey ponchos covered her to the shins, boots and baggy black pants peeking out with her stride. She had her hood up, filter mask over her face, and shuffled along at a slightly hurried pace, glancing left at the kids every few steps.

The fourth time she peered in past the fence, she wound up staring at Maya and slowing down.

"Oh, crap," said Maya. "Here we go."

"What?" Sarah grabbed the concrete step on either side of her legs. "It's an old woman."

Maya sat up from leaning on the wall. "She's looking right at me."

The woman moved to the breach in the chain link and stepped through into the parking lot. Sand brown hair hung down from the hood a few inches past her shoulders, and the bit of skin around her eyes above her breathing mask had no wrinkles.

"She's not old." Maya scooted back.

"Why's she hunched over like that?" asked Sarah.

"Maybe has a spinal malformation."

"Huh?" Sarah nudged her. "English please."

The woman straightened her posture and walked toward Maya as if in a trance.

"Get that Hornet ready," whispered Maya. "Dammit. I screwed up."

"How did you screw up?"

Maya wiggled her toes. "I'm not wearing shoes. I'm going to be kidnapped."

"That's nothing but a stupid jinx. Going without shoes isn't going to make you any more likely to be kidnapped."

"Are you trying to make a correlation vs. causation argument?"

Sarah gave her a flat stare. "I have no idea what the hell you just said."

Ji Yeon stopped laughing along with Emily and watched the woman intently, though she kept swinging. The boys ignored the stranger entirely.

"Maya," whispered the woman. She stopped a few feet away, peering down at her.

"Who are you? What do you want?" asked Maya, trying to sound polite and not as worried as she felt.

The woman reached into her poncho.

Sarah whipped the Hornet up in a two-handed grip. "Careful."

Oblivious to the stunner pointed at her, the woman withdrew a small electronic device. Sarah relaxed a little, lowering the Hornet, but kept it poised.

"Maya..." The woman took a knee and held the device out in her palms, as if making an offering to a goddess in a temple.

Before Maya could figure out if she wanted to touch it, the device projected a holographic image of a woman in a white doctor's coat. Too much shadow obscured the face to recognize her, nor did the voice that followed sound at all familiar.

"Maya, please listen carefully to what I am about to say. It is not safe for you there. I am not threatening you, but warning you of danger. Meet me at Ground Zero. I must speak with you as soon as possible." The hologram woman reached up as if to turn off the recorder, but paused. "Oh. Sometimes it's easy to forget you are a child. I mean Ground Zero the restaurant, not the crater to the south. Please hurry. You are not safe. I must speak with you as soon as possible."

The hologram flickered out. Sweat beaded on the forehead of the woman holding it. This close, Maya figured her for no older than thirty. Her hazel eyes stared unfocused and glazed, seeing neither the girls nor the building behind them. The woman didn't move, still kneeling with her arms outstretched, offering the device.

"Maybe we should check this out." Maya reached for it.

"Are you crazy?" Sarah grabbed Maya's hand. "This is obviously a kidnap attempt."

Maya pointed at the woman. "She's being controlled by nanobots. Just like that reporter. That woman in the hologram is the same person who probably sent that man to watch me."

"Yeah," said Sarah. "Exactly why you shouldn't trust this. Get Mom or Dad."

Maya curled her toes over the edge of the step. "They're raiding a food warehouse."

"So? We ask them when they're home from work."

The strange woman blinked rapidly and looked around. She jumped back from the girls with a startled yelp, muffled under her facemask. After looking around with an expression of abject confusion, she sprinted across the lot, darted out the breach in the fence, and ran away.

Ji Yeon resumed laughing while swinging.

"Let's get our shoes and go talk to her."

"No!" yelled Sarah.

The boys looked over at them.

"But she said we're not safe here. What if something bad happens?"

Sarah squeezed her wrist tighter. "Something bad happening is exactly why we should stay right here where we're supposed to be. A strange woman carrying a hologram is not an emergency. You said you didn't want to do crazy stuff anymore, right?"

"Yeah." Maya looked down. "You're right. That is really stupid to run off."

"It is." Sarah put her hand on Maya's forehead. "Are you feeling okay?"

Maya glanced sideways at her. "What?"

"You don't feel feverish."

"I'm not."

Sarah smiled. "You gave up on that dumbass idea pretty quick."

"Well..." Maya huffed. "You're right. It *is* dumb. I just thought if that woman wanted to kidnap us, she wouldn't *ask* us to go anywhere. And I guess it's pretty easy to say I'm in danger because of who I am. I'm *always* in danger." She scowled.

"Right. We wait for our parents and tell them what happened. They'll know what to do."

Maya scratched her foot on the edge of the stair. "Yeah."

"I'm not gonna let go of your arm." Sarah squeezed her wrist. "I don't want you running off."

"I don't mind."

"If you run off again, Mom's gonna handcuff your leg to the bed again."

Maya laughed. "She's *so* guilty over that. She'd never. Besides, I'd escape. It's just a matter of time running all permutations of the code."

"Wow. Just wow." Sarah shook her head.

The boys resumed pirating. Maya couldn't stop thinking about that message. Everything about it felt like a trap, but somehow, it gnawed at her that simply sitting here and waiting after receiving such a warning amounted to stupidity as well.

A few minutes later, Ji Yeon stopped swinging. She glanced at the road, then jumped from the swing, dragging Emily toward the door.

Maya sprang to her feet. "What? What's wrong?"

"Ow!" yelled Emily. "You're pulling my arm too hard."

An echo of squealing tires came from the street.

"A large vehicle is driving faster than it should here," said Ji Yeon. "It sounds like an Army transport."

Sarah jumped upright. "Everyone inside *right now!*"

20

THE KISS OF DEATH

Ji Yeon whipped the heavy door open with one hand and held it.

The boys stood on the car, looking around in confusion.

"Dammit! Get your asses inside right now!" shrieked Sarah.

Pick jumped down and ran for the building, startled by her language and tone. The twins followed. Maya shoved Emily inside, and stood there waiting for Pick. She waved him by, staring at the twins running closer.

A white armored van with six wheels screeched to a halt by the chain link fence. The side door slid back, exposing a group of people in white Ascendant armor. Before Maya could even scream, Ji Yeon grabbed her and tossed her inside the building. The twins ran in after her.

"Follow me!" shouted Maya, flailing her arms for balance. *The secret passageway!*

She ran down the short hall to the central elevator lobby—and right into about nine blueberries piling in the front door, all pointing combat rifles in their general direction.

Sarah swooned to the side at the sight of them, near to fainting.

"Kids, get down!" shouted a male blueberry.

Ji Yeon hit Sarah and Maya with a flying tackle, knocking them flat. Pick dashed over to the main stairwell. The blueberries opened fire, shooting over the kids at the Ascendant troops entering via the back door. Emily shrieked in a continuous wail of panic. The twins got stuck on a loop repeat of "Oh shit!"

A man in Ascendant armor booted the door in and started to raise his rifle. Ji Yeon grabbed a plum-sized chunk of concrete from the floor and threw it at him hard enough to crack his helmet and knock him back a step before he could shoot.

Maya screamed at a sudden eruption of gunfire. The other kids probably did as well, though she couldn't hear anything over the shooting. Brass casings rained to the ground from several blueberries' rifles, others had more modern ones that spat tiny foil squares.

A female blueberry rushed forward out into the open; the others fired faster. Pings and snaps came from everywhere, bullets bouncing off the floor and walls. The woman grabbed Pick and Emily and slid them toward the stairs across the floor like curling stones. "Get outta here."

The woman grabbed Maya's dress at her back and launched her into a spinning slide with a stiff shove. A loud plastic *clack* came from behind, and the blueberry groaned in pain. Ji Yeon scrambled on all fours into the stairwell, dragging the twins.

"Harris!" shouted a man's voice, crackling with helmet speaker static.

"Argh!" roared the woman who'd tossed Maya at the stairs. "I'm okay. In the arm."

Maya slid to a stop with her toes touching the door, facing back at the blueberry who'd fallen over on her side clutching a bullet would in her left shoulder.

The silver-visored helmet tilted toward her. "Kid, get outta here, now!"

She ran into the open to protect us...

Two other blueberries rushed out to Officer Harris and dragged her out of the line of fire, one of them taking a round in the back that knocked him into a stumble, but it didn't penetrate his armor.

Hands grabbed Maya by the ankles and pulled her backward into the stairwell. She twisted around to lock eyes with Sarah.

"The place," said Maya, scrambling upright. "Come on."

Maya ran past her friends and led the way. A chorus of pattering feet on concrete steps echoed off bare cinder blocks. At the second floor, the fastest access to the secret Brigade hideout, she darted out into the hall—but stopped after only three steps when a horrible truth hit her. She spun to face the others.

"Guys... they're after me. Go to Barnes' apartment. He'll protect you."

"No way." Marcus stepped close to her. "We ain't gonna leave you alone."

"I'll be fine." Maya backed up a step. "They don't care about any of you. If I stay here, I'm putting all of you in danger. I should be okay, but even if I'm not, my life isn't worth all you guys getting hurt."

Ji Yeon started crying.

Sarah backed up another step. "We should *all* hide in you know where."

"It's not safe down there." Maya shook her head. "It could collapse. Protect the others like you always do, okay? I'll hide until it's safe."

"No way." Sarah grabbed her arm. "You are *not* going anywhere alone."

Maya started to protest, not wanting Sarah to get hurt, but the idea of going off alone terrified her too much. Even if it made her a little selfish, she needed her sister with her.

The gunfire grew more intense, and louder. A ricochet bounced into the stairwell.

"Crap!" yelled Maya. "I gotta go right now."

"No way." Marcus grasped her by the shoulders. "You one of us now. We all stay together."

Maya stared at him. "This isn't your fight. This isn't kid stuff. They're *really* trying to kill me. I don't want any of you to get hurt. I never belonged here in this place."

"Bullshit." Anton pointed at her. "That's bullshit and you know it. You one of us."

Tears rolled down Maya's cheeks. "I'm sorry. But right now, I need to go somewhere else so you guys don't get hurt. Trust me. I will come back. Marcus, protect the others until Sarah's back."

"Until you're *both* back," said Marcus, his lip quivering.

Maya looked down. "Right."

Another ricochet pinged around in the stairs.

"Eep!" yelled Maya, trying to jump back, but Marcus didn't let go. "Come on. I gotta go."

He stared at her for a long few seconds, then leaned in and kissed her on the cheek.

Anton gasped.

"Whoa," whispered Pick.

"Okay." Marcus let go of her and nodded. "Do what you gotta do, but get back here, okay?"

Stunned, Maya couldn't think of anything to say. She blinked once, nodded, then hauled ass for the 'broken' elevator door while the rest of the kids scrambled up the stairs. The button sequence worked despite her shaking hand. The instant the 'broken' doors popped open, she ducked inside. Sarah jumped onto the ladder above her and kicked the door shut, plunging the elevator shaft into darkness.

Maya cringed at the greasy metal rungs under her bare feet, caked in some manner of slime. "Dammit."

"What?"

"No shoes again."

Sarah giggled.

"It's not funny. Whatever we're stepping on is disgusting."

"I never had shoes until Genna got me some. In eleven years, I've only been kidnapped once. And it's not because I had no shoes on, it's because people came after you."

Maya cringed. "I'm sorry."

"No!" rasped Sarah. "I didn't mean it that way. I'm not mad at you. I'd get kidnapped twenty more times if I had to for bein' your best friend."

Maya stepped off the ladder at the bottom. As soon as Sarah reached the ground, she pounce-hugged her. "You're my sister. We have the same parents now."

Sarah sniffled. "Yeah. Don't forget it."

In the dim light of a faltering LED brick, they stared at each other. Their clean, intact clothes made the filthiness of the tunnel around them feel ten times worse. After a moment of trying to stay quiet while listening to gunfire above them, Sarah got the giggles.

"What?" whispered Maya.

Sarah kept giggling, muffling her mouth with the crook of her elbow

—since her hands had turned black from the ladder.

"What are you laughing at?" whispered Maya.

"Marcus kissed you."

Maya folded her arms. "That's not funny either."

"Yeah it is." Sarah giggled.

"No, it's not." She rolled her eyes.

"Sure it is."

Maya squeezed her hands into fists and tried not to yell, or sound angry. "Sarah, he doesn't think he's ever going to see me alive again. He just kissed me in front of *everybody* after I've constantly told him I'd slug him in the mouth if he did it. He legit thinks I'm going to die." She bit her lip. *He's not the only one.*

Sarah stopped laughing and stared down. "Oh. Sorry."

Watching her mood crash that hard made Maya feel like a monster. "Ugh. Sorry. Hey. I don't plan on dying, so it's fine. Go ahead and laugh."

Sarah's expression didn't change much.

"Did you see the look on his face right after? He totally thought I was going to hit him."

"Yeah." Sarah managed a weak smile.

"Ugh. Sorry. We'll be fine. All we have to do is sit right here until our parents are back."

Sarah exhaled hard. "You're right. No one knows about this place."

"C'mon." Maya walked over the dirt floor through two ankle-deep puddles of icy water onto clammy concrete in the main tunnel. She headed down the hall to the nearest cot and sat on the edge.

Sarah settled down beside her and put an arm around her back.

"Did you see the look on Anton's face? He was totally waiting for me to hit his brother."

Sarah laughed. "Yeah."

"All we have to do is stay quiet." Maya glanced down at her feet, already filthy. She raised and lowered her toes. "Great. Not only is Ascendant trying to kill me, Marcus kissed me in front of everyone. That's *so* embarrassing, I'm tempted to let Ascendant catch me."

"That's a joke, right?" whispered Sarah.

"Yes."

Sarah let out a whispery giggle.

21

HIT THE FAN

Screams of anger and gunfire echoed in the distance, muted by two stories of earth and concrete. Maya wiped her hands on the side of the cot, then folded her arms, shivering at the chill of the basement. A dress and no shoes didn't do much to keep her warm. Sarah looked around at the ceiling.

Heavier gunfire joined in, likely Authority drones.

"I can't believe they protected us," said Sarah. "I totally thought they were going to shoot us."

"The blueberries?"

"Yeah." Sarah fidgeted. "I was like six years old the first time they locked the building down. They put the zip cuffs on me and left me, Sam, and the twins in a room on the ground floor. We screamed for help for hours before someone found us."

Maya shivered, hoping it wasn't Mr. Mason.

"I was seven the next time they raided the building, almost bedtime. They pulled me right out of the bathtub, threw me to the floor, and cuffed me without letting me get dressed. They thought it was funny when I cried."

"Holy shit!" Maya gawked at her. "That's horrible."

"They arrested Dad 'cause he hit them for treating me like that. The worst one happened when I was eight. Didn't know then, but I found out later that some guy had thrown a hand grenade into a checkpoint and killed some blueberries. He ran into our building to hide. The Authority showed up early in the morning. Dad was in one of his moods 'cause we ran out of beer. I still remember it like it happened five minutes ago. I was at the table having cereal, trying to keep quiet as Dad ran around the apartment searching for 'Korean booby traps.' When the blueberries came in, he thought they were Korean soldiers and went after them with a knife. That's the time they left me hogtied on the floor for a whole day. After they dragged him out, I think they forgot about me. Usually they put us kids all in one room. I couldn't get out of the apartment and no one heard me screaming until the other kids showed up for lunch the day after. It was Dad's turn to feed everyone, but he hadn't come back. Sam got a knife from the drawer and sawed the zip ties off me. I wound up feeding them cheese sandwiches. I just remember everyone eating while I cleaned my pee off the floor, crying too hard to see 'cause I didn't know if I'd ever see my dad again."

Maya hugged her, sniffling into tears. "I'm so sorry."

"Heh, you know it's kinda funny in a way." She let off a sad chuckle. "I was just going to stay home and wait for Dad, but Genna found me and insisted I stay with her and Sam since I shouldn't be alone at eight. Lived there for a month until Dad came home. The blueberries let him go because they finally believed he was nuts—and a veteran—so they felt bad for him. Then, like a couple weeks after Dad came back, Sam got sick. He used to watch out for all of us being the oldest, at ten."

Maya cried into her hands.

"Blueberries came back a couple months after that. Every time, they treated us like crap. Maybe four months before you got here, I cursed them out for being shitty to us." Sarah put her hands together over her head. "They hung me off my feet on a thing sticking out of the wall to 'teach me manners.' Course, the plastic cuffs cut me and I started bleeding, so they took me down. Some of them just loved making us cry. Every time I see someone in that armor, it scares the hell out of me."

"I understand why Genna wanted to kill them all. The blueberries in the Sanc aren't like that at all. I had no idea how awful they were out here."

"But, that's the thing." Sarah looked up and wiped tears from her face. "It's different now. *So* much different. And *you* did that. That woman... she just got shot trying to save us from a crossfire. Like we were Citizens."

"Real cops protect kids no matter how much money they have."

Sarah shrugged. "I guess."

"Those shitheads who abused you weren't real cops. Just thugs wearing blue armor working for Ascendant. I bet they're the same people in white armor now trying to kill me. They all got fired. I don't remember Ascendant having that many soldiers."

"How many soldiers did you see?" asked Sarah.

"Okay. I admit not too many. I didn't get out much."

Sarah grinned.

"So, umm... What should we do?"

The gunfire directly overhead eased off, though intermittent shots continued in the distance.

"Sit right here and wait for our parents." Sarah put an arm around her and squeezed. "Remember, no more missions?"

Maya bit her lip. "That hologram tried to warn us. They knew the soldiers were coming. Maybe we should go to that Ground Zero place?"

"We shouldn't go outside. People are shooting. And that restaurant thing is a trap."

Maya scuffed her feet back and forth, thinking. "If they wanted to hurt us, they could've mind-controlled that woman to bring a bomb or a gun or something, not a message."

"Does the mind control work that way? She looked like a zombie. I don't think she could've operated something as complicated as a doorknob." Sarah smirked.

"I don't—"

A huge *boom* rumbled overhead, shaking the earth, knocking chunks of stone and sprays of dirt from the ceiling. Maya screamed and cringed back onto the cot, crossing her arms in front of her face.

Sarah froze. "What was that?"

"Umm." Maya stared up at a crack in the concrete overhead that she swore hadn't been there seconds ago. Dirt rained down from a gap that appeared to be gradually widening. "Sarah. We have to get out of here right now. This place is going to cave in."

"It's not safe out there."

Maya sprang up onto her knees, grabbed Sarah's head, and pointed it at the ceiling. "Is that crack getting bigger or am I imagining it?"

Five seconds passed. The concrete swelled downward.

"I-it's g-getting bigger."

"What sucks more: possibly being shot or definitely being buried alive?"

"Buried alive sucks way more."

Maya jumped off the cot. "Come on."

She waited for Sarah to stand, grabbed her hand, and sprinted down the tunnel toward the exit. Falling rocks struck the floor behind them with echoing clacks. Picturing the ceiling collapsing in, Maya emitted a continual nasal whine of terror until she reached the end and hurled her body into the push bar on the heavy steel door. Sarah crashed into it beside her and, pushing together, they spilled out onto a small concrete ledge overlooking the crater of a former high-rise basement.

"Crap! The dosers," muttered Sarah.

"Are dead." Maya picked herself up.

"Oh. Yeah."

The report of distant gunfire echoed from every direction, along with screaming, the whirr of drone fans, the thunder of heavy machine guns, and the occasional random *whump* of a car slamming into a building or squealing tires.

"Holy shit..." Maya gazed up and around at the high-rises surrounding the hole. The reek of burned gunpowder in the air settled on her tongue. "This sounds like documentary video of the actual war."

"I think it *is* an actual war..." Sarah brushed dirt off the Hornet. "Only, not with different countries."

"Ascendant and the Authority?"

"Probably."

"Ground Zero?" asked Maya.

Sarah shook her head. "We're in a big hole. Bullets can't get us here. We should stay here where it's safe."

"Okay."

Not three seconds later, a smoking four-fanned Authority drone raced into view out from between two fourteen-story towers. The craft wobbled, twisting back and forth. Something on the side exploded, and it flipped over, tumbling into the crater like a missile.

Sarah screamed and tackled Maya.

They rolled down the hilly side, bouncing and sliding on dirt as an explosion went off barely thirty feet away from where they'd been standing. A concussion wave pounded all the air out of Maya's lungs seconds before drone parts fell around them in a terrifying rain of flaming metal.

She slid into a partially buried plastic trashcan near where the ground leveled out, bounced over it, and rolled to a stop a few feet later, flat on her back. *Ow.* A few more pieces of drone landed nearby, two on fire. Maya forced herself to sit up and looked over at Sarah. Her sister sat there gawking at the blue flames burning where the drone had plunged into the side of the crater.

"Safer," said Maya. "Umm, yeah. Sarah?"

"What?" she whispered.

"Are you okay?"

"Oh." Sarah looked down at herself. "I'm sitting on the dirt."

Maya crawled over to her. "I think you're in shock, too."

"A drone crashed," said Sarah, as tonelessly as if she'd commented soup was ready.

"Yes."

"It almost hit us."

Maya shook her by the shoulders, hating the way Sarah seemed to stare straight through her. "Can we freak out once we're somewhere safe?"

"I think I'm freaking out already."

"Yes. You are. I'm sorry. This is all my fault." Maya patted her lightly on the cheek a few times. "I need you to protect me right now. Can you freak out later?"

Sarah's eyes fluttered, and she screamed as if the crash had just happened.

"Screaming is good." Maya nodded. "Are you back with me?"

"Holy shit!" yelled Sarah. "That thing almost pasted us!"

Maya stood, and pulled her upright. "We have to get out of here."

"Okay." Sarah stooped to pick the Hornet up.

The same route they took to the surface last time remained, a series of desks, cargo containers, and a half-buried box truck formed a pathway up to a long dirt trail. Maya ran and hopped from surface to surface, making video game noises each time she jumped.

"This isn't funny," called Sarah, a desk behind her.

"I'm trying to distract myself from how scared I am."

"Oh." Sarah made a *'bwoing'* sound effect when she jumped.

At the end of the last cargo box, Maya crawled through the tangled mass of sharp rebar and dragged herself onto the open dirt trail that led to the crater edge at street level. She waited for Sarah to emerge, then jogged up to the concrete ridge. Fortunately, no new dosers had moved into the spot.

She waited for Sarah, then dashed over to the one doorway out, peering into the street. A few blocks down, groups of blueberries traded fire with Ascendant troops. The occasional civilian joined in, surprisingly on the side of the blueberries.

"Crap. We can't get back to the building. It's a warzone." Maya bit her lip, looking around.

"Ascendant's still going to be trying to find you there."

Maya turned toward her. "I don't think this is *all* about me anymore. It's open war. That woman from the hologram had a lab coat. Maybe she works for Ascendant and is trying to hurt them from inside?"

"If she works for Ascendant, going to see her is the stupidest thing you could do."

"And that zombie woman had a message, not a hand grenade." Maya headed down a side street. "If she wanted to kill me, she could have done it right there. We can't go back to our building and anywhere we go right now is going to be dangerous."

"Okay. Okay. Fine. I know the place. I used to go scrapping there a lot."

"Really? Lead the way."

"Yeah. Sometimes the people that run it would feed me since they said I was like a 'mood element.'"

"Huh?"

"The place has a nuclear war theme. I looked like a post-apocalyptic street kid or something in that crummy curtain."

Maya stopped, turned toward her, and grasped her cheeks in both hands. "Sarah... we *are* post-apocalyptic street kids."

"Not really. I mean, yeah. We're kids. I guess the apocalypse happened. But we're not street kids. We have a home."

"The population's at like eighteen percent of what it was before the war. That's an apocalypse."

Sarah resumed walking, still holding Maya's hand. "Okay. Maybe they were being nice and feeding me, but they said I looked like part of the scenery."

"Why haven't you gone back?"

"It's a long walk. There's dosers in the way, and you were here."

"Me?"

"Yeah. The food there is good, but it's not worth the danger. Besides, a lot of, umm, not nice people go there to eat."

"Oh. So it's a place criminals hang out?"

"I guess."

They rushed to the end of the block. Sarah tucked up to the corner of the building and peered around. Snaps and pops filled the Hab like a massive fireworks extravaganza. Distant metallic pings and weird twangy sounds came from ricochets every few seconds.

"Run as fast as you can across the street when I move."

Maya nodded.

Sarah waited a few seconds, then dashed out.

They sprinted across the paving. The patter of bare feet on road distracted a man in white armor into pivoting toward them. A spout of blood shot out of his helmet in time with a gunshot from farther down the street. Maya squealed and looked away. Barely a second after they passed the corner into the next block, a bullet glanced off the road nearby.

Sarah darted half a block down and dove to cover behind a wrecked car that still smoked from the rear end. Maya scooted up beside her. They simultaneously peered over the hood, watching a trio of men in white armor trade bullets with an Authority drone that weaved back and forth in the air. Sarah pushed her toward the rear end of the car.

They raced to the other side and ducked into an alley barely forty feet away from where the Ascendant guys took cover behind another car. The drone picked that moment to open up with a long burst, the .50 cal rounds Swiss-cheesing the car. Maya screamed and hit the ground, rolling onto her side a second before the vehicle detonated into a blast of sparks and metal debris. All three men collapsed in place, their armor perforated with holes.

Grunting, Maya sprang back to her feet and ran toward Sarah. They dodged from street to street, staying behind cars, flipped trucks—or in one case an Authority troop transport—continuous gunfire everywhere around them. Sarah appeared to be heading generally east, and after a few more blocks, they reached a part of the Hab with a considerably more rundown look than where they lived.

The rumble of an approaching heavy vehicle made Sarah dart into an alley, surprising a pack of gang members huddled behind dumpsters near the corner. One cross street farther down, three blueberries used a flipped truck for cover, pinned by a hail of fire from nine or so Ascendant troops. Three blueberries lay dead or dying nearby.

Maya looked at the twelve or so older teens, all of whom had armed themselves with rifles likely taken from blueberries or Ascendant dead. "Are you guys fighting or looting?"

"Uhh, looting," said a boy about nineteen with lime green hair.

She pointed. "It's nine on three. Those blueberries need help. You gotta help them!"

"Fuck blueberries." A young woman with black and purple hair raised a middle finger down the alley.

"I used to think that, too." Sarah stepped up. "They were *really* shitty to me. Used to leave me hogtied all the time because it made them laugh."

About half the gang punks grumbled and nodded.

"I hate that shit," said one.

"Ripped my pants off every time." The same teen girl with the multicolored hair scowled.

Sarah gave her a sad look. "They were really cruel to me, too. But... it has been different lately, right?"

The gang punks kept quiet.

"I know it has." Maya jumped at a nearby ricochet. "Those shitty blueberries that abused us? They're not blueberries anymore. They're wearing the white armor, thugs for Ascendant. You wanna pay them back for how they treated us?" She crouched and patted one of their rifles. "Now's your chance. Help the real blueberries."

The girl with black/purple hair clenched her jaw. "Fuckin' a right."

She popped up over the dumpster and fired at the Ascendant troops. The other gang members rushed to different spots, covering behind doorways, dumpsters, and—in one idiot's case—a plastiboard carton.

"Get outta here, kids," yelled a guy with black hair and a clear plastic jacket.

Two of the remaining blueberries glanced toward the new incoming fire, seeming stunned at the assistance from street punks. Ascendant troops scrambled to retreat as their position offered zero cover toward the angle the gang fired at them from; four of them went down.

Sarah shoved Maya out of the alley and jogged to the next street. After rounding that corner, they ran, ducking whenever a *bang* happened too close. Four blocks later, Sarah jumped up onto the hood of a large sedan, slid across, and landed in a sprint. Maya clambered over it and followed to a hiding spot against a concrete stoop on the left side of the road. Sarah peered over the top of the banister and gasped. Maya rose up to look, but Sarah pulled her down. A blaze of intense gunfire accompanied bullets bouncing everywhere, shredding the windows out of cars and striking the wall of the building above them. Broken glass fell to the sidewalk only a few feet away.

"Shit, this is bad," whispered Maya. "What's got the blueberries going nuts?"

"Not sure."

"This doesn't look like a great part of town."

Sarah cringed as a bullet pinged off the banister overhead. "It's not. It sucks. Bad."

"I don't care if dosers steal our shit. I won't even argue with them. We gotta get there."

"Uhh, I don't think there's any dosers out right now. They're probably hiding in basements... you know, where *children* belong in the middle of a damn war."

"Sorry," whispered Maya. "We tried to hide in a basement but it kinda collapsed."

Sarah huffed. "Well, we're already in the middle of it. Ground Zero's not far from here."

"I think we're *at* ground zero already."

"We're not—oh, duh. There's like twenty blueberries and more than that in white."

Maya blinked. "Where did they all come from?"

"Why are you asking me that?"

"Maybe I wasn't. Maybe I meant it as a rhetorical question."

Sarah sighed. "Why do you use big words?"

More bullets clicked and pinged off the building above them.

"Are they shooting at us?" yelled Maya.

"Umm. I don't think so. They're shooting at the blueberries, and missing, and those bullets are coming down the street."

"We should stay down."

Sarah stared at her. "Uhh, yeah."

At the whirr of drone fans approaching from behind, Maya looked up. Two white Ascendant drones, the three-fan types that used to orbit her penthouse prison, snuck up the street, flying barely five feet off the ground. Fortunately, their weapons didn't swivel toward a pair of unarmed children.

Maya eyed the edge of the stoop. She leapt to the right enough to stick her head out and shouted, "Blueberries! Look out! Drones behind you!"

Sarah screamed, grabbed her, and hauled her back behind the concrete.

Rapid rifle fire chattered, rattling Maya's brain inside her skull. She curled up in a ball with her hands clamped over her ears. Sarah squeezed her tight. A fusillade of clanks preceded a sharp *bang*. The drone on the left swerved and flew into the window of a building while the other one started shooting in the direction of the blueberries. It only managed a few seconds of fire before it flipped over and smashed upside down on the road. A baseball-sized chunk of concrete exploded out of the stoop three feet to Sarah's left.

Maya decided not to point that out, or even let her look in that direction. She grabbed Sarah by the hand and dragged her into a run powered by blind panic. They dashed across the street and into a narrow alley. Momentarily safe, no longer stuck behind a small porch right next to a gunfight, Maya wrapped her arms around Sarah and held on, trembling.

"I'm so damn scared right now," whispered Sarah.

"Me too."

"It's not your fault. We couldn't stay in that tunnel. It was collapsing."

Maya sniffled.

Another drone zoomed past the mouth of the alley, rushing toward the fighting. A long, low squeal of tires, like a huge truck sliding sideways, preceded a great *thud* that shook the paving beneath her feet. Maya stared down at her toes. All around her, the ground lay scattered with abandoned needles, derm sheets, pill bottles, beer cans, and objects she had no names for—but knew they related to illegal drugs.

"Umm, something really big just hit a building," said Maya. "And watch where you step. This alley is full of needles."

"Probably an APC," said Sarah. "Might've scratched the paint."

"Come on." Sarah held her hand and tiptoed around the deadly junk.

At the next possible chance to, she took a right turn. This street had no active fighting, which bothered Maya only because it felt strange not to see people trying to kill each other.

"Ugh."

"What?" asked Sarah.

"We're both going to be psychologically traumatized."

"So is everyone else who lives in the Hab." Sarah sighed. "No one is 'not broken.' It's really a question of how messed up we are."

An e-car raced out of a side street and screeched to a stop a short distance ahead of them. Maya flinched, but the man emerging from it wore the nice-ish clothes of someone who worked in the Sanc, but had a shell-shocked look to him suggesting a harrowing evening commute.

Maya sprinted up to him. "Excuse me."

The man paused halfway across the sidewalk to the nearby building, eyeing her warily. "What is it, kid?"

"Can I borrow your minicomputer for a sec?"

Sarah walked up beside her.

"You're going to steal it," said the man.

"Seriously?" Maya glared at him. "Do you know who I am?"

He looked her over. "Umm."

"Picture me in black pants and a black shirt instead of this dress."

"Oh!" His eyebrows went up, suspicion replaced with concern.

"Maya? What on Earth are you doing out in the streets right now? It's absolute chaos!"

"Trying not to die. Can I use your minicomputer for a sec? Please?"

"Sure." He fished it out of his pocket, typed in an unlock code, and handed it to her.

Maya opened a recording app and held the minicomputer up, looking into the camera. She appeared thin and waiflike on the screen, her dress somewhat dingy but not 'street rat' filthy. Intermittent, but frequent, gunfire provided the background music for the video she planned to make.

"People of the Hab and Citizens of the Baltimore Sanctuary Zone, it is important that you listen to me. Weeks ago, I spoke to you and tried to peel away the lies that Ascendant had been feeding you. As you can see, I'm a child. I'm nine years old. When I recorded that message, I thought the truth would go out there about Fade and everything would be different and nice like *that*." She snapped her fingers. "It didn't work that way. Real life isn't a kid's story.

"The truth didn't make the evil queen go away in a flash. But, look around you. The blueberries are *helping* us. Sorry, I know you guys hate that term, but I'm scared out of my mind right now and it's easier. Ascendant troops tried to kill me, an unarmed child, a little while ago. Blueberries saved my ass. I'm a Non now. Just like a lot of you out in the Hab. The fake Authority who were so mean to us aren't wearing the blue anymore. They're the creeps in white, working for that woman who wants to own you all."

Maya glanced down, pausing a few seconds.

"If you look outside, you'll see there's a war happening around us. I don't know where that woman found so many thugs, but the Authority are fighting in the streets *right now* trying to protect you and me. They're *dying* to help us. If you have a weapon, a gun, a sword, a *car*, anything... help them. Support the blueberries. Don't just sit back and let Vanessa keep owning you. We need the Authority, but they're outnumbered. Some of them even came from other Sancs to help clean ours up. They need you, too."

She paused for a few breaths, summoning up her most earnest pleading stare.

"I hope I'm still alive when this is over. But just in case I don't get the chance to say it then, I'll say it now. Thank you."

Maya flicked her thumb across the button at the bottom of the screen, stopping the recording. A few clicks opened an email client, and she sent the video to Zeroice with the message: 'get this to our friends. It needs to go out *ASAP*.'

Maya handed the minicomputer back to the man. "Thank you."

He dabbed a tear off his cheek. "Come on inside. You can shelter here 'til this passes."

"I can't. I've gotta get somewhere specific, but thanks."

"Okay." The man nodded. "You gotta stay alive, kid. Baltimore ain't got much heart left these days, but you're it."

Maya smiled at him and walked onward. At the end of the next block, she stopped and glanced at Sarah. "Where is this place?"

"Two blocks that way." She pointed. "You still want to go?"

"I'm scared of every option at this point, and this is closest."

Sarah chuckled, but sounded more nervous than amused. "Yeah."

22

GROUND ZERO

Sarah took off at a sprint. Maya groaned in her mind, but bolted after her, trying to keep up as they weaved around trashcans and a few pedestrians, none of whom paid two children any mind. At the first side street, Sarah stopped to check for cars or bullets passing by, then darted onward.

Blaring noise erupted from every speaker, car, drone, terminal, and minicomputer all at once. The horrendous, disharmonic wail lasted only a few seconds before Maya's voice flooded the air, playing the message she'd recorded only a moment before. Her image appeared on a giant screen a few buildings behind them, so sad and forlorn, even a non-sentient android might've pitied her.

"Wow. Do I really look that... that... umm, terrified?"

Sarah glanced back and forth between the screen and her. "Yeah." She held up her trembling hands. "Don't feel bad. I'm still at 'never been this scared before' levels of oh shit."

"I'm a bad influence. You're starting to swear."

"I think it's more the influence of being shot at."

"Hey." Maya forced a cheesy smile. "At least they're not shooting *at* us this time, like in the woods, right? Just stray bullets."

Sarah stared.

Maya hugged her. "Yeah. C'mon. we're almost there."

She jogged to the next corner and stopped at the curb, gazing across the intersection at a huge one-story building. A rusting metal arc cut to resemble a massive bear trap wrapped around the corner over the entrance. Welded-on rebar bent into letters spelled out 'Ground Zero' at the midpoint of the 'trap.' Barbed wire, old tires, sandbag bunkers and a whole bunch of fake 'nuclear bombs' decorated the walls. Three spiked-to-hell cars added to the décor as well, clearly props and not recent crashes.

Maya gulped. That place didn't look like anywhere a child should even look at much less enter. Despite the continuing gunfire echoing off the buildings in every direction, she momentarily considered trying to go home instead. Ground Zero worried her more than the prison she'd waltzed into to save Genna. Maybe that woman wasn't even here since they took too long. Of course, home sat far away behind a lot of bullets.

Might as well at least check it out. The owners fed Sarah, so maybe it's not as dangerous as it looks.

She took a few breaths for courage, then rushed diagonally across the intersection, ignoring the intermittent flash of gunfire in all four directions blocks away. A pair of double doors at the corner covered in dented hubcaps and faux bullet holes opened with far less effort than she expected. Maya padded over rubberized floor mats to a second set of doors, empty aluminum frames with no glass inside them. She didn't bother opening those, instead ducking under the push bar into a room heavy with the smell of spicy food. Aisles to the right and left led past dozens of booth seats. The middle portion of the restaurant contained a bar with a few grey-poncho-clad Nons munching on food. A guy with a ten-inch purple Mohawk and no shirt behind the bar poured another drink for a laughing woman in normal clothes.

Almost everyone in the place except for the staff stared at minicomputers, watching the last few seconds of Maya's video message.

Four or five women in skimpy outfits involving leather, license plates, metal cups over their chests, or old sports padding, waited tables along with two men dressed like skeevers. Maya stopped short, breath caught in her throat at the memory of thirty or so people surrounding them in the Humvee. *They look* too *much like wildland cannibals.*

"Aww, hi girls," said a friendly-sounding female voice on her left.

Maya glanced to her left at a six-foot-plus woman in a tiny black sports bra with white skulls over her breasts and leather skirt. The left half of her head sported a buzz cut, but long blonde hair hung down to her waist on the other side. Streaks of lime green decorated the shaved portion. A leather strap across her stomach held a holster at her hip, and the gun in it looked fairly real. Despite the outfit, she held a menu tucked under one arm.

"Are your parents outside?" asked the woman.

"Technically, yes, they're outside." Maya gulped. "But not close outside. I'm supposed to meet someone here."

The woman's eyes narrowed. "Oh, hell no. What are you kids doing? Meeting a stranger? That's dangerous."

Maya shook her head. "No. It's not like that. They're helping me."

"I was starting to doubt you'd make it," said another woman from the right, her voice on the deeper end of female.

Sarah jumped with a gasp. She spun away from the waitress and grabbed on to Maya.

The second woman wore an ordinary grey poncho bedecked with tiny hoses and wires like almost every other adult in the Hab. The high collar, a wall of fabric as tall as the tip of her nose, surrounded her head. Silvery-white hair cascaded over it to mid chest, and her right eye glowed bright red. The left eye appeared normal except for a scarlet iris. She extended her right arm, an artificial limb of dark blue metal engraved with a thorns-and-roses pattern. A black fingerless glove somewhat covered the hand.

"My name is Reykjavik. I've been sent to protect you."

Maya looked the woman over. Aside from her metal arm and obviously electronic eye, she didn't have any wounds or damage and appeared on the young side, likely still in her twenties. She did not, however, radiate much warmth, instead giving off an unsettling blankness, neither threatening nor reassuring.

"So, would you three like a table?" asked the half blonde.

"Thank you," said Reykjavik, "but we don't have time."

A loud *crash* of plates and metal pots came from the back of the restaurant. Men shouted, one yelled in alarm. Everyone in the room shifted to look toward a pair of flapping plastic doors spray painted with 'Death Alley' and a crude skull.

Maya smirked. *Not the best thing to put on the doors to the kitchen.*

Two men in white Ascendant armor, both splashed with blood and grime, burst into the room. They appeared more intent on getting away from whatever chased them than bothering with the people in here, and hurried toward the exit.

People in booths ducked down as the men advanced, waving their rifles back and forth at everyone as if they expected the entire room to pull guns on them. Reykjavik grabbed the girls, tugging them behind her and edging out of the way. Maya scooted back before the woman's heavy boot crushed her unprotected toes. The half blonde waitress rushed off and took cover under the table of an empty booth.

"Hey," said the lead trooper. "That's her..." He swung his rifle toward Maya.

Reykjavik sprang forward with such speed her body appeared to stretch into a blur of color, a long, curved blade extending from her metal arm. She punched it into the chest of the closer man, wrenching his aim away from the girls as she catapulted herself up and over him. Bullets sprayed the left side of the room, detonating drinks and food in explosions of white foam or orange sauce. A few screams of pain rang out.

The second man squeezed off a single bullet in Maya's direction, but his cringe from Reykjavik's charge sent his shot high, striking something above and behind her with a dull metal *clank*. Maya shrieked and dove to her knees under a rain of sparks falling on her. Reykjavik ripped her blade out of the trooper's chest. He swooned forward and fell to his knees, staring down at the gaping wound in his chest.

Growling, the second one tried to bring his rifle around on Reykjavik. She kicked it aside while swiping her blade downward in a slash that cut the top two-thirds of his head off at an angle. Before Maya could even scream, the woman sprang up, punched the blade in and out of his chest, and finished with a spinning kick that threw the body over a nearby table, splattering a burger and beer on the window. The meat patty slid a few inches down the glass, smearing ketchup, then plopped back to the table.

Two guys hiding under that booth didn't complain about their food being ruined.

The severed portion of Ascendant trooper head hit the ground with plastic *thunk*, like a dropped bowl of raw meat.

Sarah started to scream, but collapsed to her knees, vomiting.

Reykjavik stabbed her arm blade into the back of the first trooper, picked him up by it, and hurled him across the restaurant into the bar, where he lay draped for a few seconds before slithering onto the floor out of sight. After slinging that arm to the side to flick blood from the blade, she made a fist, and the wicked thing snapped back into the limb with a *shink*.

The woman fast-walked over to the girls. "We have to go, *now*. Maya, come with me."

"I'm not going anywhere without Sarah."

"Then both of you come with me right now."

Maya shook her head. "You should stay with us until our parents are home. I don't think I should go anywhere with someone I don't really know."

"Yeah." Sarah coughed and spat bile to the side. "'Specially someone with a blade in their arm."

Reykjavik managed something approaching a sympathetic expression. "There's no time. Look. If I wanted to hurt you..."

"Sorry." Maya held up a hand. "I'm at my lifetime limit for kidnappings. I can't approve another one."

The woman sighed. "This isn't a kidnapping. Authority and Ascendant are actively shooting at each other. The Sanc is on lockdown. The Hab's about to be on lockdown. You've got a giant target on your back."

"I knew that already." Maya frowned. "Who is it this time?"

"People who want to wrest control of Ascendant away from Vanessa," said Reykjavik.

"Been there, done that. I'm highly allergic to needles full of neurotoxin."

Reykjavik took a knee in front of the girls, a hand each on their shoulders. "I understand your worries, but the situation is dangerous. We don't have time to wait."

"I'm sorry. You seem like a really nice highly trained killer, but I can't go anywhere with you until my parents are here." Maya smoothed her hands down the front of her dress. "Do you have a minicomputer? I can send a message to them to meet us here."

"There is no time." Reykjavik bowed her head and sighed. "Dammit."

"What?" asked Sarah.

Reykjavik looked up and pulled the fabric wall half covering her face down, exposing lips painted dark violet. She opened her mouth and exhaled faint white fog in the girls' faces.

Maya tried to hold her breath, but a tingly numbness spread up her nose. "Crap," she muttered as her legs turned to jelly. "Not again."

The room melted into a haze of color, then the darkness of her face mushing into Reykjavik's poncho. Maya vaguely noticed Sarah pressed against her before blacking out.

23

UNTIL THE DUST SETTLES

F oggy thoughts swirled around Maya's head while the faint taste
of mint lingered in her mouth, its coldness reaching up into her
sinuses. She gradually became aware of consciousness while
alternating between a sense of free fall and lying upon something soft.
Eventually, the feeling of a padded cushion beneath her overpowered
the vertigo.

Dammit. Dammit. Dammit.

She remained still out of dread, not wanting to move and find herself
tied up. A moment or two later, the wooziness of whatever knocked her
out faded. She couldn't detect any tightness around her wrists or ankles,
so she opened her eyes.

Maya found herself in a clean but small room, flat on her back
upon a twin-sized bed. She reached with one hand to rub her face, then
sat up. Sarah lay next to her, already awake, staring at the ceiling.
Windowless walls of pale grey surrounded them in an approximate
cube, though it had more space than her bedroom back home. Two
LED tubes behind frosted plastic in the ceiling glowed painfully
bright. An industrial type steel door painted dull red offered the only
way out, though she expected it to be locked. A squat table opposite the
door held a flat panel monitor and a video game system hastily stuffed
into a shelf, not even hooked up. One blue throw rug provided the only

break from the otherwise bare concrete floor. Cool air that smelled like damp sneakers blew in from a square vent near the ceiling in the back corner.

"We got kidnapped again, didn't we?" whispered Maya.

"Yeah. They took the Hornet. And my tools."

Maya glanced at her legs for the visual reassurance of not being tied up, and sighed in frustration and mild relief. "Sorry for not believing you."

"It's okay," said Sarah, sounding *way* too calm. "I still don't believe it's because we aren't wearing shoes."

Maya laughed.

"Any idea who they are or what they want?"

"No." Maya climbed over Sarah to get off the bed, and stood on the rug—watching the walls sway closer and retreat. "Whoa..." She fell backward to sit on the edge of the mattress. "Dizzy."

"Yeah. I got up a minute ago and checked the door. The room was spinning around so much I almost threw up again."

"That woman really needs to brush her teeth," said Maya. "Her breath could knock out a moose."

Sarah laughed. "What's a moose?"

"A big animal." Maya breathed in deep and exhaled hard several times.

"What are you doing?"

"Trying to get rid of bad crap. Fresh air. Clear my head."

"Oh."

Maya glanced back at her. "Are you freaking out again? You sound way too calm."

"I was thinking about what that woman said." Sarah pushed herself up to sit. "She killed those two guys in like three seconds. If she wanted to hurt us, she could've killed us easily. Maybe these people aren't dangerous."

"I have trust issues with anyone who kidnaps me."

"Genna?" asked Sarah.

Maya smiled. "I don't consider that a kidnapping. They rescued me... well, at least Genna did. Okay, maybe the mercs kidnapped me, but Genna saved me from them as well as Vanessa."

"Hey, what's that on your back?" asked Sarah.

"Eep!" Maya froze, terrified at what that statement could mean: wound, giant bug, dart, electronic bug.... "What?"

The bed shifted with Sarah's motion. She pulled Maya's dress down off her shoulder a little. "Oh. It's a bandage. You've got two of them."

"Bandage?" Maya shivered. "Oh, crap. What did they do to me?"

"There's some blood on your dress. Maybe you got hurt?"

Maya curled up in a ball, chin on her knees. "Or maybe they put a tracker chip or something that'll like release poison in me if I don't do what they want."

"They can do that?"

"I dunno."

Maya heaved with a sudden upwelling of fear. "Or, maybe they gave me those mind-control nanobots."

"Umm." Sarah poked at her back. "There's holes in your dress by each bandage. I think you got hurt." The mattress wobbled again. "Hey, I've got some bandages, too."

Maya looked. A few small gauze patches clung to Sarah's left arm, left calf, and right thigh. None of them looked large enough to be worrisome, and it didn't seem likely that their mysterious captors would do something nefarious to Sarah.

"I gotta pee," whispered Maya.

"Did that already." Sarah sighed.

"Eww." Maya started checking the bed.

"No, not here. When that .50 cal hit the porch near my head."

Maya gulped. "You saw that?"

"A giant bullet hitting the wall two feet from my head is kinda hard to miss." She shivered.

"I'm really sorry. For everything. We're gonna be messed up for life."

Sarah chuckled. "I'm already messed up for life. The blueberries did that. Being close to a gunfight isn't as scary as when they left me zip tied all day not knowing if I would ever see my Dad again. It's not like those guys were *trying* to shoot us. We were just too close to a fight."

"Yeah."

After sitting there for a few minutes, Maya got up and roamed around the room. Of course, she had to try the doorknob, but it refused to turn. Her pacing eventually stopped beneath the air vent.

"Let's escape. Boost me?"

Sarah rolled off the bed and trudged over. She squatted by the wall, allowing Maya to climb up to stand on her shoulders. As Sarah rose to her feet, Maya hand-walked up the wall until Sarah reached her full height.

"Wow, it's a good thing you weigh like only ten pounds." Sarah giggled into her hand.

Maya raspberried. She tugged at the vent cover, but it refused to move. Eight screws, two at each corner, held it fast. Gazing down into a duct plenty big enough for them to crawl into behind the bars teased her with unattainable hope.

"Argh!" She banged her fist on the vent. "We need a screwdriver to get this open."

Sarah eased herself down again. Maya hopped off her and folded her arms, scowling at everything.

"I'm so sick of being kidnapped."

"Hey, maybe this'll work out. If Ascendant loses, I mean."

Maya collapsed to the floor and sighed. "Yeah. If."

"Ugh. I hope they let us out of here. A bathroom would be nice."

"You said..."

"Trying to cheer you up with a joke."

"Oh."

"Should we try the 'banging on the door and begging' thing or just wait?" asked Maya.

"I dunno."

They sat in silence for a few minutes until the soft thumping of boots approached outside. Maya leapt up to her feet, but Sarah moved protectively in front of her.

Two soft clicks preceded the door opening inward. Reykjavik, no longer wearing the poncho, stood in the gap. Her black T-shirt bore white-green letters with a fuzzy quality that read 'Echo Overdrive.' The woman's matching black BDU pants made Maya miss hers. Under the glow of the ceiling light, her metal arm glimmered, the decorative engraving of roses and thorns all the way from wrist to shoulder.

"Don't take it personally," said Reykjavik. "I didn't have time to argue with a pair of kids in the middle of a warzone. We're trying to help you. C'mon. Doctor Haas wants to talk to you."

"I'm not really inclined to trust people who lock me up." Maya met the woman's gaze with 'polite defiance.'

Sarah nudged her.

"What?" rasped Maya.

Sarah glanced back and whispered, "Might not wanna piss off a woman who can kill two guys with rifles in three seconds using a blade."

"So? Mom can do that."

Reykjavik grinned. "It's cool. I like her attitude. C'mon. The doc will explain everything."

"Bathroom first, please," said Maya.

"Yeah, sure." Reykjavik backed away from the door.

"How did you lose your arm?" asked Sarah.

"I didn't. Born that way, only a little nub. My employer helped me out with this." She held up the metal hand, opening and closing the fingers. "Not much market for a merc with one arm, and I couldn't afford this sucker myself... so, we helped each other."

Maya walked out into a corridor lined with numerous doors on both sides, as well as pushcarts and gurneys. The overwhelming whiteness despite the grunge of abandonment suggested a decommissioned hospital basement or something along those lines. Reykjavik walked close behind, one hand on each of their shoulders, steering them gently down the corridor.

Though she didn't squeeze or grip roughly, having a metal hand so close to her neck made Maya doubt she'd make it to the toilet in time. This woman had killed those two Ascendant troops with no more emotional reaction than sweeping the floor. It seemed likely she'd be capable of hurting young girls if they tried to run away.

They reached a small one-person bathroom. Reykjavik waited outside while the girls took their turns, then led them back the way they'd come and down another hallway past several rooms that appeared to be former operating suites repurposed to labs. Sarah looked around, every so often trembling hard enough that her body shook visibly. Maya's fear receded at that, replaced with anger at these people for frightening her 'big sister.'

Reykjavik stopped at a black metal door. She let go of Maya to slide it open, then encouraged her with five prodding fingers at her back to step inside a large rectangular room, crisscrossed with plastic hoses.

Maya gasped at the freezing metal floor. Scientific equipment packed a table along the opposite wall, most of it reasonably modern in appearance—and quite functional. Maybe twenty feet from the door, pushcarts, junk, and discarded food cartons littered the area around a desk where a woman in a lab coat typed feverishly at a computer terminal.

"Ooh," whispered Sarah. "So cold!"

Reykjavik guided the girls over to the desk. Maya watched where she stepped, avoiding hoses, wires, and the occasional metal bracket.

"Doctor Haas?" asked Reykjavik.

Maya looked up at the same moment the doctor peeled her gaze off the terminal screen.

A bob of super-pale blonde hair framed the face of a woman in her late thirties with a narrow nose and sharp chin. A pervasive sense of exhaustion radiated from her, along with a feeling somewhere between 'I could be mean to you but I'm too tired to bother' and 'someone just shoot me.'

Sarah hugged herself, shivering. Small puffs of fog appeared at her mouth. "Why is it so cold in here?"

"Hello, Maya. I am Doctor Nora Haas. I apologize for your involuntary relocation. I'd expected you to be willing to at least meet with me."

"That's a funny way to say kidnapping. And I *was* willing to meet with you—after my parents came back." She held her arms out to the sides for a second before letting them flop down. "Well, I'm here. What did you want to tell me?"

Dr. Haas rubbed the bridge of her nose. "I used to work for your mother's company."

"Stop right there." Maya held a finger up. "That woman is not my mother."

"All right. Vanessa's company. I was working on an advanced, secret project, but the woman appropriated my research and was planning to use it for nefarious purposes."

Maya tapped her foot. "Exactly what other sort of purpose does mind control have?"

"Huh?" asked Sarah.

"Nefarious means evil," whispered Maya.

"Then why not just say 'evil,'" whisper-shouted Sarah.

Maya scratched her head. "I dunno. 'Nefarious' feels more appropriate when it's someone really smart being evil."

Dr. Haas bowed her head. For a second, she appeared about to fall asleep, but sighed. "I know. I know. Mind control is evil. I wasn't given much of a choice insofar as developing the nanomachines that could effectively manipulate a person's thoughts and moods. However, once chaos erupted within the Sanctuary Zone, I managed to wipe the files and destroy the prototypes while making my escape."

"If you destroyed the prototypes, what are *you* using? That woman who brought the hologram was clearly under the influence of your project."

Dr. Haas smiled, her eyes half closed. "You are as smart as your reputation claims. I do have a little left, though I have no plans to use it."

"Yeah. That's what every mad scientist says," muttered Sarah.

"All right." Maya scratched her head. "So, umm... that still doesn't explain why you needed me."

"You are here to keep you safe. While I was purging the Project Unilateralis files, I stumbled across a mis-sent email that contained orders to Ascendant security forces to terminate you."

Maya closed her eyes in thought, mentally going back over old e-learns. "Orph... No Ophiocordyceps Unilateralis. Nice. That's seriously effing creepy."

Reykjavik, standing behind the girls, emitted a faint grunt of confusion.

"Don't keep primitive girl in the dark." Sarah nudged her.

The augmented woman smirked at Sarah.

"Not you." Sarah tapped herself on the chest. "I'm talking about me."

Maya grasped her sister's hand. "It's a fungus that takes over ants' brains. She named her nanobots after a creepy brain-control spore."

Dr. Haas' eyebrows went up. "Very impressive, Maya. And yes, I thought it was appropriate. Though, the intent behind Project Unilateralis was not to cause the subject's demise. Initially, the work started as an effort to conquer fear, hesitation, and self-doubt.... Something we could market to people who would willingly take it in order to overcome their inhibitions. But, Vanessa wanted to use it for military applications."

Maya shuddered. "She wanted to make the security troops as cold and heartless as she is. Totally obedient."

"Indeed. I feared the same as you. And, she seemed rather fascinated by the potential to expose unwitting people to the agent and control them like robots. Alas or fortunately depending on how you look at it, I have not been able to fine tune that control. People under the effect of the nanomachines are quite zombie like and unable to perform complex tasks. Even opening doors is a little beyond them."

"I noticed." Maya frowned. "Speaking of which... what did you do to us? The bandages?"

"Oh." Dr. Haas finally gave off a sense of genuine concern. "Please relax. Both of you had numerous bits of concrete debris embedded in your skin, as well as some minuscule bullet fragments."

Maya narrowed her eyes. "I didn't feel anything."

"Of course not. You would have been in shock. Fragments like what I removed from you appeared consistent with shrapnel from high-energy projectiles striking hard surfaces, no doubt while you were caught out in the fighting. Your adrenaline and, dare I say, shock, didn't give you the chance to notice such superficial injuries. I simply removed the foreign objects from you and gave you both a fairly potent dose of antibiotics."

Maya measured the woman for a few seconds, then accepted she'd done as she said. "Thanks."

"So that's it?" asked Sarah. "You just wanted to keep us safe from Ascendant?"

"Well, there is a small favor I was going to ask in return," said Dr. Haas.

"I'm nine and I've come *way* too close to getting killed *way* too often over the past two weeks. I'm sorry, but I'm done doing missions. I really want to make it to my tenth birthday. All I want to do is go home and be a normal damn kid."

Dr. Haas smiled. "I'm sorry, Maya. But you can't be normal. You are exceptional. Please never settle for normal. Also, do not worry. The favor I would ask of you is simply information. You don't need to *do* anything but talk to me."

Maya's teeth chattered. She glanced down at her numb toes,

desperately missing the shoes that sat on her bedroom floor... and her socks. "What?"

"I need your help to know where Vanessa is."

"Seriously?" Maya's mouth hung open. "Why do you think I give a shit where that woman is, or would have any way to know? She disowned me and I don't care. I was nothing but a piece of property to her."

Sarah bounced, rubbing her hands up and down her arms. "Could you maybe like interrogate us in a warmer room?"

Dr. Haas tried to project sympathy and didn't quite manage it. "Maya, we know about a particular individual who used to live in your building. A man who rather deserved what happened to him."

Maya cringed, sick to her stomach. "Mason."

Sarah wrapped her arms around Maya. "Die, bastard."

"Yes. Some associates of mine and I know that you planted certain information in his possession that resulted in Ascendant security carrying out 'enhanced interrogation' on the man, which he did not survive."

She's probably at the Shroud. That's the one almost no one knows about. Maya clenched her fists at the sudden thought that maybe Vanessa *did* order her killed to safeguard those addresses. The worry passed as fast as it appeared. The woman had ample time to kill her when they'd been at the penthouse. If she'd been worried about security, she'd have quietly done away with her instead of forcing her to film a video trying to lie her way back to power. And, she couldn't forget the look of utter shock in Vanessa's eyes when Maya had begged Genna not to kill the bitch.

No, on some strange biological level, a thin strand of familial loyalty did exist between them—though one would need a scanning electron microscope to find it. She shivered at the cold, figuring Dr. Haas did that on purpose as an interrogation technique, making her want to get out of here as fast as possible to a warm bed again. Still, she couldn't quite find enough hate for Vanessa to want the woman assassinated, much less help it happen. No, better for her to fall from power and be imprisoned.

She thought of claiming 'child' as a defense, but Haas knew she'd provided addresses to implicate Mason in something he had no knowledge of. Of course, Haas did not know *which* addresses, or she wouldn't have needed to ask Maya anything. She pictured the list of nineteen she'd handwritten.

"Vanessa has eighteen locations that can serve as her 'away office.' Three of them are top secret and only a handful of people know about them. If she's gone into hiding, she'd most likely be at one of those three. Either Pimlico, Graceland Park, or Beechfield. Those are the three super-secret ones."

Reykjavik reached between the girls to grab a tablet from the desk and handed it to Maya. "Here, kid. Just type them in, okay?"

Maya took the tablet, already open to a notes application. She entered the physical address for the Pimlico Secure Facility, buried under an old racetrack. Next, she keyed in the Graceland Park bunker, and last, the address for an Ascendant distribution center in Beechfield. That place had no secure office for Vanessa to hide in, but hopefully, these people would believe it merely difficult to find and waste a bunch of time searching a useless place.

"There." She handed the tablet to Reykjavik. "Those are the top three."

"Might as well give us the whole list, just in case," said Dr. Haas.

Maya let the cold seep into her thoughts, shivering out of control. "It's so cold in here. Can't we go somewhere warmer? Please?"

"Just type the addresses out and you can warm up." Reykjavik smiled, though it came off mildly psychotic coupled with a glowing red eye.

Sarah squatted and wrapped her arms around her legs, shivering.

"Okay. Okay." Maya tried to act more childlike than usual in hopes they'd think she routinely did as she was told. Of course, if they knew about Mason, they also knew how crafty she could be. Maybe Haas would recognize her overdone 'little girl trying to make adults happy' act as the manipulation it was.

Shaking from the cold, she typed out the other fifteen addresses, marking the ones she believed to be decoys as such. Neither Haas nor Reykjavik reacted at all to when she said eighteen, so she had a good bit of confidence neither of them knew the true number. She kept one address to herself—the Shroud at Double Rock. If Vanessa really had gone into hiding, odds favored she'd be at that one.

Maya hated that place because of the super fancy carpet and

furniture. Vanessa never let her touch anything there, veritably locking her in her bedroom so she didn't 'contaminate' the rest of the bunker with fingerprints, dirt, or the swath of destruction the woman believed followed in the wake of anyone under eighteen years of age. That site offered the greatest amount of security as well as the largest floorplan, nicest accommodations, and longest-lasting supply of resources.

"Here." Maya handed the tablet back. "That's all of them. I have no idea which one she'd go to, but probably not the decoys. But maybe she would use one of those since they're decoys and she wouldn't expect anyone to look there. Those top three are the best options since only like six people know they exist."

Sarah paced back and forth, shaking. "My feet are numb."

"Come on, kids." Reykjavik walked up behind them and pressed a hand to their backs. "You can warm up in your room."

"Umm," said Maya. "I gave you the addresses. Why are you keeping us?"

Sarah stepped on a plastic hose, lost her balance, and fell against the desk. "Sorry." She slid down to her knees and sat on the floor. "Ow."

"Are you okay?" Maya rushed to help her up.

"Yeah. Stupid hoses." Sarah stood and glanced back at the desk, specifically at her Hornet. "Hey, can I have my Hornet back? My father gave that to me. It's sentimental."

"Later, girls." Dr. Haas read over the tablet. "You don't need it right this moment. You're perfectly safe here."

Reykjavik grasped the girls each by one wrist and led them out of the freezing lab, towing them back to the room they woke up in. After ushering them inside, she eased the door closed.

Two soft *clicks* came from the knob.

"How long are you going to keep us captive?" Maya glared at the door.

"You're not captives," said Reykjavik. "You're in protective custody."

Maya raised a middle finger.

"We'll be okay." Sarah pulled her into a hug and patted her back.

A tremor in her sister's voice betrayed the lie of her words—or at least the doubt. Sarah probably fought the urge to burst into tears in an effort to make Maya feel better. She couldn't quite figure out what Dr. Haas would do with them, though it probably involved being held prisoner until her people killed Vanessa. After, they'd undoubtedly force her to give up any claim on inheriting Ascendant under pain of death. That, Maya had no problem with. She'd be overjoyed to walk clear away from that company without looking back, like peeling the target off her back and burning it.

But... she didn't fully trust Dr. Haas would let her live.

24

WOULD YOU RATHER

Eyeing the ceiling, walls, and floor, Maya paced around their holding cell-slash-bedroom. An unpleasant crustiness to the oval blue rug suggested this room had once been flooded. At least the place didn't stink like mold. She couldn't find anything that looked like a camera or listening device, but still didn't expect they enjoyed any semblance of privacy. Haas probably had a video feed on her desk, watching every move they made. The woman had known she'd set Mason up for death, so she would most likely anticipate Maya doing as much as possible to escape, and that she'd be difficult to contain.

Or she'd overestimated the power of a video game system to keep her attention. It did, however, tempt Sarah, who'd already hooked up all the wiring.

A small shelf between the head end of the bed and the wall contained a number of random things likely grabbed in haste. One teddy bear, a couple dolls, some 'action figures,' toy space ship, two mini electronic games, and a kiddie drawing tablet that used a 'pencil' with a magnetic tip to 'write' on a grey field of tiny hexagons. Maya grabbed it, crawled onto the bed, and waved at Sarah who sat cross-legged on the floor in front of the TV.

"C'mere," she whispered, then ducked under the sheets like a tent.

If nothing else, curling up in bed under the covers *totally* beat that freezing cold room.

A few seconds after the sounds of video game paused, Sarah scooted in headfirst. "What are you doing?"

"I'm cold," said Maya, a little louder than normal. She pointed at the toy tablet and wrote, ‹Cameras and microphones.›

"*Yeah.* Me too."

Maya swiped the bar back and forth to erase the screen, then wrote, ‹I didn't give her all the addresses.›

Sarah went bug eyed. She swiped the erase bar and wrote, ‹Y? Help V bitch?›

‹She's not in those places. Somewhere else.›

"*Why...* is it so cold in there?" muttered Sarah.

"I'm not inclined to trust people who kidnap us and keep us locked up."

"Okay." Sarah took the plastic 'pen' and wrote, ‹I got my lock stuf. Fake tript.›

Maya giggled, erased the screen, and wrote, ‹Nice! You ARE a pickpocket. And you can't spell.›

"No, not really. Just sneaky." She grinned and scribbled, ‹Can't steel from pokitz.› She stuck her tongue out and added, ‹Don't right much.›

"Ouch. Just ouch." Maya grinned.

"Miss smarty pants," muttered Sarah.

"I don't have pants right now." She tugged at her dress.

Sarah rolled her eyes, erased the pad, and wrote, ‹What plan?›

‹Plan is get outta here!›

"Oh, yeah, obviously," whispered Sarah. "How?"

Maya swiped the bar back and forth to clear the screen, then wrote, ‹Wait for dark. They'll think we're trapped and can't get out. When they sleep, we go.›

"Okay. Oh, I think I can feel my toes again."

"Ugh." Maya rubbed her feet. "Yeah. That room was way too cold."

"Hey, how does that magic thingee work?" Sarah poked the tablet.

Maya doodled some lines. "Metal shavings. The pen's a magnet that makes them stick to the top."

"Oh."

Their plan established, Maya threw the blankets back and crawled to the floor, sitting in front of the video game unit. Sarah joined her, and they spent a while playing a co-op fantasy game running around killing orcs and goblins. The simple hack-and-slash mechanics didn't involve any sort of character advancement, merely score and occasional power-ups that gave temporary abilities. Normally, Maya would've thought it annoying and simplistic, but the mindlessness of it did help make the waiting bearable.

A *click* at the door preceded it swinging inward. Reykjavik stepped in far enough to set a tray on the floor by the girls, which held two bowls of breaded chicken nuggets and a pair of juice cartons.

"I'll be back in about half an hour to take you to the bathroom. After that, it's bedtime."

"Sorry to be such a burden," said Maya. "If you didn't lock the door, we could go to the bathroom ourselves."

Reykjavik patted her on the head. "Nice try. Look, kid. We know more about you than you think we do. I totally get that you're unhappy being here, but you're locked in so you don't run off and get yourself hurt. Things are... chaotic out there right now."

"If you're worried about us, why won't you let us call our parents?" asked Sarah.

"Wouldn't matter." Reykjavik stood, her red, glowing eye gazing straight ahead into some other reality. "The Hab and the Sanc are in total lockdown mode. No one who isn't Authority or Ascendant Military can travel even two blocks."

"They don't have a military," snapped Maya. "They have assholes in armor."

"Who's winning?" asked Sarah.

"Can't say. There's more blueberries, but Ascendant seems to have better equipment. You two eat now, then get ready for bed. Nothing can hurt you in here short of another nuke landing right on top of us."

Maya shot a sour look at the bowl of nuggets while Reykjavik backed out and locked the door. "I *hate* being a prisoner."

"Who doesn't?" Sarah shrugged and picked up one bowl.

"I know, but... most people don't get kidnapped four times in like three months."

Sarah grinned around the nugget she bit in half. "Are you a professional kidnap victim yet?"

"No, just experienced." Maya grumbled and picked up her bowl. "Professionals get paid."

A sad giggle leaked out Sarah's nose.

They ate the bland nuggets in silence. She neither liked nor disliked them, though did appreciate their warmth. A few minutes after they resumed the video game, Reykjavik returned.

"Maya, come on." She pointed at Sarah. "You stay for now."

She got up and walked over. The woman took hold of Maya's left wrist with her metal hand, though didn't squeeze uncomfortably tight. Reykjavik guided her out of the room, locked the door again, then led her down the corridor. Maya walked slow, peering into all the doors on either side as much as she could. Most appeared unused and full of junk, but one room on the right contained something akin to an operating table and numerous white storage cabinets full of tiny bottles. *That's the clinic...* Reykjavik tugged her onward past several more storage rooms packed with moldy furniture to a small one-person bathroom. The woman nudged her in, and waited outside.

"What if we have to go in the middle of the night?" asked Maya at the closed door. "Will you hear us if we shout?"

"I'll leave a bucket. Gonna be away for a little while, and Haas won't unlock the door when she's here alone."

Maya pulled her dress up and took a seat, shaking her head. "That woman's seriously afraid of *us?*"

"Heh. Not quite in that way. She doesn't trust her reaction time if you two try something reckless and run off."

"She does look exhausted. Does she ever sleep?"

"Dr. Haas is very busy trying to save everyone from Ascendant."

That's my job. Maya narrowed her eyes, but wound up sighing. *No it isn't. I'm a child. The Authority is supposed to protect everyone from Ascendant.* Finished, she flushed, stood, and walked out.

Reykjavik grasped her wrist again and brought her back down the hall. She unlocked the door with her left hand, not releasing her hold on Maya's arm until she stepped into the room. Sarah ran over and pounced on her, then burst into tears as if she'd been gone for weeks. Confusion at the girl's overreaction lasted only a second before the press of something inorganic touched her chest. Maya clutched the object, which felt like a few pencils wrapped in fabric. She assumed Sarah's outburst to be a distraction meant to hide the thing, and did her best to conceal it from the woman.

"I was afraid you wouldn't be back." Sarah sniffled.

"Really, kid, calm down. It's only a bathroom break." Reykjavik waved her out. "Your turn... unless you think you can make it all night."

Sarah wiped her cheeks and went out into the hall. Maya kept standing with her back to the exit. Once the door closed and locked, she looked down at the object in her hands: a thin black nylon bundle with a tiny metal clip on the side.

The lock picks. Sarah usually wore it at her beltline, held to her pants, skirt, or whatever by the little clip. Normally, it would be invisible, but the doctor probably discovered it while checking them over for injuries. *Does she think Reykjavik is going to search her?*

Maya climbed into bed and lay down on top of the lock pick case. It didn't take long for her to begin worrying she might not ever see Sarah again. Being in this room alone frightened her. Each minute that passed staring at the pale grey walls heightened her fear. About ten minutes later, the door opened again. The sudden scrape made Maya jump.

Reykjavik guided Sarah inside, then set a big plastic bucket on the floor. "Okay, bed time."

Sarah kept her head down as she crossed to the bed and climbed in.

The door closed with a soft *thump*. A *click* came from the lock a second after, and the lights went out.

"Wow, it's totally dark," whispered Sarah.

"This room has no windows."

Sarah rolled toward her and clung. "There's no light coming in under the door."

"Maybe the hall lights are out, too. That woman can probably see in the dark. Or there's a rubber thing at the bottom." Maya paused, worry clouding her thoughts. "Can you, umm, do that thing without lights?"

"It's working by feel, so it doesn't really matter if I can see."

"Whew." Maya let out a long breath. "Wonder what Mom and Dad are doing now?"

"It's hard to lock down the Hab because it doesn't have walls around it like the Sanc. They probably went back home and know we're missing again. I bet they're either looking for us... or maybe they're fighting Ascendant. The Brigade wouldn't just sit there when actual war broke out. They could be kicking ass and not even know we're kidnapped."

"We're not kidnapped. We're in protective custody," deadpanned Maya.

Sarah snickered.

Maya giggled.

They both erupted in laughter.

That lasted about twelve seconds before they clung to each other, crying.

A few minutes later, Maya wrestled her fear under control. "I guess I'd rather be locked in here than having bullets go by my face."

"Yeah. But it's scary here because we don't know if this doctor is gonna kill us. She's weird."

"It's not easy to trust someone who thinks it's a good idea to make a mind-control device, but she said Ascendant forced her to. Not sure if I believe it. If she really hated it, she'd have destroyed *all* of it. Not kept some."

"Yeah. Do you think she used some on us?" Sarah shuddered. "I don't wanna be mind-controlled."

Maya mulled the idea. "I can't think of a reason why she would do that to us. She'd save it for..." *Holy shit.* "Whoa. What if she's not gonna kill Vanessa, but hit her with that stuff? She could control Ascendant much more easily with a proxy."

"Why do you keep using words I don't know?"

"Sorry. It's the easiest way to describe. Umm. Puppet?"

"Okay. I know puppet. So she's gonna make Vanessa a puppet?"

Maya shrugged. "Actually, it's useless if the Authority wins. If they declare Ascendant in violation of the law and Vanessa wanted, it wouldn't do Haas any good to control her. But if Ascendant wins, then it would. So maybe she wants to kidnap Vanessa, too."

"Ugh. I hope she doesn't put that woman in our room."

Maya leaned close, her lips almost touching Sarah's ear, and whispered, "We won't be here long enough to find out."

Sarah shook with silent giggling.

They lay for a little while listening to intermittent pops of gunfire, muted by distance and thick basement walls. Maya thought about Ji Yeon, imagining her to be a real child stuck on the war-torn streets of

Seoul, trying to fall asleep every night with sounds like that in the distance.

"Don't fall asleep," whispered Maya.

"Oh, no chance of that." Sarah squirmed an arm up between them, probably wiping her face. "So, how long do we wait?"

"It's gotta be nine or ten. 'Kid bedtime.' Haas is a workaholic, so she'll most likely stay awake late. But, that woman with the red eye is gonna go after Vanessa. She won't be here, and I don't think Haas will try to stop us herself."

"Okay."

Worry made it easy to stay awake. Maya tried to count off time in her head, but the repetitiveness of it began to lull her to sleep, so she stopped. After a while, she sat up, debated a moment, and lay back down.

"Too soon?" asked Sarah.

"Maybe we should wait some more."

"Would you rather have cold eggs or hot cereal?" asked Sarah.

Maya blinked. "Hello, random. What?"

"It's a game." Sarah giggled. "'Would you rather.' Something to pass time."

"Oh. Umm..." Hot milk with Megawaffle sounded disgusting. "Cold eggs."

"Your turn."

Maya grinned. "Would you rather, umm... never run out of food but you had to wear shoes every day, or, umm, not know if you could eat but not be forced to wear shoes."

"Duh. Food of course. Shoes feel weird but it's not something I'd starve over. Who do you think I am, Emily?"

Maya giggled.

"Would you rather," asked Sarah, "live in that nice fancy penthouse knowing you and all of us were totally safe, or be with us but not know if we're gonna die at any moment?"

"Umm. You mean like be alone in that place, but I knew nothing would ever hurt you, Genna, or Pope, or any of our friends?"

"Yeah."

Maya choked up. "I, umm. If it would keep you guys totally safe, I'd live alone."

"Really?" asked Sarah. "You'd leave us?"

"Not like that. You're asking a theoretical question about impossible standards of safety. In that made up ideal world where my choice to be alone in that place would guarantee all of you would never be hurt, my happiness wouldn't be worth your lives. But it's a logical fallacy considering such perfect safety is unattainable."

"Wow, okay. I'm really not sure what you just said... Umm."

Maya squeezed Sarah's hand. "The short answer is I would give up anything to keep you guys safe, no matter how much it hurt me. Wow, these questions can get deep."

"Yeah."

"Would you rather...?" asked Maya, thinking. "Have unlimited cheese sandwiches but you could never eat anything else, or be able to have other food but you had to have Tuna Blast once a day."

"Tuna Blast. Eating the same stuff all the time would make me hate them. And I don't mind that casserole, even if it is supposed to be for cats."

"Eww," said Maya. "It's not a 'casserole,' it's cat food."

Sarah chuckled. She kept quiet for a little while, then asked, "Would you rather get robbed by dosers and stuck in the wildlands with no clothes, or have the blueberries leave you zip-tied for a whole week."

"That's easy. Stuck outside with no clothes. The other option would kill me. I'd dehydrate or starve if I couldn't move. And plenty of Frags have nothing on."

"Oh, yeah." Sarah tapped her feet on air. "That makes sense."

"Would you rather?" asked Maya. "No, wait that's a bad question."

"What?" Sarah poked her in the side.

"I don't wanna say it. It's mean."

Sarah rolled toward her. "Is it about my dad?"

"No, not that mean. I wouldn't even think that."

"Okay, well ask it."

Maya sighed. "Would you rather be locked in a room with Vanessa or Mr. Mason?"

"Wow." Sarah blinked at her. "Why would you think that?"

"I know. Sorry. He like scared me so much I keep thinking about him. That's a stupid question. Totally Vanessa. She's a bitch but she wouldn't hurt us personally."

"No, she'd just have someone else kill us. The woman basically told you she'd kill me if you didn't listen to her. I can't answer that one. I wouldn't want to be anywhere near either one of them."

"Me neither."

Sarah let out a sad chuckle. "I guess you win."

"Huh?"

"That's how you win that game. Ask a question the other person can't or won't answer."

"It wasn't a fair question. I'm sorry for making you think of that man again."

"He's dead. And I think he died painfully."

"Probably," said Maya. "Still. It's a cruel question. Would you rather kiss Anton or a random blueberry?"

"Anton huh? Marcus yours?" asked Sarah with a big grin in her voice.

Maya narrowed her eyes and initiated a tickle war.

Once the laughing and squealing died down, Maya, out of breath, rasped, "He is not mine."

"Hey." Sarah grabbed onto her and went still. "No one yelled at us for making noise."

"It's so quiet. Maybe it's safe."

"Let's try."

Maya sat up again. "Wait. Got an idea." She climbed over Sarah and slithered to the floor, feeling her way over the crummy rug to the video game. A few minutes of groping at the dark later, she found the power button for the monitor and turned it on. The blue system screen with a list of games to select illuminated the room like a strong nightlight. "There. It's 10:26 p.m."

After a yawn, Sarah grabbed the lock pick case and hopped out of bed. She padded over to the door, went down on one knee roughly eye-level with the knob, and unrolled the case into a flat cloth panel about six inches long with numerous thin metal rods tucked in fabric loops.

Sarah bowed her head and sniffled.

"What?" Maya hurried over and knelt close by. "What's wrong?"

"I'm sad about Dad. I always kinda thought he was crazy or stupid for teaching me all these weird things, but it really is saving our asses.

How to escape being tied up, how to pick locks, how to use a Hornet. He's gone, but he's still protecting me."

Maya hugged her. "I'm sorry."

"Now what are you apologizing for?"

"You probably wouldn't have needed to use any of that stuff if you didn't know me."

Sarah leaned close, touching foreheads, staring into her eyes. "I don't wanna have to say this again. It's not *your* fault. It's the fault of the people who are being crappy to you. If I'm upset with anyone for all that's happened to us, it's them. Not you."

Sniffling, Maya nodded. She sat back on her heels in the blue-saturated room, lit in the glow of the monitor behind them. While Sarah got to work on the doorknob, Maya amused herself by making shadow puppets on the wall.

The soft ratcheting of lock picks competed with far away gunfire over the next minute or two for the 'loudest sound in the universe' award. Sarah emitted a tiny nasal squeak, then twisted her whole body to one side while turning the knob and pulling the door inward two inches. Hallway light leaked in as well as a brush of cooler air tinged with the stink of mildew.

"Yes!" whispered Maya.

"Hold the door," said Sarah.

Maya grabbed the edge with both hands, keeping it as close to shut as possible. Sarah repacked the picks, rolled the case up, and tucked it in the back of her skirt. She got to her feet and tugged the door open, grabbing at her empty right hip.

"Gah!" whispered Sarah. "I feel naked without the Hornet."

Maya stifled a giggle. "What?"

"Something Dad always used to say if he didn't have a gun on him." Sarah sighed. "I'd trade my clothes for it right now, I swear."

Maya gasped. "You would not."

"I sure would." Sarah glanced over her shoulder. "The Hornet would do more to keep us from being re-kidnapped."

"So let's get it back."

"It's in Haas' office!" whisper-shouted Sarah.

"The Dad gave it to you. I'm not gonna let that woman take it."

Sarah's lip quivered.

"Follow me." Maya crept into the hall, waited for Sarah to let their cell door close silently, then headed off to the right.

She navigated the old hospital basement passageways, following the route Reykjavik had taken to lead them to the bathroom, only she didn't go all the way there, instead ducking into the medical procedure room. The table, likely where Dr. Haas had cleaned them up, appeared quite old, it's black cushions riddled with cracks that revealed beige stuffing inside. Dark patches of discoloration all over the cinder block walls showed where a nasty growth of mold had been, though scratch marks said someone had spent long hours cleaning. None of the fungus remained, but no amount of scrubbing could cure such deep stains.

A blend of antiseptic solution and wet dog flavored the air, and the near-immaculate linoleum floor held an uncomfortable chill. Six white cabinets stood in a line along the innermost wall next to an open shelf holding boxes of gauze and linens. Used gauze pads smudged with blood and dirt sat in a sink on the right, perhaps left over from their last (unconscious) visit to this room.

Sarah slipped in behind her and tugged the door closed before whispering, "What are you doing in here?"

Maya crossed to the first white cabinet on the left and peered at bottles, phials, and boxes inside. Not finding what she wanted, she stepped one space right and searched the next cabinet. On the second shelf, she spotted several large multi-dose bottles of Placinox. The top shelf had boxes of empty syringes. She grabbed the handle, but the door refused to open.

"Can you unlock this?"

Sarah approached and examined the small lock on the handle. "Maybe. But not unless you tell me what you're doing."

"Placinox." Maya pointed at the bottles. "I figured they had it here since there's no way whatever that woman breathed on us would've kept us unconscious long enough to be brought here, go through a medical exam, then be moved to that room before we woke up.

"Why do you want it?" Sarah pulled out the picks again.

"The Authority uses it as a chemical restraint. It's extremely fast-acting. If I sneak up on her and give her a shot, she'll pass out in ten seconds. Or you can distract her and then I ambush her from behind. It won't hurt her, so if she really *is* trying to be nice to us, we don't have to feel guilty." Maya grinned. "Dr. Haas is working herself too much. The poor woman is so exhausted. She really needs some sleep."

"Oh, I love it!" Sarah stifled a giggle and had the cabinet open in forty seconds.

Maya jammed her hand into a cardboard box, pulled out a skinny syringe, and grabbed one of the big Placinox bottles. After biting the safety cap from the needle, she stuck it into the bottle, held it up, and drew three CCs of fluid. *That should be plenty to knock her out for a while.* She replaced the safety cap over the needle before putting the bottle back in the cabinet.

"Wow, you look like a miniature doctor."

Maya smirked. "My handwriting isn't *that* bad."

"Huh?" asked Sarah.

"I'll explain later. No time." Maya scurried out into the hallway, heading back the other way toward Haas' office. At the sliding black door, she paused, listening to the soft click-boop of electronic keypresses.

Wow... this woman is like Vanessa. Never stops working.

She paused, her heartbeat gaining speed. Sneaking up on and ambushing a grown woman, even a scientist, sounded a *lot* better in her mind than in reality. The rogue character she'd played in video games made it look so easy, but she doubted reality would function the same way. *Hmm. If sneaking doesn't work, I can trick her with cuteness, get close...* Maya peered up at a small, square window in the door, too high for her to see through. Grumbling in her head, she crouched low and gingerly tugged the sliding door until it opened a quarter inch. Eye to the gap, she peered in and surveyed the room, squinting at the blast of freezing air leaking into the hall.

Numerous machines on the far wall flickered and flashed, clearly more active than they'd been before when she'd provided the addresses. Dr. Haas sat at her desk, facing toward the left side of the room. The doorway entered at that corner, so any attempt to go into the room would get her caught. Maya knelt in place, waiting and watching. *Hmm. I guess I do the cute and innocent thing and try to make it close enough.*

Haas plucked a near-full mug of coffee up from her desk and sipped. Frozen in doubt, Maya couldn't quite work up the nerve to stroll right in and hope the doctor didn't completely flip out. After a few minutes, the woman walked over to the machinery, her back to the room while she tapped at an embedded terminal screen.

Yes!

Maya eased the door open a little more, enough to slip into the ice-cold room. With the Placinox syringe clutched in her teeth, she crawled to the nearest hiding place from the desk, a large pushcart. She squatted behind it, observing Dr. Haas still tweaking dials on the large machine. Nervously confident the woman would be at least a moment more at that task, she scurried onward to the narrow end of the desk opposite the doctor.

Okay. I'll wait for her to sit down and jab her in the leg with it.

The doctor moved two machines to the right, closer to the desk, but still had her back turned.

"The process is taking too damn long. I can't believe the calculations proved inaccurate again. Ugh. What do I have to do?" Dr. Haas scoffed. "Maybe that little girl can figure this out. Indeed. IQ of 147-155. Hah. If only. She's smart, but I'm sure they padded those numbers to make Vanessa happy."

Maya leaned up over the side of the desk, watching. Her gaze settled on the large coffee mug. *She could see me coming and grab my hand... Ooh! Better idea!* Up on tiptoe, Maya squirted the Placinox from the syringe into the coffee, and ducked back down. Curled in a ball, she gingerly slid the plastic guard back over the needle.

Something beeped. "There. That should do it."

Stifling a gasp, Maya huddled against the desk. Dr. Haas' shoes clicked over the floor, coming around the desk on the side away from the exit, trapping her. If Maya moved from her spot, the woman would easily see her. Chair springs creaked. She glanced to her left, relieved at finding the door closed all the way again. *Thank you, Sarah.* She bit her lip. If the woman saw the door open at all, she'd have flipped out.

Dr. Haas took a swig of coffee.

Eyes closed, Maya tried to ignore the frigid floor sapping all the life from her feet. Like the phantom hands of Death himself, the air conditioning reached up her dress and raked his icy talons down her back.

The soft chirp of a touchscreen registering taps continued for several minutes, along with the doctor grumbling about the calculation still not looking right. Finally, she took a few more sips and set the mug down.

Dr. Haas yawned. "Come on, coffee. Kick in already."

Yeah, seriously. Maya furrowed her brow. *Shit. Will Placinox work orally? Will heat denature it? Effect onset injected is five to twenty seconds. Three CCs on her probable body weight would've been more like eight seconds. Administering it orally will be slower by a factor... probably five to ten minutes.*

Dr. Haas yawned again, muttered a few curses about her equations *looking* right, and proceeded to complain to no one in particular about how the 'control' aspect of the nanobots couldn't achieve anything more graceful than a lumbering zombie state.

"If those Authority fools aren't able to get rid of you, Vanessa... sooner or later, someone you will never expect will. You act like you own the world, but I know you live in constant fear of betrayal."

Maya rubbed her toes, trying to revive them. The over-cranked air conditioning made the floor colder than ice. With only a thin dress on, she had little protection. *Okay, mind control is evil as hell, but she's trying to get rid of Vanessa. I'm way too scared to debate the ethics of using immoral means to achieve a noble goal.*

Dr. Haas slugged the rest of the coffee in a series of gulps. "At this rate, I'm going to need another whole pot. Damn, this stuff is weak. It's like the more I drink the more tired I get." She chuckled. "Maybe I've reached a critical point of caffeine saturation."

Maya covered her mouth to stop herself from giggling.

A few minutes passed. Maya shivered in place, no longer able to feel anything below her ankles. Her hiding place against the narrow end of the desk didn't offer much room for error. Any slight movement could easily give her away. Sarah had to be losing her mind. Hopefully, the relative calm inside the room kept her from panicking too much.

Dr. Haas yawned again and emitted a soft burp. "Oh, what's going on? Everything's hazy." She burped again, smacking her lips a few times. "That doesn't taste right. Uhh. Oh, drat. Maybe that IQ *was* right. You... sneaky little..."

Thud.

Maya waited another ten seconds, but no sounds of motion came from the doctor. Gingerly, she grasped the top edge of the desk and pulled herself up to peek.

Dr. Haas lay unconscious, face down on her keyboard.

"Sarah! It's clear."

The door slid open. Her face wet with tears, Sarah hurried in. "Holy crap. I thought you got busted."

"No, just had to hide and wait. It took longer because I put it in her coffee. Less chance of her catching and overpowering me." Maya picked up the Hornet and handed it to Sarah. "This is yours."

She frowned at the machines and the terminal. "Maybe I should wipe this out, but I don't need another person trying to kill me. I'll let the Authority deal with this if they want to." She looked down at Haas. "Sorry, but you really looked like you needed the sleep."

"Yeah. Let's get the hell out of here. Leave this stuff alone." Sarah jogged for the door, peering back at Maya every few steps. She stumbled over a thick plastic hose, but caught her balance before falling.

"Was that one on purpose?" asked Maya.

Sarah stuck out her tongue.

Back out in the hallway, Maya glanced left and right. Having no idea which way led out, she randomly went to the left, running from door to door, peeking in each one. After several minutes of searching, they arrived at a dead end. An open doorway on the right looked in on a bedroom filled with computer equipment, robotic parts, and numerous weapons hung on the wall, everything from sniper rifles to pistols to swords.

"Oh, this must be Reykjavik's bedroom." Maya whistled. "Wow, she's a real Murder Barbie. Crap. Should've gone to the right."

Sarah gripped the Hornet in both hands like a movie cop and jogged back the way they came from. Maya followed, trying to run without letting her feet make noise on the tile floor. Sarah kept going straight past the left turn that would lead to Haas' office. They peered in a few more rooms of old junk, likely doctors' offices prior to the hospital's shutdown. Another room held tons of filing cabinets, the one after that copiers. That hallway ended at a leftward corner.

"Eep," whispered Sarah.

"What?"

She pointed. "This is the way out but there's lasers."

"That's not real. This isn't a video game."

"No." Sarah poked her. "Not like laser guns. Laser tripwires. Watch the dust near the floor."

Maya peered around the corner. A sixty foot long corridor ran past a few side doors to a set of metal double-doors at the end. Tall, narrow windows in each door crisscrossed with wire offered a view of concrete stairs behind them. Here and there, thin lines of light flickered in and out of visibility in dust whorls about four inches up from the floor.

"Oh. Umm. What happens if we touch one?" asked Maya.

"Hopefully, only an alarm. But it could be sleep gas or explosives... though I doubt it. They wouldn't want to blow up their research. Follow me and move exactly as I do."

"Okay."

Sarah edged forward, staring at the walls. Whenever she raised her leg as if stepping over something, Maya imagined a line of fiery death in that spot and avoided it. After stepping over six invisible wires, Sarah broke into a run over the last ten feet and shoved one of the doors open. Maya chased her up two switchbacks and stopped at another metal door with a push bar.

A piece of paper hung from a piece of tape.

"Kid," said Sarah, reading the note. "Figured a decent chance you'd wind up reading this. Hope you didn't give Haas a heart attack on your way out. That room might've been locked, but it is safe. Doc's a little odd, but she wouldn't hurt kids. Best of luck with whatever you choose to do. – Reyk."

"Wow. Do you think she saw the lock picks?" asked Maya.

"Dunno. If she did, wouldn't she have taken them away?"

"Yeah, probably. Maybe she's guessing. If we didn't escape, we'd never see this note, so we wouldn't know she assumed we'd get out." Maya shrugged. "This way, she looks cooler than she might be. Or maybe she doesn't agree with the mind control thing, saw the picks, and let us escape."

"You are scary." Sarah blinked at her. "Are you gonna like get smarter as you grow up or are you already there?"

"How should I know?" Maya flapped her arms. "I'm only nine."

"So, should we go back and be safe?" Sarah grinned.

"Would you rather risk being held captive by a crazed mad scientist or run off into the Dead Space with just a Hornet?"

Sarah laughed, and shoved the door open.

A short concrete porch led to a crumbling parking lot surrounded by the ruins of a once-dense city. Shadows leaned away from old, wrecked cars, cast by a great light source behind the hospital building. Maya hurried into the parking lot a ways, then turned to look. The massive glowing rise of the Sanctuary Zone loomed over them less than a mile away. Unsure if she should be alarmed or reassured at their proximity to civilization, she gazed around while thinking of what to do. Three white e-sedans sat in a row near a fence bordering one side of the lot, all with Ascendant markings.

"Crap. We're far from the Hab." Sarah pulled her hair off her face and bit her lip.

"Idea." Maya pointed at the cars.

"Ooh!" chirped Sarah, breaking into a run toward them. "Looks like I get to play *RoadBlasters* again."

Maya hurried around to the passenger side door and got in. Sarah climbed behind the wheel. After a quick glance at the interior, she plucked a clear card from the underside of the sun visor and slotted it in the dash.

"How the heck did you know to look there?"

Sarah pushed the on button. "Remember when we scavved and had those carts going to Foz's place?"

"Yeah."

"Remember that guy who told me I'm too young to drink?"

"Yeah." Maya scratched her head. "He told you about stealing cars?"

"No. That place. Dad used to bring me there sometimes, and the people who hang out there talk about stuff like this all the time."

"Insert one quarter to continue." Sarah dropped the car into drive.

"Please don't kill us." Maya pulled the seatbelt on. "We just escaped."

Sarah let out a gleeful laugh and mashed her foot down on the pedal. Tires spat dirt, and the car careened around in a chirping donut twice before she got control and steered for the gates out of the lot.

"Well, you're getting better." Maya glanced nervously at the side mirror. "You didn't hit anything this time."

Sarah raspberried, and pressed down on the pedal, speeding up.

25

OFF-ROADBLASTERS

O nce Sarah drove out of the lot and found a strip of paving to follow, she slowed down almost enough to mimic the feeling of being in the car while Pope or Genna drove.

"Wow. You're even on the right side of the line."

"Ha. Ha. Okay... so home?"

"The Sanc and the Hab are in lockdown with Blueberries and Ascendant all over the place shooting at each other. It's a real war. I don't know. We can't get into the Sanc, and we could be shot if we try to go to the Hab. This car has Ascendant logos on the doors. The berries would Swiss cheese us before they realized we're kids."

Sarah glanced over at her. "What does cheese have to do with being shot?"

"Swiss cheese is full of holes," deadpanned Maya.

"Umm." Sarah shivered, taking a few rapid breaths as if about to burst into panicky tears. "So, what are we gonna do?" She sniffled, almost straying out of the lane. "Are they gonna kill us just for being in this car?"

Maya put a hand on her shoulder. "Give me a sec to think. Don't go nuts. If we see blueberries, stop the car and get out with your hands up, okay? If they see a pair of kids before they notice the Ascendant logo, they'll probably be nice to us."

"Okay." Thirty seconds later, she looked over. "Think of anything yet?"

"No." Maya sighed. "Still trying."

Sarah slowed to take a left turn.

"Nice. Almost feels like you know how to drive. So, umm, where are you going?"

"Back to the Hab. Unless you have a better idea."

"Not really." Maya looked down, and wound up staring at the Hornet on the seat between them. A metaphorical light switched on in her head. "Wait! Idea." She picked the stunner up. "Remember when I thought Genna died, how I swore I'd shoot Vanessa in the face?"

"Umm... yeah," said Sarah in a hesitant tone.

Maya grinned. "I didn't specify it had to be a real gun." She pointed off to the right. "Drive."

"Huh?" asked Sarah. "What are you gonna do?"

"The one address I didn't give them is the Shroud at Double Rock. That's where she is. We're going to go in there, dart the bitch, and bring her to the Authority. That'll stop this war."

Sarah laughed. At Maya's continued serious expression, her laughing melted to tentative giggles, then a flat stare. "Wait. You're serious?"

"Yes."

"That's stupid and ridiculous."

Maya nodded. "You're right. But that's exactly why it might work. No one, not even Vanessa would ever imagine it happening."

Sarah whined.

"We can't go into the Sanc, and going to the Hab has a really good chance of getting us shot. The worst thing that will happen if we get caught at the Shroud is locked in a room together again."

"You're so sure she won't kill us?"

"I..." Maya looked down. "I can't see her doing that. Especially when she has nothing to gain from it. Yes, she's cruel and heartless, but it's not *pointlessly* cruel. She isn't unkind to people purely to be nasty, only if it's a means to an advantage for her."

"The woman killed thousands and thousands of people for money." Sarah slowed to a stop and pulled off the road.

"Yes. Obtaining money is an advantage to her." Maya shed a few tears and stared off over the rubble, thinking of little Ashley and her half-grey face, wondering what she looked like now... if color had returned to the Fade-ravaged child.

A band of glimmering blue sky hung low to the horizon on all sides over endless fields of rubbled city. Above that, dark indigo flecked with stars and smog clouds bled gradually to perfect black overhead.

Maya shied away from the desolation, caused by worse people than Vanessa. "You've played video games. Do you feel guilty about killing soldiers or people in them?"

"No. They're not real."

"That's how Vanessa sees things. Stats on a screen, theoretical concepts that a normal, non-insane person would think of as people. But to her, they're numbers to be manipulated for profit. Remember Ashley?"

"I remember you talking about her. The five-year-old with Fade?"

"Yeah. I think if I brought her face-to-face with Vanessa, the woman would probably have given her Xenodril. She wouldn't have the stomach to murder children, even me, with her bare hands. Pushing a button or sending an email to dispatch a drone to drop Fade on a map sector isn't people to her, only statistics in a spreadsheet."

"No, she'd probably use a gun." Sarah rolled her eyes. "Especially if you're waving the Hornet in her face."

"A scenario in which we're captured is already past me waving the Hornet in her face. We don't have a lot of time. We're probably the only two people in the world other than Vanessa who know where she is."

"You don't *know* she's there. You're guessing."

"I've been to the Shroud. It's the nicest and most secret of all her bunkers. She could stay there for twenty years and no one would ever find her. But she won't just sit down there. Vanessa is going to keep doing awful things, and it'll get worse if she thinks she's losing control of her company."

"Okay. Okay." Sarah cranked the wheel to the left and pulled a U-turn across two lanes. "Where is it?"

Maya entered a non-suspicious address in the car's navigation system that would bring them within a half mile of the Shroud. "Go there first."

"How am I supposed to look at that screen and the road and the speed thing all at the same time?"

"You don't have to look at the map screen constantly. Just every few seconds to make sure you're not missing a turn. Besides, most of those roads are gone. All the buildings here are gone, too. Just try to go in the same direction as the line and don't hit stuff."

Sarah spent a minute or two glancing at the navigation panel while tooling along around forty miles per hour. She decided to try the 'as the crow flies' thing, and pulled off the road onto dirt. The car bumped and wobbled, but the ride could've been worse.

A few minutes after leaving the pavement, a strange, soft wailing noise approached from behind.

"What's that?" gasped Sarah, eyes wide. "Sounds like ghosts."

Maya twisted around in the seat. Five leather-clad figures on e-motorcycles converged behind them, rapidly overtaking the car. "Skeevers. On bikes."

"Oh." Fear left Sarah's voice. "Hang on. Gonna drive faster."

She accelerated, veering around hunks of former buildings, collapsed traffic light poles, and derelict cars. One guy on a bike zipped up even with the driver's side window and raised a metal pipe. Sarah whipped her head to the side, stared at the guy, and swerved into him. His bike bounced off the car and went careening away; two seconds later, he crashed into a giant block of concrete rubble, detonating in a flash of blue light and creeping electrical arcs.

"Ouch." Maya cringed.

"We're doing ninety. He didn't feel a thing."

"Ugh. This is really turning into that game you like. *RoadBlasters.*" Maya gulped. "And if you hit something at ninety, *we* won't feel a thing either. Slow down."

A crossbow arrow came in the rear window and pierced Sarah's headrest, the jagged razor tip hovering two inches above her head. Growling, she jammed on the brakes. The guy who fired it crashed into their rear bumper, landed on the roof, and slid down over the hood to the ground before going under the wheels. Sarah stomped on the gas, the car bouncing over the body.

Maya closed her eyes and tried to think about cartoon bunny rabbits and rainbow-maned unicorns instead of her sister running a guy over on purpose.

"I'm not sorry. Much." Sarah glanced up. "If I was three years older, that arrow would've killed me."

The passenger door opened without warning. A howling man covered head to toe in leather scraps reached in and grabbed Maya's arm. She screamed. Sarah tensed as if about to ram the guy, but hesitated.

"Veal!" shouted the man.

Maya thrust the Hornet up with both hands, jamming it under his chin before squeezing the trigger. A pneumatic *pthoonk* preceded a spritz of blood from his mouth. Tiny electric sparks shot out between his teeth and from his nostrils. The man screamed and recoiled, thin blue arcs lapping over his face. Only a few millimeters of Hornet dart protruded from under his chin, the point-blank shot having embedded the inch-long cartridge in the roof of his mouth, completely through his tongue from below.

Convulsing, the man fell out of the car, disappearing into the billowing dust in the car's wake. Maya slammed her door shut and screamed.

"You forgot to switch it to contact mode," deadpanned Sarah.

Maya turned only her head, staring at her sister in disbelief.

"It's dangerous to use darts at short range. You could injure someone."

"You're being sarcastic. Oh, remember what I said about slow down? Yeah. Forget it. *Go!*"

Sarah steered around a derelict bus with one hand while pointing at the arrow sticking out of the seat above her head. "This is why I don't care what happens to those skeevers. Still. Ow."

The last two bikes broke off the chase after a few near misses with lamp posts and sizable hunks of former building. Maya knelt in her seat, watching to the rear. Sarah slowed down again and ceased white-knuckling the steering wheel.

"Okay, maybe it wasn't all lies about the Dead Space."

"No." Sarah shook her head. "They lied about the wildlands. The Dead Space really is dangerous."

Maya blinked at her. "We got attacked by *thirty* skeevers in the wildlands. Only five here."

"Yeah, but those guys out there wouldn't have eaten us... maybe."

"Ugh." Maya shuddered. "I think I'd rather be eaten than, uhh, yeah."

"If we ever play 'would you rather' again, please don't ask that."

Maya drew an X over her chest. "Swear."

Satisfied that nothing continued to chase them, Maya flopped around in her seat to face forward and watched ruins go by for about ten minutes. The navigation system chirped.

"Keep left and turn onto Taylor Avenue."

"Where?" yelled Sarah, gesturing at the debris. "There is no Taylor Avenue. There aren't even roads anymore. Ooh, I think that's 'Blown-to-crap Avenue.'"

Maya pointed at a green spot on the nav. "That's where we're going."

"What's that green for?"

"I think it used to be a park or something, with trees. The war kinda burned them all down. It's scary how much plant life the Earth lost. We're probably at a dangerous level for oxygen replenishment."

"What?"

"I'll explain later. Too long now. Just go kinda over here." She tapped the screen again on the green spot.

"Turn left in six hundred feet onto Deckerts Lane," said the navigation system.

Maya pushed a button to turn it off.

"You erased it?"

"That wasn't really the address. Don't know if these things still talk to Ascendant or something. I didn't want her detecting someone putting the real address into the system."

"Oh."

"It might not matter. If Ascendant is losing..."

"So, umm... what are we looking for?" Sarah slowed to about ten miles an hour once the terrain became rough.

Maya leaned forward, gripping the dashboard with both hands to fight the constant jostling of uneven ground, and scanned the area ahead. After a few seconds, she caught a glimpse of a familiar giant slab of concrete. The eighteen-foot-tall wedge jutted up from the dirt like a titan's trowel left in the garden. Two thicker, square columns at the edges in lighter grey supported the darker center.

"That. It's a memorial to fallen soldiers. There's a plaque on the base with a holo-emitter that reads off the names of soldiers who died in the war."

"Why would anyone bother putting a memorial out here in the Dead Space where no one can get to it... at least without"—Sarah again pointed at the arrow above her head—"new body piercings."

"Exactly. Building the memorial was a cover for the true project... Vanessa's hideout. There's a big ass elevator behind the memorial that can fit a car. That's how we went there last time. But, she'll definitely know we're coming if we use it, and we don't have the codes to make the wireless control work. There's another way in though. We can leave the car here."

Sarah pushed the off button and the dashboard went dark. "Okay."

"Ready?" asked Maya.

"No." Sarah took the Hornet from her. "I know you promised to shoot her, but one, I've had more practice with it. And two, I think you'll chicken out. She is kinda related to you."

"Don't remind me." Maya smirked. "But, yeah... you're right. I probably would chicken out."

"And besides. That bitch killed my father." Sarah shoved her door open.

Maya eased her way out of the car. She wasn't about to say she thought Sarah better off. Not that she wished the man dead, but he should've been in a hospital for mental health, not entrusted to look after a child—or be looked after *by* a child.

She also preferred having a sister to a best friend. Ashamed of that thought, Maya sighed at her feet—and sighed again at once again being stranded out in the middle of nowhere without shoes.

Sister or best friend... There's another 'would you rather' I can never ask.

26

DOUBLE ROCK

Maya crept across the rubble-strewn ground, careful not to step on any glass or metal. Here and there, splintered stumps of former trees stuck up from the ashy dirt. Not far past the memorial, a small creek cut across an area that used to be a park, with a few sparse signs of new plant growth along its banks. The same water provided for Vanessa's hidden sanctuary—after being filtered.

A huge disc of concrete around the memorial made for a welcome safe surface to walk on without having to worry about stepping on sharp things. Seconds after she had both feet on it, a ten-inch holographic soldier appeared floating over the plaque at the base of the enormous wedge, reciting names. Hundreds of thousands of them repeated in an endless loop that only played when someone entered the area. A poem dedicated to the soldiers who gave their lives in defense of the country had been engraved in the wedge.

Sarah approached the base and paused, head bowed. Maya kept going past the slab, but stopped to wait for her at the other edge of the round platform. A minute or two later, Sarah looked up and walked over. Maya gazed around for a few seconds to get her bearings, then continued walking over dirt. At least this side of the monument had less dangerous debris. Roughly fifty yards away from the platform, Maya reached the creek and turned left, following the water's edge for a little while until she spotted a metal plate on the bank.

She waved for Sarah to hurry up, then ran to it, squatting in the loose soil beside the burbling water. Raised letters on a hatch read 'Baltimore Municipal Water Authority.' A giant, rusty padlock, bigger than the palm of a man's hand, secured it.

"Not sure I can pick that one," said Sarah. "It looks fused."

"No problem." Maya headed around to the other side of the plate and crouched at the corner. It had been a little while since she watched the bodyguard open this, but she remembered the basics. "There's a switch somewhere."

After a few minutes of poking around, she located a small flap at the edge that concealed a button. Pushing it caused a soft *clank* to emanate from the hatch, and it rose up on mechanized struts, padlock and all.

"The lock's fake." Maya grinned as she stepped up onto the plate and moved around to the front of the moving hatch. "Well, not *fake*. Just not meant to be opened."

She scurried down a ladder into a six foot concrete shaft above a wider area full of derelict pumping equipment and old fuse panels. Sarah lowered herself onto the rungs above her, but let out a soft 'eep.' Maya looked up. Her sister ducked away from the hatch, motoring closed on its own. Maya climbed to the bottom and backed up a step to give her room.

"We're in."

Sarah blinked. "We're trapped."

"Nah. It's on a timer." She pointed at a red valve mounted to a rusted pipe. "Twisting that will open it."

"This crap is old as hell." Sarah turned in place, looking around, then pointed at an overhead bulb that resembled something made forty years ago. "How is that light still even on?"

"It's not a real incandescent. Just looks like one. This is all fake. None of this machinery ever worked. It's all junk they moved here to conceal the hidden entrance. Well, technically, this is the emergency exit, like if the power goes out and the elevator stops working. They only made it look like a pre-war city water station or whatever."

Sarah jumped as a big centipede scurried over her toes. "Umm. How do you know about it?"

"Vanessa had her people teach me how to use it in case anything ever happened. She didn't want her investment to be lost." Maya scurried around bugs to the other end of the short tunnel opposite the ladder, a concrete wall covered in a nest of small pipes and green-painted water meter boxes. "Okay, now this part..."

"Investment... that's so sad. Guess we both had broken parents."

Maya folded her arms, studying the pipes. "There are a few things wrong with your statement."

"Such as?" asked Sarah, head tilted.

"One. I don't consider Vanessa a parent. Two... well, okay. The Dad was kinda broken. But I'd take ten of him before Vanessa."

"That doesn't say much." Sarah chuckled. "You once told me you'd rather live in a plastiboard box with no clothes, eating rats like a Frag instead of be with Vanessa."

"True. Aha!" Maya reached up and grabbed a suspiciously thick fitting where one of the three-quarter-inch lines went into a meter box. She twisted it a quarter turn.

With a *click*, the whole back wall came away like a door, all the pipes and meters swinging with it.

"Wow," whispered Sarah.

Behind the fake wall, a clean, modern chamber contained a spiral stairwell that led deeper into the earth. Maya ducked around the slab of concrete and padded down the hall, leaving dirty footprints on the white surface. Sarah walked heavily, as if leaving darker prints somehow got back at Vanessa.

Maya descended three stories down the spiral stairs to a chilly metal-walled chamber with one door. *Moment of truth time.* She pushed the only button on the wall beside it and the door slid open without a noise.

"Guess she didn't change the password," whispered Sarah.

"This is an escape. It would be somewhat inconvenient to try and remember a long password when you're running for your life. The odds of someone accidentally finding that entrance from the outside are pretty damn low."

"True." Sarah raised the Hornet. "Okay, where's the bitch?"

"Probably in her office. Follow me."

Maya stepped through the door into a hallway covered in plush beige carpeting that reminded her of the penthouses. Conical frosted glass lights adorned the walls every twenty feet above bands of gold trim.

"Whoa," whispered Sarah. "This is just like the penthouse."

"Yeah." Maya looked down at a rug so thick her toes almost disappeared in it. "Is it bad that I kinda miss these rugs?"

"Nah. They're nice. If I lived in a place like this, I'd never wear shoes."

Maya smirked. "You never wear shoes anyway."

"Okay. But I never had them before. I promise I'll put them on for our next kidnapping."

"Don't even say that." Maya groaned. "*When* we get home, I'm going to chain myself to the wall so I *can't* be abducted."

Sarah snickered. "With your luck, if you do that, the building would burn down."

"It's a concrete high-rise. It can't burn down."

"Well, collapse or something then."

Maya turned and put a finger over Sarah's lips. "We should stop talking or she'll catch us."

Sarah nodded.

Room by room, Maya crept down the hall, checking three bedrooms (including the one she spent ninety-five percent of her time here in) as well as Vanessa's room. She nearly let out a yelp of alarm-slash-excitement at the sight of her former mother's bed appearing slept in. That meant two things: the woman *was* here, and she came alone. No staff to make the bed for her.

Maya kept going to the end and peered around the corner into a huge sunken living room.

Electronic screens on the walls mimicked a view of a forest outside, but also doubled as a movie-screen-sized television. A wraparound sectional sofa had enough space for all her friends to sleep on—not that children would ever be allowed to touch it. Especially not grimy Hab residents. Maya resisted the temptation to fling herself on it and frolic to smear dirt all over the immaculate white cushions.

She crossed the main area without going down the three steps into the living room, bypassed the empty kitchen, and entered the second interior hallway that contained the executive bathroom. Maya tiptoed to the last door at the end, Vanessa's office, and waved Sarah over.

Her sister hurried close and tilted her head, asking 'what' with her eyes.

Maya held her hands in a gun pose and pointed at the door.

Sarah nodded and stepped in front of her. She glanced back and made a kicking gesture.

Maya shook her head.

They waited for a moment, listening to dead silence.

Sarah grasped the doorknob with her left hand, twisting it slow. When it would turn no more, she pushed the door in enough to peek, leading with the Hornet. She exhaled and shoved the door open the rest of the way, then clutched the stunner in both hands.

"No one there," whispered Sarah

Maya frowned, shimmied past her, and stormed into the giant office with cloud-soft blue carpet. Another huge electronic screen spanned the entire wall opposite the door with a fake window view of a nighttime city, likely Baltimore before the war. Beneath it, a low black shelf ran wall to wall, only as tall as a windowsill, covered in a scattering of trinkets, various promotional items to sell drugs, office awards, picture frames, and other kitsch. Books crammed the inner shelves, easily hundreds of titles, all of which appeared to be either university textbooks or medical research, including a handful on Eastern philosophy.

"Wow. It's almost like we went back in time," whispered Sarah.

"Yeah." Maya walked around the desk. Two modern terminals took up the center of the workspace. An old computer at the left edge covered in stickers bore the faces of comic book characters.

What the hell? Vanessa would never have cartoons on her computer. Did she have another kid before me?

She lowered herself into the chair and tapped the keyboard of the modern terminal. The black screens flickered to life, displaying a fairly standard background full of icons. It didn't seem useful to go rooting around the computer at the moment, but her hope that Ascendant would be going down in flames might just be that—hope, the same sort of idealistic nonsense that made her believe her first video would fix everything overnight.

Maya opened an AuthNet browser and went to a resource page Brennan had set up for her where she stored important information, like ooFC.18D4.98A0.0153, the network address Zeroice gave her. She figured it connected to whatever server he used to conduct his digital espionage forays. After copying the numbers out of her text note, she opened a messaging client and initiated a connection to that address.

"What are you doing?" whispered Sarah.

"Opening a door so I can throw anything useful into it if I find something."

She perused the icons, looking for anything noteworthy while Sarah pulled open the desk drawers one by one, peering at the contents. She took something out of the bottom drawer on the right. "Hey... who's that?"

"Hmm?" Maya peeled her eyes off the computer screen full of uselessness.

Sarah held up a clear plastic picture frame holding an image of a young woman with dark brown skin in a glittery blue evening gown, standing beside a man with a lighter complexion like Maya in a sharp black suit. They both looked to be in their early twenties. The strange familiarity to the woman's face clicked after a few seconds of staring.

"Holy crap. That's Vanessa." Maya brushed her fingers down the photo. "It's so strange to see her smiling like that."

"Like what?"

"Genuine. I don't think I've ever seen her look *really* happy before. It's..." Maya sighed. "Almost like she's a real person. I wonder what she was like."

Sarah leaned close, almost touching ears with her. "Who's the guy?"

"I dunno." Maya shrugged.

"Terrence Parker," said Vanessa, from the doorway.

Maya jumped, dropping the picture, and stared over the desk at her ex-mother.

Vanessa Oman stood in the doorway with one foot inside the room, a gun in her hand, but not raised. Her puffy white blouse sparkled with silver flecks, though it had a disheveled quality like she'd worn it for days in a row. Strangest of all... the woman wore sweat pants. That alone stunned Maya mute.

Sarah dropped to her knees and started to hide behind the desk.

"I already know you're there, girl. No point hiding."

Maya didn't like the 'tired' tone in Vanessa's voice. Much like the smile in the photograph, she'd never heard the woman sound so close to defeated. With a slow creep, she slid her hands over to the keyboard, hoping her former mother couldn't see through the monitors.

"Who's Terrence?" asked Maya, eyes locked on Vanessa's.

The woman sighed out her nose and glanced off to the side. "A man I used to know."

‹Vanessa got me. Send Mom and Dad ASAP!› typed Maya into the message client she'd opened to Zeroice's server. ‹Double Rock Park. Metal plate by creek past the memorial. Hidden bunker. Help!›

"You liked him?" Maya eased her hands away from the keyboard after minimizing the chat window.

Vanessa walked closer, stopping in the middle of the room, watching Sarah. "I know you've got that stunner pistol."

Sarah didn't flinch. "I know you've got that real pistol. You're going to tell me to throw it aside, but that's stupid of me. You won't put yours down, so why don't we both just keep them and agree not to hurt each other?"

Vanessa's fatigued expression gave way to an impressed look. "Very well. But you should be careful not to move in a way that makes me think you're trying to use it. Are you sure you wouldn't feel safer putting me at ease?"

"If you shoot Maya, I'm going to put a dart right up your nose." Sarah narrowed her eyes. "And you won't last long enough to wake up."

"Touchy little thing, aren't you." Vanessa almost smiled. "I suppose I'd have to shoot you first then."

Sarah's eyes widened as if she hadn't thought of that.

"I'd rather not. No matter what you may think of me, I don't wish to harm children."

"What about all those kids in the Fade wards?" asked Maya. "That didn't bother you."

"Ascendant has a program to provide Xenodril to children under eighteen. People had only to ask for it... but they rarely did. Saving kids for free is good PR."

Maya doubted such a program existed, though she'd never found anything proving it didn't. "They probably didn't bother because they thought Ascendant's too greedy. And let me guess, it required going to a clinic in the Sanc, which most of the people out in the Hab are terrified of doing. Why did you set Fade loose?"

"Xenodril was an unfortunate necessity. Without it, this company would never have become what it is. Ascendant would have died with Terrance, in obscurity. Ninety-four life-saving medicines exist now that would not be possible if we didn't have the funding provided by the Xenodril project."

"It's evil," said Maya.

Vanessa took a step closer. Both girls stared at her weapon, though her arm remained slack at her side. "What is the greater evil, dear? A few hundred people a year to Fade, or many thousands lost to conditions and diseases we can now cure because of that funding? What I did enabled humanity to rise from the ashes and thrive. Were it not for Fade, we never would have had the resources to bring the Sanctuary Zones into the modern era. We would still be dying of diseases eradicated a century before the war as well as cancer, diabetes, and genetic anomalies. Babies that only ten years ago would have lived as freaks—if they lived at all—can now enjoy a normal life. Is the small percentage of those who succumb to Fade truly too great a price to pay to prevent all that suffering?"

Maya's throat swelled with a lump, picturing Ashley's half-grey face as well as Genna whenever she talked about Sam. "I know you're looking at numbers. You don't see the real people behind it. I can understand you soaking Citizens for money, but why did you have to let anyone die when Xenodril is so cheap to make?"

"Fear," said Vanessa, absent her usual imperious gloating tone. "A tiger without fangs is nothing. If we gave away Xenodril to the poor, the Citizens would demand it for free, too. If Fade ceased being a threat, it would be worthless."

"Xenodril's going to be worthless soon." Maya squirmed. "Ascendant's big now. You don't need to keep using Fade."

"I'm aware you incinerated the Rosedale stock. And no, I didn't send those troops after you. The site manager did that without my authorization."

"Is he still trying to kill her?" asked Sarah.

"No." Vanessa glanced at her handgun. "I fired him."

Maya stared open-mouthed at her for a few seconds, unable to believe the woman had shown something akin to parental wrath. "For losing the Fade or for ordering me killed?"

"Does it matter?" Vanessa plucked a bit of lint from her blouse and dropped it.

"Well, if you say it was for losing the Fade, I'd think 'yeah that pretty much figures.' But I'm not sure how I'd process it if you were pissed off he wanted to kill me." Maya leaned over and picked up the picture. "You were pretty."

Vanessa emitted a scoffing chuckle.

"You still kinda are... when you're not staring at everyone like you want them dead," whispered Maya.

Sarah clenched her jaw, her cheeks reddening, a mixture of fury and terror in her pure blue eyes.

"Trying to appeal to flattery now?" asked Vanessa.

"No. Just saying. I never saw this photo of you. Or this man. Who was he?"

Vanessa glanced to the right at the false window as if gazing out over the ghost of a city long ago burned to ash. "Terrence Parker was my husband. We met in college and married not long after, in 2071."

"Three years before the war started," said Maya in a half whisper. "Did he die during the war?"

"No. He was right there with me during the worst of it, after the first wave of nuclear detonations. You think Fade is evil, but you've never seen hundreds of thousands die over the course of days. Compared to that, what Fade took is nothing." Vanessa looked down. Her grip on the handgun had loosened enough that Maya almost considered trying to steal it from her, but the shock of seeing Vanessa appear almost... sad caused her brain to seize up. "We founded Ascendant together. The name was his idea, that we would be the agents of humanity's ascendance from the ashes. We would revive medical technology and keep it going no matter what the warmongers did to us as a species."

Sarah shifted her weight onto one leg.

Vanessa glanced at her.

"Relax..." Sarah raised her left hand. "Not gonna shoot you. Just tired of standing."

"You could sit," said Vanessa, her voice devoid of energy.

Maya stared at the photo of Terrence. "But something went wrong?"

"You remind me of him in some ways, even though you don't share a single chromosome with him. My husband had a soft heart, much like you. He would value helping people over profit, even to the point the company would fail. The man couldn't see that if Ascendant collapsed, any future good we could do would not exist. But, back then, I would've agreed with him."

"So, what happened?" asked Maya—trying not to sound too accusatory.

"The military came to us because we had reestablished some ability to manufacture drugs on a scale mostly lost due to the bombardment. They wanted Fade. Or, at least, something like it. A nanobot-enhanced biological weapon that could be selectively programmed to attack enemies while ignoring friendlies. Terrence didn't want any part of such a project, but the amount of money the government waved at us was too much to ignore. But, before we completed the agent to their specifications, Terrence's soft heart killed him."

"He couldn't finish it." Maya traced a finger over his image.

"Correct. He naïvely thought the government would simply allow us to abandon the project on moral grounds. They shot him claiming that in a time of war, his refusal amounted to treason... so I gave them what they asked for. Only, it hadn't been complete. Fade didn't possess any ability to distinguish friend from foe, child from adult, innocent from combatant."

Sarah gasped. "It killed people I knew. A friend of mine, Sam. He was only ten years old. How could you *do* that?"

Vanessa gazed out at the 'window.' "I was destroyed with grief. Angry. Like you are over what I did to your father."

Maya's breath stalled in her throat at hearing her mother admit to killing The Dad. Sarah trembled with rage, but somehow kept herself quiet.

"You know exactly how I felt back then." Vanessa shifted her gaze to Sarah. "I wanted to burn the whole world to a cinder, finish off what the nukes started. But, I didn't. Terrence wouldn't have wanted me to go that far. I reverse engineered Fade to make Xenodril. The bastards who killed Terrence believed me when I told them Fade had come from the Koreans, that our NVFP-8 agent would only infect people with certain genetic markers indicating Korean, Russian, or Chinese heritage."

"They bought that line of bullshit?" asked Maya.

"Yes they did." Vanessa chuckled. "And they believed I made a wonder drug that would cure the Koreans' weapon as well as ours. We gave them vaccines for the soldiers, but that was around 2080 when the war stopped being a war and turned into a whole bunch of overgrown little boys with guns playing king of the hill."

"Dad said the war ended in 2083," whispered Sarah.

Vanessa glanced down at the gun and flicked the safety on with her thumb. "In 2080, most governments collapsed. Soldiers kept on fighting because they didn't realize the countries who sent them into battle no longer existed. It wasn't until 2083 that everyone more or less gave up on any sort of organized combat and the survivors tried to go home. I'm sure you've heard the stories about North Korean, South Korean, US, Chinese, British troops all riding together back to their villages or heading for the nearest port to hop on a boat. By that point, almost no functional aircraft remained. Men and women who'd have shot each other on sight days before shared bus rides or sat together in the backs of cargo trucks."

"Yeah," said Sarah. "And there's *still* soldiers out there in little 'tribes' fighting each other."

Maya stared at this woman who she once would've given anything to have love her, once hated more than anything, and now couldn't quite figure out how to feel about her. Much like her 'what would you rather' question about Mr. Mason, Vanessa's quandary about Fade had no answer. Maya thought any avoidable death—much less intentional murder via Fade—was evil. But, could she really claim that several thousand people dying every year to things Ascendant could treat because of the money generated by Xenodril sales would be better? Logic called a few hundred deaths a year less tragic than thousands, but understanding that point made Maya hate herself. It condoned what Vanessa had done.

"Terrence was too caring. Too weak. His soft heart cost him his life, and I resolved never to be weak again." Vanessa reached over and took Maya's hand. "There are two kinds of people in this world, Maya. People with the strength to pave their way... and everyone buried under that road."

She stared at the woman's hand so much darker than hers, neither cold nor warm. Nowhere in her memory had Vanessa ever touched her for any reason even approaching an emotional moment. "That's sad. Were you so cold to me because you wanted to protect yourself from any pain if something happened to me? Or did you really think of me as a possession you purchased."

Vanessa's jaw twitched. Maya thought the woman's face would sooner shatter into a thousand pieces than release one tear. "I promised myself I would never be weak again. My position as the head of Ascendant made me a target. The lives of everyone who depended on our medicines demanded I not allow myself to be vulnerable in any way." She dragged her gaze up from the floor to meet Maya's stare. "I didn't truly regard you as a company asset, though I did create that appearance to protect us both. Terrence wouldn't have approved. Perhaps if I had the ability to rewind time, I would do things differently. Perhaps I wouldn't. I killed the man who sent the security team after you because he ordered you dead."

She squeezed Vanessa's hand, unable to believe herself for doing it.

A moment of silence passed between them.

"I guess Ascendant couldn't make a pill to cure a broken heart," said Maya in a small voice.

27

THE QUEEN'S CASTLE

Awry smile spread across Vanessa's lips. "I see you do have my sense of humor."

"What happened in the Sanc?" asked Maya. "Why are you hiding down here?"

Vanessa heaved a deep sigh. "I'm weeding out traitors."

"By traitors, are you referring to Authority officers who realized who they're supposed to be working for, or something more internal?"

"The Authority is the last vestige of a government that obviously failed. The people in control of it are the same ilk who destroyed our world." Vanessa released Maya's hand and paced around in front of the desk, gesturing her gun randomly around at the wall. "They needed to be controlled or they would've eventually evolved into the same nuclear warmongers they once were. You may call me a dictator, but Ascendant's goal has always been *improving* the human condition."

"They treated us like complete shit!" yelled Sarah. "At least once a year since I've been five years old, I've been slapped around and left hogtied on the floor for hours—once more than a whole day. A month ago, one of them gave me a concussion cracking me in the head with his rifle."

"Almost everyone who's grown up in the Hab has PTSD at the sight of blueberry armor," said Maya. "But they weren't really Authority. They worked for you."

Vanessa ran her left hand up over her head. "It is an unfortunate aspect of humanity that some percentage of those given power exploit that power. The division between Citizens and Nons formed on its own, nothing I had intended to orchestrate."

"What's unfortunate is you didn't do anything to stop them. Why?" Maya held the photo up at her. "You were once a human being."

"There are things I didn't exactly see from my position, Maya. It's not that I approved of it... I simply had too much else in my sphere of awareness to manage everything down to the fringes."

"Now I think you're making excuses, but I guess it's kinda late. What were you going to do with the Unilateralis project?"

Vanessa whipped around, staring at her.

"Yeah, I heard about it. Mind control nanobots." Maya leaned back in the chair.

"How?" asked Vanessa.

"A conversation during my weekly kidnapping. Though, I'll admit the accommodations weren't as nice as your penthouse."

Vanessa resumed pacing. "If you would have stayed there, you'd be perfectly safe and wouldn't be abducted and threatened so much. This... this... *war* going on now, might not have happened."

"You did kinda murder Sarah's dad and threaten to hurt her if I didn't do what you told me to. Oh, and you also threatened to kill all the kids in our building. Sorry, but that kinda caused some trust issues."

The Hornet creaked from Sarah squeezing it.

"I was bluffing." Vanessa stopped walking back and forth. "You, Sarah, those poor children, none of you were ever in any real danger from me."

"Wait," yelled Sarah. "You expect us to believe you actually care about Maya now? And you still *murdered* my father. Why? What did he do to you?" Tears poured from her eyes. "He was a harmless messed-up veteran who liked to shout swear words at football and drink beer. You told those mercs to just kill Maya 'cause you'll make another one."

"That wasn't easy to say." Vanessa picked at the handgun. "It was only possible because I'd spent nine years keeping her emotionally distant for that exact reason. I knew it was extremely likely that she would be kidnapped or killed before reaching adulthood because of who I am. I couldn't allow myself the vulnerability to be affected by that. The more I showed the world that it didn't bother me one way or the other what happened to her, the safer I thought she would be."

"I'm giving that about a twenty-five percent on the bullshit-o-meter" Maya held her hands up mimicking a needle gauge.

"Only twenty-five?" asked Sarah with a raised eyebrow.

Vanessa gestured at the redhead. "Your father was... not equipped to take care of a child. His status as a veteran would have bought him sway with the Authority, and likely would have complicated even my offering you a better home. You accuse me of treating Maya like a company asset, but he treated you like a domestic servant. Cooking for him, cleaning up, doing his laundry."

"That's what people who love each other do for each other," said Sarah, barely able to speak, her voice warped by grief.

"A *better* home?" Maya thrust her arms out to both sides. "That was a prison. A big, fancy prison. You shut me away from everything. I never even saw another kid my age until I wound up in the Hab. You couldn't even be bothered to return my calls to say good night."

"I was wrong." Vanessa looked away. "I thought shielding myself from any attachment would make the inevitable easier."

Sarah crumpled to her knees, sobbing quietly.

"What inevitable?" Maya slipped out of the chair and sat on the floor with her arms around Sarah, rubbing her back.

"Losing you." Vanessa rubbed the bridge of her nose. "I thought setting your friend free from that man would help her acclimate to a proper environment."

Sarah tried to lunge to her feet, but Maya held her down. "Set me *free!*? You killed my father!"

"In an emotionless, logical sense, she thinks it was better for you," said Maya. "The woman lost her empathy."

Vanessa opened her mouth, but closed it without saying a word.

"I hate her so much," mumbled Sarah in a teary whisper. "Why did she have to kill him?"

"What about those mind control nanobots?" Maya glared at Vanessa while squeezing Sarah tight. "Were you going to use them on me so you had the daughter you always wanted?"

"No, Maya." Vanessa made eye contact. "You are so young. Your heart hasn't been torn out, stepped on, and lit on fire by the world just yet."

"It's kinda trying." Maya scowled. "You let me think Genna died."

"*I* thought that woman died." Vanessa shifted her jaw side to side. "That was not an intentional infliction of emotional cruelty. Those nanobots were for... security personnel. The Authority cannot function efficiently when they're all thinking for themselves. But it's a little late for that at this point."

Sarah whistled in a 'this woman is effing insane' way.

"Wait, you *hadn't* used it yet? Where did all those thugs in white armor come from?" Maya relaxed her hug since Sarah had calmed, but didn't let go completely.

"Former Authority affected by the purge, Nons thirsty for citizenship, existing security officers eager for more power. I didn't need mind control machines to turn them against the Authority. All it took were a few believable stories of Korean influence, a bit of flag-waving, and a heap of misinformation laced with a tiny grain of verifiable-but-misleading truth. Oh, and the former Nons were the cruelest of the lot. Offer a man who has nothing a little power, and they suddenly think themselves above where they once were." Vanessa gave a blasé shrug. "It's not exactly difficult to get people to do things, even atrocious things, if it's what they can be convinced needs to be done for the greater good. Give a man an outsider, an enemy to hate, and the rest is simple. And you did observe how cruel the Authority had been to those people. It didn't take much when I offered them a chance for revenge."

Maya cringed, simultaneously feeling a little sympathy for Vanessa along with a lot of revulsion. The woman had lost a man she evidently loved so much his death destroyed her. That, Maya could understand. But she could blame only Vanessa for the woman she'd allowed herself to become.

"So, what are you going to do now?" asked Maya.

"Well, I obviously cannot allow you two to leave this bunker. But, you will not be harmed. We will stay here until I either have Ascendant firmly back under my control, or die trying."

Maya looked down and shuddered, already homesick for her real parents, friends, and the dingy little bedroom she shared with her sister,

Magic cards and all. "Doctor Haas is trying to kill you. She kidnapped me and made me give her the addresses for the safe locations, but I didn't give her this one. I... promise I won't tell anyone else about it if you let us go."

"There's no point," said Vanessa. "It's too dangerous out there. You are already here where it's safe. People will go after you for being Maya Oman, even if I am gone. This place is far nicer than that crumbling high-rise back in the Habitation District. The two of you will have a fine, comfortable life here."

"You never let me touch anything but the carpet in my bedroom." Maya frowned.

"We should start over," said Vanessa. "I've already lost everything. There's no reason for me to stay so distant."

"You loved that guy once." Sarah pulled her hair out of her face. "Are you still even capable of feeling anything for your daughter?"

"We only share thirty-seven percent DNA," whispered Maya. "She's more like my aunt."

Sarah narrowed her eyes. "How do we know you're not bluffing again?"

"What do I have to gain from harming you two?"

"Only the security that we couldn't escape and give away this location," said Maya. "Why do you want us to trust that you won't hurt us but you won't trust that I can keep my mouth shut?"

"Well..." Vanessa folded her arms and tapped a finger to her lips. "You released details of the Fade program to the public. You somehow hacked into the system to steal the Xenodril formula, and released that to the world. I'm sure you're going to tell everyone about the Unilateralis project—don't bother, it's destroyed by the way—so you do have a track record of not being able to keep secrets."

"That stuff is horrible and evil!" Maya flailed her arms. "And against the law. I *had* to do that. You might've thought you were 'ascending' humanity, but you created a totalitarian dystopian nightmare corporatocracy."

Sarah gave her an epic side eye. "Can you say that again in English?"

"Shithole," yelled Maya.

"Dear..." Vanessa attempted a warm expression. "We have a lot of ground to retrace. Our relationship can be different. But I can't let you leave. One of these days, I'm sure the world will make you regret your strong sense of compassion, but I give you my word, I will not harm either of you."

Maya swiped the Hornet from Sarah and leapt up, pointing it at Vanessa. "What if I really don't feel like being kidnapped again?"

"You wouldn't shoot that thing at me," said Vanessa, her voice soft and calm.

Maya trembled with anger, confusion, and determination. "When I thought my real mother was dead, killed by men you sent to kidnap me, I promised myself I'd shoot you in the face."

"She didn't necessarily say it had to be with a real gun." Sarah folded her arms.

"This won't kill you." Maya squeezed and relaxed her grip on the handle. "But I am leaving. I will promise not to give out this address. Whatever you did wrong, I'm too little to clean it up. I just want to go home and be a child, have friends, and *stop* being kidnapped every damn week."

Vanessa glanced down at her gun, clutched in both hands against her body like a tiny purse. "I understand you have created emotional attachments to that woman who originally kidnapped you from your home. Perhaps I can see my way clear to accepting her presence in your life. You say you wish to no longer be abducted. Remain here and that is a guarantee. Why do you have such difficulty staying here with me, where it's safe?"

"Because. This isn't my home. We're leaving. Are you going to try and stop us?" asked Maya.

"*Why* do we have a problem with it?" shouted Sarah. "Because *you killed my father!*"

The door flew open at the behest of a boot.

Genna stomped in, rifle pointed at Vanessa. "Prepare to die."

28

ABSOLUTION

"Wait!" shouted Maya.

Genna froze, arms twitching, a hard glare aimed over her weapon at Vanessa.

Pope eased in the door. Barnes and Weber entered behind him, all three carrying combat rifles.

Vanessa's dark face paled a shade. "So... I finally meet the Brigade."

"About one-fortieth of us, yeah." Weber smiled. At twenty-four, his brush cut had gone prematurely grey, but the look worked for him.

Maya forced herself not laugh at his wise-assery and stared at Genna. "Mom, please don't kill her."

Pope raised an eyebrow at Maya, then shifted his gaze to Vanessa. "Well, if this isn't going to end right away in a hail of bullets, you might wanna drop the gun."

"Well... I suppose this is it then. If you're here to engage in some manner of protracted fistfight, you may as well pull that trigger and save us all the time."

"Nah," said Genna. "I already found out one damn punch will put you square on your ass."

Vanessa raised an eyebrow at her. "You're former military with augmentation. It's sad you're proud of your physical superiority to a civilian who rarely sets foot outside of an office or lab."

Genna growled.

"Perhaps we can reach an amicable arrangement?" Vanessa lifted both eyebrows a tick.

"Oh, this better be *damn* good," said Barnes. "I can't wait to hear this."

Weber tilted his head side to side, cracking his neck. "Exactly what are you going to offer people who've spent the past ten years trying to take you down?"

"He doesn't necessarily mean kill you." Maya held up a finger. "Just topple Ascendant."

"You real damn sure you don't want me to end this... woman?" Genna adjusted her grip on the rifle. "After all the shit she put you through?"

"Yeah." Maya looked at the picture frame on the desk. "I kind of understand why she's the way she is now."

Vanessa turned in a slow, graceful circle to face the adults, handgun still pressed to her front. "Ascendant could give you back something you lost. We could clone your son, Sam."

Genna's eyes bulged.

"Oh, shit." Maya darted over and wrapped herself around Genna—as if she had any chance to hold the woman back.

"It..." Genna shuddered with rage, glancing off to the side and down. "It wouldn't be him. The boy would look like him. Might even sound like him, act like him, but it wouldn't be the same. I can't just 'make another one.'"

"You don't seriously believe in that 'soul' nonsense, do you?" asked Vanessa, a hint of amusement in her smile. "Humans are a result of the interaction of billions of neurons and brain chemistry. Metaphysical fairy tales have nothing to do with it. The boy would be no different."

"Umm," said Maya in a small voice. "Can I ask a stupid question?"

Everyone looked at her except Genna and Vanessa who continued to stare at each other like a pair of lionesses about to throw down.

"Why didn't you clone Terrence?" Since it didn't seem likely her mother would pounce on Vanessa, Maya let go, backed up, and widened her eyes. "I'm not trying to be sarcastic here. That's a real question."

Vanessa flinched as though she'd walked face first into a cobweb.

"The technology to do that didn't exist until a year or two ago. Terrence's remains are too far deteriorated."

"That's not true." Maya shook her head. "They can clone dinosaurs if you find DNA. Age of the remains doesn't matter."

"I don't know where his remains even are," said Vanessa, a hitch in her voice. "They never returned him."

"Are you sure they even killed him?" asked Sarah.

Vanessa glanced at her. "I was standing right next to him when they shot him."

"Oh." Maya looked down, lowering the Hornet. "Sorry. Didn't know that. I thought you maybe like kinda really believed there might be a soul involved and didn't think a clone would really be Terrence."

"Fuck this," muttered Genna.

She blurred at Vanessa. A fleshy *smack* preceded the handgun flying toward Maya. It whizzed past her head, missing her by inches, and bounced off the wall behind her. Genna leapt on Vanessa, throwing her into the back wall next to the fake window.

Maya tossed the Hornet to Sarah and ran over, jumping on Genna's back as the woman punched Vanessa over and over again. "Mom! Mom! Mom! Stop!"

"Baby." Genna paused, right fist raised, left fist holding a bundle of silvery-white sweater blouse at Vanessa's chin.

The former CEO of Ascendant Pharmaceuticals grabbed at her wrist, feebly trying to shove her way free.

"Mom. Please don't kill her. Please!" Maya wrapped her arms around Genna's neck, clinging and crying at not wanting to witness her mother kill someone.

"How can you forgive this bitch?" wheezed Genna through a clenched jaw.

"I didn't say I forgive her. I said I kinda understand why she is who she is. That's not the same as forgiving what she *chose* to do. And, I really don't want to watch you do it."

"Barnes, get her out the room, please?" asked Genna.

"No!" wailed Maya. "It's not worth it. Do you really want to have the memory of killing her?"

Genna tilted her head in consideration, a few strands of her dreads fell from her shoulders and dangled. "Yeah, I kinda do."

"But it's killing," whined Maya.

"Baby, she'll be another tick mark on a long line of tick marks. And a lot o' them poor bastards only crime was carrying a rifle for the wrong goddamn flag."

"Okay." Maya huffed. "Don't you think she'll suffer more in prison? If you kill her, that's the end. If she answers for what she did, she'll have to live with no longer having power, no fancy apartment, no limos..."

A clamor arose in the hallway outside.

"Aw, shit," muttered Weber in a jovially-annoyed tone. "Who the hell invited them?"

Maya twisted to look at the door as a swarm of blueberries entered.

"Sorry. My bad." Barnes held up a hand. "Kind of expected a bigger party here. Thought we could use the backup."

"The hell is going on here?" asked a female in Authority armor.

Pope stepped in front of her and rapidly explained the situation in a low murmur.

Genna bowed her head and muttered, "You are one lucky bitch. Dunno what you said to her, but this kid is the *only* reason your ass is still alive."

Vanessa reached toward Maya. Blood oozed from her nose and lip, though her jaw didn't appear broken this time. "I'm sorry for how I was to you."

For an instant, Maya considered ignoring her, but couldn't bring herself to be that cold, not after learning about Terrence. Suppressing a distrustful sigh, she clasped hands.

"I hope you find peace," said Maya. "What you did with Fade, from a pure numbers standpoint, I can understand. But no one with a working heart could've made that decision. There is always a better way to make money than killing. It might've been fewer people dead, but *choosing* to kill is a lot different from people getting diseases because of bad circumstances." She released Vanessa's hand and stepped back.

Genna hauled the woman to her feet one handed and dragged her around toward the blueberries. After a pat down search, they put binders on Vanessa and walked her out. Maya stood beside Genna, barely breathing as the woman who had caused so much suffering disappeared down the lush hallway. Vanessa's angry shouts blared in her memory, ordering her into her room, not to touch anything here lest she make it dirty, to smile wider for the camera, shouting at various employees about being late for a meeting and to 'get on with it.'

It didn't seem totally genuine for a woman who had been so icy to her for so long to sincerely apologize for it, but perhaps knowing *why* she had become that woman had allowed her a peek of the person she'd been twenty years ago. At one point in time, Vanessa had been human. And to protect herself from tragedy, she had traded away that humanity.

"I can't hate her anymore," said Maya. "I pity her."

"You're too damn nice for your own good." Genna took a knee and grabbed her in a fierce hug. "Baby, you scared me to death."

"We didn't *want* to go anywhere." Maya rushed a story about the secret tunnel, the collapse and running through a warzone, Dr. Haas, and everything.

"You ain't in no trouble, but there ain't gonna be no more missions for you."

Maya grinned. "I'm okay with that."

"You know." Genna bowed her head. "I think Sam would'a wanted me not ta kill her, too."

"Yeah," said Sarah. "Sam was sweet, like Maya."

"Ready to go home?" Pope hooked his thumbs in his pockets.

"Yes!" Maya bounced. "Umm. Sec." She walked over to pick up the old picture of Vanessa. "Sarah?"

"Hmm?"

"I want to keep this. But if you don't want it in our room, I'll leave it here."

Sarah frowned at the picture. "You're not gonna like put it out on display are you?"

"No. Just keep it in a closet or something so I can sometimes look at it and remember that woman wasn't always a monster."

"I don't want to stare at her every day, but if you keep it hidden, it's okay." Sarah tucked her hair behind her ear. "I understand. I have pictures of Dad before the war made him nuts."

Maya hugged her.

"All right." Pope collected the girls and ushered them toward the door. "You two are up way past your bedtime."

29

THE BOARD

Over the next two weeks, Maya spent most of her time at home, or at least not leaving the building. Her friends also wanted to avoid the outside due to lingering skirmishes with groups of former Ascendant thugs. The kids haunted the basement play area or sat in Book's apartment listening to stories when they didn't descend on the Changs' place to watch movies on the tiny laptop screen.

Nightmares happened often, mostly of being trapped outside in the middle of a rolling gunfight, trying to get to Sarah before one of them took a bullet. Fortunately, since she shared a bed with her sister, whenever one of them woke up screaming, the other woke up, too. Each had become the other's living teddy bear.

Once, the second night back home, they'd both woke up screaming so badly they couldn't console each other. Pope carried them down the hall and the whole family piled into one bed for the night. But, as the days passed, the harrowing dash through streets awash with gunfire drifted farther and farther away, becoming more like an awful dream than something she'd experienced for real.

Fifteen days after watching blueberries escort Vanessa away, Maya rolled out of bed and went straight to the bathroom. Genna stood by the mirror fussing with her hair. Maya gave her a quick hug, pulled off her nightie, and hopped in the tub to clean up. Genna walked out after a few minutes amid a soft clatter of wooden hair accessories. Having the bathroom to herself lasted only a little while before Sarah stumbled in yawning and sat on the toilet.

"So jealous," muttered Maya.

"What for?"

"You get to sleep. I hate waking up early."

Sarah let off a whispery giggle, sounding still mostly asleep. "Pope's still snoring."

"It's okay." Maya stood and stepped out of the tub at the same moment the toilet flushed.

"See you later." Sarah threw a towel over her as she walked out.

Maya dried herself, then returned to her room, where Sarah had already fallen asleep again. Grumbling at not really wanting to be awake, she put on the shimmery, pinchy super-expensive dress. None of her clothes qualified as 'nice.' Her wardrobe went straight from grungy Non clothing to ridiculous. Considering the only reason she owned the stupid thing was Ascendant, it felt appropriate to wear it. She stepped into a pair of black ballet flats, which she liked *way* more than the heels she usually wore with the thing, and hurried out to the front room where Genna waited for her in a dark grey skirt suit.

"You look really weird in a dress," said Maya.

"It's a skirt. Not a dress." Genna swatted dust off it. "And it's not mine. Only borrowing it from Arlene. Little tight in the shoulders."

"The woman's a twig."

Genna laughed. "Says Princess Noodle Arms."

Maya raspberried her.

"You ready?" Genna patted her on the head.

"No, but let's go."

Genna chuckled. "Oh, one more slight change of plan."

"What?" asked Maya.

Infuriatingly, Genna said nothing as she headed for the stairs. When she exited on the sixth floor, Maya's confusion deepened. She stopped at the Chang's place, and knocked.

Zoe answered. "Hey, Gen. What's up?"

"That little thing we talked about. Is it still okay?"

"Oh sure. Hang on." Zoe zipped into the apartment, leaving the door open.

"What are you doing?" asked Maya.

Genna grinned.

Ji Yeon appeared in the doorway, dolled up in a clean white dress and pink shoes, a blue ribbon in her hair. "Good morning!"

Maya gawked. "You're... Hah! Awesome! I can't wait to see their faces! Umm. Is she okay with it?"

"I am." Ji Yeon smiled. "It is the least I can do for my friend."

Ascendant Tower had long been a place of misery for Maya Oman.

Usually, whenever she visited, people scurried away from her or shot dirty looks at her when they didn't think she'd see. No one wanted to be caught up in whatever shitstorm might fall on them for merely being in her vicinity.

Today, however, the employees all stared at her in much the same way as she imagined people used to ogle celebrities before the war. The blueberries at the Sanctuary Zone entry had been friendlier in a way that made her feel like 'Baltimore's mascot' or something. Odder still, they left the gates open and merely observed people coming and going rather than searching every car.

A thirtyish man in a nice suit, his light brown hair short and neat, met them in the lobby. He introduced himself as Mr. Chandler, then escorted her, Genna, and Ji Yeon to an elevator, up to the fortieth floor, and down a sedate white-and-cyan corridor to a set of rosewood double doors. The place smelled as antiseptic and perfect as ever, with the faintest hint of mint cleaning solution.

Mr. Chandler pulled the door open for them. Genna stepped in first. Maya followed, suffering an immediate cringe reaction to the same long conference room table she'd been forced to parade around on in high heels, 'practicing' her ad spiel in front of the board. She strolled into the room under the spell of a weird mood. She somewhat channeled Vanessa's 'I own this place' confidence, but not her '... and everyone in here' arrogance.

She locked stares with Jerry Michaels, the man whose coffee she'd tripped over, or more accurately, accidentally kicked into his lap while trying not to break her neck. Ever since, he'd referred to her as 'the klutz.' At his nameplate reading 'VP – Marketing' instead of junior VP, she quirked an eyebrow. Jerry appeared to sense something different and held back any snide remarks that might've been circling his brain.

Mr. Chandler took the seat at Genna's left, Maya at her right, facing the fourteen members of the Ascendant Executive Board.

The instant Ji Yeon entered, most of the board froze statue still, staring at her. Humming merrily to herself, the artificial child walked around the side of Maya's chair and scooted into it with her, fitting comfortably, but snug.

Much to Maya's delight, Jerry Michaels broke out in a cold sweat, unable to stop staring at Ji Yeon.

"Good morning everyone," said Izuki Yamamoto, the chairman. "As I'm sure you are all aware, we've assembled today to discuss the matter of Miss Oman's interest in Ascendant Corporation."

As in, I have none. Stakes, yes. Interest, no way.

"Good morning, Miss Oman." Yamamoto rendered the briefest of bows via nodding.

She stood. "Good morning, everyone. Thank you for inviting me to this meeting. I understand I am in a uniquely awkward position for you, seeing as how I have a forty-nine percent controlling interest in the company. I'm also aware that the fifty-one percent once held by Vanessa has been forfeited due to her facing multiple felony charges and the action of this board to sever her control of the company."

Murmuring went around the room.

"I am inclined to accept your offer and divest all interest in Ascendant Pharmaceuticals under certain conditions. I'm too young to take any active role with the company, nor do I really want to. However, I am not as naïve as my age would imply, and I will not be cheated."

Again, the board members muttered amongst themselves. Jerry Michaels rolled his eyes.

Maya pointed at him. "Pardon this one bit of immaturity, but I *am* still nine. If that idiot calls me a klutz again, this whole deal is off and I'll do everything I can to kick his butt straight out the door. It wasn't my idea to walk on the table. What kind of idiot makes an eight-year-old in high heels strut around on a polished table?"

Most of the board chuckled. Jerry cleared his throat and straightened his tie.

"Anyway." She gestured to her left. "This is Genna Washington. She is my legal guardian, and is here to act on my behalf for anything that may need to be signed since I am, well, nine. With us is Mr. Chandler, our Authority Counsel."

"What conditions are you referring to?" asked Anna Rivera, Senior VP of Human Resources.

"Hopefully, they are not greatly impactful to Ascendant and you will have no problems agreeing to them." Maya cleared her throat. "My conditions are spelled out in detail within the documentation Mr. Chandler is about to share with everyone. There are only two. First: Ascendant will destroy any remaining quantities of NVFP-8, or Fade as it is more commonly known. You have no reason to continue producing it as it is both a violation of human decency and useless as a profiteering scheme. Every pharmaceutical company in the world now has the means to produce Xenodril."

"You torpedoed your own company's flagship product," said Ron Wadsworth, CFO.

"No, we stopped a rogue element within Ascendant's leadership from committing war crimes. As I understand, the board didn't have knowledge of the top secret project..." Maya raised an accusing eyebrow. "Or did you help cover up mass murder?"

Rapid murmuring rose and settled among the board members.

Maya waited a few minutes, but no one said anything. "Good. It's reassuring to see that such an upstanding company would not be party to turning biological weapons on innocent citizens for profit. My second condition is that Ascendant will not interact financially with the Authority or any agents of the Eastern Seaboard Provisional Government in any way that implies reciprocal favoritism, influencing policy, or application of law."

Ji Yeon hummed to herself, playing with her hair ribbon, swinging her feet idly.

"If I may," said Mr. Chandler. "The second of Maya's conditions is largely ceremonial as the Authority and the Eastern Seaboard Provisional Government are making internal changes to prohibit such things from the other side. While it would be a nice gesture for the board to officially state your acceptance of such a condition, an arrangement wherein a company such as Ascendant exerts financial influence over the Authority would constitute a crime once the ink on the new legislation is dry."

Mr. Yamamoto gestured at Chandler. "If you would be so kind, please share the documentation and we shall review your offer."

Chandler plugged a small fob into the table, and within seconds, amber holographic documents appeared floating in front of the executive board. They soon entered a discussion of terms amongst each other. None appeared to want to deal with the mess of having to go through whoever wound up appointed to manage Maya's share in the company as a trustee. Had Vanessa died or retired, Maya would've inherited full control, though several of the board members continued insisting that Ascendant was not a monarchy, and hereditary inheritance wouldn't transfer control of the company. Upon Vanessa's death, the board would have appointed a new CEO. Wadsworth pointed out that how corporate law worked before the war didn't mean a damn thing.

Ji Yeon hopped out of the chair and wandered around the room, touching all the plants and whatnot on the way before pausing at the far end to stare out the window at the street so far below. Most of the board members eyed her warily as she went by.

Mr. Chandler translated things from legal speak into plain English for Genna. From their conversation, Maya figured the board attempted to wheedle out with as low a payoff as they could manage, but had no interest in an ongoing mess that might put a child at the head of the company. At least three of the board sounded like they had their eye on the CEO spot and didn't want Maya in the running.

That suited her fine. She didn't want to be assassinated or kidnapped.

"We have reviewed the terms," said Mr. Yamamoto, "and have submitted a counteroffer."

Ji Yeon scrambled back around the table and hopped in the chair with Maya again, grinning at her. She launched into rapid whispering about how amazing it was to be so high off the ground.

Mr. Chandler examined the floating holographic documents in front of him, then leaned over to Genna and Maya. "They've come back with an offer fifteen percent under our initial figure."

"Are they screwing her over?" asked Genna.

"It's not quite low enough to fall into 'screwing' territory, but it's definitely a lowball."

Genna glanced at him. "Can we get her more?"

"We could. Depends on if you want to be here all day, all week, or go home in an hour or three."

"What do you think, baby?" asked Genna.

"See if they'll go for seven percent lower instead of fifteen," whispered Maya. "But I don't wanna be here all day. It's a shitload of money either way. I really only want to peel this stupid target off my back."

Genna hugged her.

"You don't have a target on your back," said Ji Yeon. "Your back is only half covered by that dress. I can see it."

Maya giggled.

Mr. Chandler spent a few minutes typing. "Members of the board, please find a suggested amendment."

The board discussed again for about fifteen minutes before the terminal pinged.

Mr. Chandler leaned over and muttered, "They came back with ten percent."

"Okay," said Maya. "If you think it's fair, it's fine with me. I'm not too concerned with getting as much money as possible. I just don't want to be cheated."

"What do you think?" whispered Genna to Mr. Chandler.

"It's a reasonable offer. Considering how quickly they agreed to it, they either want to be rid of her fast or think a protracted process could cost much more."

"Should we do it?" asked Genna.

Chandler eyed the screen. "You could do a *lot* worse."

"All right." Genna nodded. "I'll sign it for her."

"We accept your proposal," said Mr. Chandler to the board.

The board members, except for Jerry Michaels, all pressed their thumbprint onto the terminals in front of them. Chirping went around the room. A box popped up in front of Genna. She pressed her thumb to it, and Mr. Chandler 'signed' his copy as well.

Jerry Michaels fidgeted, but reluctantly touched his terminal.

"Agreement accepted," said an electronic female voice from a ceiling-mounted speaker.

"There is one problem." Jerry Michaels tapped his fingers on the table, causing an irritating thumping.

"What is your concern?" asked Mr. Chandler.

Michaels pointed at Ji Yeon. "This entire proceeding might not be binding due to coercion."

"Coercion?" Mr. Chandler blinked. "In what conceivable manner do you feel coerced by a small child?"

"You brought a damn nuclear warhead to a board meeting." Jerry Michaels gestured at her. "That's a rad orphan, isn't it? You brought her here deliberately as a threat. We know that Maya is hostile to Ascendant and would think nothing of literally destroying it, as opposed to financially, as she did with Xenodril."

Maya stood. "Jerry, *dahling*, do you honestly think I'd blow *myself* up? She's my friend. Ji Yeon isn't armed, and we never threatened anyone."

"Her mere presence is a threat. You brought her in here deliberately for that reason. Why else would you bring some random child with you?" Jerry Michaels pointed at her. "That thing could kill us all."

Ji Yeon looked down and sniffled.

"The contract's signed already, isn't it?" Maya peered up at Mr. Chandler. "Is it too late to demand they fire this asshole?"

Half the board chuckled, a few gasped.

"But seriously. Don't call her a thing. She's sentient." Maya scowled.

Ji Yeon looked up before fully erupting in tears, and hugging her.

"Go right ahead and scan her. There's no weapon." Genna grinned and put an arm around both girls. "Ji Yeon is no different from any other child. We kind of adopted her. Besides." She grinned. "We're in the Sanc. This many people in one place? If she was armed, she'd already have gone off."

Mr. Chandler covered his mouth to stop from smiling, and muttered, "No bloody wonder they agreed so fast."

30

ALL THE TOPPINGS

A tremendous explosion shook the walls of the apartment and knocked a can-turned-vase off the tiny table at the end of the couch.

Maya, and all her friends screamed.

"Gah!" yelled Pope from the kitchen as a ripple of machine gun fire rattled the walls. He poked his head into the living room. "Turn that down a bit. You'll have Barnes going crazy."

"Sorry," yelled Sarah over the continuing onscreen battle. She grabbed the remote for the giant new TV and stared at it. "Which button does the volume?"

Anton swiped it from her. "I got it."

He, too, stared at it for a moment in confusion.

Marcus snagged it from him and held it out to Maya.

She lowered her hands from her ears and tapped the volume down a bit. For the first few minutes of the level, the sound had been quiet. The booby trap mines had caught everyone off guard.

Pick (still refusing to wear a shirt) currently had the controller, guiding a space commando around the jungle of an alien world. Ji Yeon sat beside him in a fluffy white dress, wide-eyed, staring at the screen bigger than most bathtubs.

Maya set the remote down beside herself and smiled. She swam in her new shirt (she'd opted for pink on a lark) so big on her she'd likely be able to wear it until thirteen. It had enough length that it completely hid her shorts (also new). Her toenails sparkled with purple glitter polish (as did the nails of Sarah, Emily, and Ji Yeon).

None of the kids had spoken again of Marcus kissing her in the hallway. Maya cornered him in the basement long enough to tell him she understood why he did it, didn't necessarily mind it, but would probably punch him in the lips if he tried it again anytime soon—unless more people showed up to kill her.

He hadn't found that funny.

Despite the money Ascendant paid her to buy out her interest in the company, she wanted to live at *home,* in the same apartment where Sarah used to live with The Dad. Moving all her friends and their families into the Sanc had been the other option, but she didn't want to uproot everyone, nor did she need anything fancy. Also, she hadn't received *that* much money that she could've paid the obnoxious Sanc Zone rents for everyone for too long. No, this place had everything she needed—family and friends.

And a new video game system.

Of course, she had to share her windfall. The kids all got some new clothes. She bought Pick some toy spaceships, one even had blinking lights and made sound effects. Anton and Marcus got e-readers and a slew of books. At the clothing shop with the old woman and strange twins, May and June, Maya had found a few more overly ornate tiny dresses, which she gave to Emily. Ji Yeon wanted dolls—which Maya thought oddly ironic. And despite Sarah's protests, Maya had to get her something. Since the girl had gone so long with so little to wear, she got extra clothes. And, well, the video game system belonged to both of them.

She also made a standing offer to help anyone in the building out with food if they needed it.

Speaking of food, she'd bought Hydras for Book as well as Naida. The Changs already had one, but rarely used it. Her parents had both been impressed with her restraint, having expected a nine-year-old with so much money to go completely nuts. Of course, it all sat in a Sanctuary Zone bank account that her parents managed for her. Not that she minded.

Ji Yeon integrated herself with the group of friends rather well. Everyone liked her, though her tendency for constant random hugging did annoy Marcus. She'd admitted her android-ness to the other kids, both as a gesture of sincerity into being their friend and because it had been somewhat hard to hide. After Maya and Sarah had escaped via the tunnel, Ascendant thugs had tried to chase the other kids upstairs, not realizing Maya hadn't gone with them. Ji Yeon held the doors shut, overpowering two grown men. When more had showed up, she scared them away by making her eyes glow.

Maya had managed to sell the Ascendant Executive Board on the idea of sponsoring a 'proper' clinic out in the Hab as a public relations maneuver. Nothing massive, at least not yet, but Doctor Chang had a new practice only three blocks away from the building, allowing their apartment to go back to being a home.

The only crummy thing to happen was having to sit through an interview with Elsa Saeed, the same woman who only weeks earlier had kissed Vanessa's feet while she lied about Maya never existing on an AuthCast bulletin. So, once again, Maya's face appeared everywhere in the Boston Sanctuary Zone. They wanted to do a 'human interest' story on the child who saved the Eastern Seaboard. Maya downplayed her role to 'only making a video to inspire people.' At least, she used the interview to make it clear that she no longer had any connection whatsoever to Ascendant.

Hopefully, that would stop the kidnappings.

Being utterly severed from Ascendant gave her enough confidence that she didn't even mind running around barefoot. Of course, she made sure all her friends owned shoes, even if Emily refused to wear them, Pick 'forgot' them at home all the time, and Sarah rather disliked them—though she did say she'd put them on if they went scavving again.

It didn't hurt that the entire planet, or what remained thereof, had heard by now about how Vanessa Oman had deliberately seeded the air with Fade as a profit-making venture, and she currently awaited trial at the provisional government headquarters in the New York Sanctuary Zone. Maya made an appeal during her news interview to spare the woman execution, calling it an easy out. Having years to contemplate what she'd done would be a far more appropriate punishment.

Whether or not anyone would listen to a little girl on such an important matter, she couldn't say. But... they already had listened to her enough once to start a revolution.

Maya adored having all her friends over, even if it meant she didn't get much time actually playing the video game. She could play it any other time, since she lived here. Sarah loved the racing game they'd played while trapped in the penthouse. Surprisingly, it didn't bring back any bad memories. Most likely because the game had been the only tolerable time there—doing something fun with her sister and forgetting for a while how much trouble they'd been in.

Over the next hour or so, the controller passed from kid to kid, each taking their turn with the space commando. They eventually switched to the racing game which allowed two to play at a time via split screen. The game could support up to eight simultaneous players, but Maya didn't bother asking for VR headsets.

A loud triple-knock came from the left. Maya jumped at the sound, but knowing who probably pounded on the door chased her fear away in seconds.

Sarah grabbed the Hornet and aimed across the living room.

"It's okay," said Maya.

Pope reappeared in the archway to the kitchen, pointing a real gun at the front door.

"Guys!" yelled Maya. "It's cool!"

Genna got up from the sofa and approached the door, reaching for the knob with her left hand while her right hovered by a knife on her belt. She leaned over to the peep hole, and relaxed. The instant the tension left her, the kids all started breathing again—except for Ji Yeon.

Genna opened the door.

"Hey," said a man out in the hall, holding a stack of four large, flat, white boxes. "Umm. Not sure I'm in the right place."

"You are." Genna grinned and handed him several NuCoin chips. "Thanks."

"No problem." The guy nodded at her, waved to the kids, and hurried off.

Genna backed inside carrying the boxes and shoved the door closed with her foot.

"What the heck is that?" asked Marcus.

The aroma trailing behind Genna as she walked to the kitchen washed over the twins, Pick, Emily, and Sarah like a snake charmer's music.

Maya stood and thrust her arms outward. "It is time for you guys to experience... pizza."

"What the heck is pizza?" Marcus scratched his head.

Ji Yeon sniffed. "It smells like food. And good."

"With all the toppings." Sarah winked at her.

"Yeah." Maya let her arms fall against her sides. "Maybe now you'll understand that metaphor."

"A what-a-for?" asked Anton.

Sarah scratched her head. "No idea."

Maya sighed hard enough to puff her hair away from her face. "Guys, really?"

"Food's gettin' cold," called Genna. "Who's hungry?"

With a big grin, Maya scrambled into the kitchen with her friends, swarming around four large pies... with all the toppings.

fin

ACKNOWLEDGMENTS

Thank you for reading the Faded Skies series!

Also, thanks to Lee Sheridan for editing and Ricky Gunawan for the amazing cover and artwork!

Additional thanks to my beta readers: Dianne Webb, Louise Feagans, Leslie Whitaker, Brandy Yassa, and David Lee Cox (not related).

ABOUT THE AUTHOR

Originally from South Amboy NJ, Matthew has been creating science fiction and fantasy worlds for most of his reasoning life. Since 1996, he has developed the "Divergent Fates" world, in which *Division Zero, Virtual Immortality, The Awakened Series, The Harmony Paradox, and the Daughter of Mars series* take place. Along with editing for Curiosity Quills press, he has worked in IT and technical support.

Matthew is an avid gamer, a recovered WoW addict, developer of two custom RPG systems (paper & dice), and a fan of anime, British humour, and intellectual science fiction that questions the nature of reality, life, and what happens after it.

He is also fond of cats, presently living with two: Loki and Dorian.

Visit me online at:
  Facebook: https://www.facebook.com/MatthewSCoxAuthor
  Amazon: https://www.amazon.com/author/mscox
  Pinterest: https://www.pinterest.com/matthewcox10420/
  Goodreads: https://www.goodreads.com/author/show/
7712730.Matthew_S_Cox
  Twitter: https://twitter.com/mscox_fiction
  Instagram: https://www.instagram.com/mscox.author/
  Email: mcox2112@gmail.com

OTHER BOOKS BY MATTHEW S. COX

Divergent Fates Universe Novels
Division Zero series

- Division Zero
- Lex De Mortuis
- Thrall
- Guardian
- Harbinger

The Awakened series

- Prophet of the Badlands
- Archon's Queen
- Grey Ronin
- Daughter of Ash
- Zero Rogue
- Angel Descended

Daughter of Mars series

- The Hand of Raziel
- Araphel
- Ghost Black

Virtual Immortality series

- Virtual Immortality
- The Harmony Paradox

Prophet of the Badlands Series

- Prophet's Journey

Divergent Fates Anthology

(Fiction Novels - Adult)

The Roadhouse Chronicles Series

- One More Run
- The Redeemed
- Dead Man's Number

Faded Skies series

- Heir Ascendant
- Ascendant Unrest
- Ascendant Revolution

Temporal Armistice Series

- Nascent Shadow
- The Shadow Collector
- The Gate to Oblivion

Vampire Innocent series

- A Nighttime of Forever
- A Beginner's Guide to Fangs
- The Artist of Ruin
- The Last Family Road Trip
- The Phantom Oracle
- How Not to Summon Demons
- Ordinary Problems of a College Vampire
- A Vampire's Guide to Surviving Holidays

Standalones

- Wayfarer: AV494

- Axillon99
- Chiaroscuro: The Mouse and the Candle
- The Spirits of Six Minstrel Run
- Sophie's Light
- The Far Side of Promise anthology
- Operation: Chimera (with Tony Healey)
- The Dysfunctional Conspiracy (with Christopher Veltmann)
- Of Myth and Shadow

Winter Solstice series (with J.R. Rain)

- Convergence
- Containment
- Catalyst

Alexis Silver series (with J.R. Rain)

- Silver Light
- Deep Silver
- Silver Quarrel

Samantha Moon Origins series (with J.R. Rain)

- New Moon Rising
- Moon Mourning

Vampire For Hire series (with J.R. Rain)

- Moon Master
- Dead Moon
- Lost Moon

Maddy Wimsey series (with J.R. Rain)

- The Devil's Eye
- The Drifting Gloom
- Dark Mercy

Samantha Moon Case Files series (with J.R. Rain)

- Blood Moon

Immortal Operative series (with J.R. Rain)

- Broken Ice

Young Adult Novels

The Eldritch Heart Series

- The Eldritch Heart
- The Cursed Crown

Evergreen Series

- Evergreen
- The World That Remains
- The Lucky Ones
- Nuclear Summer

Standalones

- Caller 107
- The Summer the World Ended
- Nine Candles of Deepest Black
- The Forest Beyond the Earth
- Out of Sight

Middle Grade Novels

The Adventures of Ubergirl series

- My Dad is a Mad Scientist
- Aliens Ate My Homework
- The End of all Halloweens

Tales of Widowswood series

- Emma and the Banderwigh
- Emma and the Silk Thieves
- Emma and the Silverbell Faeries
- Emma and the Elixir of Madness
- Emma and the Weeping Spirit

Standalones

- Citadel: The Concordant Sequence
- The Cursed Codex
- The Menagerie of Jenkins Bailey

www.ingramcontent.com/pod-product-compliance
Lightning Source LLC
Chambersburg PA
CBHW030602180626
46816CB00005B/1646